GW00949942

A CIRCLE AROUND HER

BOOKS BY
JONATHAN STRONG

THE HAUNTS OF HIS YOUTH
(new edition of Tike and Five Stories)

OURSELVES

COMPANION PIECES

ELSEWHERE

SECRET WORDS

OFFSPRING

AN UNTOLD TALE

THE OLD WORLD

A CIRCLE AROUND HER

JONATHAN STRONG

Z

ZOLAND BOOKS
Cambridge, Massachusetts

First edition published in 2000 by
Zoland Books, Inc.
384 Huron Avenue
Cambridge, Massachusetts 02138

PUBLISHER'S NOTE
This book is a work of fiction. Names, characters, places, and incidents are either the product of the author's imagination or are used fictitiously. Any resemblance to actual events or persons, living or dead, is entirely coincidental.

Cover painting, *Ferns*, by Rudy Burckhardt, oil on canvas, 36" x 32"

From the collection of Roland and Lori Pease

The author wishes to thank the Tufts University European Center, Talloires, France, where this book was begun.

FIRST EDITION

Book design by Boskydell Studio
Printed in the United States of America

07 06 05 04 03 02 01 00 8 7 6 5 4 3 2 1

This book is printed on acid-free paper, and its binding materials have been chosen for strength and durability.

Library of Congress Cataloging-in-Publication Data
Strong, Jonathan.
A circle around her : a novel / Jonathan Strong. — 1st ed.
p. cm.
ISBN 1-58195-014-4 (acid-free paper)
1. Middle aged women — Massachusetts — Fiction. 2. Country life — Massachusetts — Fiction. 3. Massachusetts — Fiction. I. Title.

PS3569.T698 C57 2000
813'.54—dc21 99-089681

for Morse Hamilton

A MAY MONDAY

I

WHEN MARY LANAGHAN'S husband left her in 1985, she took her four children to the country — or so it seemed then — and found a house by a lake in the woods. She was unable to afford as much land about her as she would have liked, but for some years she and her two girls and two boys lived with the sounds of birds and at night only starlight. It was a refuge from the suburb where her neighbors had watched her marriage come apart. Her children went on to the regional high school, which was a step down from their old school system, but Mary no longer cared what colleges they got into; she wanted them unambitiously near her and refused their father's offer to send them to boarding schools. Divorce had at last allowed Mary to live somewhat closer to the politics she had formerly only sympathized with at a distance.

There were two further addresses out her road, first a ramshackle cottage rented only in the summer months, then a flimsy-looking winterized boathouse lived in, most recently, by two men who ran a diner. Drew Hale, the landlord who owned both, lived down in Leominster now and no longer had any interest in parceling off a small lot here or there, as he had once done to the builders of Mary's house. In his opinion, the whole area had been spoiled when a string of vacation homes, as he called them, went up along the shore of the main lake. He was waiting for some big developer to buy all of Hale's Cove, and he enjoyed reminding Mary of this whenever he drove up to tend to his property.

For ten years, he had been holding forth his threat, but builders had favored the other end of the road, where public water and sewer lines now reached. Ill-proportioned garrison colonials with large attached garages had been set down, each in its own swath cut from the woods. When the trees were bare, Mary could see them marching toward her; one more and she would practically have a next-door neighbor. These were year-round people, suburbanites as she had once been, expanding suburbia to reclaim her.

But her house, an unlovely version of an Alpine chalet resting on a concrete-block basement, resisted this claim. Finding a house that could not be neatly subdivided into living room, dining room, and kitchen, one that required its own new rules for family life, had been a sign for Mary. Her sons had slept in the loft on one side, her daughters on the other. They would descend their ladders to the main room, which was open to skylights in the high ceiling, and she would make them their oatmeal and rye toast and send them hiking off to the bus stop. Under the girls' loft was what she dubbed the free-for-all; under the boys', her own quiet inviolable room, which even Shirley, her youngest, had accepted as such from the start. And in good weather, before and after bug season, they mostly lived on the balcony that wrapped around three sides under broad eaves. Back then, Mary had already imagined her eventual child-free days there: a rocker, a sunshade, and a book about birds or wildflowers on her lap. It had seemed a happy prospect, but that was because getting her brood through adolescence proved such a load of work.

Now, alone on a peaceful spring morning, with chickadees still at the feeders and her familiar cardinal returned, Mary heard Drew Hale's failing muffler pass behind her house, followed by another, quieter car. From the northeast corner of her balcony she watched flashes of steel through the budding trees, but when Drew shut off his engine, the other car made a short screech and Mary heard gravel crunch as it reversed and turned. With one more flash in the trees, it was gone, back out the road.

As rarely as she saw Drew and as touchy as their encounters usually were, Mary nonetheless felt the need of a walk in his direction. She had not seen him all the cold winter since November, when he brought new storm windows to Victor and Ron, his boathouse tenants. She called Hilda, her old German shepherd, pulled her rubber boots back on, and grabbed her jeans jacket off the back of the rocker.

Hilda waited to see, through her cataracts, which way they would take. Mary chose the path along the water past her son Martin's trailer, up on blocks with its tires off the ground; she tried to give one a spin but it barely budged. The dog was following slowly. Far from snooping, Mary might have seemed merely to be out looking for lady's slippers and bluebells. One of her new hobbies was identifying things in nature, and Drew plainly appreciated her exploring his woods. His sense of property came from an era past, when the woods were open to everyone, no matter who held the deed, because everyone knew how to use them. If this was no longer true, on Hale's Cove Drew chose to stand by the old rules — that is, until he passed it over to the bulldozers.

He was unboarding the cottage windows when Mary hailed him from the path. He nodded at her and kept working, assuming if she wanted to discuss something with him, she would come closer so he would not have to shout.

But first, she stopped and watched him, and Hilda, who instinctively shied away from Drew, busied herself by the water. Mary had learned this slower use of time since coming to the lake. It had been both too late and too early for her children to learn it, but thirty-eight had been a good age for someone who had not learned it at three, as Drew obviously had. Ten more years, and now it was second nature to Mary, and she wondered if she could ever speed up again if she needed to.

She always thought of Drew Hale as part of another generation, but he was not much past sixty and vigorous in his steady precise way. By trade he was what is known as a curious artificer, which is to say a maker of irreplaceable parts. He would fashion new cogwheels for old clocks, duplicate elaborate bits of brass moldings; he would restore obsolete farm implements and rebuild mill machinery — or firearms, for he was also a gun dealer. Her neighbor Ron Starks had once shown Mary a wooden sign he had found — D. HALE REPAIRS ALL — from when the boathouse was a workshop and Drew himself lived in the cottage with his wife and daughter. Now he went about pinning back the shutters as if each window disclosed a scene from a happier past.

When Mary came at last in range, Drew began to speak: "I drove all the way up from Leominster to show the cottage to some damn woman. When I met her in Haviland Center she was already looking at me a bit sideways. Then she followed my car out here, and the next thing I see is her taillights backing up in my face and she's barreling off down the road again. I guess she took one look at this place and one more look at old me and figured I might be some kind of crazy rapist."

To remain neutral, Mary asked, "Who was she?"

"Oh, some damn woman. She wanted a lakeside vacation home for the month of June. She couldn't believe it was only three hundred a week. On the phone I told her I hoped she liked rusticating. She said that's just what she liked. She was going to bring her computer and get some work done."

He swung out the last shutter and pulled up the hook, then walked around to the water side, expecting Mary to follow. She noticed the long cuffs of his green work pants scuffing under his bootheels. The white paint on the cottage had a light green mold growing on it in the shady corners, and the gutter above her head was sprouting weeds already.

"You're a woman, Mary," Drew was saying, "is that what it was? Did she think I was some kind of old rapist?"

"I suppose she might have," said Mary, who had learned to take her time with Drew's questions, not to fall into a trap where he could get her arguing with him.

"Very nervous woman," Drew said, fiddling with the padlock on the crawl space under the screened porch. "I'm getting the water up and running. We've had the last of the freezes."

"Let's hope," said Mary. "Can I help with anything?"

"I told her in the village," Drew went on, "that she didn't have to worry about her neighbors. One was a nice quiet divorced lady and the others were two fairies."

"Come on, Drew," Mary said. She knew she could sometimes keep him from stepping too far over the line if she spoke up quickly enough when he began that sort of thing.

"Well, but I told her you'd never know they were fairies."

Mary ignored that, and he just chuckled, opening a valve with the wrench from his back pocket. "She was . . . a very . . . nervous . . . woman," he repeated, slowly, for his own ears. Mary left him when he turned to the fuse box with his handkerchief to wipe off the condensation, and she took the steps down to the little stone patio Drew had laid at the water's edge. This was what classified the cottage as a vacation home, she decided. The patios were much grander on the other shore of Lake Umbachaug, beyond the piney point that enclosed Hale's Cove. There was scarcely a screened porch to be found over there; the houses all had plate glass and screen combination sliders, but people tended to keep the doors closed and their air conditioners on.

Hilda was sniffing around the extension of Drew's dock, which was still up onshore for the winter. Mary considered if she would offer to help him with it the way her sons used to. Last spring, Victor and Ron took charge because Drew had broken an arm in a fall on the ice, and it was months before he could lift anything.

Now he joined her by the water. "Are the frogs out at dusk yet?" he asked.

"Oh yes," Mary said, "for some days now. I've been listening. I have a tape of pond sounds I study."

"I've read that frogs are disappearing all over the world," Drew said. "I think it said there are only a quarter as many as there used to be."

Mary was looking deep into the dark green water. "Are Victor and Ron going to help you put in the dock?"

"I'll give them a call. They know what to do," said Drew. "I've got my daughter wanting to use the place before it's rented. She just got out of her marriage."

"Oh no," said Mary, but she realized she had no reason to assume he wanted sympathy.

"That boy was the biggest bum I ever ran across," Drew informed her, an edge of fury in his voice. "I took against him from the first day. But I sat back and watched it happen exactly as I knew it would. Now she knows better."

"She's lucky then," Mary said. "Here, Hilda, fetch?" But the dog did not want to get her paws wet and pretended not to see the stick. "Have you got other renters lined up yet?"

"I put an ad in *The Boston Globe.* Don't worry, I won't have back those wild partiers."

"Oh, it was just a few weekends," Mary said, having already made her point last summer.

But she decided not to invite Drew over to her house for tea or a muffin. Their relations were fine as they were, and whatever kindnesses she offered would not ensure the future of the woods. "Well, I'll take the old dog for the rest of her walk," she said.

"Can you understand that woman turning her car around and taking off like that? Did she expect a country club out here? Either that or she decided I was a rapist and panicked. Or else she was plain rude."

"She was probably just rude," Mary said. "Most people are. If they don't want what you've got, they hate to waste time making excuses."

"Most people . . . are . . . rude," Drew concurred, nodding at the water. "Will you look after my Peggy when she comes?"

Mary knew she had a way of making herself available without meddling. It seemed to draw people to her more than if she went knocking on their doors. "Of course I will," she said. Then she decided to make a joke about Drew's car as she left. "Oh, I see D. Hale repairs all but mufflers."

He pointed a knowing finger at her, as if to say, "You got me there." She was up the steps with Hilda shuffling behind and about to round the corner of the cottage when she heard him say, "I'm too busy these days to keep up with my own stuff. All these house restorers and antiquers keep coming around. They're trying to hold on to what little past they think they have left. I don't have much to say to them. They think I'm a man of few words. They see me as some kind of old Yankee codger."

"You make them feel they're getting the authentic experience, Drew," Mary said.

He pointed the knowing finger again and chuckled, but before Mary and the dog could slip out of his sight, he was going on: "Yeah, they love authentic. My dad built this damn cottage in the Depression, and we moved out here from the village when I was almost three with only the woodstove and the hand pump. Some people's authentic is other people's bitch of a life."

Drew was edging toward his favorite topic: self-reliance. Mary felt the trap about to close. "Oh, you loved it," she said as lightly as she could, hoping for the knowing finger again, but it did not emerge from his clenched right fist. She imagined him starting up about how his tax dollar was going to welfare mothers and how environmentalists were putting restrictions on land development. "Say hi to your wife for me," Mary said quickly, as if she had something she had to go do now. "Bring her along next time. Maybe you'll both come visit Peggy."

"Say, when you see him, would you just ask Victor to put that dock in?" Drew asked. "I'm not going to bother calling him."

"Sure," Mary said, moving her feet at last. She would keep going, nudging Hilda along. "I'll ask him. Ron's the one who'll do it, actually."

"I mean whichever one's the little muscleman," she heard Drew say behind her. "The taller one's not good for lifting much."

She and Hilda passed the big Chevrolet parked on the pine needles. Drew had fiberglassed the rust spots and sprayed on rustproofing paint of somewhat duller red. Mary found herself smiling again when she reached the old railroad bed, which ran like a raised dike through the woods, straight and flat all the way north through Parshallville to the New Hampshire line. The rails had been pulled up in the thirties and the abutting land auctioned cheap to people like Drew's father, but a century ago excursion trains ran up to Lake Umbachaug from Worcester and Leominster and stopped right on the cove, where there was, according to an old photograph Drew had once shown Mary, a picnic pavilion and bathing cabins. Most of the trees had grown up since then; indeed, few big ones had survived the 1938 hurricane. Mary's woods — Drew Hale's woods — were actually rather young.

It was a strange sort of woodland walk, striding ahead of the dog along the level bed. Usually, Mary took the rambling side paths, but to stretch and feel her lungs and her heart, she preferred the old railroad. It moved Hilda along more easily, too. Drew probably considered her a city person with no real knowledge of the woods. He knew the names of everything that grew or swam or scampered or flew while she was barely learning. Besides, she wore a wool-lined jeans jacket from a classy catalog and expensive running shoes though she never ran, and she had put up her long brown hair, slightly streaked with gray, in the sort of stylishly loose bun that could never be mistaken for a severe farmwife's. Something in Mary wished she could be worn and weather-beaten like Drew, but she had not properly hardened her eyes or her lips, and her skin was too milky, too apt to blush. To Drew Hale she could not possibly ever belong here.

The motorbikes would be coming out on weekends soon — they were local, they belonged — and Mary would begin to hear gunshots again; there was no more hunting near the lake, but people came from miles around to shoot targets in the regional landfill to the west. And then the motorboats — but, luckily, Hale's Cove was too mucky for them, and if they came in at all, they slowed way down and steered clear of the lily pads. The partiers in the cottage last year had kept a motorboat at the dock. They would wait till they were drunk in the middle of the night to take it out and by moonlight edge it past the rocks off the piney point, but they started whooping and whistling as soon as they revved it up. One very early morning Mary had listened to two drunk young women floating about on rubber rafts and trading detailed information about the men they had just been with. Mary would have enjoyed eavesdropping more if she had not been so dead tired from all the loud music and hollering.

Now it was quiet: birdsongs she was unsure of, wind whirring in the pines, the panting dog. Mary would be turning forty-nine, and then quickly, as she knew these years seemed to go, she would turn fifty. And she was a very lonesome woman now. She knew that, and she did not know what she could do about it.

II

LOUISE THIBAULT LIVED with her brother, Charles, in what had been their grandmother's house, a little box with a high-pitched roof and ancient green asphalt shingle siding. It sat only ten feet back from the busy Leominster Road leading southeast out of Haviland Crossing, one of several villages that made up the towns that made up the regional school district. Louise and Charles had lived in one village of Haviland or another all their lives. Their father used to hunt and fish with Drew Hale. He drove the snowplow for the town and sold tires and exhaust systems out of a barn in North Haviland before Midas arrived and he and their mother took off in a trailer for Florida. When their grandmother died, the kiddies, as their father still called them, moved from an apartment above the pharmacy in Haviland Center to the one house anyone in their family had ever owned. It was known as the cross-eyed house because the only two windows in front were set close on either side of the door. Brother and sister each took a room and shared the kitchen and bath in back. Charles wanted to finish the attic, but he was far too heavy to make it up the narrow stairs, especially carrying lumber or sheetrock, and Louise was heavier still. From fat children they had grown huge in high school, where they were nicknamed Watertank and Corncrib. It never really bothered them. They each had a good strong laugh and no enemies. Charles worked at the new convenient mart next to Midas up the road, and Louise was a nurse's aide. She took shifts caring for old people in their homes and was interning as a counselor to help the dying.

Whenever Mr. Hale drove through Haviland, he tended to check in on the young Thibaults for his old friend Albert. Louise had not gone to work yet, but Charles was still sleeping off the night shift, so she asked Mr. Hale to slip quietly by his room on their way back to the kitchen. She squeezed around him and shut the kitchen door to let her brother rest.

The kitchen was cramped and dark. The blue-and-white-checked oilcloth on the table had been there for decades, wiped clean thousands of times. Louise pulled the string to the overhead light, and Mr. Hale settled onto the sturdy bench against the wall and placed his sharp elbows on the table. "Black coffee," said Louise to let him know she knew what he wanted. "And a doughnut?"

Mr. Hale smiled. "I called your poppa on his birthday," he said. "He's proud of you, Louise."

"I know, that's what he tells me every time he calls," she said and set down the mug and a box of doughnuts to choose from. Then she poured herself a huge glass of grapefruit juice and sat on the other end of the bench. "You're up here turning the water on already, Mr. Hale?"

"It's not going to freeze again," he said. "But that was some long cold dry winter, wasn't it? And I keep reading about this so-called greenhouse effect."

Louise shrugged because she was not sure one way or another what the greenhouse effect was supposed to be up to. She did prefer cold to heat; cold helped her burn calories, and she always felt too warm inside her skin regardless of the weather.

"It was a wasted trip, though," Mr. Hale said. "Some damn computer woman called me about the place. She wanted it the whole month of June. I warned her she wouldn't be getting a country club at that price, but she said it was what she wanted, genuine old lake cottage, just pine boards and beams and screened porch and tin sink. Beds are a little swaybacked, I said, but that was fine with her. So I come meet her in Haviland Center, and I see right off she's a fussy sort after all. I keep forgetting most people are these days; on the phone they sound easygoing and they turn out fussy as hell. To shorten the story, she follows me out there, but as soon as I step out of my car, she slams her Camry, or whatever the hell it's called, into reverse and turns around on me, and that's the last I see of her! She was probably thinking I was some old rapist, do you suppose?" A good smile broke out all over Louise's face. Mr. Hale started to hoot but stopped himself so he would not wake Charles. He leaned over his coffee mug and patted Louise's hand. "That'd be my guess, anyway."

"Too bad, though, you didn't rent the place," she said.

"It'll still rent. I got an ad in *The Boston Globe.*"

"But get the right sort of renters, Mr. Hale, not those college boys you had in last year."

"No single young men," he said with a shake of his gray head, and he picked up last week's *Haviland Vigilant* to check out rentals and see just what a good deal he was offering.

Louise had heard about the upset over the all-night parties from Mrs. Lanaghan, who volunteered regularly on the hospital desk. Back when Louise was in school, Mrs. Lanaghan was a volunteer parent at Umbachaug Regional, and she was always nice to Louise. Martin Lanaghan had just entered her class, and he finally learned to call her Corncrib like everyone else, but it took a while. He was nice like his mother. Louise had helped him feel at home in his new school. And once, she had been invited to the Lanaghan house for a picnic with all the other kids on the Haviland bus, and Martin had showed them his family albums of their old life in the suburbs near Boston. That picnic had reminded Louise of when she was a little kid herself, playing with her brother in the sand when Martin's house was just getting built and her poppa was visiting Mr. Hale over in the gun shop. She remembered Mr. Hale's sign nailed to the big maple, but later when Martin took them all for a walk in the woods, Louise had looked for the sign and it was gone. She had wanted it still to be there, so she could explain to Martin about the old days on Hale's Cove in the seventies, with the fathers in the gun shop and the mothers sewing on the screened porch.

"How is Mrs. Lanaghan?" Louise asked after she finished her grapefruit juice and Mr. Hale was eyeing another doughnut. "Go ahead," she said, "that's what they're for."

"I saw her this morning," Mr. Hale said. "She's a bit lonely, I'd guess. I don't think those children of hers pay her enough attention. I'm not sure what the hell she does with all her time."

Louise was about to tell him she volunteered at the hospital, but Mr. Hale was going on, raising his voice a little. "That husband must have settled a pile of money on her. Imagine being able to live the way she does without any kind of paying job. And let me explain something to you, Louise. She's one of those liberals that wants people like you and me to pay more taxes to take care of people that won't take care of themselves. No skin off her nose."

"But how's Mrs. Lanaghan doing, really?" Louise wanted to know.

"Well, I'd say she has to be an unhappy woman," Mr. Hale said. "But I'll give her one thing: she never lets you know it. On the surface she's always mild. She never leans on you."

"So you saw her just now?"

"She came by with that half-dead dog. They're always out looking for wildflowers with nothing better to do."

"What's this commotion?" said sleepy-eyed brother Charles, pushing in the kitchen door and filling the frame with his blue-striped pajamas.

"Go back to sleep, Charles," said his sister.

"Not when I smell a fresh box of doughnuts." He edged into the room and noticed the coffee was getting low, so he dumped the old grounds and set about making a new pot.

"I called your poppa on his birthday," Mr. Hale said.

"You still miss him, don't you, Mr. Hale," said Charles.

"Well, why he ever moved to Florida . . ."

"No snow, and it's flat," Charles said and grabbed himself a Bavarian creme. He pulled out a vinyl-cushioned bench from under the table. His rear end covered it entirely.

"He said he's coming to see his kiddies this summer and bringing your momma this time," Mr. Hale said. "Elizabeth and I had damn well better get to see something of them."

"This is a fine little doughnut," Charles said, devilishly raising his thin eyebrows. Mr. Hale passed him the box across the table for seconds. He probably would have begun to tell his story of the computer woman to Charles, but Charles had a way of getting a conversation going in his own direction: "It's a temptation on my new job," he said. "Imagine spending all night surrounded by good little things in plastic packages. I like the cream pies best, especially if I nuke them quick — not so long as to melt the frosting but just to make them go a little limp; fifteen seconds about does it. Then I like a Slim Jim now and then. There's always Little Debbies, though. They come out with different cakes for each season — heart-shaped pink ones, orange pumpkin ones, whatever. If someone asks me what's a good cheap snack, I point them to the Little Debbies. There's Hostess, there's Drakes, but I tend to go with Little Debbie. The varieties of chips is another thing — sour cream and onion, sea salt and vinegar, mesquite ranch. We also sell those sandwiches in Saran Wrap you can nuke up nice and tasty — ham and cheese; egg, cheese, and sausage." Charles stopped himself to get up and pour a big mug of coffee, ladle in some sugar, and tip the cream in right to the lip.

"Your poppa told me you loved your new job," Mr. Hale said. "He's proud of you both."

"Well, we're managing fine without the old folks," said Charles. "They felt bad leaving us, especially Momma. It was her decision, of course. She's the one who decided Poppa had plowed enough snow for a lifetime."

"Elizabeth misses her," Mr. Hale said. "In Leominster she's only got her bingo friends."

"Let me tell you about the late night crowd, Mr. Hale," Charles resumed. "You get into these kinds of conversations with them. Some weirdo wanders in at three A.M. for a pack of Kools and it's like I'm the only other person awake on earth to them. People passing through, restless people out driving, people on break from the night shift somewhere — a woman came in at four this morning getting away from her husband. They'd been up late fighting and he was only getting worse, so she took off. She leaned up against my counter and had a few smokes and we solved the world's problems." He grabbed for the last doughnut, a glazed cruller at the bottom of the box.

"I don't know about you two," said Louise, who had been staring out at the just blooming forsythia zigzagging across the square window above the sink, "but I have my afternoon shift with Mrs. Germaine. She's not long for this life, so I'd better get over there fast." Her smile broke out and then she lifted herself up from the bench and squeezed past Charles. "Glad you stopped in, Mr. Hale," she said. "Don't let him chew *both* your ears off."

Charles's voice had started up again when Louise got to

her bedroom. She picked out a green-and-yellow rayon scarf and stooped to comb her wispy hair in the tiny mirror over her grandmother's bureau. She had never gotten around to hanging it up higher for herself. Her grandparents' old four-poster bed was just right for all of her, but Charles had propped it up with extra legs. The only item she had to bring was her own TV because Charles put their grandmother's console in his room by his big mattress on the floor.

Louise took the car keys from the hook by the door and stepped out into the spring weather. They still drove their mother's aged Lark, loyally maintained and now slathered over in flat white paint with a few rusty spots bubbling up. She and Charles could not handle the bucket seats you got in newer cars.

As she drove, it occurred to Louise that she might go out to Hale's Cove when she had finished at Mrs. Germaine's. She figured it would be all right to drop in on Mrs. Lanaghan. Martin used to say how his mother depended a lot on her friends. They had once been a family in the suburbs with everything you could ask for — their next-door neighbors even had a swimming pool they could use. Martin had said he was not bitter, but he could not believe his father had broken the commitment to their family that Martin himself could never break. Then he told Louise that he had been named after Martin Luther King. His mother had chosen names like that for all of them and their father did not even realize it. She had waited till the divorce came through to explain it to them. "I always belonged more to my mother than my father, so this is home now," Martin had told Louise ten years ago. But after looking through those albums of all the fun times they must have once had, Louise knew he was being a good sport.

She pulled into Mrs. Germaine's long driveway off the Fraddboro Road. She would find the old lady waiting, sitting up in bed with her oxygen in her nose. In the kitchen, Louise arranged the lunch tray and found the double-crostic book open to yesterday's completed puzzle. "I can still do them," Mrs. Germaine bragged. "I have watched every other part of me slowing down and stopping, but my brain is still up to speed. The things it thinks up for me after dark, I can't tell if I'm awake or dreaming. Last night I was hurtling along in a train across a blue landscape. Picnickers in old-fashioned blue bathing suits were waving at us as we passed. The train, Louise, was absolutely silent, and everything inside it was also blue. Blue, I discovered from the little pamphlet the conductor was handing out, was the color of good-bye."

From her Death and Dying class, Louise knew now to take whatever elderly people said as part of the real truth of life, so she made herself try to see the blue landscape and the blue train, and there they were. She had seen them, too.

III

ROUTE 108 TRAVERSED in an S-shape all five towns of the Umbachaug Regional School District. The contours of the land had determined the course of the highway three hundred years ago, when it was a mere footpath; the course of the path, when it became a wagon road, determined the main streets of the settlements; the locations of the settlements, determined by a spring, a stream, or a hundred acres of good flat land, eventually implied a region, and the region gradually assumed a unity, despite the differences in the towns or indeed the differences in the villages within them.

Victor Bardonecchia had grown up in working-class Parshallville on the New Hampshire line. He was dark and mustached and thin and looked older than Ron Starks, but in fact the two had overlapped in high school. When Victor inherited the family business, a diner between Parshallville Common and Old Fraddboro, Ron had begun working there with him and slowly buying up his half share, but they still called the place Ugo's Original 108 Diner, after Victor's father. Victor had recently invested in a CD jukebox and made his own personal selection of titles from the distributor's extensive catalog because he did not trust Ron, whose idea of a preference was anything with an easy beat.

When their old school friend Stewart Tomaszewski showed up for an early lunch and ordered his usual western sandwich, Victor made him settle in with a cigarette for a CD demonstration. Suddenly, from the little speakers in Stewart's booth, came the song about all being bound for Mu Mu Land. "Tammy Wynette," Stewart said. "That crazy song got going through my head for weeks." Victor was watching him closely and could tell he was not really impressed; Stewart had a CD player in his new car and one he carried strapped to his waist when he went running, and of course a big loud system in his apartment over his mother's garage. Behind the counter, Ron was singing along with Tammy about being justified and ancient, a phrase he admitted made no sense, but the tune always set him waving his hands in the air. It was one of the few songs where his and Victor's tastes coincided, but what made the song for Victor were the unexplainable words. He was drawn to the peculiar. He felt the same about Kraftwerk's Autobahn song, which took him back to his monotonous days in the service in Germany before he and Ron had teamed up. That was a song that really drove Ron nuts.

"So she's out of your life?" Victor heard Ron ask, bringing the order around to Stewart's booth when the song was done. Stewart nodded. He stubbed out his cigarette, picked up the sandwich in both hands, and suspended it before him, looking at it hard, then bit out a big chunk and got ketchup all over his lips.

"She's out of my life," he said in the silence between songs. Victor punched in "Smells Like Teen Spirit," but Ron made him turn it off, so he punched in "Because the Night," which was mellower and did not bother Ron as much.

"There's a volume control on your unit," Victor called over to Stewart, who shook his head; the loudness was fine with him. Obviously, Stewart did not want to have to talk about his marriage to Peggy Hale, but all the same Ron would make him talk about it. Ron was not particularly respectful, but Victor did admire the way he kept at people till they said the things they really did need to say. Maybe Stewart had come into the Original between the breakfast and lunch crowds so Ron would have a chance to pry out of him what he was truly feeling. Stewart took for granted Ron's being there to look after him and did not seem to mind the huge crush Ron had had on him since high school. Stewart had been through three wives now and never once followed Ron's advice, but it seemed to comfort him knowing he could still get it, however many stupid mistakes he kept making.

Ron had taken a seat opposite Stewart in the booth. "No fraternizing with the customers," said Victor; Ron gave him the finger and looked Stewart straight in the eyes. "So did she leave or did you?" he asked.

"She left," Stewart said. "But I wanted her to. From the first date I should've seen it wasn't going to work. Even then she was planning for us to get a place of our own."

Victor looked at his watch and went behind the counter, put some bacon on the grill, and began slicing tomatoes. With the music he could not really hear what Ron was getting out of Stewart, but he knew he would hear it all, with commentary, when they got home that evening. He wondered how Ron could be so fascinated by Stewart's boring life. Women always started off thinking he was wild and fun and, being a Tomaszewski, a good catch; then they got tired of living in his mother's garage apartment. Sometimes, he had already married them; sometimes, he claimed he was going to. With the first one he had had a son, but those two were long gone out of his life now, and maybe Stewart had learned at least one lesson: Ron advised him to tell the women he was with that he was not ready to lose another kid.

Victor could barely hear Ron's voice rising above the music. "When it's right, it'll ... your reactions ... start buying a car or a CD system when it gets ..." Victor remembered the time Drew Hale had come out to bring them the storm windows and how Ron had tried to justify Stewart's sudden need for a '95 Neon with air to his latest father-in-law. "What kind of name is Neon for a car?" Drew Hale had asked. "It's named after a fish" was Victor's contribution. So Drew had asked, dryly, "Who names a car after a fish?" Ron told him that the car you drive has a lot to say about who you are and Stewart was getting into electronics sales and needed it for the road. "So what does that Korean shitbox say about who you are?" Drew wanted to know. "Well, what does that rust-bucket Chevy say about you?" Ron fired back. Their landlord shook his head and started pulling out the storm windows stacked across his backseat.

Victor wondered why such a stupid scene stuck in his head. He often felt plagued with meaningless memories, which was partly why he could not listen all over again to Stewart's excuses for himself; he did not want them flying around his brain all night.

As the song ended, an athletic young woman with dark hair and a pale face walked in and took what Victor thought of as the fifth stool, counting from either end. He decided not to make another musical selection. This woman looked somewhat familiar, but Victor could not place her. Her hiking boots meant she was probably from Boston; no young woman from around Umbachaug would wear boots like that, and her sweater was too bulky, but in Boston that did not seem to matter. Bostonians acted like they already knew what to order to cover up being unsure if they belonged in the Original 108 at all; Victor could always spot them.

"I'll have a grilled cheese on rye and a V8," she said. He smiled and nodded and then she asked him, "Are you Ron or are you Victor? My mom's your neighbor."

"Victor."

"I'm Rosa Blakey. We met once walking along the railroad bed." Victor suddenly saw Mary Lanaghan in her features, but she was heartier, surer.

"I'm Ron," Ron said from the booth. "And this here is Stewart, but you don't want to know *him.*" Stewart gave Ron the finger. "You wish," said Ron.

Rosa seemed to take their horseplay in stride; her Boston air was falling away. "So you went to Umbachaug Regional?" Victor asked.

Rosa swiveled back around on her stool. "Three whole years."

Victor poured her the V8 and popped a slice of lemon in it. He looked closely at the smooth young skin of her face. She had her mother's pale cheeks with a touch of freckles, but her hair was much darker, nearly black.

"Your mother never told us you were married," he said.

"I'm not. Blakey's my mom's maiden name. I prefer using it. By the way, she says you've been great neighbors." And then another thought struck her: "I bet the last time I was in this diner was when your dad still ran it."

"I was probably in the service then," Victor said. Rosa seemed to be looking more closely at him. It made Victor look away, but he thought about how Ron always looked right back at people, even closer than they looked at him.

"People must miss him. He took care of everybody," Rosa said after a sip of V8. "I don't get down here much. Now I live in northern New Hampshire, way up past the mountains where the Connecticut River starts. A couple more miles and you have to speak French."

Victor was at the grill flipping her sandwich. She was certainly trying to befriend him. Was it because her mother had told her he was gay? When he and Ron moved in a year and a half ago, Mary Lanaghan had made it clear right off that she totally accepted them as a couple; it had seemed so Bostonian of her.

Victor would have asked Rosa what she did for work up there, but when he turned around she said, with her mother's way of curling up her lower lip, "My grandfather Blakey was probably as much of a jerk as my dad, but my grandmother's maiden name was Toole so I went with Blakey." Victor managed half a smile back.

In his booth, Stewart was looking relaxed, sipping the coffee Ron had brought around to him and acting as if he was not overhearing the talk at the counter. Then right at eleven, in walked Mr. Zart from Zart's Dry Goods down the road for the BLT Victor always knew to have ready for him. He looked warily at Rosa and gave Victor a squint. Rosa was way too Boston for Mr. Zart's taste.

"You visiting your mom?" Victor asked, hoping it would explain her to Zart.

"She doesn't even know I'm coming," Rosa said. "I wanted to stop here and eat first, because she never has enough in the house when it's just her. I'm on a covert operation. I've got to help convince her it's okay my brother Martin moves back into the old trailer for the summer."

"We've been looking after your mom for you," Ron called from the back room, where he was now washing up the last load from breakfast. "The only one we see much of is Bayard. That's you guys' old trailer? I figured it was Drew Hale's."

Rosa contemplated the grilled cheese Victor had set before her, then she continued her conversation with the back room. "Martin got it during college when he had his — I don't know what he'd call it now — his retreat? His retreat from life. He wanted to be safe near Mom but under his own roof."

"It's real seventies, it's like aluminum siding with wheels," Ron called out over the steaming water.

Victor had placed himself at the other end of the counter from Zart to form the fourth corner of the square of men around Rosa. Why did he think of something as bizarre as that? It was as if he had to complete the geometry; if he moved two steps closer to where she sat at the counter, he would unbalance everything.

"It's a Nomad," Rosa said. "I was so jealous. He got to drop out of U Mass and Dad was ready to give him whatever he wanted to get him going again. He got that funky trailer to fix up like his own little house, with his tapes and sci-fi books, and I had to go practically to Canada for a place of my own and had to finish at UNH first."

"I'd been wondering about that trailer," said Ron, leaning in at the pass-through. "I'd been thinking about asking Drew Hale about me using it. You just blew that idea."

Victor had not heard him mention this particular scheme before. Sometimes it scared him that Ron could be so independent, but it was also what he liked about him. And here was Stewart still living above his mother's garage, and this Martin Lanaghan — what was it about these straight boys and their mothers? Ron had gotten away from his mother early, and Victor's own mom had died long ago.

"Victor, your dad had some cousins in Quebec," said Mr. Zart, catching up with Rosa's earlier remark. Then, mostly to himself, he went on: "Ain't never been to Quebec, and there it is, so close."

"You think you're surrounded by woods," said Rosa in a chummy voice, "and you come to the border and suddenly it's all farms and little French towns. You thought it was moose and bear all the way to the North Pole."

"Actually, Zarts never went much of anyplace," said Mr. Zart, not even looking in Rosa's direction. "*I* certainly ain't gone much of anyplace."

Victor was feeling claustrophobic. It was the way those three customers out there seemed to inhabit different worlds. Usually, he liked it when the diner was filled with a random assortment, but now there did not seem to be enough air. Maybe it was Stewart's silence. Victor slipped into the back room and told Ron he would finish the dishes. Ron could tell exactly what his tone of voice meant; when Victor needed to be alone, Ron never questioned him. And now he put his hands down into the hot water and scrubbed, but he could still glance up and out the pass-through if he got curious.

He saw Rosa widen her staring eyes when Ron instead of Victor reemerged. She had an idea. "Hey, Ron, can you tell me something special about my mother these days, something she does?" she asked him. "I want to know something about her that she won't know how I know, something I can spring on her."

Ron loved tricks and surprises, so he spent some time cogitating. "Here's one," he finally said. "You can tell her you just had this *Psychic Friends* kind of vision and you had to come down to see if it was true. You can say you saw her walking in the woods with Hilda. See, I watched her yesterday when I got home from work; it was sunset and I was at our kitchen window with the lights off, so she wouldn't have seen me. And she and the dog were walking along toward the railroad bed the way they always do. But this time — in your vision, see — you saw your mother leap up in the air and grab hold of a branch of the old maple there and start swinging and swinging back and forth like a kid. And then a sunbeam shot through the trees and struck her face, and she hung there in it — "

"You saw this?"

"She'll totally freak. You can say you felt this mystical experience all the way across New Hampshire."

"This is perfect," Rosa said.

"Don't believe a thing Ron says," said Stewart from his booth. "He always makes up shit like that."

"Yeah, and you're Mr. Trust Me Trust Me," Ron said. Rosa had swiveled to assess the cigarette-smoking fellow behind her, but she did not look impressed when she turned back. It occurred to Victor that Stewart had the kind of style — hair just too long, gold earring, a purple suede jacket — that probably would not go over with the hiking boot crowd, however irresistible he was to Ron. "You try it on your mom," Ron was saying, leaning in close to her. "You can pull it off."

Rosa looked up past him and caught Victor's eye in the pass-through. There were her soft cheeks nestled in that thick blue turtleneck. Victor could tell she was hoping the story was for real, but Ron had not said anything to him about Mary Lanaghan swinging on the maple tree last night. It was the sort of thing he would usually have mentioned. Things tumbled out of Ron, though sometimes he dolled them up a bit; maybe Mary had just stretched to touch a low branch as she passed by.

With his hands all hot and slippery, Victor still felt the tension out there. What was Mr. Zart, his father's poker buddy, thinking down the counter? The old man had been miserably low for months after Ugo Bardonecchia's death. That was the generation where the men hung out with the men, the women with the women. As a boy, Victor had felt happier with the women, and he took a deal of ribbing for it. Uncomfortable memories. Why could he not just scrub away and think of nothing but soap and grease?

"Let me get it straight," Rosa was saying. "My mom leaped up and grabbed the tree, and the sun — "

"I believe it's the God's truth," Victor could hear Mr. Zart interrupting. "I once saw my mother in a vision. After she died. She was all in a ray of light, at peace. That was nineteen hundred and fifty-nine."

Stewart was back by the window drawing a long breath through his cigarette and then shaking his head. Rosa looked as though she was thinking hard about something else, and Ron was standing by the grill with his thick biceps crossed over his chest, pleased as punch with himself, Victor could tell.

IV

ROSA BLAKEY LAY still on her old bed in the loft. When she had tugged at the long curtain on its wooden rings, the clicking sound had brought her teenage years to mind. It was a sound of morning, when she and Shirley were getting dressed for school and it was time to sweep back that great yellow veil through which sunlight was already shining. Their brothers' orange curtain was usually still closed, and they would hear stumbles and mumbles and groans from behind it as they descended their ladder to take over the bathroom first. On Sundays, her mother would be resting, waiting for the four of them to bring her breakfast in bed, the one time they were invited to relax with her in her room. Where had such rituals come from? They had fallen into them so readily, as if after the divorce they had all agreed on an entirely new and simpler way of life. Mom had done it well, Rosa decided, because instead of remembering those days as the most disrupted time of her life, Rosa held on to them for comfort even now. The sunny colors of the hemmed-up bedsheets, hung on wooden rings and sent along their thick dowels by an exuberant morning welcoming sweep of the hand, lent their hue to her memory. Fifteen, sixteen, and seventeen had been her bright yellow and orange years and as much so at night when reading lamps shone warmly through the curtains, auras of home and study and peace.

And now, the accustomed reading hour her mother always insisted on had brought with it that old mood of contemplation that had salved Rosa's late youth after the hectic tension of life with her father. She had no longer been expected to get up and do anything, not to practice her flute or figure her math or go play tennis. She had been allowed to stare up at the skylight and out to the high branches, which she came to know in every season. Now, the yellow-green maple flowers quivered there in the wind. Up in New Hampshire, Rosa had many such moments of respite, but the tradition had begun here, in the shape of a particular branch she had traced across the nearer skylight, ten years ago.

Today, her arrival after lunch had first startled Hilda, who had let out a sad yowl and begun to tremble but not to bother getting up until Rosa had climbed the steps to the balcony, and then the dog had edged her way across the rough planks to nuzzle and wag. No matter how old, a dog must do this, Rosa had told herself. At such a moment, a dog must immediately show all its love; it cannot have a bad mood. But taken by surprise, Mom had been a little cross at first. "Why didn't you call? I never know what you're up to, Rosa. What if I'd had to be out all day?" "I would've waited," Rosa had said, placidly, to take the sharpness out of her mother's tone. But she had stared hard at Rosa: it was not what Rosa said but how she looked that must have quickly softened her temper, and she could not help wrapping her arms tight around the big bulky navy blue turtleneck sweater and rediscovering how strong her older daughter really was. "Oh, Mom," Rosa had wheezed out, caught in the embrace.

Then she had explained in some detail how the lodge never knew ahead of time when she would get a day off and she had not wanted to set up a plan that might fall through.

She had reminded her mother that one of the family rules when they moved to the new house was not to overschedule their lives again. Even Shirley, who was only eleven back then, had tried to slow herself down. "But, darling, those were the days when I knew you would always be coming home," Mom had argued, sounding more resigned than plaintive, but it was getting harder and harder to read her. The brothers still had no idea how complicated their mother was. Rosa surveyed their orange curtain across the chasm of the main room. For a moment, she pretended that Martin and Bayard were asleep behind it as they once might have been. And then the sound of footsteps swept the past out of the loft and Rosa was there alone, resting, and Mom was downstairs putting a kettle on.

The precise moves, repeated a half dozen times a day for three years, were still in Rosa's body; she swung herself around, hand on the ladder's left pole and, in the same motion, let down her foot the distance to the next rung. At the stove, she gave her mother another hug — "I had a great nap," she said — and they went out to the balcony to have their tea.

It was a brighter day down here than any yet up on her First Connecticut Lake. Spring came so late there. Settling onto one of the white plastic nesting chairs like the ones the lodge had by the dozen, Rosa realized what a strong effect sunlight had on her. She was ready again to come awake, to get past the winter slowness. Just the touch of heat on her elbows, where she had rolled up her sweater sleeves, was enough to revive her.

Mom, in her rocker, opened a package of imported cookies and spread them out on a white plate. A thin coating of dark chocolate over orange marmalade on a butter cookie was a treat to savor only in tiny bites with each sip of lemon tea. Typical Mom, thought Rosa. "What were you reading?" she asked.

"*The Body Language of Dogs*. Some silly thing from the library," her mother said. Library books seemed to pass more quickly through the house now that she was alone there. She must have read every nature book and travel book and homemaking book in the Haviland Public Library, not to mention art books and American history books, but no psychology books ever, Rosa had noticed. She wished her mother would look more into her own self sometime.

The two of them had already caught up on the family goings-on except for the question of what Martin was going to do next, and Rosa had not yet figured out how to bring up the plan about the old trailer. She was trying to move the conversation around to it naturally when she remembered the story Ron had told in the diner. It had gone out of her head as soon as she arrived home and had not come back to her even in the entire hour up on her old bed, yet the picture was suddenly vivid again, Mom swinging from the bough like a grade-schooler. Rosa was not sure if she still wanted to try the hoax. She had a vision of herself, last night at sunset, sitting alone on her own lakeshore, watching the returning ducks paddle about, quacking in the stillness. Her boyfriend, Nat, was spring skiing in the Laurentians. The two of them had made it through another winter in the wilds, and soon the tourist season would crank up again. She had to admit it was not only Nat's hesitation that held them back from what he termed total commitment; she had her own doubts but had not wanted to go into them earlier with her mother. Her brothers made the mistake of involving their mother in every passing agony of their lives, but the sisters knew better.

"What's the latest on Martin?" Rosa surprised herself by asking.

"I was going to ask you," Mom said, rocking slowly and thoughtfully with her teacup at her lips.

"I had this idea," Rosa said, completely plausibly, she thought. "What if he took a real break and lived in his old trailer for the summer? Maybe it would get him out of the dumps again." Rosa had been saying the opposite to Martin on the phone: he should take a bus west, anywhere, find himself a dumb job in a new place, shake himself up a little. But their long conversations always brought her around to a pledge of support.

"I'd like that," Mom said, "but would he? Doesn't he really want to be on his own now, like you?"

"He thinks he does," lied Rosa, "but I was just imagining how it might be good for him to take the stress off for a while. It's not like he'd move back in the house."

But there was the issue of what he would do all day, so Rosa, the devoted sister, contended that Martin had a hundred hobbies to keep him occupied and maybe he needed time to indulge in them, maybe that was why he was so low lately.

"There is such a thing as a job," Mom said.

Rosa amused herself with the thought that they were each arguing the other's position. "But he's had jobs, he's saved up. He's stashed away a lot more than me." And that annoyed her, but she did not say so because she had always been determined not to allow her mother to see inside her private jealousies.

"Have you suggested the trailer to him?"

"We talked about it some," said Rosa, pondering.

"But I wish he had something to structure his time. The day camp? Maybe he could do something over there."

"Mom," Rosa said, "the whole point is for him to take the stress off." The job idea was merely her mother's face-saver, and Rosa could already sense from her a new cheerfulness at the prospect of having Martin around home.

"I think, though, I should put a condition on him, Rosa, that he line something up for the fall — " She turned her head because a car had pulled onto the gravel behind the house and then a door slammed. Hilda's tail hit the floorboards a few times to show she was on duty. "I'm not expecting anyone, but then I wasn't expecting you — " She was giving Rosa a suspicious look.

"Maybe it's Martin already with all his crap," said Rosa to be funny. Her mother just listened. Then came heavy footfalls up the stairs.

"Mrs. Lanaghan?" piped a voice, and an immense female shape, shadowed by the sun, rounded the corner of the balcony. "It's me, Louise Thibault," she said, turning into the light. "Oh, is that Rosa, too?"

"Corncrib!"

But she was larger than Rosa remembered. Her pant legs stretched to contain random bulges of flesh. The loose tent of her smock was topped with a very undersized yellow-and-green scarf. She leaned over to try to pat the dog, but she gave up, said "Hi, Hilda," and lumbered on. Rosa could see that Mom was touched Louise had come by. She was unnesting another white plastic chair, but their visitor quickly, and prudently, took a seat on the bench by the door, so Rosa poured out a cup and passed the cookie plate.

"Mmm, these are a new variety, Mrs. Lanaghan," Louise said with interest.

Rosa watched Louise pop one in her smallish mouth as Mom explained, "I got them at the Old Fraddboro Store."

The notion of going to Old Fraddboro for imported cookies, of going to Old Fraddboro for anything really, was clearly outside Louise's frame of reference. Rosa would have dropped the subject, but her mother now elaborated on it, telling about all the good things you could find only over there, as if maybe to encourage in Louise an entitlement to Old Fraddboro, too.

"Well, I don't go that way much," Louise said. "Except I have a client in Basswood, and all those elderly know each other. I'll probably get more referrals."

"And how's the work going?" Mom asked next. Rosa saw that Louise was unable to resist an immediate second cookie.

"Mrs. Germaine down the way — do you know her, Mrs. Lanaghan? — oh, she's difficult. She's so scared once she's not going to get her crostic right and then that'll be curtains. She makes herself do one a day. Mostly I sit there on her chaise lounge and she asks me what this or that word might be. I always don't know, but she keeps asking. It's better than having her just talk to herself. Another gal comes in for the overnight, so I leave her with soup and the radio on to her *Fresh Air* program. She can automatic-dial the hospital if she's got an emergency."

"And how's the training?" Then Mom turned to Rosa to explain how she had learned at the hospital volunteer desk that Louise was joining the terminal home-care program.

"I hope I'm cut out for it," Louise said. "They tell you the calmer you are, the better. You have to learn to accept things. They don't just mean death itself but all the stages leading up. I never used to realize life was a bunch of stages you're at. Even what they call denial is a kind of stage for a lot of people."

"You've always been good about accepting things, Louise." Rosa was content to let her mother do the talking.

"That's what they tell me," came the cheerful reply, and then a third cookie darted between her lips as if self-propelled, Rosa imagined.

"So what brings you round to see us?" Mom asked next, allowing no awkward pause.

"Well, I was at Mrs. Germaine's, and since I only do five hours there I had some time, and I was thinking about you today, Mrs. Lanaghan. I don't know. What brings me round? Well, I was thinking about Momma and Poppa coming by the lake in the old days before this house got put up and about Charles and me playing in the sandpile. I know: it was Mr. Hale, he came by this morning and he was telling me about seeing you out walking."

"We had a nice chat."

"Hey, Mom, what's old Drew been up to lately?" It was Rosa's sudden attempt to enter the conversation.

Her mother had a wry smile on her lips. "He's still an old devil. I like to think he means well, but I'm not sure he always does."

It looked as if their guest could already use some more tea with plenty of sugar and milk, so Rosa attended to her cup while Louise went into a discourse on Drew Hale. She hasn't asked us about ourselves yet, Rosa noted: we're feeding her and asking her questions. It bothered Rosa that her mother was such a practitioner of self-obliteration, the result of an Irish Catholic upbringing, she would have said to excuse herself, but it only made Rosa mad. Here, drink this, Corncrib, she thought, and scarf another handful of these!

". . . and Mrs. Hale was real close with Momma," Louise was saying. "Thanks, Rosa. But the thing about Mr. Hale is, you know, he's always trying to convince you of something. You should've heard the fights him and Poppa used to have. See, Poppa was union from his mill days."

Rosa watched her mother rock back so the sun was on her cheeks. "I'm always careful what I reveal to Drew," she said. "This morning he had a story about some possible renter thinking he might try to assault her out here in the woods and I didn't know what to say to him."

"He thinks he's such an old bull," Louise said.

"He's an old coot," said Rosa, aware she was talking about Mr. Thibault's best pal but somehow needing to put an edge on the chatter. Mom darted a frown her way, but Louise was smiling. Edge was something unknown to her. Her body, Rosa decided, spread out in such a way that she must never know quite where she ended. Her body flowed into the bench and stuck to the wall behind and absorbed the cup she held.

"Working with elderly," Louise said in the new professional voice she seemed to be learning, "you get used to that sort of thing. Old men think they can make little remarks, but you go along and ignore them."

Then Mom asked Louise how her brother was, but before she could say more than that he was doing fine, Rosa decided to jump in with "Speaking of brothers, Louise, you'll be interested to know your pal Martin may be coming back to the lake this summer."

Louise looked up at her, perhaps for the first time since she had sat down. It was strange now to look her in the eyes. Ah, that is where her edge is, Rosa saw, it's in her eyes, the place she looks out at the world from. "He might move back into his trailer," she told Louise, somewhat softened. "I know he'll be wanting to see you."

The eyes appeared to twinkle at her. And up from the interior of Louise, a voice emerged full of sweet memory: "Gosh," it said, "so how's Martin doing now? Where's he been at?"

Rosa thought of a photo in one of their family albums of Corncrib Thibault peeking in the trailer door, which was in fact too narrow for her to get through without squeezing. Martin had snapped it from inside, and you could see his feet in white socks stretched out on the bunk in front of him. She would leave it to Mom to tell the public version of Martin's peregrinations from dorms and apartments all over Amherst and Northampton to rooms in Boston and, briefly, to the attic of their father's new house back in Newton. Martin had had, including the trailer, fourteen abodes since high school, but all within fifty miles of home. And he had worked in copy shops and secondhand record stores and as a groundskeeper and waiter and delivery boy. He had mooned after uninterested or unavailable women and talked about them to his sister as if they were really part of his life. Rosa wondered why she had to hear the details of her brother's fixations and why he could not find people in his own life for confidants. All he had were his computer newsgroups.

"Can you think of any place around here he might make a little spending money?" Mom was asking Louise.

"The mart, I suppose, where Charles works. I'll ask."

"But not till fall," Rosa stipulated. "He wants to take it easy for a while."

A big smile broke over Louise's face. "So wouldn't I!" she chortled and swung out her fat calf, a quick jab at the air. The peach-colored stretch pants flashed then disappeared again under the smock. "I get pretty beat. Oh, and with summer coming up and all the humidity — I guess I'm a working gal by nature, though. Martin sure never had much of a problem lazing around. He could lie there and listen to tapes and read books and be happy."

Louise had just conjured up for Rosa the old image of

Martin in retreat. Would it be like that all over again? In her mother's faintly blushing cheeks and around her eyes, Rosa perceived the strain of time passing. Mom was not the same as she had been. These ten years had taken from her the last touches of girlishness and supplied the first hints of age. There she was, in the same sunlight that, sinking to rest across the road last night, had found an arrow's path between a hundred branches to strike her face all golden in the surrounding dim greens and grays. To hear of it had nearly made Rosa cry, sitting there in the diner, happy to be coming to see her mother again. But she had deflected the emotion then. Instead of her lonesome mom, she had tried envisioning her own Nat, skiing up in Quebec. In those northern mountains, where there is still snow, she had told herself, there is this man with large crooked teeth but the gentlest eyes swooping down a silent white slope alone. She would be glad to get back to him tomorrow night. It was always best with them after they had been apart for a time.

"And so what are you doing with yourself these days, Rosa?" asked Louise at last. "That your Wagoneer with the New Hampshire plate?"

Rosa's chance had come. She could do Mom's thing, a blithe account of her lodge life and throw in that it was a transitional job and she would probably want to move back to civilization in a year or so but it was a great experience for now — that sort of stuff — and maybe she could add something jolly about Nat Speradakis. Mom was looking at her eagerly.

"Oh dear." Rosa sighed, to her own surprise. "It's been so cold and dark up north. I don't know if I can take much more of it. I've got this boyfriend who's driving me crazy." She was discovering, as she spoke, that she merely wanted some sympathizing. She could make a story of it — the woods, the freezing lake, the isolation, her unsureness about marriage — and Mom could listen and worry, and instead of sitting there feeling angrier by the minute, Rosa could set aside her duty to Martin and get some attention for herself.

V

JIM PFLUEGER had found himself a way out of his former life. It had taken some time, and he had made several bad turns on the way, but his daughter and son no longer resented him; they seemed to understand what it had been like for him and even appreciated how he had stayed the course. Now they were as likely as not to drop by his place in Dowland on their way from college to their mother's in the city. It was never for much of a visit. Monica, especially, acted as though she did not mean to intrude, but there she was anyway, for an hour or two; once she had even brought along a sort of boyfriend, another time she had her roommate with her. And Eric came to work on his car or help Jim at tax time. He never had much to talk about but had the need to do something, occasionally, with his dad. Jim tried to make clear to the kids that his little house was theirs, too. It was not their home, he knew, but it was a place on earth that would always belong to them. He had yet to absolve himself for his disappearance during what he called his Kathleen time, and he still questioned why it had taken him so very long to realize what he was doing. In therapy, it remained an unending mystery: that a man, hurt and confused and angry as he may have been, should put aside his own children for even a week — a woman, he felt, would never have done that. No, Dr. Forest kept telling him, a woman might; it was a whole mature adult who would not. He was mistaken to blame his past behavior on his maleness. Did he think there was something wrong about being a man? Forest had laughed and said, "In that case, there's not much I can do to help."

Jim had been at the computer all afternoon, tinkering with the awkward prose of some nincompoop, hacking away at civilization's general decline. Bad as the writing was, he enjoyed stuff that taught him something, manuals on boat maintenance or bird-watchers' newsletters, even if he never intended to make use of the information, but today it was an extensive fund-raising brochure for a suburban church, and he had a moment of despair. I'm fifty, he thought, looking up past the pale blue screen to the pasture across the road. Is this my life? But Dr. Forest, in another quadrant of his head, spoke up quickly: No, this is not your life, Mr. Pflueger, this is a job. Besides, you're keeping the English language up to snuff. You could do worse.

When Jim had been obsessed with Kathleen, it had not seemed to matter so. He had slashed his way through paragraphs like a cavalier. Everything he did had mattered. He wanted to live in the moment like that again, he had told Forest yesterday. And then they had talked, as unashamedly as he could, about sex and how it felt in the moment instead of in anticipation or retrospect. Kathleen had always made him feel in the moment, totally engaged with her body. He could not stop running his fingers all over her. "In the moment" seemed another of those therapy phrases he found himself thinking in lately. He did not like doing so, but if there was a subtler way to examine his psyche, he had not arrived at it yet.

"Good for you, Dad," Monica once said. "Most men your age won't go into therapy at all. They blame it all on the woman and don't want to think about it." Jim knew this was high praise from a college girl of the current generation, however much it made him feel condescended to, but the truth was that Monica's new stepfather had turned out to be an exemplar of "most men" once the honeymoon ended; Donna was no longer as blissful as she had thought she would be. If I can be patient, thought Jim, if I can let natural affections rise and fall, I'll have Monica and Eric back in my life again for good.

He stepped out onto his porch. The pasture across the road was turning a fresh golden green. It was to be its last spring if the town meeting did not reverse its vote. Everyone except immediate abutters like Jim had been persuaded they needed a stronger tax base. A hundred years ago, the little triangle of Dowland, two miles on each side, had snipped itself off from the manufacturing town to the east and allied with Umbachaug in hopes of retaining some rural simplicity. Now, the town's share of the regional school budget, the landfill, and road maintenance was gobbling up its resources. It seemed Jim had found Dowland just in time to say good-bye to it. I'm always doing that, he thought. I did it with Kathleen.

So he sat on the front step and picked at the peeling gray-blue paint and simply watched the sun declining beyond the pasture. He allowed himself a reminiscence of two summers ago, making love by moonlight over there with Kathleen before they went their separate ways. He was easily aroused, thinking of her, still. He could have gone back inside the house and indulged the fantasy further, but he felt, at that moment, he should try instead to concentrate on the pasture. Wait till after sunset. This was a time to store up in his memory every hillock, every clump of grass.

If he were a painter, he would have painted this view in a hundred lights and seasons like — who was it? — Monet. Jim had loads of snapshots, of course, and they would remind him in his old age of the lost beauty, but none captured it as his eyes did now. In fact, you could not shoot into the sun and get anything like a true representation of the varicolored scene.

A crow flew from a telephone pole along the road and landed on the grass to peck about. Jim even loved the way the phone lines drooped gracefully across the sky. He loved the dusty road he had to travel for a whole mile to reach Route 108. He had only lived there for three years but had totally forgotten the views from his Cambridge apartment after the divorce and from the house where they had been a family. I will never forget this pasture, he told himself now. I am at last old enough to know there will be nothing more beautiful in life than this. I have to look at what I have. There it was again: "in the moment." But he heard the voice of Dr. Forest saying calmly across the cinder-block cubicle where they met once a week, "We do not have the perfect words for things. We have to keep talking with the only words we have. Maybe we'll find better ones if we keep at it."

Forest was not much older than Jim. Jim had resented older brother figures until now, perhaps because he had been one himself. His sister had followed him so faithfully he was embarrassed by it now. What had he known more than she? How had he even managed to act as if he had known so much more? Of his own children, Monica had always seemed such a reasonable older sister for Eric; she had no tyranny in her.

Jim got up and walked toward the road, taking very slow steps, wondering if he even really wanted to cross to the pasture. Watching it so hard had made it seem an unreachable green and golden land. His boots struck the lumpy pavement and crunched in the sand left by the winter plows. He was under the phone lines now. Now he was descending the ditch and rising again through the weeds. In a bound he was over the low stone wall. There were several crows down the way who paid no attention to him. Yes, it is real, and I may still touch it, Jim thought, and he lay down on a patch of soft grass. This was not where he had last lain with Kathleen. This was a spot he had perhaps never stretched out on before. Whose bedroom will rise above where I am lying? he wondered. What will it be for them to look from their window back across the road at my dilapidated dump of a house blistering in the setting sun? Will they have any idea what their presence has done to confine my soul?

That was how Jim Pflueger meditated after a dispiriting afternoon of churchy prose. The winter, which had seemed interminable, had closed him in and shut him down but then begun to open him up again in strange ways. He had put his television in the closet. He had let his America Online account lapse. "Is this some sort of menopause?" he had asked Forest, who smiled like the Buddha and said, "Well, yes, I suppose you could put it that way."

What had truly surprised Jim was that, when he went to the Dowland Free Library for the latest volume of Elmore Leonard, he had also, hardly thinking, grabbed Walt Whitman off the classics shelf. Were his college days drifting back to him? Did he want Monica to think better of him? Whatever it was, he now read a little over breakfast every morning and then at night before sleep. Some of it was wordy and overly declamatory, but then he would reach a line that caused a shiver inside him. "When the lilac-scent was in the air and Fifth-month grass was growing . . ." That was one. He could not get it out of his head.

And as he turned on his side, there it was, that very grass, looming tall from his nestled vantage point. There are only two things that really stop people in their tracks, he thought: lovelessness and disease. As long as we are healthy and loved we chug along obliviously. His sister had become a different person, in a philosophic sense, when she first got sick, and now, perhaps, Jim thought, now that he was living alone, he was becoming a different person as well.

Still, what he really wanted to do right then — he could not deny it — was stroke the skin up Kathleen's thigh and reach around the smoothness of her hip and up her backbone to make her tingle, but not exactly Kathleen anymore, rather some other soul in Kathleen's body. And if he could stop thinking of precisely that body — he had tried simplemindedly with magazines and videos, but Forest had a more complicated approach: stop thinking of *only* Kathleen's body; think of her body and her character together, associate them, see them as one and the same, and gradually she won't seem as exciting to you. Perhaps. Forest always added a *perhaps* or a *maybe* to everything he said.

The shadow of trees was approaching Jim across the pasture. Just as he got up, intending to go sit on the stone wall awhile, he barely heard the phone ringing in the house. For all his newfound pensiveness, Jim was not one to let a phone ring. He sprinted to his door and caught it as the answering machine began its salutation.

"Let me shut this thing off. Hold on. There. Hello?"

"Dad," said Eric.

"Hey, where are you?"

"Mom's."

"What's up?"

"Exam week."

"So what are you doing in Cambridge?"

"Studying mostly."

"Well, don't miss your exams."

"Dad!"

"Stop by on your way back to Williamstown."

"If I get time."

"Well, I'm here."

"Here's the thing," said Eric. "I got this data processing job for the summer but it means living with Mom and Chucky, and I can get a place with some friends if I can do the last month deposit now, but Mom said I had to ask you this time. I'll pay you back at the end of summer."

"Fine," said Jim. "How much you need?"

"Five hundred?"

"Wow."

"Well, it's Cambridge."

"That's okay," Jim said. "Stop by, I'll write you a check. Or should I mail it?"

"If you could like mail it to me at Mom's, Express Mail? Actually, I need it tomorrow."

"I can just make it to the post office before they take it in to Fraddboro," Jim said.

"Sorry, Dad."

"It's fine. You'll pay me back. You'll be taking care of me in my old age anyway."

"Dad!"

"But I better get a move on."

"Thanks, Dad."

"You call him Chucky?"

"Chucky," Eric confirmed, and they both laughed and said their quick good-byes.

Jim went to get his checkbook feeling rather happy. Then he hopped in the sole remnant of all his midlife indulgences, his classic 1950 Rambler with the Smith College decal Monica had made him stick on the rear window, and headed down the long narrow road to what passed for the village: a general store with gas pump, a post office with a library in back, and the veterinarian-approved health-diet dog food outlet, the only thing for which people made a special trip to Dowland, Massachusetts.

VI

HAVING SPENT ALL DAY over the grill, Ron Starks certainly did not feel like cooking when he got home. First, he had a workout in his very own weight room, where Drew Hale had stored lumber in the old days, then he emerged, sweat dripping from his chest into his faded purple URHS shorts, and leaned into the fridge for a protein shake. He spooned in some glutamine powder and stirred it up. Victor looked over from the TV. He was snacking on breadsticks and carrots and having a beer watching Dan Rather, who never seemed all that fascinating to Ron. He would wait for *Entertainment Tonight* to join Victor on the couch.

"Take a shower!" Victor said. Ron wandering around the house in his frayed old shorts seemed not to do all that much for Victor anymore; even Stewart took more notice. Last week after they'd run together and showered back at his garage apartment, Stewart had said, "God, Ron, you sure are bulking up these days." Ron responded with a seductive flex. "The bigger the better!" he said. "I guess you'd be the one to know," said Stewart, but Ron got him right back: "Well, it's true, Victor's hung like a horse . . ." Stewart shook his head as if to say, "I don't know why I put up with such shit from you," and Ron did not know why he did either, but he did. Me and Stewart just have our old thing going, he told himself now. Victor thinks I actually want to get into Stewart's pants, but why would I go and spoil my lifelong instant turn-on?

There sat Victor in his gray sweatshirt and jeans and moccasins with his can of Bud, and he was lifelong, too, of course. Ron was about to remind himself how lucky he was when the thought of his virus passed quickly through his head. He immediately decided he was lucky anyway. Very lucky. He had been staying totally healthy, and it was only a couple of years since he got infected. He had friends. He had a home. His family didn't bother him much these days. He was buying into the diner, and he was safe, for really the first time in his life.

When he had showered, he took a fresh pair of white sweats off the bathroom shelf and sauntered naked out past Victor to the phone. He wanted to leave a message on Stewart's machine about the note Mary Lanaghan had tacked to their door. Ron could put in the dock, no problem, but the news about Drew's daughter moving in next door was definitely going to bum Stewart out.

After four rings some music came on — it sounded like Barry White — and Stewart's voice said he was having way too much fun to come to the phone. "Hey, we're getting your wife for a neighbor, you asshole," said Ron, and then Stewart picked up.

"I was sleeping," he said. "What did you say?"

"Would you take that in the other room?" Victor asked

as soon as Ron launched into his news, so he dragged the phone across the floor and into his weight room. He lay down on the mat and managed to do a few sit-ups with the receiver tucked under his chin while he listened to Stewart rave. Then he pulled on his sweatpants and started trying to quiet his buddy down.

When *E.T.* was about to begin, Ron cut it short, having agreed to perform nightly surveillance of Peggy on Stewart's behalf. He draped the sweatshirt around his shoulders and sat down beside Victor. All he got was the "why do I put up with your shit" shake of the head that Victor had picked up from Stewart, a way those two had of bonding, Ron figured, to cover up how much they aggravated each other. But Ron sort of liked being thought of as impossible. He had grown up getting the same treatment from his parents.

"You'll love this," Victor said, scratching at his mustache. "They're doing a spot on Keanu Reeves."

So they settled in to watch, Ron chomping on a raw carrot, Victor nibbling breadsticks.

"One thing's for sure," Ron said at one point. "When I watch a show like this, I realize everyone else in America thinks about sex as much as I do." Victor snorted. "Well, you're just as bad."

"Worse," Victor said with his dark heavy eyes staring at the TV. Ron slung his legs around and pressed his thighs into Victor's lap. Victor reached over to clasp Ron's feet, now propped on the arm of the couch. Then they both looked back at the TV. It was getting dark out the window behind it. Even as he watched Keanu Reeves talk about performing Hamlet, of all stupid ideas, Ron found himself thinking of Mary Lanaghan swinging on the maple tree last night, and then he remembered about Rosa and wondered if she had pulled off the *Psychic Friends* routine.

A commercial came on. "What, that's it? They're not going to show him working out?"

"Sorry, Ron," said Victor.

"Fuck this. Hey, let's go drop in on Mary and find out more about Peggy moving in."

But Victor was too beat. He called the diner to make sure that boy Kevin was handling the cleanup and then headed downstairs to the bedroom level, where the boat slip had once been. Now it had sliders out to a deck, the feature that had sold them on the place; the only water inside was encased in the king-size water bed Ron had insisted on buying when they moved in. After the foldout canvas cot of his youth, he had been ready for luxury. In exchange for getting his weight room, he had helped Victor set up his own hideaway in the attic. He got him a deep-pile carpet remnant, a papa-san chair, and big foam throw pillows, and arranged all Victor's magazines, model kits, whittling sticks, and business files in old milk crates under the eaves, but Victor seldom went up there; at home, he was either on the couch or in bed.

So Ron put on his running shoes and went out alone. He sprinted past the dark cottage and turned toward the distant twinkling on the corner of Mary's balcony. Passing through the twilit trees, he could see the boxy silhouette of the Nomad down by the water. Ron did not really know why he coveted it so — just as another place to fix up, probably. Victor could set up his hobbies there, or Ron could make it his own little fuck palace; that was what he usually fantasized about. "Too Much Monkey Business," the vintage Chuck Berry tune, started running in his head as he picked up the pace.

Below Mary's balcony, in stripes of light from between the planks, he stopped, untied the sleeves from around his neck, and pulled the sweatshirt over his cold perspiring skin. He listened for signs of life, heard none, then clomped up the stairs shouting, "Mary Lanaghan, this is a home invasion!"

That set Hilda off. Soon Mary was at her door saying, "Well, Ron, come in, come in, you have to meet my daughter Rosa, we're just finishing dessert." The dog gave one last woof, then took her spot by the table to await leftovers. Rosa alerted Ron with a forefinger to her lips before her mother looked her way to make the introduction.

"Well, now I've met all four of you guys," Ron said. "You look like your mom." He pulled out a stool and sat down.

"She's got my complexion, but all my kids have raven hair like their father. He's what they call black Irish," said Mary. 'Let me give you a slice of this pound cake. And peaches from a can." Ron was always glad for a bite, since he and Victor seldom sat down to a meal but just snatched what they could at work. "They're not bad, though," Mary said. "From the Old Fraddboro Store."

"You keep telling me about that place," said Ron.

While he tried to eat the dessert in modest forkfuls, Mary told him most of what he had already heard from Rosa at lunch, about her job at the lodge up north and about Martin coming home for the summer and why Rosa called herself Blakey not Lanaghan. Rosa smiled cheerfully through all of it, and Ron enjoyed the odd sensation of sharing a secret with this girl he hardly knew. Mary seemed older in her mother role. He was not used to her acting so picky and so almost bossy, a toned-down version of his own overwhelming mother. That's the problem with families, he decided, they trap you in your age bracket. But when he ran into Mary alone, she never seemed like a mother; she was funnier and gentler, just herself. Last fall they had had some long talks down by the cove. Mary was the only person besides Victor and Stewart he had talked to about his virus. She worried about it more than Ron did himself and read up on the latest research and left photocopies in his mailbox of scientific articles he could not understand. She was always upbeat. She believed in his vitamins and supplements and in exercise and said there was no reason, what with the new antivirals, that he would not die of plain old age. She had been on the hospital desk once when he went in for a checkup, and he showed her the printout of his blood work to prove the stability of the T-cell counts. He told her his doctor was on the lookout for change. Then he might want to start treatment.

When Mary paused in her recap of family news, Rosa asked Ron if he knew those humongous Thibaults, and he said he had definitely seen them from a distance. "You could hardly miss them," said Rosa. "Well, Louise Thibault came by earlier this afternoon . . " But Ron was getting bored with the chitchat and wanted to get at what he had really come over for.

"So what's this about Peggy Hale — I mean, Tomaszewski — moving in next door?" he asked.

Mary was pouring herself some more decaf and offered a cup to Ron, who figured why not. "Weren't you somehow connected to her?" she asked.

"You mean because of Stewart?"

"Who's Stewart?" asked Rosa.

"Stewart Tomaszewski, you saw — he's a friend of mine." Ron had covered in time. Rosa was looking at the crumbs on her plate. "He's still married to her," Ron said, "but they're separating. I've told you about him, Mary. He's the one I run with."

"I can never remember all the names in your life," Mary said. "Ron has about ten siblings, Rosa, over in Sewall."

"There's eight of us," Ron said.

Then Mary settled down and told Ron about Drew Hale's visit and began to sound more like herself again, not someone's mother. It was the kind of gossipy talk Ron loved. "This woman wanted to rent from him," she was saying. "I was sitting on the balcony and heard their cars drive in, and then suddenly the woman took off. Drew was convinced she was afraid he'd get her inside the cottage and throw her across a bed, and he didn't mind telling me about it, either."

Ron shook his head. "That's like the time he told Victor and I some fag joke. He wanted to see how we'd react."

Rosa had put her plate on the floor for Hilda to lick off the peach juice and cake crumbs.

"Drew likes you two despite himself. You've got him all confused," Mary said. "Anyway, I'm supposed to keep an eye on his daughter while she's here."

"Hey, so am I!" said Ron. "For Stewart. He thinks he's a gift to the ladies, so he doesn't get it when one of them's had it with him. He's hurting bad."

"What's Peggy Hale like these days?" Mary wanted to know.

"I hope you two aren't going to start couples counseling on this poor woman," said Rosa, tipping about impatiently on her stool.

But Ron was intrigued at the prospect. Victor always said Ron was like high school over and over again, but why not? Across the table, Mary was saying she could do couples counseling on Rosa, too, if she didn't watch out, and Ron found himself thinking of last fall, sitting by the cove and piling up tiny haystacks of pine needles as he tried to nudge

Mary back toward her own life, to convince her there was nothing to be so timid about. "Play around a little, Mary, have some fun for a change," he had told her. "And look what playing around got you, Ron," she had said, her voice serious and shaky. But he had still tried to lighten it up: "Well, at least I ain't letting moss grow under me." He had not meant to put her down, but she choked up for a second and then gave him a tight sad hug. That was when she admitted she had not been with a man since her husband — well, except for a couple of awful dates that went nowhere. But this year she was getting asked to hospital board dinner parties with some likely candidates. Ron had hopes for her.

Hilda came around to sit by him, so he set his plate on the linoleum floor, too. Rosa and Mary were spatting about why some guy named Nat had gone off to ski by himself and not even offered to take Rosa with him, but the conversation would eventually wind its way back to Peggy Hale. Ron wanted to tell Mary what a decent girl Peggy was, despite the impossible men in her life.

VII

EVERYTHING HAD BEEN put away. Mary had kissed her daughter good night and watched her haul herself wearily up the ladder to her old familiar bed. Rosa must have awakened very early at the lodge to have stopped for food somewhere on the way and yet gotten there by noon; all their talk must have tired her out even more. Safe at home, Rosa would soon be sleeping soundly, but Mary's pulse, which had leapt at the first sight of her, was still coursing too fast for sleep. Her job, Mary could not stop herself from thinking, was hardly over. She had always acknowledged the evidence of generation upon generation that motherly influence could only go so far, and with her children living at a distance now, Mary had managed to relieve her constant watchfulness with perhaps a bit more attention to her own requirements. She was reading more, for one thing, and getting more exercise. But that quickened pulse was a reliable sensation, and truly it was so very natural for Mary to focus on her children, ever shepherding them toward an elusive state she would like to think of as adult happiness. It was instantly fascinating to discuss Rosa's uncertain attachment to Nat or Martin's recurrent aimlessness, to consult with Shirley planning her honors thesis or Bayard vacillating between girlfriends. Mary's concern for Ron Starks or even Louise Thibault could never spring from quite such an interior source. She was compassionate — she allowed herself that — but the feeling in her tonight, as she pulled up to her neck the quilt she had managed to sew herself, went even deeper than compassion. It was unthinking as breath, and she could take no credit for it.

There had been one startling moment that evening. As Mary was setting the table, Rosa had come in from walking the dog, perched on a stool with the warmest glint in her eyes, and said, "Mom, do you ever just go swing on a tree out there? I can picture you taking walks, with your woods all around you, and just — I don't know — leaping up and swinging on a tree branch." All Mary had answered then was, "Oh, maybe sometimes," but down in her body, all through it, she had felt, if such a thing possible, the very circulation of her blood.

She knew Rosa had been looking carefully at her face

then, and Mary had been unable to stop her lip from curling up in a tiny sign of satisfaction, which, surely, Rosa had noticed. Quickly, she had set down the wooden bowl of lacquered gourds for a centerpiece and two sturdy candles in their squat wooden holders on either side and puttered about at the sink, washing and peeling. Then Mary had handed Rosa a cutting board and a knife to slice up the vegetables while she prepared the couscous.

This May night was not quite warm enough for an open window, but now in her bed Mary had a sudden yearning for a whiff of the outdoors. She slipped from under her quilt for five seconds to raise the window a mere inch, enough to hear more clearly the wind in the pine trees and an occasional distant sound, a plane overhead or a truck rumbling out the Fraddboro Road.

A chill reached her. She was now as close to everything as she could be and yet as far away. That was how it felt. Soon enough, she understood: her own parents, long gone, were weaving themselves in faded threads through the pattern of her thoughts. Mary remembered how she had thought of them yesterday when that ray of the setting sun had warmed her face and thought of them again in the cold light of that morning, walking through those woods with the dog and hearing what was surely a rifleman shooting targets in the regional landfill. The curious artificer, Drew Hale, had left her unsettled; the blank panes of his former workshop had almost scared her. But old Hilda had gone on, compelled to trace a path from scent to scent with some presumable pleasure. Mary, too. She had found the expected patch of bluebells in the dell beyond the railroad bed, she had heard the cardinal singing, and eventually she had cheered herself up.

Maybe what had saddened her that morning was the vision Drew Hale had insisted on calling forth of his fearful prospective tenant. Simply rude, Mary had decided, but clearly Drew's interpretation had lingered in her thoughts while her own had vanished. It was the terrified woman she still saw. If only Mary had taken her walk fifteen minutes earlier, she might have encountered her on the road and encouraged her to stay. It would have been pleasant to have her next door for the month of June.

Mary sat up in bed. It was not yet ten; there was time to call Christina in Newton. They usually talked on Sundays but had missed each other yesterday. Of all her old friends, only Christina had fully comprehended what had gone on between her and Dermot; Christina alone had insisted on taking sides. It had meant an end to neighborhood pool parties. The other families went instead to Crystal Lake to avoid the awkwardness. But Mary had sat with Christina in the sun on canvas deck chairs and talked softly while Bayard and Shirley splashed about with little Gus.

She pulled the receiver with its bellyful of lit-up numbers back under the quilt with her; eleven punches produced a tune she could practically whistle by now. At the sound of Mary's voice, Christina said, "I knew it would be you."

"So what are you doing?" Mary asked. "What were you doing the moment before the phone rang?"

"The moment before?" Christina gave it some thought. Oh, she had to confess she had been thinking about Bosnian relief, no, really, she had. She knew it sounded awfully earnest of her. Why did she get so swept up in such events? She had joined a community organization raising money for Sarajevo. Old Mrs. Friedenheimer across the street was very active in it.

"You're making me feel guilty," said Mary.

But that was not the effect Christina had wanted. "No, but you see, Mary, here I am in Newton. We have a swimming pool, for God's sake, so who's feeling guilty?"

Mary countered that Christina always used what she had, she connected herself, she brought up her son to be connected, outgoing. Mary's own kids were self-absorbed, she said, but here Gus was, a member of the Gay-Straight Alliance at his high school and he wasn't even gay.

"Most of those kids aren't gay," said Christina. "It's the cool thing to do. It upsets their parents, and they get to put strange objects in their earlobes and dye their hair."

"Nonetheless, it's being connected," said Mary.

"It's called teen rebellion, Mary," Christina said in her soberest voice.

Then Mary said, "Well, I wish my kids were more rebellious. For a social life Martin e-mails girls he meets on the Internet."

Christina said she was glad to hear Mary in a whimsical mood; after their last talk, she had feared she was hitting another low. Or was it just hormones?

"I seem to be staving it off," Mary said. "Sometimes I wish I'd get one clear sign. Would it be a relief?" Underneath her quilt, she was conscious of her whole warm body, how it was hers and only hers now, how she had held herself close over the cold winter but now felt, even in that night air, the relaxation of spring that allowed her toes to uncurl, her spine to stretch out, ready for the new season. She would not have to light the woodstove again.

"Kurt keeps telling me when it happens it won't be a big deal to him. He loves me now, he'll love me then. I'm supposed to find that a comfort."

"And you do," Mary said, thinking of Christina with Kurt near her somewhere in the house and her son living at home for a few more years. "Has Gus done something weird to *his* hair?" she asked.

"Just that shelf effect, two layers, it's already out of style. But he pierced the top of his ear, the cartilage, and it was a lot more painful than he thought it was going to be."

"What does Kurt say?"

"Kurt tries to be easygoing. Gus thinks everything Kurt does is dorky. He bought CD versions of his old rock albums and thought Gus would be interested — the Byrds, the Animals."

Mary was picturing Christina in her usual wing chair in her high-ceilinged living room with all the lights on and thought she could hear the bass from Gus's room pounding in the distance. She imagined Kurt in the adjoining study catching up on legal work with his laptop and all around them the airy space of that old house, bookshelves crammed, Oriental rugs askew on the hall floor, hats and jackets thrown down on chairs, cat litter scattered across the tiles in the back entry. Outside, there was that set of canvas chairs by the pool and the old uneven stockade fence with the gate, which always stuck, leading to next door, the companion Queen Anne with its wraparound porch and curved glass in the corner windows, the stained glass on the stairwell glowing red and yellow and blue at that hour. What an unreal stage of my life that was, Mary thought, when I was only thirty and found myself living there with four kids and Dermot.

She told Christina that Rosa had shown up that morning, and soon they were off on a discussion of Rosa's serious relationship versus Bayard's dates and of how the divorce had hit those kids so differently. As usual, Christina insisted that all children were individuals and you could never fathom the million sources of either their discontent or their resilience. Mary agreed but was sure it was possible to perceive patterns, at least, to know what to look out for, to guard against dangers.

"And to blame yourself for," said Christina. "You know that's what you do, Mary."

Mary curled up tighter under her quilt between her blue flannel sheets in the light of the twelve little buttons on the receiver. "Well, I was raised Catholic," she said.

"So was I," Christina said. "You don't have to be Boston Irish, you know. And who says I got over it either? I'm knocking on doors for Bosnia."

Mary's chest suddenly ached from missing her old friend, and she heard herself saying, "I wish you and Kurt would rent the little cottage down the cove from here for a week. You've seen it. Remember? It's cheap. He hasn't got anybody for it yet."

The idea had come forth with the words. It seemed now to be what the whole day had been tending toward. And so Drew's terrified woman was nothing more, perhaps, than an element of her own self, Mary thought, the fearful part, being chased out by the advent of spring. And then Rosa had come and, as her retinue, Louise Thibault, too, and Ron Starks had appeared at dusk to set some blessed seal on the day. Now all these benign forces had converged in Mary's brain, creating a moment of certainty that, of course, Christina must come and bring Kurt and even drag along Gus if she could, and — Mary suddenly remembered — Martin would be around by then in his trailer and maybe the other kids would come — her racing thoughts turning to words again — "for my birthday, Christina. I'll turn forty-nine in June. We'll have a picnic down by the cove and swim and float about. Wicker basket and bedspread and bottles of wine . . "

"Maybe, well, we could look into it," said Christina.

"He's in Leominster. Let me get the number. Call him first thing in the morning. Drew Hale. H-A-L-E."

Christina was chuckling on the other end of the line while Mary reached out from under the quilt for her address book somewhere on her bedside table. Her bare arm felt the chill. She wanted to stop everything in the universe at that precise moment, before she had a chance to find out if Christina would take her up on the idea. It was a delicious feeling not to know yet.

A JUNE TUESDAY

I

IN INDIAN TIMES Lake Umbachaug had been a good deal larger. Much of the land Drew Hale owned — Mary Lanaghan's smaller piece as well — was underwater then, and the piney point was a sandbar. But white settlers widened the breach at the southern end, where a slender brook had skimmed off the lake's surface, and a torrent rushed out, fertilizing the homesteaders' farmlands before collecting itself again within modest banks on its way to the wider Quidnapunxet. The reservoir of Umbachaug remained low. From the shoreline the land stepped up to a flat sandy sill on which, one day, Mary's chalet and Drew's rental cottage would rest, and then it rose again, rockier and ragged, where it had never been smoothed out by pre-Columbian waters. Swamp maples invaded the muddy corners of the new cove while pines took to the sandier soil and maintained their claim for three centuries of growth and harvest.

Martin Lanaghan, sitting on the doorstep of his trailer in the warm month of June, was remembering when he first saw his mother's property. Mr. Hale had walked them through the woods and, at one stopping place, turned to Martin like a high school teacher putting him on the spot: "Why do you suppose that rocky hill cuts off at this dirt road where we're standing?" Martin had no idea. "This was a sacred lake, son, and the hills," Mr. Hale explained, "came right down to its edge. We're standing now in the phantom waters of ancient Lake Umbachaug. What do you think of that?" At sixteen, Martin had not liked Mr. Hale, had felt uneasy around him, the more so because Bayard had taken a sudden interest in his workshop, especially the guns, and learned to clean rifles and pistols and gone along with him to shoot targets in the regional landfill.

Hale's Cove had been a strange relocation for the brothers. It counted as Haviland, but their high school was in Parshallville, an entirely separate town. Their classmates came from Fraddboro, too, and Dowland and Sewall, and it seemed to matter which you called home. Bayard soon found himself a set of pals in Haviland Center, but with only his senior year to go, Martin developed no loyalties. He missed his old suburban Newton. He had loved having the Ostermanns next door, the Friedenheimers across the street; they had known him most of his life. His mother's woodland refuge was Martin's place of exile. He never let on how he felt because he did not want her to worry about him on top of everything else. He and Rosa, the eldest two, made a private pact: they would tell their fears and sadnesses to each other alone. For Bayard and Shirley, sharing sleeping lofts with their big brother and sister was a treat, and the free-for-all room almost beyond believing; their father would never have allowed such pillow fights and Nerf ball games in the old house, such loud music, would never have let them scribble and paint all over the walls. They forgot Newton; the Ostermanns' pool was nothing beside Umbachaug. Bayard rowed the entire lake to build up his arms, Shirley climbed trees and built leaf forts, even Rosa jogged the railroad bed with Hilda to work off her fat thighs, she said, but Martin let a veil fall between him and the peaceful countryside. He thought only of backyards and sidewalks and old neighbors as he helped his mother insulate the basement ceiling and install storm windows. He did love the new place in one unexpected way, though: it had caused him to see her at last as she really was, gardening, cooking, sewing, reading. And somehow it left his father back in another time, leaning out the driver's side of his Saab, smiling with all his teeth at Martin while a shadowy unknown woman sat in there beside him offering nothing but a cautious wave.

Martin, in U Mass T-shirt and cutoffs, sunlight on his pale hairy knees, was wondering now if he had returned because the cove, through memory, had become home to him at last. Back when he dropped out of college, his parents' gift of the trailer had seemed some late acknowledgment that he had lost more than the other kids. That particular portion of guilt had persisted, Martin knew, because this time his father had offered to pay for his America Online account if his mother would arrange for a phone line.

Martin dug his toes into the soft pine needles and closed his eyes. He was suddenly a lonely wayfarer, a hermit in the desert. He imagined total solitude. But then a ghostly impression of being underwater filled his thoughts. The surface of a pristine lake shone in sunlight somewhere above him and muck was oozing between his toes. He blinked and reached behind for his curled-up copy of Frank Herbert's *Heretics of Dune* and, for a while, took himself to a yet stranger world, but he kept sensing water rising about him.

These two lakes, the one he saw and the one he dreamed of, were the subjects of his e-mail the night before to his friend Suzanne in Tesuque, New Mexico. He had never seen Suzanne, but more than Astrid in Amherst or Rachel in Newton, more than any of the women he had ever been able to tell his thoughts to, she was becoming his true soul mate. They wrote each other about the books they read; they traded cassette mixes and then critiqued them in Internet chat sessions. They had met through the Peter Gabriel newsgroup. Suzanne did lots of poetry and had written two complete fantasy novels; she worked at a resort called Rancho Escondido, which Martin imagined as a cluster of bungalows and corrals on a vast dry plateau of sand and sagebrush. She probably had an equally perfect vision of his New England, but their correspondence was more about feelings than about daily life, about universalities they could relate to without knowing what the other looked like beyond the blurry photos they had scanned in when they first linked up. His two lakes had been symbols of what Martin wanted to express, that the imaginary is always deeper than the real, that their friendship, existing only in lights on a screen, was deeper than most of his so-called friendships in reality. And yet, he had also admitted in last night's e-mail, he often did find himself trying to imagine the actual Suzanne.

She would be reading his letter now, before work. It was only seven out there, but she got up earlier than Martin and always read her mail first thing. He realized he was as expectant as he was fearful but resolved not to turn on his computer until after lunch. He had probably said too much. In all their confidences, neither had ever touched on a mutual attraction. Suzanne had told him about the guy in his late thirties who ran a textile gallery in Santa Fe and kept wanting to start seeing her again, and he had told her about Rachel and somewhat less about Astrid, but they had both moved on quickly to an assessment of the emotional issues, and that had taken them to books and movies and mostly to music, where they understood each other instantly by mentioning particular songs.

Martin was looking across the shallow cove, picturing the scene he had described in his letter, the point submerged as a treeless sandbar with an Indian wading knee-deep along its length, searching for fish to grab with his bare hands. There was no distant sound of a motorboat, such as Martin actually heard, no far-off shouts from the day camp up the lake. But suddenly, something orange and pink was floating into the corner of his left eye, and a breathy voice said, "Hey, Marty!" or "Mah-ty," really, in the Massachusetts accent everyone in Newton either never had or quickly tried to lose.

"Hi, Peggy," Martin said in a quiet voice. She lay on that orange rubber raft in her pink bikini, paddling herself along with her too yellow hair blowing out behind. It was hardly hot summer yet, but she was making the most of her vacation.

"Just waking up?" she asked as she ran the raft onto Martin's tiny beach.

"I'm not sure I'm up even yet," he said to excuse his lack of enthusiasm.

"So I heard your radio last night," Peggy said, hopefully.

"CD actually," said Martin. He was annoyed at himself for not seeming friendlier. He did not know why he had such trouble managing to.

Peggy stretched herself up on her elbows, like a sea lion, and Martin got a glimpse of the tops of her breasts, pink as her bathing suit. Then she nestled down on her crossed forearms and splashed at the water with her toes.

"Did I keep you up?" Martin asked, fearing he was guilty of the unneighborly behavior his mother had cautioned him about.

"Oh, I was up, too. I can't get to sleep out here alone. I'm not used to it."

She was obviously waiting for Martin to help her get the

conversation going, so he said, "Nice of your father to let you have the place."

"Let's say I didn't have much choice," Peggy said. "Come home now and get a job or hang out here and cool off first."

Martin squinted at her. She seemed sad. It made him glad for his own wishy-washy dad, his well-meaning mom; he could not imagine them pushing him into anything. That was an advantage of their being divorced.

"So what I want to know — " Peggy said, "I'm out here because of that fucker Stewart fucking me over; who are you out here because of?"

"What makes you think I'm out here because of somebody?" Martin stretched his pale legs out, and his toes almost reached the lip of the pine-needled slope where the sand began. If Peggy reached out her arms, she could have tickled them.

"You're too good-looking not to have had a girlfriend," she said, smiling up at him as easily as if she had simply said good morning.

It was unexpected. Martin did not know how to react. He drew his knees up again and bored his toes into the pine needles.

"So?" said Peggy.

"She lives out in Santa Fe," Martin decided to say.

"She run away from you or you run away from her?"

Martin wondered how deep he should get into this — there were endless possibilities with an imaginary girlfriend — but before he could answer, Peggy started to tell him about her own situation, how it was she who finally left him, Stewart, her husband; how it was a relief at first, it was still a relief, except being out here in the woods did not help much, it made her think about it all the time.

"And the weirdest thing is," she said, "Ron Starks, his best friend, lives in the boathouse next door. So I have to put up with seeing Ron, and I swear he's trying to get me and Stewart back together. My dad definitely didn't realize."

"What's Stewart have a gay best friend for?" Martin asked, but he did not mean it to sound disapproving or suspicious; he was just curious.

"They go back to high school. Stewie probably used to have Ron blow him, I wouldn't be surprised," Peggy said.

Martin was unsure how to respond. Maybe Peggy was being funny, or needed to unload a little.

She reached out her arms, shoved the raft off the sand, and paddled herself around. "You should come in, Marty. It's not too cold."

He found himself standing up and trying out the water with his feet. "It's not too warm either," he said.

"Yeah, but it's not too cold."

He waded in up to his knees and stopped. Peggy was paddling around him in a wide circle. Water drops glistened on her back. "Ron and I skinny-dipped last night," she said. "It felt great."

"I thought you tried to avoid him."

"I avoid him talking about Stewart. Ron's fun to hang out with. We were dancing and singing and driving Victor crazy."

Martin felt lonely and awkward. The side of himself he rally hated was forcing itself into his thoughts. Peggy had swept her raft around and was making for his knees. He saw her hands reach out to grab him when it was too late to catch her first, and he buckled. Then she splashed his T-shirt, and it was a question of whether he could join in cheerfully and splash back or sink neck-deep into cold water to keep things from escalating. That was easier, he decided, and it was not as cold when he got all the way in.

"See, the sun warms up the shallow parts," Peggy was saying. Martin knew she was disappointed he had not tried to tip her over. "Take off your shirt," she said, "start getting rid of that pale." When Martin stood up, he realized he would be warmer without the dripping T-shirt, so he tossed it up on land. "After Stewart, I'm not used to guys being shy," Peggy said.

This was better. She had given him his traditional excuse for himself. He shrugged in what he had learned was an appealingly helpless fashion. Peggy tipped herself off the raft and dived after his ankles, so he leapt on the raft and made for shore.

"You bastid!" Peggy spluttered behind him. She caught up soon enough, but Martin was off onto dry land. He made it back to the doorstep of his trailer, and she ran up dripping and flopped on the pine needles at his feet. "Basically," she said, "I let you win."

The cold water was slipping right off him in the morning sun. It felt better than anything had felt in months. He had been so numb in Boston. He remembered a frozen walk to his father's house and sitting by the fire to thaw out, the last time he had sensed his skin coming alive like this.

"So you're here to get over a girlfriend and I'm here to get over a husband," said Peggy. "We definitely got something to talk about."

"Would you like tea and a muffin?" Martin asked.

"Tea? Sure. I don't usually have tea. What kind of muffin?"

"My mother got them. Lemon–poppyseed. Or I've got bagels."

"You eat weird," said Peggy, pronouncing it "wee-id."

She was looking at him now as if from behind a screen, not as sparkly eyed as earlier. Martin felt she had made up her mind to lay off him until she puzzled him out better. He generally had that effect on women. He and Suzanne had e-mailed on the subject, but she never attributed his slowness to fear or prudishness the way Rachel did. Suzanne believed in taking time to experience things totally. She had a sort of Native American philosophy about love having to do with planting and growing and harvesting and storing away. Now Martin was all of a sudden aware he was getting nervous about checking his computer.

When he had heated two cups of water and warmed the muffins in his dad's old microwave and toasted a bagel in his mom's discarded toaster oven, he brought it all out front on a tray and Peggy looked up from her catnap. "I should be feeling better," she said. "Great weather, almost summer, I'm making a new friend, I'm safely out of a shitty marriage . . "

"What does your dad think about it?" Martin asked, knowing Mr. Hale would have a strong opinion one way or another.

"Let me tell you about my dad," Peggy said. "He was on to Stewart, but he's such a peach he doesn't rub it in. He says I need thinking time. Gives me the cottage for a month. Who's complaining? my girlfriends say. They don't know what it's like having a dad a step ahead of you."

This was tricky. Martin was not sure he should say it, but he did: "I always found your dad to be sort of a pain."

Peggy seemed pleased and took a bite out of her bagel. "You got any jam?" Martin reached into the trailer and handed her an unopened jar from his box of Old Fraddboro supplies. "What's lingonberry?" Peggy asked.

"Mom bought it."

"Let me tell you about Stewart's mom," Peggy said, spreading the jam thickly. "His mom does his laundry and she tiptoes up the steps to our apartment and just leaves the basket on the landing. I come to the door and she's on her way down. 'Didn't want to disturb you, dear,' she says. That's such bullshit!"

Peggy was sitting up now, and Martin could tell she did not mind being there nearly naked. He thought back to his earlier retreat time, when the only visitor to his trailer had been Louise Thibault, four times the size of Peggy Hale and all encased in gray sweat clothes. They used to listen to They Might Be Giants and Jonathan Richman and laugh and talk about what the people they knew in common were up to. Louise thought his music was oddball, but she was comforting. She came again the week he moved back, for old times' sake. Martin worried that he condescended to Louise, and to Peggy, because of their accents and the things they talked about. He could actually see some blondish pubic hair peeking out of Peggy's bikini the way she sat, cross-legged, on the pine needles. She had pink nail polish on her toes.

"I don't blame his mom," she was saying. "She's widowed. What else has she got to do? But let me tell you about that fucker Stewart." She began with the story of their courtship at Ron and Victor's diner, then talked about Stewart's place above his mother's garage with the Jacuzzi and the round bed, which somehow made you go wilder than usual, and about their wedding, how they chose their own vows from a book of love poems Ron gave them and how blown away she was at first, marrying one of the Tomaszewskis, getting in with Stewart's older crowd. "Marty," she said, "you got to put a lot of the blame on great sex. I thought I could live forever on it."

Martin realized she could just as easily have said, "Great sex is definitely the key to a lasting relationship," and she probably would on some other day. Nevertheless, he did not want to discredit her wisdom. She seemed sad again. He reached over, and what he touched was her big toe. He gave it a brief squeeze.

That brought the sparkle back into Peggy's eyes. "Not that I have anything against great sex," she said. "Hey, Marty, what do you think is going on with Mary — I mean, your mom — and that guy from Sewall?"

"I haven't met him," Martin said.

"Ron's from Sewall, and his aunt works for him. The guy's on the hospital board. Ron's always on your mom's case. But she won't tell him if it's like heavy."

Martin did not know what to add. He did not like thinking about his mom's desultory social life. For years she had been going out for dull evenings with dreary people and coming home cheerless. This hospital board guy was undoubtedly the same, even if she tried talking him up more than usual, his poor mom.

It was half a minute before Peggy went on. First, she asked Martin exactly how old he was, and he told her twenty-six. Then she wanted to know about the girl in Arizona. "New Mexico," he said. "Her name's Suzanne."

"So where'd you meet?" Peggy asked, reaching over to return the toe squeeze, but she held on awhile.

"Boston," Martin said, which was true insofar as he had met her at all. "By the way, I've been meaning to check my e-mail," he said, "to see if she wrote yet today. It's crazy. We e-mail every day. Mind if I just check?" He stood up, and Peggy had to let go when he stepped into the trailer, though she tried to reach for his ankle to hold him. "I'll be right out," he said.

"You're definitely still hurting, Marty," he heard her say.

"I'll be right out," he said again. He did not really want to find out what Suzanne had written but could not help himself, either. Maybe there was nothing.

He logged on and tried not to think as he waited for it to say, "You've got mail," in its Elmer Fudd voice. He clicked on the mailbox, feeling his heart in his chest, and there was only one subject heading: *You and Me.* He was afraid to click on it, but he did as soon as he heard Peggy saying, "What the hell are you doing anyway?"

"I'll be right out," he said once more as Suzanne's words came up on the screen.

> I try to imagine the actual you too. This is what I see. This quiet man with dark dark hair long and straight like the Indian you wrote about. I see him standing up to his knees in a lake. Which of the 'two' lakes you have to guess. At sunrise watching the light come through those green green trees you have back east. Nothing is dusty or dry. Instead its all moist and fresh. He's part of the blessing of morning. He understands birdsong and the ways of the waters. He slowly dips his bare body into the coolness as he does every day in his forest refuge. To become newborn. So, the actual you is not the lonely sad Martin in his trailer with his desktop and aol account. The actual you is what you think of as the imaginary you. You do not know the imaginary me that has to go serve breakfast now and strip the beds and lead fat old city dudes on trail rides. You alone know the actual me. The naked dawn dancer me. Think about it. Peace!
>
> Suzanne

Martin sat back, the folding metal chair cold against his skin, and thought it out as she suggested he do. She had seen him as the wading Indian he had imagined seeing across the cove. He did not know why her words now made his heart sink. In a way, she was right. That image was a deep part of him. But what he had meant by his e-mail was that he was beginning to want to know her more on the surface, too. He wanted to know about stripping beds and trail rides at Rancho Escondido and all the stupid details of her boring day, but she did not want to know his.

II

DREW WAS STANDING on the dock Victor and Ron had put in for him. Where the hell was Peggy? It was ten o'clock on a Tuesday morning, and she had left the cottage wide open. His daughter was not the sort to go for a walk, even on such a nice day. He had come to check up on her and do a quick inventory of the place for the people Mary Lanaghan had got in for him the last week of the month. He was sorry he was going to send Peggy home, but all she did was complain about being there, and Elizabeth was sure she would be happier back in Leominster. Drew had hoped Mary Lanaghan could talk sense with Peggy better than he could. It was strange, he thought, how he had respect for that woman despite her unearned income. Of course, her little slice of land was surrounded by his acreage, and he could choose to do whatever he liked with it — the very trees were awaiting his decision. He had no reason to feel beneath Mary Lanaghan, but, yes, he did respect her, he hated to admit it.

The dock needed paint. It needed a few planks replaced. Those Boston people would sue if they stubbed their toes, so he had better get around to it before they came. Christ, the whole damn cottage needed paint. But Drew had made the decision last year never to paint it again; it would meet the bulldozers sooner than he would paint it. He remembered the first paint job back in '39 after the hurricane. He was only five. His father had given him a big dripping brush, and he had carefully swiped away at the lowest clapboards. Some of the paint was still under there, seven coats later.

He climbed back up the stone steps to the porch door and banged it open. Peggy had dragged a quilt out to the wicker settee. She must have spent the night there in the freshness. Kleenexes were all over the place. Did she have a cold, or had she been crying again? The Chinese checkers board was on the floor and some of the marbles had spilled across the straw mat. There were four Rolling Rock bottles lined up against the screen. Maybe Victor and that other one had been over. Peggy herself was never much of a beer drinker until Stewart came along with his all-night parties. Drew knew Peggy was really a quiet girl at heart, more like Elizabeth, a homebody.

He picked up a paperback book from under the settee, some long-haired big-chested pirate clutching a busty blonde from behind, the same sort of book Elizabeth read. As far as Drew could tell, they were all exactly alike. He stepped into the main room and reassured himself that the real books were still on their single shelf above the windows, his favorite *Drums Along the Mohawk* and others from his youth, *Two Years Before the Mast* and *Rabble in Arms.* The place smelled of cigarettes. Peggy could never quit for long, and Drew supposed, with all the strain she had been under, she had to have a puff.

He caught sight of a photo of Stewart Tomaszewski on

the kitchen counter. The guy was smiling up at Drew as if he had won a prize. What was Peggy keeping his damn face around for? Drew was tempted to put a match to it and watch it burn, but he set about counting plates and bowls and silverware and pots and pans. The inventory was almost complete, and he found the missing cereal bowl and spoon on the table by the bed. So maybe she had not slept on the porch. No, this bowl was all dried up and crusty; it had been there since yesterday. The girl is still depressed, Drew decided, and he took a seat on the squeaky bed, his mother and father's.

Thoughts of them were closer in his mind than they used to be. As time went on he seemed to remember more of them rather than less. Sights he had imagined were forgotten would come to his mind at odd moments such as this: his mother sick and cold in this same bed calling to the kids to come down from the attic and sit by her and cheer her up. Her face was long and pale and scary, except it was his mother's and he wanted to hold on close to her. He remembered the way she had rubbed his back round and round in slow comforting circles, even when she was the sick one. He could still feel the sensation on his skin.

How could he be contemplating the destruction of this little house? When he sat peacefully inside it, it seemed eternal. It would mean nothing to the Boston renters; it would hide its soul for the week but miraculously reveal it again as soon as everything was back in its place and no one was there. Peggy did not understand this historical soul, but despite herself she was part of it. When she set a cereal bowl on the table, it added to the sum of history. Whatever the renters might do was quickly erased, for the house retained only what Peggy did, and Drew and Elizabeth, and the long gone family of his childhood and youth.

Everything — the forty-eight-star flag furled in the closet, the Parcheesi board and Bill Ding blocks and dominoes, the coal shovel, the drain stopper on its chain — outlasted those people who passed through. A drinking glass broke, a plate cracked, a fork disappeared mysteriously, but the greater part of Drew's life remained, and all his spanking new things in Leominster were of no account.

Maybe Peggy was over next door, but surely those two had been at the Original since six. The idea of eating food prepared by someone who might well have AIDS always gave Drew a chill. After Ugo died, he would never eat there himself, but he kept quiet about it. You could not know what you were eating anywhere anymore.

Drew hesitated at the door. He did not suppose his daughter would go barge in on Mary Lanaghan's morning unless they had become real friends these past weeks. Somehow he hoped that might be the case but decided to check the boathouse first.

He let the front screen door slam the nicely satisfying whack he missed in his new aluminum-paneled door in Leominster with its pneumatic gizmo. Drew often found himself in a quandary: technically, he favored improvements; he wanted to see the pains of human life alleviated through ingenuity and imagination, but he did not see how his new screen door, for all its cleverness, was a civilizing agent. True, you did not have to paint the frame, and it doubled as a storm door in winter when you replaced the upper screen with a glass panel, and perhaps the rusty spring that caused the old slam was a device annoying to sensitive ears. But his new door disconnected Drew from the outside, not that the outside in Leominster was more than a tidily mowed patch of lawn and some hedges Elizabeth trimmed obsessively. His new door was one of thousands, of millions, as were those molded white plastic chairs they had on their patio — even Mary Lanaghan had chairs like that: they were taking over the world. Give Drew a broken-down wobbly kitchen chair of unpainted wood, or maybe one painted up cutely by Elizabeth with flowers on the backrest.

But he could not figure how to reconcile these inclinations of his heart and eye with the notions of freedom he treasured. After all, were not his new screen door and his plastic chairs the results of private enterprise? The only people these days who seemed to care for worn-out things were the Mary Lanaghan set, the antique-collecting Boston snobs who had plenty of comforts to make up for the severity of an occasional revivified object. Drew told himself, as he walked along the dirt road to the boathouse, that perhaps he was a kind of museum curator, a respectable enough job even in a moneymaking society. He had been appointed, because of his particular skills, to preserve bits of history for the enlightenment and instruction of coming generations — how a musket actually fired, how an old banjo once sounded, how a cider press operated — and could he help it if he fell somewhat in love with the aura of those old things, if he was still in love with these woods all about him that might soon — would certainly soon — fall and make way for what the next crop of humanity would imagine to be a better life?

Victor was sitting out on his stoop. Drew never knew what to say to him. The man was long and lanky and dark, like his father, Ugo, but with a droop to his eyelids and to his mustache that made him look like he was hiding something. In a way he was, Drew realized, and Drew did not want to know anything about it.

"Your daughter and Ron kept me up last night," Victor

said in a dry voice. "So I told Ron he had to work the whole morning."

"She go help him out?" Drew asked.

"Could be. I didn't see her." Victor motioned to the lawn chair, a rusted-out aluminum one with woven plastic straps for a seat. Drew eased himself onto it so they would not give way.

"You should get some of those molded plastic chairs," he said. "Two for twelve bucks on sale at Osco." He smiled at himself for loyally promoting progress. Maybe Drew liked it best when everybody else moved on and left him the sole inheritor of the rough past.

Victor shrugged. "We don't sit out all that often," he said.

"You been seeing much of Peggy?"

"Last night I did. Of course, she stays away when Stewart's here. He's been coming by a lot. Him and Ron go jogging out the railroad bed."

Drew had not realized how much of a connection his prick of a son-in-law had with these guys. He knew they knew him, but he never would have given Peggy the cottage if he had known Stewart would be coming by. He kept the thought to himself and said with a twinkle, "Now don't you go to Tomaszewski's for those chairs. Osco's got 'em cheaper."

"I don't suppose I'll be getting 'em from anywhere," said Victor, leaning back against the doorframe and sipping his coffee.

"So how's Peggy doing in your estimation?" Drew asked him.

Victor seemed to be counting something, the stripes on his coffee cup maybe. "Huh?"

"How's Peggy doing, you think?"

Victor sat for a few seconds. "I'd say she isn't over it yet,

Mr. Hale. I'd say she needs to get away and start up something else to convince herself men can be decent sometimes."

"You don't think much of Stewart."

Victor shook his head. "He's Ron's friend."

"I surely don't think much of him," Drew said.

The wind picked up and rustled the pines and all the maple leaves over their heads. The two men, whose families went way back in the region, one to an Italian stonecutter and his wife a laundress, the other even further to a Scottish mill girl and a Scots-Irish farmhand, did not have to say anything for a while. Victor just sipped and seemed to be assessing the arrangement of tree trunks across the road. Drew's thoughts had wandered to a day when his dad took him on a job up to Parshallville and they stopped at Ugo's Original 108 and had scrambled eggs and home fries and sausage and coffee, for something like thirty cents each. It was a lot of money to spend on a luxury when his mother could make a perfectly good breakfast at home.

"You're in luck," said Victor. Drew looked up and heard a motor. In drove the despicable Dodge Neon with Stewart Tomaszewski at the wheel. Ron hopped out the passenger side. "Who's behind the counter?" Victor wanted to know.

"I called Kevin. He wanted the hours. Don't worry, it's the slow time. Hi, Drew," said Ron, stepping into the house.

After what must have been a little thought, Stewart emerged from his car wearing some kind of nylon black shirt and shorts and very elaborate rubber shoes. Drew decided he would sit stolidly on his own property and see what the boy came up with.

"Hello, Drew," Stewart said in a measured voice. "We're going for a run." Drew nodded. "How you doing, Victor? Hear you didn't get much sleep," Stewart said.

"No thanks to your wife," said Victor.

Stewart laughed a little. Victor was getting up. The air was so charged, Drew figured shy Victor wanted to get out of the way; it was not his burden, after all. "Hey, Ron," he yelled through the door, "how long's Kevin there for?" Conveniently, Ron did not answer, so Victor had to go on into the house.

Drew gave Stewart a hard stare.

"I guess I haven't seen you since the separation," Stewart said.

"So you go out running with your fag friend, eh? Sounds about right," Drew said.

Stewart turned and walked back to his car, then turned again, looked at Drew, and shook his head. "Forget it," he said. "I'm not tangling with you."

"Good," said Drew.

That was it. They each waited for Ron to come out. He did not have a fancy jogging suit, just URHS shorts and a T-shirt that read, "If you don't like my attitude, Dial 1-800-GRANDMA." Where would anyone get a shirt like that, and why would anyone wear it? Drew wondered. Ron was a meaty little fellow, not the type you usually associated with being queer. Victor was more the type, but maybe it was the Italian in him.

Stewart and Ron were already off down the road, and now Victor was standing in the doorway. "Well, Victor," Drew said, getting carefully up out of his seat, "I guess I'll go look for Peggy at Mary Lanaghan's. I got renters coming in next week. Friends of Mary's. So it's time Peggy came home."

"Don't worry, Mr. Hale," Victor said. "It's over. Stewart never goes back to his old women. That doesn't work for him. He'd say it's his pride."

"I could tell you what I think it is," said Drew.

III

MARY WAS SITTING on the glassed-in veranda at the southern end of Ara Zeytoundjian's house in Sewall. Sun from the southeast warmed her back and brightened the view west to the Quidnapunxet, which took a broad bend at the foot of Ara's bluff and almost seemed a lake. No other house was visible, no road, only a rowboat near the opposite bank with an immobile fisherman in it. Ara had gone to select a bottle of wine. This house was strange to Mary, not because she had never been entertained on such an elegant scale but because it had been so long ago and she had changed so much since.

After her hospital hours, she had driven over for one of Ara's lunches. She was more comfortable with lunch, although her first visit had been a dinner party with doctors and board members, twelve people and she the only single one other than Ara. Ara's wife had died two years back, and he was coming out of his period of mourning. His children were all married and living in cities, doing well for themselves. Ara's own business dealings had been consolidated in the seventies and now took care of themselves. Mary remembered how Dermot used to fume at the thought of men like Ara, not with political disdain but with envy. And here Mary was now.

Am I disdainful myself? she wondered as she took in a view like a painting from her American art course at the community night school last year, right now an Eakins, in afternoon light a Hopper, finally at sunset a Frederick Church, and all private to this man. But he had shared each with Mary. In her Newton days, she would have felt more uncertain how to behave and have tried not to admire with eyes too wide. Her parents had had a few fine things, of course, as fine perhaps as this small marble-topped table, this Wedgwood, this bouillon spoon with his wife's monogram, but not enough to fill a twenty-room house and a cottage on Nantucket as well, where Mary had been invited for the Fourth of July with a party of Ara's friends. She was telling herself it might do her good.

Mostly, she was looking forward to Christina's arrival next week and to Shirley coming home for the summer. Ara still seemed strange to Mary. She did not know if she could be said to be dating him. What was it exactly that they were doing? Now here he was, showing her a bottle of Pinot Grigio in his large hands. "This one is special," he said. "I think you'll like it."

"I'm afraid I won't be the best appreciator, Ara," said Mary.

"You're a great appreciator," he said.

"But I won't know the difference."

"As long as you like it," he said easily and poured her delicate glass two-thirds full, sat down, and poured himself precisely the same amount.

"Oh, I will." She took a sip as he raised his glass to her and then added, "Mmm, and I do."

Ellie Starks, Ara's cook, came in and cleared away the empty bowls and the tureen of cucumber soup; Ara seemed annoyed she had not done so sooner. The unfortunate fact that she was one of the Starks clan had once required him to assure Mary that Ellie was among the better bred ones. When Mary told him how fond she was of Ellie's nephew Ron, it had suddenly seemed a point not to pursue. There were two distinct sides to Sewall, the gentlemen's farms by the river and then the small houses strung along Railroad

Street with smudgy-faced barefoot kids climbing on porch railings and mothers screaming at them.

"Ellie's poached a salmon," said Ara when she had retreated to the kitchen. "As far as I can tell, she's the only one of that whole family who knows how to do anything."

Mary smiled. He was probably right. Ron really did not know how to do much, except be cheerful despite everything, but to Mary that was, perhaps, the higher achievement. "Who'll be in Nantucket?" she promptly asked, to return to a neutral subject.

Ara went on to enumerate the guests with thumbnail sketches that included family background, educational affiliations, current social and even psychological status; one of the wives, for instance, was climbing slowly out of a depression brought on, Ara quipped, by her husband's propensity for relating movie plots. Mary found herself hardly bothering to sort out what Ara clearly felt was an amusing cast of characters. They were all a bit older than her Newton friends — at least the husbands were; there was a second wife or two. Mary now recognized it was indeed disdain she was feeling, so she nudged herself to take a broader view. Who was she to harbor secret criticisms of the world inhabited by this perfectly nice and generous man who seemed to admire her so much? And he did make her feel good about herself; that he was hardly an old Yankee had modified the self-effacement her parents had taught her to practice before the sorts of people who lived in such houses. It amused Mary that the only real Anglo-Saxon she seemed to know lately was Ron Starks.

Mary's mind ran on through these odd byways while Ara talked. She had attentive eyes and a responsive smile, so he would not detect her lack of engagement. And she managed to interrupt her speculations on the Zeytoundjian family, before its alliance with Harvard University and the Quidnapunxet Club, just as Ara reached the end of his guest list.

"It sounds like a lively group," she said, mostly as a compliment to his narrative powers.

"You'll enjoy some of them, anyway," Ara said modestly, and Ellie Starks — Aunt Ellie, as Mary had heard tell of her — entered again with a platter of beautiful orange fish and gray-green asparagus. Ara apologized for the absence of hollandaise; he had to watch his cholesterol.

A gentle sip of the wine prepared Mary for the first bite of salmon, the central moment of a carefully arranged experience. She would try to sustain this mood now. She would think about Ara, focus on appreciating him and not be distracted by her whimsical imagination. She knew her tendency to undermine possible intimacies with an ironic attitude. It seemed to happen only in situations where sex was a consideration — think of Dermot and the bitter irony he aroused; Mary had never found herself ironic with her children, or Christina, or her neighbors here, not even with Drew Hale, really. Again, she was lost in reverie. Listen to Ara. Treat him as a full human being, she told herself, but the phrase turned ridiculous as soon as she thought it, so instead of thinking she determined to watch.

Ara was taking salmon in bites of equal size, separated by sips of wine and nibbles of asparagus. His shock of gray hair hung over his wide dark brow; his nose was impressively unlike Dermot's Irish pug, his lips fuller. He spoke carefully but with an appealing lightness. He did not seem to require Mary to be anything but a companion; he was taking a most gentlemanly pace. She had to admit she found him attractive. He truly was not a pompous business type, whatever her preconceptions had been; this comfortable world came effortlessly, unpretentiously, to him, though it may not have to his father, who had made his fortune in metallurgy during the Second World War.

"We might go for a paddle this afternoon," Ara suggested.

"I'm not used to being fed so well at lunch," said Mary.

Ara set down his fork and looked at her warmly. "Last time you were here," he said, "you got me to talk about my family, and about Charlotte's death. You listened a lot. I wish you would tell me something more about you, your family, your divorce. Beyond the facts, I mean. Only if you feel you want to. I'd like to know what's happened in your life. There seems to be a big weight on your back still, Mary."

"I suppose there is," she said.

"How does it feel? I know that sounds silly," Ara said, "but it's what they made us talk about in the bereavement group at the hospital. I never thought I'd let myself take part in such a thing, but there I was."

"How does it feel?" Mary repeated, and again, "How does it feel?" She gazed out the perfectly clean glass at the scene below them, the graceful river; the fishing boat had drifted out of sight. "It feels as though no one is there most of the time," Mary said. "I like the feeling usually, especially in the mornings. I feel fresh each day. Back in Newton I was under a daily sentence. Then it really did seem a weight. Now it isn't so much a weight as too much lightness, too much air. Maybe that has the same effect as a weight. It's as if I must constantly breathe each breath, fill each space with something so it won't float away. I have to hold it all down."

"So it's more as if you yourself are the weight?"

"Or that I should be more of one, that I should have more gravity," said Mary, "be someone whole, myself, have a purpose, and not just to help out, but to be . . ." She smiled at herself talking so abstractly with this man. "I don't know what my interests are, Ara, maybe that's all it is," she said.

"Interests," said Ara, pondering.

"Perhaps this has happened to you," Mary said after another sip of wine, which she felt tingling in her mouth and tingling more warmly, as it went down her throat. "I fill up my days rather well," she said, "but there are moments when I think there must be something already in existence that I don't know how to find."

After a quiet space, Ara asked her, "What was Dermot like?"

This time he seemed to want a specific answer, so Mary tried: "Dermot would always do what he wanted to do. If he wanted to do something, he did it. It was the main thing I thought was so wonderful about him. He was a handsome athlete in school. He was the most popular boy I knew at Boston College."

"Interests?"

"Dermot's?"

"Well, I thought maybe you just adopted his and now you're ready to begin looking for your own."

Mary had had this thought before, had read it in some self-help book Christina had sent her once. It didn't provide much of an answer, but she could not fault Ara for hitting on it, too. He was sitting back and looking at his clean white plate. She settled back herself.

"A lot of damage can be done to a life," he went on, "in the most unnoticeable ways. I hate to think how our small mistakes, added one on top of the other, get to towering over us as the years go by. The popular view of psychology reduces it all to major traumas. I'm inclined to think of it, for most of us, though, as a veritable mountain of thin sediments, laid carefully month by month, day by day, moment by moment. But the heartening thing about my analysis, Mary, is that it's not as difficult to begin laying new sediment as it would be to mine out the mountain."

Mary was finding herself in a more spontaneous mood than she had been during the soup course. "I mean it as a compliment, really," she said, "but where did you learn to talk like that? It comes right off the top of your head. I just couldn't do that."

Ara seemed unsure of the moment. His eyelids twitched, then he almost blushed. "I was never an athlete," he said. "I was never the most popular boy. I was a nice Armenian kid at Harvard in the fifties who wanted to be refined and well-spoken."

Suddenly, Mary felt extremely fond of him. The afternoon paddle on the river had a new appeal. She wanted Ara to tell her more of who he really was.

"Mary, you keep turning it back to me," he said. "I still haven't the least notion why Dermot Lanaghan would have left behind a life with you. He must be a foolish fellow."

Ellie Starks came in with a silver coffeepot on a silver tray with a silver creamer and sugar bowl and two Wedgwood cups and saucers and a glass plate of the sugar cookies she made by the dozen for her nephew Ron to sell at the diner in Parshallville.

IV

LOUISE THIBAULT had left Mrs. Germaine listening to her afternoon Fresh Air show and driven down to Charles's store to pick up stuff. She could get Mrs.

Germaine's toilet paper and bread and Cranapple juice and whatever else at the Grand Union, but she saw no reason not to patronize the convenient mart, even if everything there cost more. Mrs. Germaine had no idea of prices anyway; she was always giving Louise a twenty, hoping it would cover it. Louise never pocketed the change, but she would just as soon give the mart the business. When Charles came to work that evening, his manager would be sure to say, "Your sister came in again today, she's our most faithful customer."

Louise was bumbling out the door with two heavy bags and a wrapped-up hot sandwich for the road when Martin Lanaghan pulled over in his mother's blue Cavalier. "Hey," she said to his "Hey!" He seemed awfully cheerful for Martin. "What's up?" she asked him.

"This is funny," said Martin. "You know I have this friend Suzanne I was telling you about?" Louise vaguely remembered but was not sure which of Martin's friends she was. "She believes in a purpose behind everything," Martin said. "I was mad at my mom for staying out so late for lunch when I wanted to use the car, but if she'd come home any sooner then I wouldn't have bumped into you."

"Or if Mrs. Germaine hadn't sent me on errands," Louise said.

"You got a sandwich there? Hey, let me get one. I'll join you at the picnic table," Martin said, so Louise set her bags on her backseat and strolled across the lot to the shady spot where two metal tables were chained to a sumac tree and settled herself slowly, testing to be sure the table would not tip. She was glad to have another chance to talk to Martin. He was one of the few people she could unburden herself to; Charles never listened long enough to catch what she really meant.

Louise unfolded the greasy paper, and hot barbecue sauce filled her nostrils. She tore off the corners of the two salt packets and sprinkled them under the top bun, then she popped the little ridges of the pepper packet and sprinkled it, too. Martin came out with a cold Italian sub and two large Diet Pepsis. "Here," he said, "you need something to rinse that down," and he sat across from her, grinning. When did Martin ever grin before?

"You the cat that ate the canary or what?" said Louise.

"Mmpf" came out of Martin's lips along with a few crumbs. And then "I'm feeling a lot better since I saw you last week."

"Win the lottery?"

"I'm just feeling a lot better. I don't know. Things are happening."

"Nothing's happening in my life," said Louise.

"Nothing used to happen in mine," Martin said. "But then today I wake up and something happens. It's pretty amazing."

Louise looked him over closely. He had not shaved and he had a film of sweat on his cheeks and forehead. His eyes were dark under his black eyebrows. He was the kind of boy who looked very tough and scary until he sat down and talked to you and then he had a quiet, almost pipey voice with a nervous giggle in it and you noticed how he moved his hands nervously and fiddled with his hair. "What is it? Suzanne moving in with you?"

"She's the one in New Mexico," Martin said. "She's definitely not moving in."

"Oh, she's the e-mail one," said Louise.

"But I heard from her this morning," Martin said, still all bouncy. "God, what am I going to tell her now!"

"Tell her about what?"

"We tell each other everything about our romantic lives," Martin said. "There just wasn't much to tell about mine since Rachel. I told you about Rachel."

"The cunnilingus one?" Louise asked, and Martin nodded with a grimace. In a way it was great how he had told her all the gory details last week. Louise had dropped by his trailer, and they had talked like old times. He helped her study her textbooks and read her a chapter out loud about dying people and then they discussed it. After that, nothing was too strange to talk about. This girl Rachel just liked to be done, as Martin put it; that was all she would allow. For a while, Martin had thought it was pretty wild, but it was not leading anywhere, obviously. There was another one before Rachel he had trouble getting it up with, as he put it, because she was so scared of it all. It never occurred to Martin, Louise was sure, to wonder if Louise had had any sex life. Like everyone else, she figured, he assumed she had written it off years ago. She would surprise him, sometime, with a story about her skinny friend Dave Paasivirta over in Sewall and the thing they used to have going. "So there's something to tell about yours now?" Louise asked.

"Maybe," Martin said, tiny sweat beads breaking out on his cheeks and a blush rising up his neck.

"Since last week?"

"Maybe since this morning," said Martin. "Let's just say, Louise, that I've finally experienced total intercourse, I mean all the way."

Louise took a bite and kept looking across the picnic table. She was aware of the sunlight creeping up from the far end and no breeze at all. Someone was dragging a whiny kid across the parking lot behind her.

"Finally," Martin said again.

And Louise had hoped, as soon as she saw Martin pull in,

that she would get a chance to talk to him about what was on her mind lately, about the fears of her own death she kept having. She had never thought of such things before, but this reading and thinking constantly reminded her of it. And Mrs. Germaine talked about death all the time. This blue business was everywhere. "You're looking a little blue about the mouth, Louise," Mrs. Germaine had said when she brought her her lunch. The lightbulb in Mrs. Germaine's bathroom seemed to shine blue off that invalid potty chair, off the stack of Depends on the dresser.

"I guess you're just the cat's meow, Martin," Louise said as affectionately as she could.

"That's about it," he said and wiped his forehead.

"Are you going to tell me who's the lucky lady?"

"You think she's lucky, huh?"

"What, she was doing you a favor?"

"Could've been that," Martin said. "I wasn't exactly a love machine."

"I'll bet she enjoyed it," Louise said, once again appraising that handsome but also scary and oddly timid face.

"I suppose it was all right for her," he said. "For me it was unbelievable."

"And no strings attached?"

"Well, no, I guess not," said Martin. "She's actually married. But she's separated. She's letting off steam. It started with tickling. Then she made it seem like the whole thing was only going to be for fun."

"Let me tell you something, stupid," Louise said. Sometimes she called him stupid in a way he seemed to like, because although he was smarter than she was, he admitted it was only in a schoolbook sort of way and Louise was wiser in the ways of the world. "Those types of girls are everywhere. You just never went along with them before.

You always had to get heavy and intense. I could tell you a thing about having fun myself. I ever tell you about my pal Dave Paasivirta?"

"He was in our class?"

"You didn't know him. He was from Sewall. One of those Finns. He knew what fun was, let me tell you."

"Are you talking fun fun?" Martin said cautiously.

Louise decided the time had come to bowl him over. "I'm talking, what did you call it, total intercourse. Him and me, lots of times."

Martin put down his sandwich and looked at her. She could see something scared in his eyes, as though the rest of the world, in this case Louise, was way ahead of him. Maybe that was what made him scary, the scared look he always had inside, but then you realized you were not scared of him, he was scared of you. In a way, Louise didn't mind her brief triumph. Here Martin was, so happy about himself, and she had brought him down a peg. "Of course, it didn't last forever," she said to ease off a little. "It lasted quite a while though. Even with him married now I get the feeling he might still be interested. I think it's because he's so bony. He likes that feeling of just landing on a really big woman."

"Why didn't you ever tell me, Louise?"

"Gosh, you never used to talk about sex. When you lived out here last time, you were like some priest in the woods. I didn't think you even knew about those things."

"And this was going on back then?"

Louise nodded. "I would've liked to have told you," she said.

The same whiny kid got dragged back across the parking lot. Louise could hear him complaining, "But I wanted the Atomic Popsicle, Ma!" It sounded like she cuffed him, but

Louise did not turn around. It came back to her that Martin was still in the middle of something — oh yes, his big breakthrough. She had better go back to asking him questions, though she was not sure she wanted to know much more. She preferred thinking of him as a priest. Somehow, that way, he reassured her.

"So who was it?" she asked him.

"You have to not tell anyone, especially my mom," Martin said, and then he went on to explain about who else but Peggy Hale.

"Hey, this is a little close for comfort," Louise said. "Peggy's practically like a big cousin from her dad and my dad being old friends, like one of those cousins you never see once you grow up but that doesn't mean you're not related."

"You wouldn't tell Mr. Hale."

"Cripes, no. He's pissed off enough already. So Peggy really does sleep around. I always figured. Tomaszewski's getting his own medicine back."

Martin's face had been taking on a stern look. He was biting his lip and his eyes had squinted up. "God, I forgot how many people are involved," he said. "I'm sure she's going to tell Ron Starks and then that's it, it's everywhere." Louise was not sure who Ron Starks was, but the name was certainly familiar. "Or will she?" Martin wondered. "I got the feeling she didn't want anyone in the world to know. She was doing it privately for herself, because she wanted to."

Louise leaned across the table as far as her bulk allowed and whispered, "And then you go and tell me, the first person you see. Honestly!" Martin was knotting up his forehead like he was getting a headache. This was the face Louise was more used to, not the cheerful one of a few minutes ago. "I'm not saying anything," she said. "I'm just saying that if you told me, she'll probably tell someone, too."

"But she really made it sound," Martin said, "like a super-private thing. I wasn't meaning to tell anyone. I was just coming to get things for the trailer, more the kind of snacks Peggy likes. If I hadn't seen you, I wouldn't have told anyone."

"All because your mother was late with the car," Louise said. "Well, I won't even tell Charles, so there! I might tell Mrs. Germaine, but she'll take your secret to the grave. I got to have something to talk to her about. She likes spicy stories. She was reading some book on Nancy Reagan, and I swear it did her heart good, she got so mad. So I got her at Osco's one on Jackie Onassis and she got all fraught up about her next."

They had finished their sandwiches and both were wadding up the paper. Martin made the tosses into the barrel under the tree, but he missed with Louise's wad and got up to deposit it properly. He seemed deflated. Louise wondered why Martin could never keep himself in an up mood; something always brought him down. If Louise had had a recent rendezvous like that with skinny Dave, she would have stayed chipper for a week.

"So anyway, Louise," Martin said, shyly almost, "are you glad for me?"

"Obviously," Louise said. "Didn't I get the message across?" She slowly got up and out of the picnic bench and started walking to her much repainted white Lark. Martin followed her. "I don't know, Martin," she said, huffing a little, "I have all this death stuff on my mind lately. I'm sorry. Maybe it's all too much for me to handle, this training. And then I have to go back and sit with that old lady. I used not to listen to her much, just let her babble along. But now I find I'm listening to everything, looking for clues about life and why we're here. Intercourse doesn't seem like as big a deal as it once did."

Martin said, "I never should've told you about it. But I wanted to share it, somehow. Really, if you see Peggy, you won't let on?"

"I never see her anyway," Louise said opening her car door.

"You off to Mrs. Germaine?"

"I shouldn't have been gabbing so long as is," said Louise. Martin seemed to need her to say something else. "Look, you can relax now," she said. "You got one thing out of the way, at least."

It was hot in the car, even with the windows open. Back in the shade of the tree a bunch of guys from Midas had sat down at the other table and opened up their lunch boxes. One of them with a black beard was looking scornfully at Martin's rubber sandals. Guys did not wear sandals like that around here. But the funny thing to Louise was that she knew Martin had just got laid in a way those Midas guys probably only dreamed of. Why did guys always have to act like they were more hot with the ladies than other guys were? Even Charles had to always brag about how the ladies loved to come in and talk to him, but when was the last time Charles actually touched a female? Betty Abbato in 1989. That was about it. Martin was still standing by her open window, leaning over with his elbow on the car roof, looking in.

"Don't keep worrying about death, Louise," he said. "Think of each morning as being born. I think being born is more astounding than dying. It makes sense how things die, life runs out, you give up, but being born, that's so hard to grasp. Something comes out of what seems like nothing at all."

Louise reached out and pinched Martin's U Mass T-shirt. "Hey," she said, "I can't take too many inspirational messages." So she backed out, and in her rearview mirror when she had turned laboriously toward the highway, she saw Martin heading off into the mart with the spring back in his step.

V

THAT WEEK the sun had reached its apogee, and from then on it would be descending from a spot imperceptibly lower in the sky and doing so slightly earlier each evening, though no one had felt the reversal yet. Indeed, the beautiful lazy time had hardly begun. For months, Lake Umbachaug would still sparkle warmly despite ever-briefer light, and when after all the brown leaves had blown away and the sun was ready to commence its long return, those wintry months — December, January, February, March, even April with its muck — would loom grim and sad in minds unconvinced of their promise of an extended day.

Victor Bardonecchia was particularly sensitive to the loss of light; for him the June solstice was no moment of celebration. He had woken up the next day depressed, not only from anticipating a slightly earlier dusk but burdened with a sense of other people's obliviousness to it. They all imagined summer had just arrived, while Victor knew it was already on its way out. Ron never noticed the deep changes; he flipped between moods ten times a day. He could work himself up into happiness through a vigorous run with Stewart on the basis of nothing but physical camaraderie, and Stewart, of course, remained placidly self-satisfied as ever because Ron was always up like that in his presence. But slip Stewart into his Neon in his sweat-glistening jogging outfit, watch him drive off alone, and then remind Ron of Kevin working solo at the counter and of the number of free hours Victor had coming to him, and then the gleam was gone from those blue-gray eyes and Ron would start stomping around the little house ready to punch a wall. Yet unaccountably, snap, Ron would remember some pleasant prospect awaiting him back at the diner, something to do with slutty Kevin or another casual buddy of his who was due in at two, and Ron would give Victor a tight squeeze and a kiss on the top of his head and say, "Okay, baby doll, I'm giving you the whole day off," and he'd pull his bike out of the shed and pedal off energetically, up the railroad bed.

And Victor was left sitting and wondering what that was all about. Ron had left the Hyundai at work and had not thought to ask Stewart to drive him back, but had he imagined he could induce Victor to bike back to relieve Kevin? — No, Victor told himself, Ron had taken one of his spontaneous flights of temper just because he felt like it, expecting all along to get himself back to work in good time.

And suddenly it came whirling down on Victor, as it always eventually did, the ineradicable memory of the night Ron told him about the results of his HIV test and the huge gaping "No!" that had escaped Victor's throat and still seemed to hang in the air above the water bed in their room that had once been a boat slip and was now, still, a kind of safe haven for both of them, where the house above with all its domestic trials was forgotten and the water beyond the sliding glass doors played in the wind and replicated itself, dry as bone, across the white ceiling. They could curl up together on their wide buoyant cushion and — even under the echo of that "No!" — retrieve a sense of belonging to each other despite all. Then Ron's whimsies, his banging the door, his coming up behind Kevin dishwashing and groping his butt, became entirely unimportant to Victor. Annoyance, Victor decided as he sat on the aluminum chair in front of his house with a stick to whittle and yet one more cup of coffee, is a natural ingredient of love.

He could hear steady hammering again down the cove. Drew Hale, who had not found Peggy at Mary's either, had then gone to Haviland Crossing for lumber and returned to repair his dock. And later, Victor had heard the hammering cease and a fatherly voice intone across the water, "Well, young lady," and so Victor had cocked his head to catch what they were saying. "Just rafting around in the sun," said the daughter, "paddled by Mary's kid's trailer." "Didn't you hear me yelling for you? Didn't you hear me hammering?" "Marty was playing his music too loud," said the same voice that had kept Victor up all night. "But then I did hear you hammering . . " And by this point she must have arrived close enough to the dock not to have to shout, and if a family argument ensued, Victor could no longer decipher it.

So he returned to his whittling, a hobby he had adopted in the service to give him an excuse to sit quietly in the barracks and leave loudmouthed volleyball and intensely silent card games to the others. He was carving an arrow, with arrowhead and feathers all of wood. He was tired of walking sticks and letter openers and wooden spoons. Ron never used the things he made him anyway, so Victor had decided to work on objects more decorative than useful; he had a growing sense of a need to make what could not be bought, what did not even already exist anywhere. He had had a dream about the attic room Ron had consigned to him, and in the dream Victor had enmeshed it in intricately carved posts and beams that formed an elaborate maze only he knew the way through.

This day was very much a loss, Victor decided, but he needed such days now and then or he might crack. Drew Hale coming by had almost thrown off what good the day was doing him, but then there was also a certain pleasure in watching the old guy stand his ground. Victor was not afraid of Drew's type now. It was all he had ever known when it came to his father's generation. He would be glad to see them gone, but as long as they were here, he had learned to handle them. He had finally handled even his own father by arming himself in the steady, slow self-respect with which his father answered any assault. Ron would flare up, but Victor just stared people down and never gave them an opening. It had worked in high school, in the army, and it still worked. On his deathbed, his father had admitted, offhand, as though it was obvious and did not need to be said, that Victor had the family pride even in his little finger, which he had then held tightly between his snaky forefinger and pickle thumb. Ron had been blathering to Antonietta and did not notice.

The strokes of Victor's knife kept pace with Drew's distant hammer in a shifting rhythm of barely discernible echoes. And then a third element intruded, the panting of an old dog, and Victor turned to see Hilda right behind him sniffing to learn which one it was, knowing that the other one was likely to give her a snack and this one was not. And then Mary appeared on the road looking tired and old.

Maybe it was the shapeless drab sweater that hung off her shoulders. "It's summer, Mary," Victor called. She shrugged her sweater sleeves to indicate she was cold anyway. Victor himself had on a flannel shirt and jeans, but his sleeves were rolled up and his feet bare on the pine needles sprinkled with chips of yellow wood.

"Day off?" she said. Victor nodded and tucked his knife and arrow under his thigh. Ever since he had met Rosa Blakey, he tended to see her mother in two layers, the Rosa layer shining below the surface of the hollower cheeks, the sadder mouth. "Peggy just came by. She's leaving us," the older Mary told him. "I'm afraid it's my fault. I got my Newton friends to take the cottage for a week, which means she has to go back to Leominster. She's ready to, she says, but still I feel guilty."

"Maybe now I'll get some sleep," said Victor.

"Oh that," Mary said, standing with her hands on her hips as she watched Hilda prowl along the boathouse. "Well, I didn't hear a peep, but the hill blocks sounds from coming my way. For me, it's been nice having a girl around."

"She was down bothering your son this morning," Victor said.

"He could use the company."

Mary sounded sad about it, so Victor said, "Want coffee?"

But she shook her head. "I had coffee, then I went canoeing on the Quidnapunxet, then I had tea. I'm fully caffeinated."

"Canoeing with that Armenian gent?"

"And I saw Ron's aunt. She said to tell him his sister Alice is pregnant."

"That'll be her number five," said Victor.

"How often does Ron get over there, anyway?"

"Ron? He made a rule. He only visits the ones who'll visit us. One visit here, one visit there. He told them so. Alice won't come. Only Martha comes, and his brother Henry if he's out of beer on a Sunday."

Victor knew that if he were Ron he would have given Mary his chair and run in the house and pulled out a stool for himself and made her drink a Cranapple juice if she would not have coffee. But he just sat there looking up at her shifting on her feet and watching the dog, so he also watched the dog. There goes a blind and deaf old animal and two healthy people are staring at it with nothing much to say to each other, he thought. He tried to think of something he wanted to know from Mary.

"So you're not going to miss Peggy?" Mary said.

"She's all right. It's when she and Ron get together."

"He didn't get very far saving the marriage, I guess."

"Not much to save," Victor said.

"That's what I decided." Mary nodded in the direction of the hammer blows. "Her father's right. She's put too much stock in men, I mean in the sense of their holding all the answers."

Victor shrugged. He did not really know what Peggy's problem was; he had never found her interesting enough to worry about. He did not have women friends, except for a few lesbians he knew from the service. Ron had all the straight women friends. Ron got involved in straight women's problems all the time, and he kept pointing out how pretty one girl or another was. Victor never saw it. It made him feel defective when Ron went on about beautiful women; it put him and Ron in whole different worlds. But he did not mind when Ron got hot over Keanu Reeves or Mark Wahlberg because he knew that he had whatever they had and more when it came right down to it. In that way, Victor was sure of himself. He could be as quiet and withdrawn and unsociable as he needed to be and yet, when the time came, work his private magic. The two of them never wanted to lose that. He wondered if Mary had any idea, if Ron had talked to her about a thing that personal. "No, men certainly don't have the answers," Victor said when words finally came to him through the long circuit of his thoughts.

"Unfortunately, neither do women," Mary said.

"Maybe dogs do," said Victor.

Hilda was back panting beside Mary. "You guys should get a dog," she said.

"Ron's more of a cat person, but he's not supposed to be around cat litter because of something you can get from cat shit. He used to have a cat."

"I guess Hilda wants to move on," Mary said.

"When's your daughter coming?"

"Oh, Shirley's due any day, and with my Newton friends coming Sunday, it's going to get lively around here. You guys haven't gotten to know Martin much yet, have you?"

"It's okay if he wants to be left alone."

"But he's so depressed." Victor could see deep inside Mary's eyes when at last she looked directly at him instead of at the dog and said, "I'm still afraid it's because of some terrible damage Dermot and I did."

What could Victor say to that? He had never heard her speak of her husband and her together having done anything. He saw the younger Mary through her pale cheeks, ruddier, fuller, smoother, and he saw her in love with this Dermot, the father of her four children, and like Victor's own family, like Victor and Ron, they would belong together even after death because of what history did to people. Maybe Mary was becoming whole in Victor's mind. He had not thought of her before as anything but a nice enough woman wandering about the woods, detached, in love with birds and greenery and even with water and sand and granite. He had not come to care for her the way Ron did. Her beauty had been lost on him.

VI

MONICA PFLUEGER and Shirley Lanaghan barely knew each other at Smith, but someone in Monica's women's group knew Shirley from softball and had told her she could go Tuesday with Monica instead of waiting till the end of the week for her other ride. So Monica took her along and let her off in her mom's driveway right on Lake Umbachaug. Neither Shirley's mom's car nor the dog was there, and Shirley told Monica her mom must have taken the dog to the vet because otherwise it never went in the car, and it never went on walks alone either. She seemed worried.

Monica had been hearing a lot about Mrs. Lanaghan on the drive. Shirley seemed proud of her for doing what their generation of young women expected of themselves but seldom saw evidence of in their elders. Shirley's mom had brought them all up by herself. Apparently, she had some part-time hospital job along with child support and alimony, and she had lots of projects and was always reading, not novels but practical sorts of books. Shirley's mom was not bitter — she still liked men — but she did not date and had found a kind of steady peace inside herself, Shirley claimed. Monica had taken all this a little personally, though she tried to sound impressed and admiring and even used the occasion to dump a little on her own mom's antidote to single life in the form of Chuck E. Cheese, as her brother called him. She got some good laughs out of Shirley but felt disloyal the whole time, and really she did admire her mom, who, despite her dad's behavior, had found a way to give her kids the life she had always expected them to have. Monica wondered if there was something selfish about this Mrs. Lanaghan taking the kids to her refuge from the world, taking them from their friends. Monica had been somewhat curious to meet her and hoped she might invite her in for cookies and tea. Other people's families fascinated Monica, partly because she was a psychology major, but partly because she was always trying to figure out what made families tick, which of course was what had attracted her to psychology in the first place.

Shirley Lanaghan was an okay kid, proudly going through a bisexual stage, though Monica could not tell if it would stick. Her own bisexual stage seemed cleanly over, but she was proud of it, too. It had given her a new freedom with the guys she had dated since. In fact, Monica had a theory that if bisexuality were the accepted norm for everyone up to, say, twenty-five, people would settle into much better relationships with whichever gender they ended up with. She had written an A paper on how male homophobia made for bad heterosexual relations because guys were always overcompensating for their unsureness. She really should do a follow-up on female homophobia, which was a little harder to write about, especially when there was so much lip service paid to women's solidarity; but it was there — Monica had felt it in herself even. That was why the affairs she had had with Liz and Danielle had made such a difference. Now that she was with Tommy, he felt mostly like her lover, not mostly like a guy. But Shirley had not wanted to hear anything about Tommy or about Monica's dad, or her brother, Eric, the little yuppie.

So when Monica pulled back out onto the Fraddboro Road, she was glad to be alone. She had been thinking about her dad a lot lately. Instead of going back to Route 108, she figured she would wend her way on side roads to Dowland. She turned left after an old white car had chugged past with an immense woman driving. Monica could not help gasping. She tailed the car to be sure she had seen what she had seen. The shape behind the wheel was two-thirds the width of the car, which was going slower and slower and tapping its brakes, and then a thighlike bare arm reached out to signal left even though the blinker was flashing, and the car turned into a long driveway marked Germaine. Pretty soon came the sign: ENTERING FRADDBORO — INC. 1696. Next year will be the big one, Monica realized, with all sorts of historical crap all over the place. Her dad liked that kind of thing.

She did want to see him. Her mom and Charles O'Keefe were expecting her for dinner, but it was only four o'clock, so she could make it by six-thirty and still spend an hour first with her real true father. That was how she referred to him in her thoughts. What else was he? But her mom had an irritating way of calling Charles "your new dad" or "your second dad," and that was not how Monica — or Eric — felt about him. He was a major butt pain, they both agreed, but they were good sports because they knew how much insecurity their mom had endured and they had to be grateful she was now on more solid ground. Monica could tell, perhaps better than her brother, that in their mom's private thoughts Chucky was not all he might have been, but Monica had come only lately to understand something about the different stages of adulthood, that what made sense at twenty-five might make no sense at fifty. Strangely, this alteration did not seem merely a loss. Monica was not as idealistically snobbish as her friends, who thought there was only one kind of romance and then you died. Well, if that was the case, forget it. Her friends did not really mean it that way — they all intended to grow old — but they had so little respect for their parents' ways of coping. Monica was not sure she would turn out all that much happier. I will reserve judgment till I'm fifty, and then some, she told herself. Look at Dad. He has changed a lot this year, and he's seeing a shrink.

It was odd to think of him living out here. Why had he moved to this nothing corner of Massachusetts? He had never heard of Umbachaug before, had never known anyone who came from here. He could have moved out to Northampton near her and still been in the country. Fraddboro sucks, Monica found herself thinking as she passed pseudocolonials tucked expensively in the woods and then the road to Basswood, the retirement community, with its gold-lettered sign: WHERE LIFE GOES ON. "Give me a fuckin' break" she said aloud.

But at Old Fraddboro she pulled over because she suddenly had a notion to get her dad a treat from the store. The place was expensive, but earlier when they had passed through Haviland Center she was eager to deposit chatty Shirley and not dawdle around looking for a gift with her. Shirley so badly wanted to make friends, but Monica had been careful not to encourage her. She especially did not need a new friend going through her dump-on-men stage. The things Shirley said about her brother Bard or Baird or whatever provided the usual appalling examples, but it seemed irrelevant to where Monica was now. She was in love with Tommy and Tommy was not like that, and her life was stretching out, even though she knew Tommy would go to a different end of the continent next year for grad school, knew they would probably not make it even through graduation, let alone thirty more years. But she was a different Monica, she had explained to her women's group. She did not need a Tommy to be herself; she was Monica without him, and that made her love him in a funny other way that had crept up on her. Her closest friends knew what she meant.

At the counter she saw a stack of elegantly boxed imported marmalade cookies that would do. Monica was no longer such a penny-pincher. She had a well-paid two-month summer job at an educational testing company in Boston, not as well-paid as Eric's job, naturally, but her wants were fewer, they really were.

"Excellent choice," said the kid at the register. In Northampton he would have been some easygoing folkie she could have had a friendly chat with, but this kid was tidy and programmed. Monica assumed he went to Umbachaug Regional and was proud to be working at the Old Fraddboro Store instead of a 7-Eleven. Store clerks would make interesting subjects for a term paper, the different styles of interaction, their attitudes toward the goods they sold. But the female homophobia idea was better, more significant. Monica had no desire to contribute to slicker marketing techniques; she wanted to spend her life getting at the essentials. Straight men did not seem as afraid of lesbians, so maybe straight women were not as afraid either. Maybe only gay men really scared everybody. Monica had to admit she sometimes felt her gay men friends were out of control, like straight men without the women to tone them down.

"Excuse me?" Monica said to the high school kid because she had not heard what he asked her.

"I said my brother goes to Amherst." Monica realized she was wearing Tommy's T-shirt. From his voice, this kid more likely went to some second-rate prep school. His parents were Fraddboro transplants, she deduced, his father commuted to a high-tech firm on Route 2, and they thought Fraddboro was the upscale place to be.

"My boyfriend goes there," said Monica.

"Good school," said the kid. "Here's your change. My brother's on crew there."

Monica tried to smile. She wished she could say something witty and incisive that would unsettle the kid's entire worldview, but she could not think fast enough, and actually she only wanted to get to her dad's.

"Enjoy," said the kid.

"Enjoy what?" Monica said under her breath so he did not hear it. She hated how people used transitive verbs without objects. Her dad had taught her to care about grammar.

When she got back in her rusted-out Fox, the last car her mom and dad had owned together, Monica had an unexpected rush of feeling as if she might suddenly cry. Where is this coming from? she asked herself. She had better back out, drive on, maybe it would pass. She had been thinking too much about men and women, mothers and fathers; she had been building up emotions inside her all the time she was doing her usual psychosocial analysis. She often pulled herself up short like this: you cannot analyze things intellectually without it having a subconscious emotional effect. Tears were brimming on her lower eyelashes, but Monica kept rolling through Fraddboro until she hit Dowland with its pathetic INC. 1899 and began to sense the near presence of her father.

She had hated Kathleen. The thought sprang into her mind, but not with the familiar rationale of Kathleen having filled her mother's place. This time she felt she hated Kathleen because she had not been as serious about her dad as her dad had been about her. But then Monica heard in her head the chirpy little voice of Shirley Lanaghan going on about how her brother Baird never stopped to notice what he was doing to women's lives, and Monica reminded herself that her dad was hardly blameless, even with Kathleen, not to mention with her mom. So which side, Mom or Dad, women or men, was making her so tearful? Maybe it was the fact that she could not tell, that it was all of them. And then suddenly she had it, the key to human interaction, the thing her friends were not willing to accept because they were still engaged in the search for rights and wrongs: no one, Monica told herself, had wanted to tear her family apart, not her mom, not Charles, not Kathleen, not her dad, but it had happened because of an absence of something she could not put words to; something had been missing in everybody's life, and that was all it was, something elusive, unnameable. I'll just call it loss, Monica thought. It's what we all must get used to.

She imagined her true father on his front porch as she would surely soon see him. He would be in his baggy khaki shorts with his bare feet up on the railing in the sun. He would have a glass of Squirt and a book on his lap. What might he have borrowed from the Dowland Library — she was passing the post office and the dog food joint when the thought popped into her head — maybe Emily Dickinson this time? Monica would love it if he had Dickinson, but she should not have imagined it because now it could not be true. He probably had Raymond Chandler. Still, she could suggest Dickinson. She could keep nudging him. And for his country life, how about Willa Cather? And then Zora Neale Hurston, and all the books she had read in her American women writers course. He would not be resistant to reading women. If anything, he idealized women too much, as if he did not feel worthy of them. Which was sort of true, considering how he fucked up with her mom and then fucked up with Kathleen, too. And he did not make as much money as Charles O'Keefe, but Monica sort of liked him for that.

The gravel road was spewing itself out behind her crunching tires in a golden tail. Her dad had told her they planned to pave it when the development went in. She would not experience the same feeling coming to visit him then. He would no longer seem to be living in a lost old-fashioned world, meditative and lone. He would be connected again, and the transformation would no longer happen when she left the main road. Monica listened to the crunches, watched the sunny billow in her mirror, and determined she would remember this feeling of retreating in time, this dust-clouded approach, for the rest of her life.

VII

MARTIN HAD HIS youngest sister home again. Talking with Rosa got too intense, and it was edgy around Bayard, but with Shirley, Martin coexisted comfortably, she in her private world, he in his. The respect between them, which their mom attributed to their age difference, in Martin's mind formed the family's steadiest link.

He had come back from his errands, which had taken him all the way to the health-diet dog food outlet in Dowland for his mom, to find Shirley sitting on the balcony wondering where everyone was. She had gone on about her friend Monica from Smith who had driven her home and about her dorm cleanup job and how much reading she had to do for her senior thesis, but she was going to get some sort of work, maybe waiting tables, and it was going to be a fun summer anyway. Soon, their mom had come back from her walk, with Hilda slower than ever behind her clomping up the stairs. Shirley had to hug and kiss her dog before she got to Mom, who stood patiently watching, knowing as Martin did Shirley's perpetual agony that Hilda would not make it till her next trip home. And then as soon as Mom had gotten her own hug and kiss, she asked Shirley why she had not told her she was coming. "None of you ever lets me know your whereabouts," she had said in the gentle complaining voice that made Martin feel guiltiest. "It's to keep you on your toes, Mom," Shirley answered. Then she went into an even longer explanation of this girl Monica and some women's group Monica was in that she might join next fall and how her work-study boss had let her leave early because the basic job was done and all they were waiting for was a dozen replacement mattresses. Martin said he had to take his own groceries to the trailer and he would see Shirley later.

There was a note scrunched in where the aluminum siding met the silver doorframe. "So where da fug are ya?" it said, but the idea that it was from Peggy disappeared when Martin noticed Shirley's typewriter-style *a.* He put down his shopping bags and unlocked the door. There was his narrow bed, which would never again feel the same to him. The spread was crumpled on the floor and the sheet wrinkled and, when he looked closer, slightly stained. He put his nose down against it and breathed the mix of faint scents. He felt tender all over, vulnerable. This was where it had finally, unexpectedly, happened.

But what was he supposed to do now? Well, he put the beer in the fridge. He did not often drink beer, but he knew Sam Adams was what Bayard drank. He put the chips and Little Debbies in the cupboard and slipped the box of condoms in the drawer under the bed. Should he wander by her cottage? Mr. Hale did not seem to be hammering anything now, and she had told Martin to come by anytime, but what if one of those gay guys was there? Peggy had a whole world Martin would not fit into. He decided it was best not to seem as if he had been blown away by what had happened; that would only give her an opportunity to kid him. So he lay down and felt himself stretching the length of the mattress, sinking close into the sheet and catching a hint of a perfumy smell on the pillow. A sudden weight seemed to press on him all over, and soon he was sleeping.

"Martin!" came a voice.

He did not think he had been asleep for even one minute, but the light was different, slanting in the narrow window above his head and hitting the rhino on his endangered species poster. In the open doorway stood Shirley in her softball jersey with her Red Sox cap, bill forward for a change, shading the soft features of her face. It took Martin a second to remind himself that she had returned home.

"I should've known you'd have a nap," she said.

It occurred to Martin that he could not see Peggy here if Shirley was going to be dropping by like this. "Hi, sisty," he said.

"Mom wants you up for dinner. She said she's going to stick to salad because she had such a big lunch with that hospital board guy, so there's enough meatballs to go around."

"How many Smith girls still eat meat?" Martin asked. "You must be weird."

"I have to eat meat in my line of work."

"What's your line of work — softball?"

Shirley doffed her cap and smiled at him. She looked around the trailer and said, "Looks better. Last time you had those black-and-silver *Star Trek* posters. Now it's not so cluttered."

"I'm simplifying my life," said Martin.

Shirley took a seat on the metal folding chair and watched the screensaver go from starlight to sunrise. "Cool," she said. "I've got a barrel of monkeys that spills out and then they get stuffed back in." For a while they compared machines and then got into a discussion of what Windows 95 would be like. It was supposed to be out by August. "I'm sure Dad will get it for you," Shirley said matter-of-factly. "You won't even have to have a job."

"But you like having jobs, Shirley, you like being busy."

"Yeah, I look forward to hustling my butt."

Martin stuck his foot out and poked at her bottom with his toe. Shirley got up and sat the other way around on the desk chair and simultaneously swiveled her cap so the adjustable plastic clasp striped across her forehead, her familiar look, with her short dark hair tucked up under. She had a button nose and fairer skin than any of them. Martin knew he had an adorable little sister.

"I wish I, too, was clinically depressed," she said.

"I'm not clinically depressed."

"But it's cool to be clinically depressed these days."

"I'm not even on medication now."

"So get a job like me," she said, but she did not seem too serious about it.

"I've been wondering about something," Martin said. He sat up on the bed, as if by doing so he could become more clearly her big brother. "Why do you think Mom has never gotten a job? I mean a paying job, even at the hospital, or anywhere. She talks about me getting a job, but she never talks about getting a job herself. I'm going to ask her. I'll sling it right back."

Shirley was looking skeptical. "Sure you're not on meds?" she asked. "You never said anything like that about Mom. I can't believe you said you'd sling it right back."

"Why's that so weird?"

"Because you always love Mom exactly the way she is. You never want her to change. You keep coming home to make sure she doesn't change on you. That's what I think. I was trying to explain our family to Monica Pflueger, the girl who drove me home. She's a psych major. Mostly, I talked about Bayard's craziness and Rosa drifting along with Nat Speradakis. But I told her how you kept on coming home. I mean, you lived at Dad's for a while, as well. Martin, it's true. Hey, speaking of home, it's great about the Ostermanns next week."

"I thought it was the week after."

"No, Mom's going to Nantucket with that guy July Fourth. It's for her forty-ninth birthday, next week. That was the whole idea."

"You mean they're staying in the cottage?"

Martin had not calculated the short amount of time he had left with Peggy next door. He felt as if his Newton past, in the form of Mr. and Mrs. Ostermann and their porchy house and their pool, was reaching out to him as he had always thought he wanted it to do, but he did not want it this particular moment, or only a part of him did.

"I wonder what little Gus is like now," Shirley said. "Mom says he shaved his head and has loads of earrings."

"Are we supposed to come up for dinner right away?"

"She said half an hour."

Martin stood up and found his sandals by the bed. He should change his T-shirt; it reminded him of being with Peggy so he had not wanted to take it off until now. He stuffed it in his laundry bag and put on a black one. "Listen, I have to send a quick e-mail, tell Mom I'll be right up."

Shirley relinquished the desk chair. "You're so on edge," she said. She was looking at him hard until he caught her eye and she squinted out the window into the sun. "Okay, whatever," she said. "Don't bring laundry. I've got all mine to do first."

When she was gone he got on the computer and began a letter to Suzanne. He wanted to free-write it the way his freshman English teacher had made them do, but he could not do it back then and he still could not. He found himself dangling at the end of the first sentence: "I have so much to tell you about and I don't know what to say or if it will even matter to you but my whole life has changed about three times today and I feel . . ." He could not see where to take it from there. Suzanne's letters were together, the way a writer would write, with imagery and philosophy and style. They probably came out that way. Martin had never been great at English and sometimes stopped reading before the end of a book because he preferred to remember what it was like living in a made-up world and not have it closed off by the last page; Bayard, the honors English major, thought it was a stupid attitude — he finished every book he started. As for writing, the more deeply Martin felt something the harder it was to put it in words, which seemed reduced, inaccurate, or the wrong thing to say. He deleted the text and decided to try again, but this time he would visualize before he wrote. That was the other thing

Cheryl, his teacher, had suggested. So he closed his eyes, and what came to him was Cheryl herself, her long blond hair, his first hopeless crush at college. Slowly, she turned into Suzanne or the way he imagined Suzanne from the one photo she had scanned in for him. Then came the sudden astonishing memory — was it truly his? — of his penis in his last and only condom inside of Peggy and what it felt like being so surrounded by her, nothing like a smooth belly to rub against or a hand or a mouth, but an entirely new sensation grabbing him, tight, soothing, tremulous. He could not visualize a thing now, only feel it, and Peggy was responding as if Martin was doing well by her, as if she was entirely happy with him. She wanted him to push hard while she squeezed, and he felt each time that they almost became one person but then they were apart again, and then again they were almost one. How could he write about this to Suzanne? It was something she must already know and assume he knew. It was what everybody else expected, and he was twenty-six and only just discovering it. He wanted it again right away. And she had said to come by anytime. On his way to his mom's he could walk by the cottage and make a date for later, casually, because he could not be with her now anyway, it was dinnertime.

But what he found out, after he had gotten off the computer and switched to his striped polo shirt and headed up to the road, was that Peggy was walking along herself, smoking a cigarette. His mom had come by to ask her over, she said, since it was almost her last night there and she wanted her to meet Shirley. "Hey, babe, that was nice this morning," she said, swatting a mosquito on her bare brown arm.

"Definitely," said Martin.

"I'm crashing early tonight, but maybe sometime before

my mom comes up to get me Thursday and clean up the place, what do you think?"

"I'm available," Martin said, just a step behind her on that sandy flatness where the lake had once reached up to the granite hillside.

"I'm going to miss having Mary next door," Peggy was saying. "She's been a good person to talk to. I wish I'd got to know her better."

A JULY WEDNESDAY

I

WHEN SHIRLEY AWOKE, she went down and swam the cove to the piney point, where she sat on the sand in rising sunlight. Of course, Bayard and Martin were still asleep, but soon she caught sight of Gus's shaved head bobbing off the cottage dock. When her mother had gone on her Nantucket trip, it had felt to Shirley almost like a Newton weekend with the Ostermanns next door looking after the Lanaghan kids. Mr. Ostermann had found the cottage such a good deal, and such a cinch to get to from Boston, that he had taken it for all of July, too, and was coming up on weekends to join Mrs. Ostermann and Gus.

This morning, with Bayard behind his orange curtain and herself behind her yellow one, Shirley had imagined the older two were off at college and Mom was sleeping in her own room, not down the road again with Bryce Murtagh, whom Shirley truly did not care for at all. It was hard to believe Mom had gone to his house the very night Bayard had come home. Bayard had probably told her she should. Shirley had only seen Mr. Zeytoundjian once, when he picked Mom up for Nantucket, but even though he was too old he seemed a much more decent guy. Bryce Murtagh was not even actually divorced yet, and he lived in one of those hideous houses with a giant-screen TV and a hot tub and central air. He sold some sort of software.

By now, Gus had noticed Shirley, had waved wildly and begun swimming across. Whether it was the difference between ages five and ten or ages fifteen and twenty, Gus had always seemed like a kid to Shirley. At five, it was water wings and sniffles when she splashed him; at fifteen, it was a sleek fish slipping through the water toward her. She supposed girls of thirteen found him totally sexy. She might have at that age, too, except for the scalp job, but somehow Gus did not seem exactly male. Lately, Shirley had been thinking about androgyny because of her thesis, which would trace changing definitions of gender in twentieth-century America, as influenced by wars, economic cycles, political movements, and how it all was distilled in books, movies, and music. Professor Woo had told her she had to focus on select instances, but in order to do that, Shirley first had to know as much as she could about everything. She liked the exploratory stage best because she did not have to come to any conclusions yet. "That's what education should be," Bayard said. "We're too young to come to conclusions. They'll just embarrass us someday." Last night he had given her his paperback of Hemingway's *Garden of Eden* because it was very intense, he said, and the man and woman try cutting their hair to look exactly alike and reverse pronouns on each other. "Macho writers can be kinky," he said. "Read Norman Mailer. *Why Are We in Vietnam?* If you're going to do this right, Shirl, you can't ignore the macho element." He was right from a scholarly point of view, but Shirley did not like reading male authors; they made her too angry. She supposed she would give Hemingway a try, though; it was funny how she and Bayard, the two youngest, were the serious students. If he went on for a doctorate, she was sure she would, too.

Now here was Gus, surfacing after a long spell underwater. He touched bottom and ran his palms over his head even though there was no hair to slick back. It must have been habit. He had his Newton South swim team Speedo on, and there was the nipple ring he acted totally nonchalant about. As he disappeared again for a submarine attack, Shirley decided it was hairlessness that made him so androgynous, because hair was a loaded concept. She could conclude her thesis at the point where androgyny was no longer a matter of veering toward the opposite gender but of obliterating all signs of either gender, returning to babyhood, maybe, where genitals alone marked the difference.

Gus's arms reached out in the shallow crystalline water, then he burst onto land dripping all over, plopped by her side, and looked out across the big lake. "All that ugly shit over there," he said, "you can't see it from your cove."

"That's the Fraddboro side. Don't kid yourself, those places are expensive. Why are you up so early anyway?"

"I'm always up early," said Gus.

"I thought teens were supposed to sleep late."

"So when you turn twenty you start getting up early again?"

"If you have a job." Shirley was working at Ugo's Original now because Victor had decided they needed more midday help. First, Mom had wanted Martin to do it, but he said he would feel funny working with those guys, so Shirley jumped at; it was better experience than scooping ice cream in Haviland Center.

"I like getting up early because you don't hear the boats yet," Gus said. "All the assholes across there are hungover still. I go back for a nap when they start up. I was up fishing at six."

"You like it here," Shirley decided for him.

"Newton basically sucks," said Gus, fiddling with a twig

in the sand. His legs were also completely shaved; he seemed made of hard brown rubber.

"As soon as we moved away, I sort of forgot about Newton," said Shirley. "Dad moved to his new house, so it wasn't like I was going to visit the old neighborhood ever."

"I can barely remember when you guys lived next door," Gus said. "I remember your mom most, sitting with my mom all day by the pool. I have this memory of seeing her cry a lot. My mom was always comforting your mom."

"That's your mom's whole thing."

"My mom's a saint," Gus said.

Maybe her own mom was over in bed with Bryce Murtagh, but Shirley had always thought of her as a saint, too. This Bryce thing did not bother her on any political or moral ground, but it felt strange, it having happened so fast. She and Martin had talked about it. At first, he said it was none of their business, but then he himself started knocking Bryce's bad taste, and then one day in Martin's trailer Shirley and he gave Bryce an all-out thrashing. When she tried to get Bayard started last night, though, he told her to lay off. "You think Mom has to get married again before she can sleep over with someone? You guys are such pigs." In a way what Bayard said had helped reconcile Shirley to their mother's occasional absence. "I think Mom's handling this beautifully," he had said from his loft across the way, and Shirley decided Mom must have been talking more about it to Bayard and suddenly regretted her own disapproving aloofness.

Gus was leaning back on his elbows now. The sun was well up over Fraddboro, turning his browned skin redder. "Do you think Martin's homophobic?" he suddenly asked her. It gave Shirley a jolt whenever she was sitting quietly with someone whose train of thought had taken an entirely different track from hers. "I mean, he get so wincy when I talk about the Alliance."

"He doesn't know how to talk about it," Shirley said.

"So he's homophobic."

"He basically hasn't been exposed to it enough yet."

"He's twenty-six!" said Gus. Shirley always made allowances for Martin, so she could only shrug. "At your mom's birthday," Gus went on, "he was really wincy with Ron Starks. He wouldn't let Ron joke around with him."

"Ron can be an asshole," said Shirley. "I'm not kidding, I have to work with the guy. Since when are you the homophobia police?"

"I think it's really interesting to watch how some people act," Gus said. "I like it when they don't have any idea where you're coming from and don't know what to say. People in Newton can get very nervous."

Shirley knew his angle on Newton was bullshit. In ten years, Gus would be like Martin, idealizing his childhood; it was what everybody seemed to do. Corncrib Thibault had been at their mom's birthday, and all she could talk about was the picnic Martin had had when they were in high school and the times when she was little hanging out with her parents and the Hales. "We had picnics all the time, right here. We had broiled fish and corn and Mrs. Hale's corn bread. Of course, we didn't have wines, we had tonics. My mom brought her pies." She went on about the food and how they spread out bedspreads just like this and took naps in the shade and on and on.

"But you're the perfect Newton kid, Gus," she told him.

When he made a face and then stretched out his legs in front of her, Shirley sensed something in herself. Her feelings about women were confusing her. They had more to do with understanding, with being close. She had wanted to be close to Monica Pflueger; she had written her a thank-you note at her summer address and never heard back. She had hoped Monica might come out to visit her dad and they could come over for a swim at the cove. Monica's dad might even be someone nice for her mom. Wouldn't that be cool? He had to be better than Bryce. Monica, her stepsister, it was a neat idea. Was it incestuous? But she did not look at Monica's body, nor even at Susanna's or Michelle's at school, in the way she was now looking at little Gus's. She wondered how bisexual she really was, wondered what it would mean to be truly lesbian. She turned to Gus and asked, to get her mind off Monica Pflueger, "So have you lost your virginity, fella?"

"Whoa!" he said, eyes wide.

"Just asking," said Shirley. A week ago she had told him about her experiments last semester, not so much to confide in him as to present herself as a role model since he was so into his Gay-Straight Alliance.

"Depends on how you define virginity," Gus finally said.

"Okay. Do you consider yourself a virgin by your own private definition, whatever it is?"

"Speaking heterosexually: not a virgin. Maybe I haven't met the right guy yet," he added with a smirk.

"You're such a bullshitter," Shirley said. "You're as hetero as Bayard. You like messing with my mind." The amazing thing was that she could see his swimsuit expanding as he lay beside her. She wanted to touch his hairless skin because she knew the two of them would feel awesome lying against each other, but she felt no desire for Gus himself; he was a pushy little kid, and certainly he felt nothing for her as a woman. They talked about issues, he complained about things, she guided him, but if he had a crush on her he covered it by being flip and bratty. Or maybe because she had no crush on him she could not imagine him with one on her; there was that five-year gap. And then Shirley reminded herself that Gus could not qualify as a consenting adult however much he wanted her. They were out on the point in full sunlight. He was looking at her.

"Why the hell do you have that stupid nipple ring?" she asked.

"You don't like it?"

"I'm not into piercing."

"I think it's suave," he said.

"You must be the only kid . . ."

"Ethan Friedenheimer got one last winter, and I know a couple of senior girls did."

Shirley shook her head dolefully. His swimsuit was not subsiding, and he was staring at her. "Hey, let's walk down the point," she said. She was immediately afraid Gus would interpret this as an invitation to go meandering through the undergrowth back where no could see them, but she had had to think of something to break the spell, and slipping into the water seemed an even more dangerous activity to propose.

II

"I'LL HAVE A NUMBER four," said Peggy Tomaszewski, as she still called herself, "with home fries and grapefruit juice. And, Shirley, I'm about ready for a refill."

Shirley Lanaghan reached back around to the counter and grabbed the coffeepot Ron was handing over to her from between two fat truck drivers. He could tell she was having a splendid time. It was stupid of them not to have hired a girl before; Kevin did everything like it was a drag.

"So how's your mom?" Peggy was asking her.

"You should come by and visit," Shirley said.

"Ron tells me she's got something new going."

"Yeah, I guess she does," said Shirley. Ron noticed she was sounding more like a local, not so much in her accent but in the way she never said too much. Local people, except for himself of course, tended to be short of speech. He was used to playing off them and never enjoyed it much being around other talkers. Sometimes, Shirley's brother Bayard was even too talky. Ron could handle Martin, because he was so nervous, and Ron knew what the story was with him; Peggy had told him everything.

"I'm super glad for your mom, Shirley," Peggy said.

"Number four with home fries," Shirley yelled to Ron, who had already gotten a start. "Yeah, I guess I'm glad, too, keeps her out of my hair," she said to Peggy. Ron could see she was not sure how long she was supposed to talk to customers she knew, or even ones she did not. A lot of people who came in liked to say something about the hot sun or the road construction down in Haviland, but usually only a comment or two, unless it was Shirley waiting on them. She had that welcoming look to her with her short hair and little nose. She was the kind of girl Ron could almost go for, but Kevin was convinced she was lezzie.

"How's your brother?" Peggy said after Shirley had gone around to get juice.

"Which one?" Shirley called back.

"The cute one."

"Bayard."

"Marty! I never seen Bayard."

Ron said, "He's a lot cuter than Martin," and got funny looks from the truckers.

"No way!" said Peggy in her booth.

Ron watched Shirley's face as she brought over the juice.

He could not tell if she knew about her brother and Peggy. She kept the friendly smile on all the time and put the small glass down with a little bow of the head.

A family came in. Ron recognized them because they were in every few weeks, but he never knew their names and figured they were from Fraddboro. Shirley went to get their order, and Ron cleared off the truckers' plates and took their money. "See you again," he said without getting much back but two nods; they were giving Peggy the once-over on their way out.

"Fat slobs," she said after the door closed.

When Shirley brought her breakfast, Peggy was clearly ready to talk some more, but not so loud, since the family was talking quietly amongst themselves in Fraddboro style. Parshallville people talked loudest but least. The more you had to say, the quieter you said it. Ron had been observing customers for a couple of years now. It was a lot more interesting than working in the laundry and not seeing people at all.

Some regulars came in next; Eddie wondered where Kevin was, and Ron had to explain his new hours. Midmorning you got people who had time to kill, loaf, chat, goof off. Then usually it went really dead till noon, when the next crunch came. Victor always let Ron run the mornings, and Victor liked the long slow afternoons till Kevin came in and Ron got his second wind after a run with Stewart or getting into some kind of monkey business.

"What're you doing up here?" he called over to Peggy, who was glancing out the window, smoking and forking at her home fries.

"My dad's seeing his old friends from Florida, the Thibaults. Maybe you'd give me a ride over to the lake later, Ron?"

"I'm not taking Shirley till two."

"Two's fine," said Peggy. "I told my dad to pick me up there. We're going out to the Yellow Barn for supper."

"Hey, my little brother washes dishes there. Peggy, I hope you're not hanging around here waiting for Stewart. He's out on the road, you know."

"I don't want to see that prick," Peggy said as softly as she could, not to offend the family. Shirley was serving their sandwiches and asking about drinks in her college-girl voice. Ron was proud to have her working for him when families like that came in.

"You talk to him lately?" he whispered over the counter.

"You should know," said Peggy.

"I don't know nothing," Ron said. Of course, he knew plenty, but he was stuck between two friends, one he really liked and the other he had a lifelong crush on. Lately, Stewart kept claiming to be frustrated and horny, so Ron told him he could help him do something about it. Stewart said to stop that shit once and for all but went ahead and showered and toweled off in front of him anyway. Victor was sick of hearing about it.

Ron selected a couple of CDs but kept the volume low. He liked moving around behind the counter to some kind of beat; the diner seemed too backwoodsy without music. Here it came: "I Can't Dance to That Music You're Playing," Martha and the Vandellas from the radios of his childhood, his mother's kitchen radio, his father's radio out in the garage, his big sister Sarah's transistor on the front porch. The old life came back to him in these songs, not that he had a lot he was happy to remember. Victor never understood why the Starkses listened to so much black music. Ron thought maybe it was because they felt like substitute black people since no actual black people lived around Umbachaug. Victor pointed out that since most of the other trashy families in Sewall played country, the Starkses must really be the bottom of the barrel.

Working the counter, Ron always had four things going at once, the cooking, the chatting, the music, and then, quite separately, the thoughts in his head. He could be having a friendly conversation with the landfill gun club types, cooking eggs once-over-easy and hotcakes and sausage as well, keeping with the rhythm of the song, and then in some other room in his mind he could be thinking the most serious thoughts. Just now he had been telling himself that because Stewart knew about the virus, he must be scared of it, in the air, in a sneeze, even in the bar of soap they shared, and yet he must also not want Ron to know it, so he talked about being horny to show he was casual. He was horny to go to bed with Peggy again because she was so good, despite the shit that came along with it. He asked Ron questions to see if she was hooking up with anyone else. Stewart did not like the idea. Ron almost told him about Martin, but Peggy had said their second time did not go so well; Ron would wait to tell Stewart when she had a more serious prospect. In the meantime, Stewart was surely finding ways to get his rocks off. Was he careful about sex? It was not so high risk for him. Ron had never been afraid, exactly, but he had always tried to be safe. He had been stupid, however, been drunk, had been sloppy and should not have gone with the one who wanted to feel it skin to skin a while first. Actually, it could have been a couple of guys, a couple of times. One's rubber slipped off. It made Ron shudder if he imagined the very moment it might have happened, but glimpses came anyway in these hotcake-flipping dancing-behind-the-counter thoughts, of someone dark-bearded in the woods at night in the landfill, of a house in Fraddboro and sitting on the deck with cocktails and being waited on by a guy in a tennis outfit who wanted Ron to hang out all afternoon in his jockstrap, and of the high cab of an eighteen-wheeler at a rest stop and tossing about on the mattress up behind the seat. Ron truly had thought he was being careful at the time.

The second song came on, "Going to a Go-Go," the Miracles. Victor had little use for Ron's music but admitted the customers preferred it to what he would have chosen. Ron glanced into the back room and saw the door open and Victor sitting on the stoop with a coffee cup awaiting a delivery. Old Zart would be in soon, so Ron started some bacon.

"Ronny, I been watching you," Peggy said now that the place was clearing out. Shirley was wiping off the table where the quiet family had sat.

"What did you see?"

"I saw little wheels going around in there."

"You going to sit there smoking till two o'clock?"

"Any objections?"

"Shirley, you go sit and talk to Peggy, she needs company," Ron said. "Here, give me that plate. No, you go sit. You both got secrets to tell, I'm sure. It's girl-talk time." He came around and took the damp rag out of Shirley's hands and held her by the shoulders and plunked her down across from Peggy.

"Hi, Peg," Shirley said. "He's my boss, I guess."

Ron saw Zart across 108 looking both ways and afraid to step out. "Victor, here's the old geezer," he yelled, and he heard Peggy start up by asking Shirley how her mother was doing, how her mother was really doing.

III

CHRISTINA OSTERMANN SAT comfortably dripping onto the red towel she had spread out on the dock before taking her morning plunge. She loved to have the sun alone dry her skin and her hair. The white two-piece was more conservatively cut than what she might have worn even five years earlier. She was in fine shape but thought it bad taste for a woman of forty-seven to show too much buttock, at least on a public lake. By her own pool she occasionally trotted out one of her old suits; they had sentimental value for Kurt. "I'll be on my deathbed thinking of you in that suit," he had said a few weeks ago, and Christina fully believed him because Kurt meant everything he said.

She studied the dock. The chipping green paint and the rotting boards pleased Christina. It was a shame the owner had seen fit to replace practically every third board with an unpainted blond one. Christina wished people could take more pride in things out of repair. For her, a creaky old dock, each board pitted and peeling in its particular way, was an object for admiring contemplation. A protruding nail, a threatening splinter, these added history, but this dock now represented two time periods, and it would never be wholly itself again; each year it would slough off planks, receive new ones, and never be allowed to die a beautiful death.

She turned on her stomach, and a fresh sensation surrounded her, warmth from the towel under her folded arms, warmth from the great sun on her bare back. This month was a gift, an escape such as Christina seldom granted herself. Her responsibilities were waiting patiently at home in Newton, and no one was expecting anything of her right now. The month had given something to her marriage, too, staying apart all week and then reuniting in a lazy forgotten place. The loud boats on the main lake and the motorbikes on the dirt road did nothing to disturb Christina's larger sense of peacefulness. And to have Mary Lanaghan again a mere stone's throw away was the final blessing.

"Mother!" She turned her head slowly over one brown shoulder and saw her son on the porch, a baseball cap mercifully covering his pate and his nose pressed against the screen. "I'm awake again."

"So I see."

"Can I have second breakfast?"

"It's almost lunch. I invited the Lanaghan boys."

"I'm hungry now."

"So eat."

He disappeared in shadow, and Christina's eyes readjusted to the sparkling reach of water before her. A boat with a tiny outboard was putt-putting along toward the foot of the cove to fish among the water lilies. Gus had discovered fishing himself. For such an annoyingly active boy, the appeal of a sport requiring patience and meditation was unexpected. Kurt had happily, and expensively, equipped him, but both parents knew better than to call attention to the phenomenon of Gus sitting alone on a boulder by the shore at dawn and dusk, sometimes for hours. Usually, he was not even plugged into his Walkman.

To have time to think was the great luxury then for everyone, time to let thought take its natural course. Christina had finally achieved a deeper understanding of her old friend Mary. In one sense, Mary had gone far ahead of her and was looking philosophically back at Christina hastening along behind in life's welter; previously, Christina had mistaken Mary's slow pace for sadness.

She could hear an increasingly furious swimmer's kick around the bend of the shore toward Martin's trailer and soon saw long arms reaching out and then a mouth turning up to breathe under the left arm, and then came the kicking legs. Even at his full growth, Bayard swam with all the determination that had propelled him as a boy, taking lap after lap in the Ostermanns' pool while Shirley splashed about with Gus at the shallow end. "Yo!" came the spluttering shout when Bayard caught sight of the old neighbor lady, as she liked to call herself in the Lanaghan kids' presence.

"Arrive last night?" she called, knowing the answer.

"For a couple of days," he said, suddenly there. His hands seized the end of the dock, and he pulled himself up in one motion to sit on the edge.

"I haven't seen you since you graduated, Bayard. A year and a half?"

"At least that," he said. He smiled a most cheerful smile. Christina was sure that, as a boy, he had modeled himself somewhat on Kurt, even catching on to his particular smile. Dermot Lanaghan had had no smile by that point, and Martin never really had one at all. When Gus was a baby, impatient Kurt had practiced his fathering on the younger boy next door, made him a swimmer, a music lover. Christina had probably not seen Bayard in a bathing suit since puberty. He had wet black hair all over his chest and legs and a purple-black cast to his cheeks, yet he seemed all alight, bright teeth, long black lashes spangled with droplets. Christina immediately saw how he must make it difficult for Martin.

"So you're all here but Rosa."

"That one," said Bayard, "it's time to drag her out of the woods. She's losing all her mental faculties. Have you met Nat? She's been stuck on the guy for years."

"I hear he's sweet."

"He's sweet, oh, he's sweet, that's the trouble with him, he's so sweet." Bayard shook his wet black locks. "I don't know," he said. "He's a ski bum. What can I say?"

A memory was rising in Christina's mind of the fourteen-year-old Rosa, parents divorcing, stumped by adolescence, gentle, pretty to the adult eye but nothing yet to boys, never coming out by the pool, staying on the Lanaghans' porch on the glider, swinging softly to and fro with a book she was scarcely reading on her lap. Christina came often to sit by her, in a patch of sun on the red-painted porch floor. She would be casual, available, she had told herself, not an intimidating adult but a friend who stretched out unself-consciously like a child on the floor while Rosa rocked herself on the squeaky couch. She had helped her, Christina was sure.

And now, again, with another Lanaghan, more than a decade later, came something of the same feeling, though Bayard certainly needed no particular help from Christina. It was rather her uncondescending adulthood he expected and would get. It was remarkable, she thought, to see that furious little kicker now, big and wet and hairy, all the implications of his undeveloped self drawn at last to the surface.

"Funny," he said, "how Rosa finds that dork at college and sticks with him when she's got a whole life ahead of her. Like she wants to repeat Mom's mistakes."

Christina smiled and said, "But where would you four children be without your mom's mistakes?"

He gave no answer but lay out on his back with his long legs dangling over the end of the dock. "You know," he finally said, "something big is happening with Mom. I came up from New Haven to psych Bryce out firsthand."

Christina, amused and touched, tried to sound reassuring: "I think he's good for your mother. She's been missing this part of life."

"I know that. I was the one telling her to date, and I'm the one she talks to about this. Mom made him sound like a live wire compared to Ara Zeytoundjian. She said she felt unironic and free with Bryce. Mom tends to get ironic about men, in case you haven't noticed."

Christina had noticed; she had often tried to ease Mary into admitting she liked one man or another, but Mary would always isolate, with absolute accuracy, what made him impossible — his passion for model trains or that he said "between you and I" or, when it came to Ara, the fact of his considerable wealth.

"But from what Shirley says," Bayard was going on, "Bryce sounds like a major candidate for some heavy irony. Our mom sitting and watching satellite-dish TV! You met him yet?"

Christina was thinking hard what would be appropriately confiding without being disloyal to Mary. "He's a different sort of fellow from most anyone she's known," she said, nodding.

"And that's probably what she needs right now," Bayard said. "I tend to bounce back and forth myself, quiet types, crazy types. You have too much of one so you try the other. I'm half quiet, half crazy. But I tend to have at least something in common with the women I'm with. I'm just saying I can't tell yet about Mom and Bryce."

"Oh, Bayard," Christina said, without annoyance because she felt none, but with a sigh of exasperation — at life, not him.

"You know he lives in one of those houses," he said. "I get the feeling to him the woods are like a design feature. I'm serious."

"I detect a note of irony," said Christina. "What do you tell your mother?"

Bayard rolled his blue eyes and did a couple of sit-ups before answering. "That's tricky. Martin and Shirley are being assholes about it. I told them to lay off. They act like kids who don't want to lose their mother. I'm trying to be supportive for now. That's what she needs. I mean, I only had a chance to say a quick hello to the guy so far."

Christina would have asked if he could at least credit Bryce with being a nice person, but she heard a distant halloo thorough the trees and realized Mary might well have overheard all this had she been paddling along the bend in the shore; luckily, she was on foot.

Bayard lowered his voice. "But I bet he doesn't go through with his divorce. Not with that new house and his wife cooling off at her parents'."

"Maybe," Christina whispered, "your mother is simply having a fling." Bayard was looking closely at her as if he expected to discover something mocking him in her eyes, but he would not because Christina had made her face as warm and soft as she knew how. She had a notion it was precisely Bayard's susceptibility to hurt that kept him on the run in relationships. She and Mary had discussed him often on the telephone. It was difficult to assess which child Mary worried about more, but Christina had certainly heard the vulnerable aspects of each. Her own Gus she loved fiercely but did not worry over, and this gave him many strengths. Christina would not rely on the power of worry to civilize her son, but she had never gotten her method across to Mary Lanaghan.

"Yeah, I should know about flings," Bayard said, charmingly, and it was apparent to the old neighbor lady that he must have a stunning effect on his admirers, his lovely smile and bright eyes but, miraculously, no calculated seductiveness, no preening. He had inherited Mary's good nature, her straightforwardness. And again Christina wondered if Kurt's attention at the crucial moment had helped save this boy but not reached out far enough to save Martin.

There Mary was with a wicker basket containing corn bread and beer, her contribution to the picnic. "Martin's on his way," she called.

"Aren't you going to dip first?" asked Christina.

"Hi, sweetie," Mary said to Bayard. She came down the steps to the dock. "Well, maybe. I have my suit on underneath."

"There's towels," said Christina. She saw the dark slow shape of Hilda padding way behind up in the woods.

Gus popped onto the porch at that moment, nose against screen again, and called out, "Mrs. Lanaghan, when's Shirley get back from work? I got to see her for something."

"I hate to think what that's about," Christina whispered to Bayard in the intimate tone she knew made him feel like one of the adults.

IV

IN NEW HAVEN, the air-conditioned bookstore had disconnected him from the summer world beyond the plate glass. Customers browsed about in shorts and sandals, enjoying a cooling half hour, while he stuck to jeans, a long-sleeved work shirt, high-tops, and socks to keep from catching cold. Here at Umbachaug he was, briefly, reminding himself of July, of using a lake to cool himself off, of heavy air laden with leaf and needle smells, and of pollen, his downfall. He had toasted himself sufficiently, so in a leap and a splash he was in again, leaving Martin to mop sweat off his face with his T-shirt on the hot planks above. "Hey, Gus, I'll race you across the cove," Bayard yelled to the boy dangling his feet off the dock.

"I'm way wasted," said Gus.

"Martin?" But Martin only shook his head and lay his cheek down on his towel. "Too much beer?" Oh well, thought Bayard, I'll race myself. He shoved off from the corner pole. Last year he had only stayed home a short week after graduation; his dad had given him a trip to Ireland. Bayard had not swum that whole misty summer, and when he got back and could no longer simply walk in and use the Yale pool, he began to feel in danger of losing muscle tone. He found running tedious, so he biked a lot until winter cut into his routine. This is what it will be like to get older, he decided; you stop doing it, you start losing it.

Swimming the cove was a little harder than it used to be, and maybe Gus would have made it ahead of him. When he got to the point he floated awhile in the shallow water and took soft breaths scented with pine, but then came one penetrating breath of gasoline fumes when a motorboat roared by on the lake. "Slow it down!" he shouted, unheard, and waited for the wake to rock him into shore.

He set about exploring the old paths and thought of high school sex there at night with other pairs panting nearby — and mosquitoes. Rosa and her crowd used to hang out at the landfill, so the point belonged to Bayard's friends. They would park down at the public landing and walk out, and his mother never knew how close to home he actually was. The paths were as well-trodden as ever. Kids probably still used them, and there were fishermen, and bird-watchers, and day campers pretending to be Indians. Bayard recognized every turn leading to the soft mossy spot where he had first made it with Karen and later Felicia, oh, and Jeannie. And there was his favorite pine trunk to lean against and listen to night sounds and point at stars. Bayard used to row across on mornings after, to throw away condoms and beer bottles. He had not wanted to give anyone cause to crack down on their regular midnight get-togethers.

His skin was warm and a tad sticky now. He climbed onto the boulder on the cove side and sat himself down in the hot sun. In their early days here, he and Shirley had called it Lookout Rock. Bayard would row her over for picnics of crustless peanut butter sandwiches and Hawaiian Punch. Their mom made Shirley wear an orange life jacket in the rowboat, even though she was already eleven, so they folded it out for a soft seat when they got to the rock, their two bottoms fitting neatly, close side by side. Bayard remembered the stories he had heard from Mr. Hale about old times on the lake when the train went through and city folks came out to swim and go boating and eat fish grilled on open fires and sing songs everybody used to know. The gentlemen wore swimsuits that covered them from their necks to their knees, and the ladies wore bathing bloomers with skirts and sun hats. Someone played the banjo and someone else the fiddle. Mr. Hale's father had worked there as a boy, tending fires and serving up the fish on white tin plates with blue rims, some of which had made their way to the cottage he built in the Depression. Bayard had seen them. Holding a scratched-up tin plate, he had conjured an entire rollicking congregation, singing, dancing, eating, out there in the woods a hundred years ago. He had determined where the picnic pavilion must have stood, where the bathing cabins were, where the long dock was with its rowboats and canoes for rent; he had seen parasols in ladies' hands as they strolled through the trees, seen gentlemen with straw hats and walking sticks, and heard the plunking banjo and the strumming mandolin over the water, and the cheerful burble of human voices; he had even heard the puff of an ancient locomotive pulling in to take them all home.

But the shore he watched now was overgrown with blueberry bushes and saplings; there was no lawn to play upon. Bayard perceived the northeast corner of his mother's balcony poking out of the branches and there, to the right, a glimmer of aluminum where the land began to curve back away from him. Beyond he could see not the cottage itself but only the small dock where Martin and Gus lay conversing head to head and then a glint on the glass doors of the converted boathouse Ron and his friend rented. It was a peaceful scene but somehow enclosed, sequestered, detached. Bayard could never live on Hale's Cove again. Besides, his nose was stuffing up as he had feared it might. He lowered himself down the boulder, knelt happily in the water to let coolness envelop him, and then pushed off again, this time with a more leisurely stroke. Bayard was aware of his whole body; it felt right. He would join the Y when he returned to New Haven. This was going to be his year to get back in shape, and he would begin to read on a strict plan, and he would definitely take the Grad Recs.

It was also time to leave his family alone, not out of disregard for them but in order to create a better sense of himself, to get separate, the way he had long gotten separate from his father, but without that rancor. Of course, he would keep an eye on Shirley — maybe it was only your elders you felt the need to separate from.

Halfway across, he flipped onto his back and stroked just enough to keep afloat. His ears, underwater, picked up motors churning out on the lake, but he transformed them into the twanging of crickets and, looking up into the blue, admired the summer picnic sky of the last century. The slowness of the past seeped into his skin. He saw himself out in a boat with a young lady, alone as they so seldom could be in those days. She let her parasol shade them from watchers onshore, and Bayard managed to plant a kiss on her pink cheek, an instant of intense arousal such as his modern self often yearned for but never achieved. In those days, Bayard was sure, he would have been a ladies' man of the most impassioned sort. Mystery would have accompanied him, surrounded him, his own and hers — she being all the gentle, covered-up young Worcester ladies on their summer outings, shyly hoping for, but fearful of, a gentleman's attentions. Those lovesick picnickers on the cottage shore knew little of what we know, Bayard mused; they had no psychological explanations but found themselves driven and confused and ecstatic but also cruel, dishonest, evasive, timorous. To fall in love must have been something overwhelming, a touch of that great unreachable harmony that hung over their singing as the fish fried, the harmony they strove for, where all notes were true and God approved of them. In such a world, thought Bayard as he ran his arms through the silken water, the stolen kiss would have dazzled him as no kiss yet ever had. But this loss did not make him sad; strangely, it comforted him to think of it as he made his lazy way across the cove.

There were voices. A car door slammed. Gus was leaping up the stone steps like a monkey, all arms and legs. When, after reverting to the crawl, Bayard struck the end of the dock and tossed his wet hair as he surfaced, he saw, with Shirley and Ron, a young woman he did not recognize getting out of Ron's car. She was calling Martin, who had slowly followed Gus, and when he reached her, she pinned her arms around him with a big loud laugh and an extra squeeze. "I missed you, Marty," she seemed to say, though Bayard was not sure; he hoped that was what she had said. He kept his head low and watched and listened. Soon, Martin and she were heading off toward the trailer. Bayard heard him mentioning Siouxsie and the Banshees, his new CD. Gus and Shirley had already ducked out of sight beyond the cottage. It was Ron who noticed Bayard peering over the end of the dock. "Hi, gorgeous," Ron called, and Bayard waved. He liked Ron. "Where's your mom?"

"Walking with Mrs. Ostermann," Bayard said.

Ron came down to the dock, looking even more pumped up in his tight T-shirt than last year, and asked him how it was going.

"Good," said Bayard. "I'm on my own. It's good." He stayed in the water, but not because he minded Ron giving him the eye. "Who was that girl with you?" he asked.

"Didn't I tell you last year about my buddy Stewart marrying Drew Hale's kid? That's her — Peggy. Now they're separated."

It came back to Bayard, before he went to Ireland, joining up with Ron on a jog and him huffing away about some brand-new doomed marriage.

"And now she's got your brother's knickers in a twist," Ron said. Bayard looked at him blankly. "Well, at least that's the way she tells it," said Ron, sitting down and running his hand along the smooth new planks Drew Hale had added this year.

V

OUT THE RAILROAD BED, quite a ways, propelled by Christina's curiosity farther than she usually walked, Mary had begun to worry about the dog making it all the way back home, so they found a mossy resting spot well off the path. After lapping up a good drink from a puddle, Hilda had flopped on a flat rock, and now her ribcage was rising and falling, assuring Mary she was all right. It was lying on her side in the woods one day that Mary expected to find Hilda dead, or that was how she hoped it would be, but she also dreaded it.

Mary had been enjoying Christina's many stories, not really absorbing details but letting them flow through her as other people's lives used to do in her Newton years when she was part of things. She felt how inadequate their Sunday phone calls and their visits every other month had been. Here, she and Christina could simply waste time together again, and wasting time was the only way you came to feel at home with someone. Except for Martin, her children hardly ever wasted time with Mary anymore. Geography has an emotional force, she thought, watching Christina's face running through its familiar animations: disdainful eyebrows for the latest owners of the Lanaghans' old house, a flash of anger — darting tongue, wide eyes, hands sweeping the air — at recent cuts in public higher education, a smile creeping across her toothy mouth when she announced Gus's heavy crush on Shirley. These attitudes had long ago been embedded in Mary's memory, and even geography had no power over them, but it was different seeing them once more in the unhurried present. Mary wondered what time and age must have felt like in the days when people passed their lives in a single village and never had to step back far enough to notice change, never had to miss the daily company of those they loved. Christina, then, would have accompanied her calmly till death.

"When the Friedenheimers come to use the pool," she was saying, "and they bring Bubbie, I know I'm in for quite an afternoon. I'll hand it to her. She's a believer in what the individual person can do." A look of profound respectfulness had come over Christina's face, in the eyes, in the tightened brow. "She's ninety by now and you can't stop her. She's on the Bosnia committee, of course."

"Mrs. Friedenheimer, the mother?" said Mary vaguely.

"Burton's mother — Bubbie. She moved in with them finally, I'm sure I told you."

"I always liked her," Mary said. She had an image of a stout talkative gray-haired lady with a strand of pearls at her neck slicing immense pieces of cheesecake at a neighborhood gathering a dozen years ago.

"She's not well, that's the sad part," said Christina. "The family's always with her now."

Mary leaned all the way back and let her head rest on moss. She made a sympathetic murmur, falling tones, a slight exhalation, and looked up into the huge branches of oak and ash unmoving above her. This is the true forest, she thought, its grandest trees unharvested. Hilda's legs twitched in her sleep.

"So how was last night at Bryce's, Mary?"

Christina's voice startled her. It had shifted registers. The talk of Newton had been spun out in an easy light thread that wove around Mary like a charm, but this sudden question was husky, intent. Mary closed her eyes. Perhaps, if she did not look at her friend, she could come up with an answer for her.

"I am not in love," Mary said. "It's something else." It had taken her a good minute to think of this, and she had said it very slowly.

"And what is it?" came the same husky, but softer, voice from the air above her closed eyelids.

Mary had to think again. "It's a renewing of my senses," she finally said.

"That sounds fun."

"It *is* fun," Mary said.

A distant annoying buzz turned quickly louder and then, for ten seconds, almost unbearably loud as some motorbike hurtled along the old railroad bed down the hill from them, but it only interrupted, did not break, the spell.

Mary had not opened her eyes, but she sighed faintly to indicate she was waiting for her next true thought. When it came to her, it was so swiftly followed by others that she found her mind leaping ahead of her words and could not stop herself. "Christina, it's all been entirely strange to me. I'm not holding on to anything — you know how I always prefer to hold on — but it's like there's no future, there's no past. Does that make sense? If I want to see Bryce, I go see him. And he's there, puttering around when he gets home from work. He's out of his suit in his boxers humming to what he calls his easy-listening station." Mary had to laugh. She wanted her friend to see what she saw. "His face lights up," she said, "and he puts his arms around me. If I think about him one aspect at a time, there's nothing I particularly want about him, but when I'm there I don't think about him like that. Ara was always over behind some table or at the other end of some couch. He approached me carefully, politely, but always there was a kind of tension, as if he might jump the gap. I said I wasn't ready for anything yet. And I wasn't, with Ara. He said he was the patient sort, but it must've embarrassed him when we had separate rooms. I don't feel Bryce always courting me so. He's simply Bryce. That sounds stupid. But Ara — it was just one time at the beach on Nantucket when I felt his penis against me — " Mary stopped a moment but realized she had to go on. "We said nothing, but it got awful after that. I felt sorry for him, and we had all his friends around. Innuendos all over the place. I think I hurt his feelings, but at the hospital we act like we're still friends. I feel terribly awkward."

"Back to Bryce, Mary. I'm not asking about Ara," said Christina firmly, in the darkness of Mary's floating thoughts.

"What about Bryce?"

"Bryce, you and Bryce. I've hardly met the man."

"You're asking why am I keeping him to myself?" Mary did not expect an answer, but she left her question in silence for a while. Christina, finally, made an inquisitory sound at the back of her throat to prompt her. Mary had never been to a psychiatrist, but she imagined this was what it might be like. It was different from when she had come to Christina for support in her year of crisis, when they had sat face to face and she had wept and Christina had hugged her. This was trancelike, dreamlike. She heard the soft panting of the dog a few feet away, slow beats of time.

"Because I know he's not really for me," Mary said. "That's why I'm keeping him to myself. If he was really for me I would want him in my life. I would want the kids to know him, you to know him. I don't mean I'm ashamed of him. I'm very very proud of him. Does that sound dumb? But I don't want anyone else to be around. This is terrible the one month you're here."

Christina's throat, the only part of her that Mary was aware of now, made an amused purr.

"What I mean is, Christina, we have very good sex. It started happening that way, I'm not sure why. I never had that sort of sex with Dermot. I don't mean to be cruel. Oh, look, Bryce is just a software marketer with a wife and two little kids who've moved out on him because I'm sure he can be a real ass. She's with her mother in Boston. Maybe the dream house finished her off. It's unbelievable the stuff he buys. We drink beer from huge insulated plastic mugs. His whole house — the windows are too small for the walls except for one picture window that's too huge. And there's a hot tub on a high deck you can't get down to the ground from. The carpets are thick, the curtains are heavy. It could be the Sheraton Tara. It's unreal air in there. My kids are appalled by my stories. Ara would've been perfect for them; they'd assume I was being taken care of."

"But you wouldn't be taken care of," said Christina. Because she had said so little, her words had astonishing force.

"Yes, because lately I feel like someone quite different," Mary said. "I was not so sure who I was. I'm still not sure who I am."

In the silence, at a far distance, she heard the crackle of rifle fire in the landfill. They should begin walking back. Bayard had only today and Thursday off, and Mary had to spend some solid time with him before she drove him to the bus in Leominster tomorrow night.

"Christina?"

"Hmm?"

Mary did not want to open her eyes quite yet. "I think I've been asleep."

"You nodded off for a minute."

"Did I? No, I mean asleep in my life." She thought of how she must look to her friend, lying on the forest floor, eyes closed, breathing in a slow rhythm. "Asleep for ten years," she said.

"No," said Christina, sharply. "I do believe you were asleep with Dermot, but these last ten years, it's been a long slow convalescence, that's all, not a sleep."

"I'm almost fifty," said Mary.

Christina said nothing. A sense of regret hovered in the air between them, but after a few minutes, surprisingly, it resolved into a calm. Maybe it came from being beside her old friend and her dog in those sweet-smelling woods in summer.

"Want to open your eyes now?" Christina asked gently. Mary looked around. She did not at first see Christina, who was to one side and behind her. She saw Hilda and reached out to touch the fur on the shaky thigh. The dog started and raised her heavy head, put it down again, then realized the time had come to trudge on. She made a low moan and stretched. Christina lay her hand on Mary's shoulder and gave it a squeeze that nearly hurt. Mary looked up into the sharp eyes that must have been watching her closely all this time.

As they let the dog lead them down the narrow trail to the old railroad bed, or bike path as newcomers called it — as Bryce called it — Mary found a lighter note. "I felt hypnotized," she said. "Did you hypnotize me?"

Christina laughed, tossing her head back as she always did when she felt happy.

"Because I'm not used to talking about sex."

"You hardly did," said Christina. "Gus talks more graphically about sex at the breakfast table."

"Is sex really the heart and soul of life, Christina?" Mary wanted to know. She had put it casually, but she did hope for an answer.

"Of course it is!" shouted Christina, leaping from a small boulder down onto the broad path. Mary was helping Hilda wind down sideways.

"Dermot always claimed it was," Mary said when they were on the level, walking side by side with the dog not too far behind. "But I don't think he understood it. He got it over with. What did I know!" said Mary.

"Poor girl, you took care of your dying parents and your babies and all you had for assistance was Dermot Lanaghan."

"And the church in the back of my head when I thought I'd got away from it."

"But isn't it something to be able to look back on all that?" said Christina. She was walking faster, so Mary quickened her step. She could never draw on the source of sudden enthusiasm that filled Christina at times like this. "Even to look back on Nantucket two weeks ago. What's done is done."

"I was dying on Nantucket," said Mary. Here came another motorbike from behind them. She grabbed Hilda's collar and pulled her to one side. The deaf old dog looked bewildered but let out a bark when the young man with a ponytail flew past. "I don't see the thrill in it," Mary said. "Isn't it boring for them? They roar to Haviland, then they roar back to Parshallville. It's what they do out on the lake, too. Now they have Jet Skis. They roar up to the Parshallville beach, then they roar down to the public landing."

Christina had her oblivious grin on. She was too happy to complain about the detritus of the modern world. That was how Mary felt with Bryce. Let her children worry about her if they had to. Was she to complain that a man, who still looked great in his boxer shorts and had a warm smile, wanted to take her in his arms, and then, for respite, cuddle with her on the widest softest love seat she had ever sat on and feed her goulash bubbling in a microwave container and watch with her on his king-size TV the stupidest families in the universe screaming at each other and patching it up over and over again into the timeless, placeless night?

VI

DREW HALE IMAGINED he was in his '71 Chevy, not his '83. He imagined that when he reached the loop at the end of his road he would find himself at the gun shop with his sign still hanging on the maple branch and Albert Thibault would soon be dropping in for a chat. He imagined he had not yet sold the chalet lot, that is was still a pinewood on sandy soil, and that Elizabeth and small Peggy were waiting for him at the cottage the way they used to do. That was two dozen years ago.

And now what he thought of as his new Chevy was ready to be retired. He drove the hell out of his cars and had no loyalty to them. Most men he knew, Albert included, cared more about their cars than anything else they owned, but not Drew. He cared about his guns, his furniture, his books, his land and the houses on it, and he cared about his two women, them most of all. Of course, Albert cared about Pauline and the kiddies, but the truth was he talked more about his car. He drove a Ford Thunderbird down in Florida.

Drew arrived at the gun shop — the boathouse — no, the rental property. He chuckled to himself. He was to pick Peggy up here at five and she had damned well better be ready. He honked and waited, but nothing happened so he honked again. The fairies were not at home. Drew felt odd about renting to the two of them; one might have been all right, but the two together made him uncomfortable. If it were not for the memory of Ugo Bardonecchia, he would never have let them sign the lease.

He revved the engine and pulled around the loop to head back past the cottage where Mary's friends were. He would have come up when they meant to leave in June, but they had called the day before and signed up for all of July. Twelve hundred bucks, no dickering, the check was in the mail. Mary Lanaghan had said something about them raising money for Bosnia, and now Drew noticed a scrawny bald boy sitting on the front stoop with the Lanaghan girl. He looked like he was fresh from a refugee camp.

Drew drove on to the turnout behind Mary's place. He honked a brief, friendly honk, but no one came and the dog did not bark. Drew looked at the chalet, blank from the rear, two narrow ventilator windows where the stove and bathroom were. Mary's car was there, but no one came down the steps that led from the front balcony. Drew remembered the sandpit they had dug before they poured the foundation there, before the concrete block basement went up; he remembered when trucks brought the lumber and stacked it under the trees and when the pump was put in, and the septic, and the electric lines. He and Albert had unofficially overseen the operation, and Louise and Charles played in the sand and talked to the construction crew, Charles asking question after question. And sometimes Peggy came and looked on, grown up compared with the two fat kiddies.

It was worth it, the profit was good; the first owners were sort of lowlife, but then Mary Lanaghan had come along. Her deference toward Drew, her sense of his senior relation to the cove, made her seem more like a self-sufficient unbothersome renter than an owner; he was still the only true man of the place.

Now he heard footsteps and turned to see the older Lanaghan boy coming up from the lake along the grassy path where his trailer was parked, and there was Peggy ambling behind him. "Wait up," she was saying, and the boy, Martin, said he thought he had heard a car. Then they saw Drew. "Hello, Mr. Hale. I told you so, Peg."

"Hi, Dad, I wasn't sure what time you were coming."

"What did I tell you?"

"You said five, but then you said you had to pick Louise up at her job."

"That's where we're going to next. Hop in, you're late." Peggy came around the car looking, to Drew's eyes, preoccupied. "How's your little brother?" Drew asked Martin.

"He's here. He was asking about you. I don't know where he went off to, maybe jogging."

"I missed him?"

"I guess."

"I wish I could stay around, son, but we've got a big family whoop-de-do planned over at the Yellow Barn."

"He went jogging with Ron?" Peggy asked, but Martin did not seem to know. Drew began backing tightly around to get pointed the right way. Peggy threw the Lanaghan boy a kiss out her window, and then Drew wheeled left and plunged down the shady gravel road.

"Bayard's the better of those two," Drew said. "That one's got problems."

"Who doesn't!" said Peggy.

"Listen, Mary Lanaghan told me about it the first time he moved back here. He's got serious mental problems is what I'm saying."

"Yeah, he's sort of sad," said Peggy. "But I don't mind him."

"You didn't meet the other one."

"I met him. We swam over when he was on the dock. He's sure cute enough. It's funny that he seems older than Marty."

Drew was glad Peggy was getting the idea that age did not necessarily indicate how grown up you were; Stewart Tomaszewski was thirty-five, after all.

"But you know, Dad," Peggy said when they hit the Fraddboro Road, "right now I think I can use a little immaturity maybe. I don't feel like taking anything too serious."

Drew grunted a noncommittal reply. He was waiting for the mailbox marked Germaine, and when he saw it and turned just in time, the Chevy rattled at all four corners. He was curious to see the big house back there, which he had last glimpsed when he was a teenager and Mr. Germaine chased him off the property. The brown paint was peeling and there was a falling eave over the screened porch, but someone must have been coming to clip the hedges and weed the garden beds; the place did not look too bad. "I don't suppose I should blow the horn here," Drew said; Peggy thought probably not.

They sat a bit. It was only five-fifteen. Sometimes, Drew did not know what to say to Peggy, especially when he had determined not to lecture her. "You went swimming with the older boy?" he asked, for something to say.

"I like Marty," Peggy said. "But I'll tell you what, Dad, I think I won't be hanging around there much anymore. It makes me feel funny being on the old place where I was a kid and seeing other people living in the cottage. Ron and Victor are great, though. I know you don't approve of them, but what can I say?"

"They're all right," Drew said. "It's their friend Stewart that bugs me."

"Oh yeah, him," Peggy said. Good, they could josh each other about it now. She was coming around. "And that's a benefit being friends with Ron," she said. "I keep thinking I want to see Stewart again, but then I remember I don't. Ron's always talking about him."

"But Mary Lanaghan, now there's a good new friend you made up here."

Peggy was quiet. She was not disagreeing; she seemed to be thinking about something else. Drew waited, patting the door panel outside with the palm of his left hand, and estimated what it would take to repair the screened porch roof.

"Yeah, but you know, Dad, after all, Mary's got Marty there, and I just don't want to get involved."

"You said you liked the kid."

"But it's hard to be friends with just Mary when I'm more his age and he's there all the time."

The kitchen door slammed, and Louise took the steps down one by one, cautiously. She was carrying two pie plates wrapped in tinfoil.

"Hi, Corncrib," called Peggy. Drew shushed her, but she frowned at him for being so sensitive; if Louise didn't mind, why should he?

"Hi, Mr. Hale, hi, Peggy." Drew made Peggy get in back so Louise could have the front. He felt the car tilt when she got in. "See, Charles has got the Lark because he's taking Momma to the hairdresser, and Mrs. Hale and Poppa are waiting at our place."

"This is quite an operation," said Peggy.

It was a rougher ride getting out the Germaine drive than coming in. Drew was worried about his suspension but covered by asking Louise how the old lady was today.

"Oh boy," she said, "at least I got my pies baked. She just wants to talk. You know, back at first it felt like everything she said had some special meaning, because I was still getting used to working with death and dying, and I thought like any day she might croak. I mean, she'd say things like 'Blue is the color of good-bye,' and it seemed so heavy. But she says weird crap like that all the time. It doesn't add up to much. What was it today? She's getting ready, she keeps saying. 'Ready for what, Mrs. Germaine?' I say. All the time I'm remaking the bed and she's propped up on the chaise lounge. 'Ready in my own mind, Louise,' she says. 'Everything's changing.' In the daytime, she says, it's like she's in a happy dream, but after dark is when she feels it — she listens to her radio all night, but that doesn't seem to be enough. She said they played this symphony and it opened up into the depth of time, she said. 'But, Louise,' she said, 'sometimes there's also this whirlwind rushing by like a train.' She has a thing for trains. So I asked her which it was more, the depth of time or the whirlwind. She couldn't say. That's the sort of thing I get every day. I also work for a lady in Basswood. Nice lady. She just wants me to change her diapers and fix her hair. It's a relief."

"Man," said Peggy, "I could never take your job, Louise."

"Louise, you're a good kid," said Drew. "Sometimes all you have to be is a listener. That's what those people need more than anything."

"I just try to be calm, Mr. Hale," Louise said. "It's not so fascinating as I thought it was going to be. I like it, I guess. It's like I'm doing something to help people. When I qualify for terminal home care, though, I hope I don't have to work with some young person dying."

"No AIDS types," said Drew.

"Oh Lord," Louise said, balancing her pies on her lap, "I hope not. But you're supposed to be ready for everything."

"What kind of pies you got?" Peggy asked. Drew could tell she wanted to get off the subject of death. That was all right. He did not like thinking about it either, but he did think about it. Seeing Albert and Pauline he had thought about it, because they looked so suddenly old.

The road through Haviland Center was half blocked off for repairs. Louise pointed out the apartment where she and Charles used to live above the pharmacy. Then she asked Peggy about Martin Lanaghan, and they sounded so concerned, the two of them, it made Drew wonder if there was something new gone wrong with that boy. "I'm going to have to drop in on Mary soon," Louise concluded as they pulled over in front of the green-shingled cross-eyed house.

Charles was waving from the door. "I got Momma. We're ready to roll. Just stay put. Mrs. Hale can hop in next to Peggy. Momma! Poppa! Louise, you stay with the Hales."

"I'm comfy," she said.

Elizabeth came out with Pauline right behind her. "Honey, what are those pies?" Pauline asked when she saw what was on her daughter's lap.

"Smells great," Drew said.

"Don't worry. They're for later, Momma."

"It's a big whoop-de-do," said Drew. He was suddenly very pleased. The two families were together. If he had seen Louise and Charles waddling along the street and did not already know them, he certainly would have made some crack about their size, but they were Albert's and Pauline's, and he loved them as much as any real uncle could. He knew Peggy was not thrilled to be thrown in with the fattest people in the five-town region at this point in her life, especially going out to the Yellow Barn, which was the sort of place where she and Stewart probably hung out, but the good-sport side of Peggy was in better working order lately. The collapse of her marriage had taught her some humility, Drew figured.

Finally, Albert emerged. Again Drew got that shock, that sense of Albert as old, and that he moved slowly, that he ached, that he was no longer the same man who had gone fishing with him on Sunday mornings and spent the rest of the week replacing everybody's mufflers and exhaust pipes for a decent price or when it snowed was out driving the town plow through the cold New England winter any time of the day or night.

VII

"TELL ME," Shirley said. Martin was looking at his feet, picking at his toenails. "Tell me, bruthy. Come on, tell."

"I don't think anything's ever going to work out for me," he said.

"So it didn't go that far?"

"It went far," he said. "The first time."

"Why didn't you tell me back then? I had to wait till she came by here today to pick up the vibe."

Martin leaned against his pillow and stuck his feet out on the camp blanket. Shirley, who had been sitting at the computer, came and sat beside him. She knew Martin would never tell her everything, the way Bayard would, but they had their own language that allowed her, momentarily, to become counselor to her oldest brother. With no one else his age had she ever been able to talk this way. She looked up at him, and he was smiling, achingly; his eyes were wet.

"It was a breakthrough," he said. "Why did she make me fall for her and then split?"

Shirley was familiar with the question. Splitting was the approved mode, she had found — no questions asked, no looking back. It was not cool to fight it, and the worst thing you could do was to let yourself be devastated. Girl or boy, it was the same. She asked Martin what would have happened if Peggy Hale had stayed on another week at the lake.

"But the Ostermanns were moving in."

"No, I mean, what if they weren't, if you'd had some space."

"I saw her a few more times."

"I know, but, Martin, what I'm saying is, basically, what would've happened if she'd stayed?"

"You're telling me she would've split anyway."

"I wondered is all."

Shirley was back in her jeans because the evening had turned breezy. Besides, she had not wanted to lather her legs up with Off when she walked down to the trailer after supper; Bayard needed a chance to catch up with Mom at the house. Martin was in jeans, too, and the Newton South T-shirt the Ostermanns had brought him for old times' sake. She nudged her denimed thigh up against his and nestled her feet in his armpit, and he threw the extra pillow to her end so she could get comfortable. This was how they had talked when she was in ninth grade and he took his year off from college; Bayard was always too close in age to cozy up to.

"Peggy's a couple of years older than me. She's had a lot of experience. She's been married," Martin said.

"And?"

"Well, I'm in a different place."

Shirley wanted to ask him where that place was, because she truly wanted to hear it from him, though he would get it wrong. He would say, she knew, that women did not take him seriously, that in his jobs he always ended up working for jerks, and that now he was in a kind of decompression chamber, finding his way back to his own self. He would not say the truth because he did not know it. The truth, Shirley was sure, was that things in his life had scared him and made him angry and the amount of anger in him scared him still more. It was a terrible circle because even this summer of freedom had made him more afraid of the world and therefore angrier, and now, because of Peggy, angrier still and more afraid. Their mom had not made him get a job, and even his inaction made him angry and afraid, but it was true that action of almost any sort might have made him even more so. So it was not a decompression chamber, this trailer, this retreat in the woods, it was only a smaller prison. The yet smaller prison, the most inescapable, Shirley realized as she looked down her legs into his dark eyes, was Martin's body itself. That was the place he was in. He had never stepped out of it and looked back. Or maybe he had, briefly, with Peggy. "Did you learn something from being with her?" Shirley asked, carefully.

"I only learned what I can't have, so now I want it more."

"Yeah, I guess I know."

"You're so experienced, sisty," he said showing an edge of sarcasm.

"Well, I've tried a few things."

Back in that sunken voice of his he said, "I suppose you have."

"But I don't know at all what I want, Martin. Unlike you. You know what you want. Let me tell you something about me." She had said it so she would have to follow up with something, but she was afraid of what she had to tell him, so she waited. Martin was silent, with his eyes like wells of sadness, his lips full from trembling. "Okay, here goes," Shirley said, then gathered her determination one more time. She pulled her cap around with the brim in front to shade her eyes from his when she looked down. "I don't know if I really like boys or girls," she said.

"You like boys, Shirley," he said in a soft voice, to reassure her.

"I also like girls, I have to say. I had experiences with two friends this year. And I'm finding myself sort of prone to crushes. That girl Monica Pflueger, who drove me home, remember? I got a stupid crush on her."

"It's from living in Northampton," Martin said to be funny, then he asked, "Did you actually do anything, with girls?"

"What's weird is, that wasn't what it was all about," Shirley said, knowing she was avoiding an answer. "It was more about being with them. I felt I wanted to be with them, first Susanna, then Michelle. I mean it was sex, too," she said finally.

"Susanna?"

"Oh yeah, and you've got your Suzanne." Shirley knew Martin had been willing to tell her about his Suzanne only because Suzanne was in New Mexico and was not real, but he never told her about Peggy until Shirley figured it out for herself that afternoon. Gus had figured it out, too. He had a sixth sense for sexual tension, being full of it himself.

"By the way, Suzanne was encouraging me about Peggy," Martin said. "She kept saying to tough it out, be steady, and understanding, available. She couldn't believe it was over so fast."

Shirley patted Martin's knee. "So what's her advice now?"

"She said maybe I should be happy for a while with the peace of the forest. She has an idealized version of this place. She thinks it's wilderness. She has no idea how close things are in the East." Then, after a quiet moment, he said, "Hey, weren't we talking about you?"

"I couldn't tell if you wanted to know about it," Shirley said.

"No, but what about boys? You always liked boys, being with boys."

"I still like boys. It's different with boys."

"Gus is after you," Martin said.

"Tell me about it."

"You should help him lose his virginity."

"I'm told he already has."

"Figures," said Martin, looking even sadder. His own virginity must have been lost in such slow stages he could not be sure when it happened. Shirley had never known the specifics, but the girl in Amherst was certainly something, and so was the one in Newton. Peggy was obviously something more. But Shirley had never seen her brother with a date he brought home and hung around the family with like Bayard. Shirley put her head back on the pillow and closed her eyes, with her left hand holding Martin's right hand down along his side.

The two of them entered one of their silent zones. It was always clear when they were in one: a slow rhythm pulsed through the air between them, like long slow waves of awareness, each in separate thoughts. Hers were, suddenly, of Gus and that morning, of how insistent he was, and slightly tempting, such a little male, but how easy he was to fend off when the moment came. "You keep it in your Speedo," she had said when he wanted to make out in the woods. His body had felt like a slippery eel when they hugged and she felt him hard against her, but he did not know how to be at all seductive; it was more like wrestling, and that was as far as it went. He was apologetic when she came home from work, afraid he had totally turned her off, so they had to go talk about it tediously in that hemming-hawing teenage way for a good hour until she convinced him she liked him just the way he was. "It'd be cool to bring you to a dance at school," he had said. "The Alliance has the best dances. You could really pass for queer. Some of the girls would go for you." She told him that was all she needed. But the whole thing had brought her more confusion. She thought of Martin being twenty-six; he was five years ahead of her, and by then, certainly, she ought to have fallen in love for life and settled down. It was not very far away, and she did not want to be lost like Martin, but when she thought of Rosa having been with Nat Speradakis since college, she did not want that either. Maybe Bayard was getting more serious lately. He was only a year and a half ahead of her, and maybe that was when it would begin to happen, but that meant she had a year and a half max. Did she have to make it happen or would it happen by itself? Shirley knew perfectly well it happened differently for everyone, but how did you practice? All she could think of was that you had to risk falling in love too early for it possibly to be right, and then you had to be willing to work it through and probably break up — but how many times?

"I've been thinking about Mom," Martin's voice said, and Shirley looked up. Usually, she was the one to leave the silent zone first, no longer able to keep her thoughts from turning into words. "Mom is changing," he said. "I wonder if it's menopause."

The idea had never occurred to Shirley. "I don't really know much about menopause," she admitted.

"She's getting to the age," Martin said. "She's probably telling Bayard all about it and she won't tell us."

"Menopause."

"It's one explanation."

"What do you know about menopause?"

"Some stuff I read on the net."

"You're serious about this," Shirley said.

"You're the girl. You should ask her, sort of offhand. Sometimes it makes you more emotional, it said. Look at her and Bryce Murtagh."

"I think it's better if Rosa asks her about it."

"Or Mrs. Ostermann. Talk to Mrs. Ostermann, Shirley."

"Martin, I'm not getting into this," she said. She felt annoyed at him for making everything about women seem like a great mystery beyond his power to know. His stuff about Peggy Hale was stupid. What could Martin ever have in common with Peggy? He kept letting that sort of thing happen to him. Shirley looked at him, his eyelashes heavy and dark on his eyes, always staring into himself. He had not even wanted to help her explore her questions about sexuality.

But then he struck her again as only sad. And his sadness was a trap, a circle, like the circle of anger and fear. How do you break a circle? she found herself asking, secretly, inside, so Martin would not sense her annoyance but believe still in her love for him. And to answer her question, all she could think of was to say, "Maybe we should go up and bother Mom and Bayard. They've had enough quality time."

When they got near the house, they heard soft voices from the balcony. Candles were lit in the glass chimneys set on the bench that ran along the wall. Shirley heard a coffee cup clink against a saucer and Bayard's sneeze. It was not just he and their mom, but Mrs. Ostermann was there, and Shirley feared Gus might be there, too, listening to his Walkman, waiting for her so they could discuss their relationship some more. She should never have followed up on her impulse to see what it would be like to grab that sleek little dude.

"You go ahead," she said in a whisper. Martin looked quizzically back at her. She used sibling code, holding up her palms, which meant she would explain it later. So he walked ahead, and Shirley stood silently on the path.

It was not really that she dreaded the prospect of dealing with Gus; at dusk he was probably off fishing, anyway. But it was a larger feeling that had come to her, unbidden. She had felt a sudden sense of her home, the home of half her life, beyond her in the trees, and felt a new fear that her mother might not always live there. If her mother could change, everything could. For ten years the family had remained essentially the same, her father with his lady friends in his new house, the rest of them in this beautiful place with their mother. The fragile balcony, candlelit behind the branches, was still the broad threshold of her home. Next summer, at this moment, it might not be the same; Shirley might not be the same. She shivered in her T-shirt when a breeze blew up and made the pines roar above her, while she stood still and waited and watched dark forms bending and waving their arms about on the balcony. Bayard was getting excited about something. She heard again his distinctive sneeze. He was telling Martin about how he and Ron Starks had nearly run down their mom and Mrs. Ostermann and Hilda, who had to get out of their way on the old railroad bed that afternoon. Bayard was not going to slow down and let Ron beat him.

AN AUGUST THURSDAY

1

MARY WAS IMMEDIATELY conscious of an irony in her waking up in Bryce Murtagh's bed in his centrally air-conditioned bedroom with curtains so heavy no morning light could peep through, while farther out the road past her own house, in the weatherworn cottage Drew Hale rented out, the man whose last name she still bore might well be hearing leaves rustling and the songs of wrens out an open window. But Dermot had never been a country person. He liked the city he had grown up in, and now he liked the suburb more, which was country enough. And he liked his comforts, none so overpadded as Bryce's but certainly an air conditioner, undoubtedly a TV with remote control, a coffee machine on a timer, and the morning paper on the front stoop. However was he faring out here in Mary's slow world, where you had to peel off the sheet, all sticky from a summer night, had to boil a tin kettle on the stove and wait till your trip to town for the *Globe*?

Dermot Lanaghan had appeared only seldom at Hale's Cove since those early years of their joint custody, when he would drive out to deposit the kids after their every-other-weekend visits. Soon it was just Bayard and Shirley to chauffeur, then just Shirley, and the whole arrangement became so awkward, so undesired by every party, that months intervened, and eventually (if the kids had occasion to see their father or, more likely, to visit Boston) they took the bus round-trip from Leominster.

Dermot had seemed not to think much of Mary's woodland life and showed little inclination toward bringing up his own children. As long as he paid for them, he considered his duty largely done. What he told Mary was that when the kids were older he would have more time and be more interested in them as adults. He had grown up without fatherly attention himself and felt he had turned out fine. His father was quite his ally now, lying bedridden in South Boston ever since Mother Lanaghan's death. Mary's kids reported sheepishly that in his decline their grandfather barely tolerated any mention of his former daughter-in-law. She knew he felt she was weak, unable to bear the suffering that women, in his day, had borne without complaint.

Bryce was sleeping soundly with a pillow over his head. Everything else about him was easygoing, but when it came to sleep, he was particular. He needed a pillow between his knees to keep them from rubbing; Mary's softer limbs did not suffice because then he got too hot. He had another pillow under his arm, two to keep his head at the proper height, and finally the one to cover his ears. By the glowing clockface Mary could make out the gray contour of the pillow pile beside her. Eight hours ago they had been as close as two people could be, for a good hour of energetic sweet sex, so she did not mind his hibernation over there, especially because she knew that when the preprogrammed soft music slowly emerged from the hum of Bryce's white noise machine and the rheostat timer edged up an electric dawn, she would see into the downy cavern and catch the pale flash of an eye; then, with a splendid stretch, Bryce would toss aside pillows right and left and spring out, all hands and arms and lips and bristly cheeks. Each morning it was as if he was discovering her in his bed for the first time.

And so Dermot's brief sojourn at the cove hardly mattered. If her ex-husband had found his way to Drew's cottage one year earlier, Mary would have holed up in her house and walked the dog down to the public landing instead; she would have agonized over each car coming and going, would have been filled with constant fury. But Dermot had only arranged for this week when invited, so to say, by Martin and Shirley, who had been careful to ask Mary's permission first; they claimed they wanted to see their dad on their own turf for a change, but Mary wondered at their deeper motive. Dermot seemed delighted to pay the five hundred a week. Drew Hale had phoned Mary to explain the hike: Bostonians were suspicious of the bargain he had been honest enough to offer in the past. But she reminded him that the Ostermanns had snapped up the month of July at the old rate. "Aw, they're do-gooders, they take in refugees," Drew retorted. "I bet that bald so-called son of theirs speaks Serbo-Croat. But I'm talking about the snooty set that expects to hand out moola wherever they go."

Mary thought she heard distant music, the lulling sound of low strings, or was it the murmur of the sleep machine? Her wrens, her goldfinches and sparrows were surely chirping for Dermot by now and no doubt annoying him. Yesterday, he had walked along with her and Hilda and complained of how noisy it was in the country — you heard everything more distinctly: buzz saws, motorboats, the damn birds; he had never been quite so aware of how loud the world was. This was his perverse response to her contentment with the peaceful life, of course. She knew he was being funny, and she also knew he would never concede her a point.

But Martin seemed pleased to have his father around. They spent a lot of time on the computer doing whatever it was people found so fascinating these days. They installed their Windows 95. They had mah-jongg and chess games and a morphing program, which Shirley thought would be useful in illustrating her androgyny project, and Dermot had brought dozens of CD-ROMs — world geography, the entire collection of the Metropolitan Museum, and an anthology of old TV commercials, which they had forced Mary to watch to see what she remembered from the fifties. Deodorant, she admitted, had haunted her childhood — smooth marble nudes artfully photographed and a pompous voice intoning, "In the mature male and the mature female . . ." It was all about armpits. Or the girl in the raincoat singing hypnotically, "White — Rain — White — Rain . . ." Or Willie the Penguin and that clean Koo-ool taste. Shirley and Martin had not expected their mother to go emotional on them; she had left the trailer feeling shaky with Shirley's "Oh, Mom!" sailing after her, but Mary did not enjoy recalling a childhood of sitting on the frayed Oriental rug in the den with her mother and father behind her on the sagging horsehair sofa, TV tables in front of them, cocktails, cigarettes, frozen dinners, and Mary yearning for a sister or brother or a friend to ask over to spend the night.

She could only hum softly to herself, now, to think of Bryce Murtagh at her side, hum along to the simple tune rising out of the mechanical whirr. She knew it, yes, Handel's Largo, it was on that restful Baroque classics cassette Rosa had given her for Christmas. She felt guilty for not listening to music more often; her children had chipped in for a decent boom box, which Shirley herself used a lot when she was home, but alone Mary seldom thought of it. It had too many small black buttons to adjust, and mostly she preferred not to intrude on nature's quiet; even the silent fall of snow in winter she wanted somehow to hear by not hearing a sound. Bryce had his music going all the time, or else it was the TV.

"Baby," his voice mumbled from under the pillow.

Mary reached across to touch his arm, which was wrapped around the biggest pillow as though he loved it more than anything in the universe. She felt his smooth muscle, felt it tense as he squeezed. The lamp behind him was glowing now, creeping up the scale to full strength.

"Mmm, baby."

It was a matter of no more than a minute before the pillows would fly. "Wait a sec, Bryce," Mary said. She slipped out of bed and tiptoed to the opposite wall, pulled the cord to sweep back the curtains, and then set about cranking out one of the panes, then another, the only two that opened. She pranced, chuckling to the far corner and pulled open those curtains, too, and that was where she found the sun, low and fierce, piercing through the pines.

"Hey, hon?"

"Don't move," Mary squealed and leapt over him back to her side of the bed, then burrowed into his lair. "This is what is called morning," she said. "When Shirley goes back to school and you start spending some nights at my house for a change, this is how it's going to feel."

He tipped the top pillow off and blinked at her, cheerful as ever. "Nature girl," he said. "I got awful lucky all of a sudden."

"How's the sun on your face?"

"Wakes you right up." Bryce scratched at his temples and fluffed back his graying mop, still blinking at her.

"How's the breeze?"

"Hey, that's my cool air escaping," he said, but he did not seem to mind. Mary could see the trees behind his house in two straight rows converging in a corner of the developer's perfectly square lot cut from the woods. Around Mary's house, maple and ash and oak encroached undisciplined, and in storms small branches fell on her roof, acorns, leaves blew everywhere, but Bryce's pines kept a safe distance. Mary told herself they were still beautiful, but she wondered if their spirits were not somehow tamer. "It's a great view, isn't it," Bryce said. "You're better at appreciating it than me."

Mary turned back to look into his open pale eyes. She had no thought in her head at all.

"I'm better at appreciating — you!" he said, and now the energy awoke in him, suddenly, as it unfailingly did. They had the usual morning tumble without enough time to make something of it because the Largo had already moved on to something Vivaldi-ish.

So Bryce vigorously took over the bathroom while Mary allowed herself to stretch and breathe and lie back again on the bed in just her panties. She did not want to shower when there was an August lake awaiting her, and she did not have to be at the hospital before ten. She could wake Shirley up in time to drop her off at the diner, unless Dermot had already volunteered, which would save Mary the trip to Parshallville, but the idea of him getting credit for favors annoyed her.

"You're thinking about your ex, I can tell." Bryce had returned, wrapped in his immense maroon towel. "The frown on your lips."

"He'll be gone in a few days," said Mary.

"Can you tell when I'm thinking about Valerie?" he wanted to know. It had never occurred to Mary. "Well, I was thinking of her when I was shaving," Bryce said. "She liked me better when I had my mustache."

He came and sat beside Mary on the bed. She pulled on a T-shirt and was up to her ankles in her madras shorts before he stopped her. "Breakfast in underwear," he said, grabbing himself fresh boxers from his dresser. "Well, I'd better close these windows up before my electric bill skyrockets. Man, it's already hot as hell out there."

Mary watched him with curious pleasure. This handsome fellow, five years younger than she was, did just about everything the opposite of her way. Now he was aiming the remote control at his entertainment unit, or whatever it was called, switching the CD off and talk radio on. Pat and Marjorie were bashing each other's politics at seven-fifteen in the morning.

"I remember your mustache when you first moved here," Mary said. "I used to see you and Valerie driving in. Your garage door would go up, and you'd disappear in there. I never saw you outside, not even your kids."

"Isn't it funny," Bryce said, "to think how I'd driven right by my neighbor with the German shepherd and never thought we'd end up in bed? Valerie called you the dog lady." He sat beside her and ran his fingers along the top of her thighs, which were brown in the sunlight. "Nice," he said, then: "Okay, breakfast time."

Pat and Marjorie were having the same argument in the kitchen. They were timed to come on with the coffee. Marjorie said Clinton stood a chance in '96, but Pat was giving her the business. Mary had a sense that Bryce did not find Pat half as appalling as she did, but she could tell he did not want to say so. In fact, he generally stayed off politics with her. There was only that one time she told him about the children's names, but he had never heard of Bayard Rustin and seemed to confuse Shirley Chisholm with Barbara Jordan. He did have a good word for Rosa Parks from what he remembered of Modern American History at Holy Cross, but he found it peculiar, her secretly naming her kids after black people. "You're not like anybody I ever knew before," he had told her then, and it became one of his catchphrases. It seemed to mean he liked her all the more. He used it when she suggested a midnight skinny-dip, which he and Valerie had never thought of doing; he used it when Mary dragged him on walks or did not know the characters on *NYPD Blue.*

Bryce stood at the counter pouring cereal, slicing up bananas, pouring one-percent milk. She watched him and wondered if she would stay this patient with him, if she would finally get bored. He was so kind, and it was not Dermot's sort of calculated kindness but seemed to be in Bryce's blood. Even if she ended up with nothing to say to a man like him, might it not be enough?

"What's this you have about breakfast in underwear?" Mary asked him when he sat beside her in the breakfast nook, bare thigh to bare thigh.

"Need you ask?"

Mary imagined he and Valerie had not eaten breakfast in their underwear since way before their kids were born. Two little kids. Mary remembered those hectic mornings in Newton with each of hers five minutes out of sync with the others, toasts popping, a litter of cereal boxes on the table, juices spilled, high-pitched squabbles, Dermot's tight schedule. Bryce must also be thinking about his kids, Mary realized. A man so kind surely missed them all the time. Their school pictures were in frames on his dresser, of course, and there was a retouched color blowup on the wall in the den, sister holding little brother on her lap, Fiona and Sean. Mary had been foolish not to remind herself constantly of Bryce's children, but usually they disappeared into the decor of the house, more evidence of comfort, along with the ice maker on the fridge and the gas grill out on the deck. This house was, to Mary, a museum of the normal.

"Here's what I'd be willing to bet," she said before she quite knew what she would say next, but it was already quivering in her mouth. Bryce turned toward her, smiling as usual, but Mary was sure she now saw a blankness behind his eyes. "You and Valerie are definitely getting back together," she told him.

He reached over to her thigh and gently placed his hand there. "We've talked about this before," he said.

"We've left it open," said Mary. "I'm only saying I'm willing to bet now which way it's going to go."

She felt the pressure of his palm, and then his little finger tucked itself under the seam of her panties and stayed there. "I feel real love for you, Mary," Bryce said. "Why would you think it's going the other direction? We just started. Besides, Valerie's had it with me. She's always got to have her way."

"But we all want to have our way, and we don't often get to," Mary said, calmly now. "Some of us aren't even sure what our way is. You're like me, Bryce. We're too eager to please each other."

"That's good," he said, "that's how it should be," and he gave her a kiss with his milky breath. She gave him back a sad look, then stared down at her place mat, Fiona's drawing of a horse, laminated. "I know, we've both got kids," Bryce admitted, "and we don't even know each other's yet. Valerie will be damned before she lets our kids see me with a girlfriend. You know, it's the goddamn house!" he said suddenly, slamming his other palm against the Formica. "It brought on everything, Mare. Why do people think they've got to have perfection to be happy? If we just got this house, I thought it'd be perfect. See, until the house, there was always something other than me she could complain about. Then she found herself stuck out here with me." He gave Mary a shrug of his bare white shoulders, a tilt of his head, and it reminded her for a second of her own Martin; it made her reach around him and hug him as tight as she could.

"Why do I always want to make love with you, Mary?" he asked after enjoying the hug awhile. "Valerie and I gradually stopped wanting to."

They held each other with the sun streaming in the thermal panes behind them. It warmed their air-conditioned backs, as if it was a brisk winter day out there and magical heat was being sent 93 million miles to this cold planet of theirs. Bryce was stroking Mary's hair, which she always let down inside his cool house because he loved to let it fall about him in bed and loved to dig his fingers deep into it when they watched TV. He would be late for work if they did not let go of each other soon, but she could tell he did not want to let go. Whatever else could Valerie have wanted?

11

THURSDAY WAS RON'S morning off. He went to his support group at the hospital, which he actually enjoyed because he was maintaining perfect health and could offer a lot of support to the others and not need any himself. Victor asked him why he even went, but it came free with the medical plan, so why not? After the bad news, he'd really had to find some things out, but now it was a way to take his mind off himself. "More high school," said Victor. But Ron knew Victor was glad he was doing all he could to look after himself, monitoring the T-cell counts and keeping up on the latest arguments about when to start medicating. It was not solely an HIV group. There were people with other things to worry about. So far no one had died; no one had even had a close call yet. It was just a bunch of people who had been told they had something that would eventually kill them so they had better start taking better care. Emotionally, too. One of the things Ron had begun to feel was that his group was no different from real life. Everyone was going to die. Everyone had better take care to last as long as possible.

Victor had the car, so Ron was in his URHS shorts, ready to work up a sweat on his bike. He had a T-shirt rolled up in the saddlepack and a towel and of course his condoms, lube, and snap-on leather cock ring in case something presented itself on the way, though the Haviland direction did not usually turn up much. He was looking forward to catching Mary at the hospital desk. With her new relationship, she was not as available as before, but Ron was used to this downside of convincing his friends to fall in love. Besides, where would he be without Victor? He wanted everyone in his life to enjoy his feeling of having a home.

And now here came Mary's ex-husband walking along the road in navy blue bermudas. "Dermot Lanaghan!" Ron called out. "I thought Mary said you didn't care for walks in the woods."

"No shit?" said Dermot as he strode nearer. "Well, that's just me ragging on her. I walk around the reservoir at home every day. A brisk walk. That's all the body needs." He was looking critically at Ron, whose body certainly indicated otherwise. "Trouble with all that muscle, my friend, is you're going to have to maintain it. It's dying to turn to flab."

"Don't I know," said Ron.

Dermot had stopped for a second; it seemed his brisk walk allowed for interruptions. "Nice bike. I've got a Peugeot at home. Julie and I take long rides on weekends. Lots of bike paths out where I live."

This man was too damn straight even for Ron. When Mary had introduced them, Ron could not imagine her with him, could not imagine him the father of her kids, but he could detect, beneath the thickness, the outlines of a once handsome young athlete. Dermot was wearing Tevas and an alligator shirt. He would fit in better on the Fraddboro side of the lake.

"I drove Shirley to your diner," he was going on. Ron glanced back at the shiny black Saab parked by the cottage. "So you're not working today?"

"We take shifts," Ron said. He was feeling bored and wanted to be on his way, so he hopped up on his bike. Straddling a bike was, to Ron, about the sexiest way to stand around. It reminded him of the boys outside his middle school, back when the Starks kids had no bikes and were waiting for the bus. "I'm off to get some exercise, too."

"Don't overdo, my friend," Dermot said. "You know, I was a real jock in college. I had to change all my habits once I got into business. Work life's a whole different kind of stress. It won't help you take it off your gut."

"You should get Martin up for your walk," Ron suggested. It seemed odd to him that Martin and Shirley had asked their father to come visit, but he figured they must have something they liked doing together.

"Oh, he's up all night on the net," Dermot said. "I wish that boy would find a job in computers. He's already taught himself a hell of a lot."

"Hey," said Ron, pushing back and forth on the pedals, "it must be nice being around your kids this week."

"We're having a hell of a time," Dermot said. "They're my oldest and my youngest, you know. There's something about your very first and your very last. You're softer on them. Of course, it's no problem when they're such good kids. I guess we did something right, anyway." And he laughed as though what he just said made him a great guy. "You're treating Shirley all right at the diner, I hear. She's a hard worker."

"Don't I know," said Ron. "Hey, I got to get going," he finally said. "How much longer you here for?"

"Through Saturday. The owner was here early this morning for his rent. Cash. Saturday to Saturday, five hundred bucks. For that little shithole."

Ron let out a laugh and was off toward Haviland Center. What a prick, he kept thinking, but soon he got into the rhythm of the bike and felt his thighs pumping and his stomach tensing and the warm air rushing at his shoulders. He had to watch it when he got to 108. The approach to the village was still all torn up with construction. He pulled over to the Coke machine outside the pharmacy, got himself a diet ginger ale, and straddled his bike along the sidewalk as he drank it down, aware of the teenage girl who worked there looking out the plate glass at him. When Ron was a kid, no one had looked at him much. He was squat and pudgy, and there was nothing special about his soft little face. That was why he liked people paying attention now, or so they told him in group. If you could not get what you wanted back when you needed it, you spent the rest of your life trying to get it, they said, but it never quite worked, there was always something you missed. And they wanted him to tell them what testing positive did to his self-image and what it was he really needed now. He felt that shudder. He was better getting at what other people should do. Giving advice was his strong point.

He got the towel out of the saddlepack and wiped the sweat off his chest and forehead. The girl was still watching him. That shrimp of a bug-eyed kid, Kevin, was the one he could really turn on this way. Ron admitted he was a little mean to Kevin. Victor was always telling him to lay off, but Kevin never seemed to mind.

When Ron started pedaling slowly up the hill to the hospital, he concentrated on the strain of each pump. He loved it, would always love it. He had never known in high school what it would feel like to make his body into something. Now every muscle counted, and his jawline was firm, even his blue-gray eyes had turned steely. This was the body he had in him, if he had only known about it when he was a kid. Back then, Stewart was already in his body. And that prick Dermot Lanaghan must have been in his, but then it left him — because he thought he was so cool. He still thought he was. And now Ron realized why: because of money. This Lanaghan was his own master. It was not about the brisk walks or taking it off the gut. It was the piles of money. Fuck that, Ron thought, puffing out, sucking in, but as he pedaled it crossed his mind that even the adorable Bayard might turn out to be like his dad. No, Ron decided, he was just too damn cute.

III

"HELLO THERE, Mrs. Lanaghan."

Louise was glad to find Martin's mother at the welcome desk. She had taken to stopping by on Thursday mornings after she finished her class and visited with one of her Basswood clients who was probably in the hospital now for good. Louise wished she was qualified already so she could be of more help to her, but maybe this time was a dry run, her teacher told her, for when she had to be the one doing all the care. That was what she started right in telling Mrs. Lanaghan, who told her, "I'm sure you're a comfort as is."

"Well, it's no fun," said Louise. "She was such a nice old lady — Mrs. Bulmer. Always wanted me to fix her hair for her and dust the place good. She didn't want to leave any dust behind her. We'd have a good laugh over that."

"I know the lady you mean. Last week she was still wheeling herself down here to the library borrowing mysteries. Mrs. Bulver, I think."

"Bulmer, Bulver. I call her Grace."

"Have a seat, Louise," Mrs. Lanaghan said. "If you've got a minute."

So Louise lowered herself cautiously onto the bench beside the welcome desk and straightened out her slacks, which had gotten all bunchy. "I prefer staying in central air on days like this," she said. "Trouble with Mrs. Germaine's is she won't believe in it. She's got to have her old fans — one pointing this way, one pointing that way. And then when the sun starts setting, she wants them round the other way. She likes to have the air blowing for her breathing."

"I hear she's hanging on pretty well."

Louise shook her head, resignedly. "Mrs. Germaine's in her own time zone, but I'll bet she outlasts me," she said with a chortle. "So how's my pal Martin?"

"You know his dad's up?" Mrs. Lanaghan asked, but in a quieter voice, as if she did not want the people waiting on couches across the hall to hear. Louise had never seen Martin's dad, except in pictures where he looked somewhat like Martin, but she knew he had hurt his son, so already she did not like him. "Martin and Shirley got the bright idea of him renting Drew's cottage," came the explanation in an embarrassed voice. Louise felt the urge somewhere inside her body, way deep, to pat this kind lady on the back or give her a squeeze, but as she could not reach across the desk, she tried to let her eyes show what she meant. Mrs. Lanaghan was not meeting her gaze. "I hope they don't think they're going to make him and me friends at last," she said. "I know it would make their lives easier. We probably should be able to be friends again. Time has passed, but time doesn't —"

"He doesn't sound like someone I'd want to be friends with," Louise interrupted, hoping she would look up at her. Then she tried something else: "How's your daughter, the other one, Rosa? Remember that time I came by your home and there she was calling me Corncrib like the old days?"

"It's high tourist season up north; she can't get away yet."

Louise was patting her knees and looking out through the vestibule now. She should get going soon. She had promised to bring Charles some fresh coffee rolls before she made her Basswood trip because Mr. Hale had stopped in earlier and cleaned them out. "You raised a nice family,

Mrs. Lanaghan," she said. "You must've got them away from that man in time. I don't mean to be rude."

"No, no," Mrs. Lanaghan said, "but I wish that was true."

"Ask Martin. He'll say it's true. He used to tell me."

"But I wonder, Louise, if Dermot and I'd stayed together and Martin had kept his old friends and had his dad right there pushing him a little — I stopped pushing the kids. I let them be. I just let them be."

A guy in a Midas uniform came in to ask for Mrs. Theodore's room number. It was his mother. She was supposed to have been moved. Mrs. Lanaghan seemed to know all about it. Louise looked off at the potted palm by the front door and hummed to herself so as not to intrude. The guy seemed awfully worried and maybe looking to complain to someone.

When he went off down the hall, Louise turned back around on her bench and realized she had been thinking about Florida, so she said, "You and Mr. Lanaghan sound like my parents, Mrs. Lanaghan."

"Mary," Mrs. Lanaghan said.

"Mary. It's sort of hard to call you Mary when you're Martin's mom. Oh well, Mary. But my parents, they never pushed me and Charles either. We could do no wrong. They said there's only one secret to being good parents: that you love your kiddies to death. And that's what they did. A lot of kids around here are hoping their parents get out of their lives quick, but we didn't want them moving. I think it's good Martin's hanging around. Maybe he's slow getting work, but some people speed up later. Look at me. It took a while finding what I want to do. Do you remember a kid named Dave Paasivirta from my high school class?"

"I remember that name from late slips."

"Yeah, that's him. His wife and him aren't getting along, so he's got whole new plans for his life. Wants to move to Idaho, I think it is. He's been coming by and I been fixing a little supper after my brother's off to work." Louise did not want to go into details exactly, but she did want to talk some about Dave now that he was around again, so she explained, "He's got to get away from that wife. She's no bed of roses. What I'm saying is, it's not too late for things to start happening. So that's my message for the day. I guess it doesn't go for old Grace upstairs, though. Not much happening there!" At last, Mrs. Lanaghan was looking at her. Louise noticed how she had her brown hair pinned up all sloppily on her head with an amber comb stuck in it, sort of Oriental, she thought. And that was a pretty lavender blouse, real silk, it looked like, it had a soft sheen.

"Louise, come by soon and visit Martin. He could use your angle. He's got some New Age e-mail friend he relies on totally for spiritual advice."

Mrs. Lanaghan had reached across the desk and given Louise's arm a pat, and Louise suddenly wondered if she knew about what had happened between Martin and Peggy and decided it might not be a bad time to say something. She knew to be discreet, so she lowered her voice and leaned closer. "Mrs. Lanaghan — I mean, Mary — I think something real good happened for Martin this summer with Peggy Hale. I know it hurt his feelings for a while, but still it was major." Her friend Mary was looking at her, unsure, a tiny twitch at one side of her mouth. "Martin's spunkier now, don't you think?"

"Spunkier?" said Mary.

"He's more like connected." Louise could almost see thoughts scampering around inside Mary's head. She should not have told her.

Then a guy in a tight white T-shirt came down the hall. He looked like a physical therapist except for his URHS shorts. He started in talking about running into that man who claims he hates the country taking a walk in the woods.

"He means Dermot," Mrs. Lanaghan said. "Ron, you don't know my friend Louise Thibault, do you? Louise, this is my neighbor Ron Starks."

"Hey," said this Ron. He was being too loud for the waiting area.

Louise gave a quick smile. She had heard about him. He was not a physical therapist. He worked at that diner in Parshallville she and Charles never went to because the booths were too close. Besides, their father had some reason for not liking Mr. Bardonecchia; Louise thought it was a poker debt going way back. The word was that those two who ran the place now were queers, or gay as they said in her class when they had to learn about AIDS. She tried to say gay now, except with Dave, who knew all about Ron Starks from growing up in Sewall. Dave said Ron used to hang around by the river and do fellatio and worse. That was the story.

"So, Mary," Ron was saying, "I got some ideas in group today. Ideas for you. I was sitting there listening to the talk about when you start this treatment and when you start that, and what your choices are, and what we know, and what we don't know —"

The old couple across the hall was looking at Ron, not at their magazines anymore. This group of his had got him all hyper. Louise bet it was the one run by the head nurse, because it was not the Death and Dying group her teacher ran; it must be that other Thursday group, probably for psychos. She was surprised she had never seen this Ron when she came out of training, but today old Grace being upstairs had kept her from rushing off to Basswood right afterwards. He's probably got AIDS, she thought. What else could a guy like that be in for? And then she remembered something Peggy said last month at the big reunion. She was talking about that gay guy Stewart was friends with, and so what was wrong with that, she said, and besides she really liked him too, and Peggy's dad was getting steamed and saying he did not really appreciate him renting the old gun shop, and Louise's dad made a crack about Bardonecchia. Then Peggy said, "I thought it was Stewart you had the problem with," and her mom was shushing her. "All I can say is, it was high time we moved you out of there," Mr. Hale said, so everyone stayed in a bad mood until they brought out Louise's pies, which made a big hit. And this is the guy — Ron, Louise realized.

". . . but it would make a difference, Mary, the way you thought about yourself," he was saying. "Even if he kept sending you the usual amounts."

"But anything I made, I'd have to deduct from it. That would only be fair," she whispered back.

"So you still don't want to do it."

"It'd be setting a precedent."

"Look, you could talk to a lawyer."

Louise was feeling bored. She didn't trust this Ron guy. He was trying to convince Mrs. Lanaghan of something she did not want to do. "I'm going down to the cafeteria before I head out into the heat," Louise said, getting up slowly. "I'll be back this way."

"Hey," said Ron with a wave before he leaned back over the welcome desk. Mrs. Lanaghan was looking perplexed. This business of her husband being around was hard on her, Louise could tell, and Ron was not helping any.

The hospital corridors were shiny gray with different colored stripes leading you where you wanted to go. You followed red to emergency, blue to outpatient, green to mental health. Louise was following yellow to the cafeteria. It was such a complicated route she would never remember without the stripes.

Charles had worked there for a while vacuuming and polishing floors. He ran a buffing machine and an industrial vac, but it got too hard on his back muscles, so then they switched him to the parking lot. He had to sit in that cramped booth with a space heater or a fan, depending on the weather.

In the self-serve line, Louise poured a tall glass of lemonade and checked over the pastries. They were too stale for her brother, but she got herself some blueberry muffins and butter pats and individual jellies. She sat on the window side of the big empty room and looked out at the trees. She remembered when her father took her and Charles to Mass General in Boston for some special tests he wanted them to have. Nothing came of it, but Louise still thought about the loneliness of that city hospital, all stony with a thousand empty windows, so many people but nobody really there. She had no desire to go back.

When she finished the muffins and lemonade, feeling cheerier, she made her way, following purple, out to the lobby.

"Aren't you running late, Louise?" Mrs. Lanaghan said, pointing to eleven on the clock.

"Where's that Ron guy?"

"He went off on his bike."

"So which of those groups is he in?" Louise asked.

"Actually, I'm not allowed to talk about other patients, even to my friends," Mrs. Lanaghan said.

"Oh, that's the same thing in class. We have to promise to keep it inside the four walls, even just us observers. People can get pretty touchy." She could ask what Ron had been saying about money but figured it might seem nosy, too. But something was keeping her from moving on, probably the heat out there, shimmering beyond the potted palm. "I didn't mean to say anything rude about Mr. Lanaghan earlier," Louise said; in the cafeteria she had been thinking over her remark.

"No, no, please," said her friend Mary. She had to get used to her being Mary; Mrs. Lanaghan fit better. The old couple with the magazines was still waiting. Mary told them the doctor would truly be down any minute, and they nodded. Louise simply could not face the heat. She could see her white Lark across the parking lot baking in the sunshine. The rest of her day was going to be hell until Dave Paasivirta came by later.

IV

THERE WERE SURVEYORS in the pasture across from Jim Pflueger's house. They were putting up little stakes with orange ribbons on them and looking down sights, one to another. If it had been any other pasture, Jim would have gone over to talk to them, find out how it was done, volunteer his help. But these men were the enemies of those particular grasses and wildflowers and that milkweed, enemies of the birds and butterflies that were used to it as it was. Jim sat at his computer but watched out the window. Monica and Eric were going to hate seeing this. They thought the pasture was the best thing about visiting. Monica went there to read books and Eric to fly his kite. Jim called it the pasture, but it had not been used as such in his time. It was more of a meadow now; soon it would be house lots.

Jim was protected on the three other sides by woods owned by someone from Fraddboro who thinned them out conservatively every other year and had already subdivided as much as he intended to, or so he said. A hundred years ago, Jim's house had been a farmhand's cottage on a large sheep farm on both sides of the road. The main farmhouse still stood at the dead end. They said it had been a hippie commune in the seventies; now an MIT anthropology professor had fixed it up. He and his wife were as upset about the development as Jim was.

Jim looked down at the screen. It was a self-help book about money management he was supposed to have in by tomorrow. It was crashingly dull, not to say confusing. He had been tempted to e-mail Eric about certain passages. It was not only a matter of getting the English right; these business types coined words such as *shortfallwise,* but if he rewrote that sentence, would it lose its precise meaning?

He got himself another Squirt and stretched. He had not yet earned a walk, so he sat down again and aimed the little desk fan at his face. The men over there must be hot in their long pants and shirts in the direct sun. One of them looked maybe Cambodian. Except for waving out the window when the professor or his wife drove by, Jim had little human contact before noon. He had preferred it so after the hectic mornings of his Cambridge years. The kids had always got themselves up and off to school on time, no complaints, but Donna had a dozen things for him to do before he left the house that she had not thought of the night before — change the cat litter, sort the recycling, put the extra leaf in the dining table — so he was rushed driving out to work, and when he got there, people were in and out of his office all morning wanting him to rewrite something or check over something else. Jim had started at PSI before computers; he was an editor, a wordsmith among people unsure of words, people who trusted him. He had a kind of marvelous edge on them. But then the equipment he had to use began to come from their world more than his, and the more complex it grew, the more they seemed to claim mastery over Jim as well. He was still in-house editor, but his salary ceased to go up the way theirs did. The company kept expanding, and then he got stuck in the back of the new building, looking at Route 2 and not the office park with its gardens and benches and walkways. He had been lucky to have the window; there were lesser wordsmiths who had cubicles with people leaning in over the dividers all the time.

So Jim now blessed his house and his quiet and his freelancing. But he was isolated. On her last visit, Monica had told him to get out more. She promised to check in once more this summer and bring Tommy, but she had not yet found the time. She was a wordsmith, too, Jim thought with pride, but with more than just grammar and vocabulary to her. She had sent him her favorite book, the collected poems of Emily Dickinson. He kept it in the john and tried to read a few each time; they were little flashes of truth, he thought, though he did not always understand them. Sometimes, a phrase stuck, like "My life closed twice before its close" or "The world feels dusty when we stop to die." What did they really mean?

They made him think of his sister Anne, who was into her second round of chemo. He wished he could see her. He was writing her postcards every day, that was his pledge — postcards, not e-mail, even though it was getting harder to find new cards. Last week, he had driven over the New Hampshire line to get some of mountains and moose and corny ones of a giant fish in a rowboat or a tumbledown shack captioned "Drop by Anytime." And he got Eric to send him a packet of Beantown cards; out in San Diego Anne would appreciate them. Today's was a scene of the path along the Charles River where Jim used to jog with Eric and Monica in the old days. He turned it over and read again:

> Dear Anne — The sun is up over the trees, shining on little puffs of milkweed dancing above the pasture. The monarchs are happy. It's that turning point of the year when everything is sensing it's coming time to hold back. It's somehow a perfect moment. You're the philosophical one now, Anne. You've looked at it in the face, and you've seen right through to the next spring. How do you do it? I should learn from you. I love you always —
>
> James

Sometimes, he wrote chat, but this serious one seemed fine. Anne had told him on the phone how she did not appreciate the avoiding her San Diego neighbors did. His poor sister — after her and Dick's first year out there, she said she had not yet met a person she would cross the street to say hello to.

Back in June, Monica and Jim had had a long talk about Anne's decision to give another go at the chemo. Monica had looked stricken at the news, and that got her asking about her aunt in a way she never had before. She had known her aunt Anne only in short visits and the one time they had all gone to California, which turned out to be their last trip as a family. Now, Monica wanted to know more about her and her dad when they were growing up in Chicago. She wanted images, she said, she wanted stories, so Jim told her about the kingdom they used to have called Pinka-nuu-nuu Land. The image he most wanted Monica to see was of her aunt Anne draped in a lavender bedspread with Gramma's necklaces around her neck and a sort of tiara Jim had made from a coat hanger wrapped in black velvet ribbon, with brooches and pins and earrings from Gramma's jewelry box stuck in all over it. They had made a Royal Progress — a term he had learned from his book about the kings of England — through the backyard, with Jim as prime minister in Grampa's derby and blue blazer with his Purple Heart pinned to the pocket. Then they sat, side by side, on lawn chairs and posed for imaginary photographers. Pinka-nuu-nuu Land was in the Pacific Ocean somewhere between Alaska and Hawaii. Jim admitted it was largely his own creation and that Anne had loyally followed her big brother, overbearing as he must have been.

"Tell me some more," Monica had said. And he had settled back on the porch with his feet up on the railing and told of Anne's dumb cluck of a first boyfriend, and her disappointment not making cheerleader, and her letters when he came east for a job. He still kept them and had given Monica the whole set to take with her if she promised to bring them safely back. Then Eric had come out for the Fourth of July in a van with his roommates after they had canoed the Quidnapunxet down from New Hampshire. They spread all their wet camping gear on the pasture and hung out with beer and radios till sunset. And then they headed back to the city. He had not seen either of his kids since then.

Jim settled back into money management, into "operationalizing" and the verb "to interface." After two hours of steady and annoying work, he determined he had need of the long walk into Dowland to mail the postcard and pick up another couple of books. Thrillers used to be his favorite reading, but they did not work on him the way they used to, maybe thanks to Dr. Forest, or maybe thanks to getting over Kathleen. Her image had lost its power, so he did not need to escape from it. Or maybe it was Anne he was learning from. Maybe it really was Anne.

He laced up his shoes and pulled on the loose T-shirt Eric had brought him from his summer job — SOFTRAM '95 — DOUBLE YOUR MEMORY, it said across the back. He hated the whole idea of it but loved anything he got from his kids. The shirt meant that Eric knew he preferred a size XL so the breeze could blow through it and that he was trying to bring Jim into his world, making him his again.

When Jim stepped up to the stone wall across the road, the Cambodian-looking surveyor gave a smile. What could Jim do but smile back, and then it occurred to him he could at least learn something about the construction schedule, so he asked. "Don't know much," the man said. "All we know we suppose measure. Get it all lay out. They in Worcester. Give a call." He told Jim the name of the developer, which he already knew from town meeting, so he thanked the man and despite himself waved to the other man across the pasture. It was not these guys' fault, he reminded himself as he set out on the road, rubber soles on gravel. That brown-skinned man, he thought, is from far away, and now he is here measuring out parcels of property. Does he have anything close to him at all that he still loves? Or has he come to love something he has found here, new and strange, fragile as his lost fatherland?

V

Mr. Zart had finished his BLT and given Victor the usual two-fifty, which only covered the sandwich and not the chips, coffee, and one of Aunt Ellie's cookies, but Victor had decided to keep charging the old guy what his father had charged and not to expect a tip. Mr. Zart spent precisely fifteen dollars a week at the Original, and on Sundays he got a free lunch at the church. Fifteen a week, say sixty-five a month, seven hundred and eighty a year — it was a lot of money from one customer. Of course, it meant putting up with his ramblings, which were less interesting by the day; the sentimental need in Victor to remain attached to his father's best friend was wearing away. Today, Zart had come in very late after a visit from the town clerk, who had helped him go over his books. It must have put him in a surly mood because he had sounded off in grumpy fashion about how Victor's mother had never truly understood Ugo. "She wanted him home," he said several times. "Do you hear what I'm saying, Victor? She wanted him home and taking care of her. She wanted him home." Victor had drifted off thinking of his mother, who had been only thirty-five when she died. And he had been only eight. In some ways, she was confused in his memory with his older sister, Antonietta. For comfort he must have slipped directly from his mother's arms into his sister's. They had each held him close and calmed him in his sadness.

Mr. Zart was dismounting the fifth stool with some distress. He usually sat at either end, where he could swing himself around more easily, but the end stools were taken when he came in. Shirley Lanaghan noticed and offered an elbow to help him down. Zart was rather smitten with Shirley. He kidded her about her short hair and her button of a nose. Victor thought of these as signs of her tough delicacy but was surprised at himself for catching such a distinctly feminine nuance; he tended to obliterate the physical side of women, but lately he had begun to take account of certain correspondences between the sexes. It was more evident in younger people like Shirley and Kevin, who was in the back room washing up after the lunch rush. Kevin was slight and soft, and it was only Victor's knowledge of his maleness, really, that brought him into sexual range, while in Shirley the same degree of softness, held up against femaleness in general, seemed taut and vigorous. It was relative. But he knew he would never want to touch Shirley. He would touch Kevin, and did, but not as Ron touched him — on the butt or tight around the skinny waist — no, only a pat on his shoulder, or at most a rap of his knuckles on Kevin's skull along with "Is anything up there?" when Kevin emptied coffee grounds in the dishwater or stacked the cups so high they toppled.

"So long, Mr. Zart," Victor called across the counter.

"This little lady's going to come work for me next," said Zart. "She'll bring in the customers." Shirley was blushing. When the door had swung shut, after Zart's slow exit had sent a great wave of heat into the diner, Victor told her she had better not take that offer seriously. Zart got five customers a day if he was lucky. Without the Parshallville cops' and public works crew's wives' patronage — in effect, town policy to support the old guy — his dry goods store would be boarded up like Pollard's Hardware and Fonteneau Brothers. Parshallville was not much of a town anymore, but the box company, the lumberyard, and the metal strapping plant kept it going for now.

Victor thought he saw Stewart Tomaszewski's Neon pass by. He had time to wipe off the entire counter before the car came back the other way and pulled up sideways in front, taking what could have been two parking places. Stewart got out the passenger side, and then Victor heard Shirley say, "It's Peggy Hale." The two of them dashed inside, from air-conditioned car to air-conditioned diner, before they could break a sweat. Peggy had on a blouse buttoned once over her pink bikini top, and Stewart's Hawaiian shirt was open all the way, crucifix nestled in curly black hair. "We're on our way to the Parshallville beach," Peggy said, "but Stewart's thirsty."

"No bathing suits or bare feet in the diner," said Victor with a fake frown.

"Bull," said Stewart.

"These are shorts. I got on flip-flops," Peggy said, but Stewart held up a bare hairy foot and gave Victor the finger with his other hand. "Hi, Shirley, don't mind Stewart," said Peggy. They plopped side by side into the center booth, and Stewart immediately began scanning the CD selection. "Where's Ron?" Peggy asked.

"It's his late day."

"Damn, I wanted to see him."

Shirley was standing there holding her order pad, probably wondering as much as Victor did what the story was with these two. He saw Kevin's small face peeking out the pass-through.

"What sort of shitty selections are these?" said Stewart. "Too much weird shit, Vic. Get Ron on the ball."

"You guys haven't been running for a while," said Victor, scraping off the grill.

"Too hot, too busy. Yeah, I'm getting a little paunchy. Next month I'm back into it."

"What am I looking at this for?" said Peggy, putting the menu down. "I know I want a chocolate frappe."

"Paunchy, paunchy, paunchy. Hey, how about a raspberry-lime rickey? I'm so dehydrated."

"I'll stick to the frappe," said Peggy.

Shirley dug out ice cream while Victor sliced limes. There was an uncomfortable level of energy over in that booth. "Hey, babe," he heard Stewart say and then some sort of wrestling around.

After Shirley ran the mixer, in the sudden silence, Victor pumped a squirt of raspberry syrup and said, "Glad to see you two are divorcing so happily."

Stewart was fiddling with the venetian blinds to keep the sun off his face. "Couldn't be happier," he said.

"Hey, Shirley, come sit down with us. We got to talk," said Peggy, so when Shirley brought the drinks around, she looked once at Victor to be sure and then slid in across from them. "You never officially met, did you? Stewart, this is Mary's kid Shirley." Stewart stuck his hand out, and Shirley shook it, her hand so small in his, Victor noticed. He sat on the freezer compartment and leaned an elbow on the counter to remain part of the conversation. He felt excluded the way he had felt with Ron and Peggy back in June, but Shirley was his waitress, he had a right to eavesdrop and to look after her. He could detect Stewart already turning on the charm.

"Your mom still seeing that guy?" Peggy wanted to know, and Shirley nodded. "Still don't approve?"

"He's harmless," said Shirley.

"That's more than I can say for this bad-ass." Peggy squeezed Stewart's arm. Victor was glad Ron was not in yet; there were enough hormones racing around as is.

"How's your father?" Shirley asked Peggy.

"Pissed as hell," said Stewart. "He found out me and Peg were seeing each other again, and he made Peg move out."

"I moved in with my girlfriend," said Peggy. "She does nail care. I'm working nights at the mall. God knows I wasn't about to go back to mother-in-law."

"It's a temporary arrangement," said Stewart. That was his favorite concept. "So you're Martin's sister?" he asked Shirley. "How's he doing now?"

"He still doesn't have a job," said Shirley. "Mom kept expecting him to do some work for the day camp up the lake, but he's busy enough with his computer."

"He still got that girl out in the desert?" Peggy asked.

Victor knew more than he cared to about Peggy and Martin, all the details Ron had gone on about, but he wondered what Shirley knew. This was getting like high school. He decided he could not stand it, so he tossed the wet rag he had been wiping the pie rack with into the cold water sink and edged around back to check on Kevin, who had finished the dishes and was standing there dumbly looking out the pass-through. He jumped when he heard Victor, who rapped the back of his head once and made him giggle. Then Kevin mouthed, "That Stewart!" and Victor told him to lay off Ron's boyfriends. "He's such a hunk," Kevin whispered.

Victor stood next to him at the sink, even close enough to put a little pressure against Kevin's hip, and caught Stewart saying, "Peggy says that brother of yours is quite the dreamboat."

Before Shirley could decide what way to take this, Peggy, in her direct way — Victor did like that side of her — said, "Shirley, your brother maybe didn't tell you, but him and me had a brief thing going in June. He's really sweet, your brother."

Victor could not hear Shirley's response, soft-spoken as she was, but she seemed to be relaxing, smiling.

"I'd like to nuzzle into *that,*" slutty Kevin whispered in Victor's ear, pointing out at Stewart.

"He's totally straight," Victor whispered back impatiently.

"So? I can still want."

"Go out and sweep up, why don't you? But don't drool on him." Once Kevin was out front, Victor started making the motions of dishwashing as he watched the booth. It was as if he were gently dipping crystal goblets with delicate stems into steamy water and pulling them out hot and glistening, one after another.

"Oh, I tell Stewart everything," Peggy said. "He can hardly mind about Martin."

"Here's the way I feel," Stewart said. "Peggy is great at getting people to relax. She says your brother was all tied up in knots. He was worried about this, that, and the other." It sounded like Shirley was meekly protesting. "Yeah, but, Shirley," said loud Stewart, confident as ever with his gold-ringed hand reaching across to give Victor's waitress's arm a soft pat, "that's how you learn. You get roughed up. So? What's the big deal?" Kevin was hovering to one side, behind Shirley. "You want to sweep under here, kid?" Stewart said sharply.

"Take your time," said Kevin, moving slowly along, sweeping around the stools and glancing back. Victor kept pretending to dip goblets, which were becoming real to him, as in the diner game he played when he was small, scrambling imaginary eggs, flipping imaginary burgers and using his rubber spatula to scrape nonexistent grease off the radiator cover in the parlor. Why had Stewart gone back to Peggy? He never went back to his women.

"It's a tough business, love is," he was telling Shirley.

"Stewart," said Peggy, "you don't know half."

"Guys don't," Stewart declared. "We're pigs. Let's face it." Shirley said something. "No, no, not your brother," Stewart conceded. He moved his hand from near Shirley's arm to drape it across Peggy's shoulder. His raspberry-lime rickey was down to the pinkish melting ice and the lime skins.

Kevin had finished the corner booth and now said, "Excuse me, folks," and swept the broom under the table a couple of times so Peggy and Stewart had to stretch their feet up and across to the seat on either side of Shirley, who gave Kevin a raised eyebrow. "Sorry about that," he said and went on to the first booth, which afforded a better view of Stewart's chest.

Victor's dishwashing game had slowed to a stop. He stood holding an invisible goblet in one hand, a real dish towel in the other, and he felt calm again. Everything was going all right for Shirley out there. She was taking care of herself. He did not worry about Kevin this way and did not know why he wanted Shirley Lanaghan to feel at home in his world, to feel safe. He had never worried about a girl before. It was probably because she was so well-educated, so likely to move on to another world, which Victor could only assume would be better for her, but he did not want her to look back regretfully on this one.

The door opened, and in came a family of six big people speaking loud Quebecois; Victor recognized it but could not understand it. They were exclaiming to each other, probably about the genuine old diner, which thanks to Ugo Bardonecchia had remained original, true to its name, except for the CD selectors and fluorescent fixtures and air conditioner above the door. Kevin came back looking flustered, so Victor went out. The parents and the two younger-looking kids took the corner booth while the taller sister and very tall brother claimed two stools at the end and swiveled around to chatter to their family. Shirley had hopped up with her order pad but was waiting as they read out the menu in jokey French. Victor picked out *ott dogg* and *omm-boor-gair;* they had a good laugh over *frappe,* which they proceeded to order six of in an over-Americanized way — *"Frrrapp!"* — and laugh some more.

"We got to get out of here," Stewart was saying. "No, I mean to the beach." He cast a critical eye at the Quebeckers, Peggy jabbed her elbow into his side, and they wrestled their way up to the counter to give Victor a five. Stewart took the crumpled dollar bill (one of Zart's) back to tuck under Peggy's chocolaty glass, and he gave Shirley the sort of bright smile that got Ron going every time. "Hey, I'm glad we met," he said. "Don't take me too seriously. I'm actually a halfway decent guy."

Shirley seemed to appreciate his style because she threw back her loveliest grin, that delicately tough sweet unscared look of hers that Victor counted on. Then she turned to the other booth and, to Victor's amazement, started in with, "Bonjour, Monsieur, Madame," and off she went.

Ron's bike skidded on the gravel out back, and soon Victor heard him goofing with Kevin in the back room. And then a black Saab pulled in up front, and Victor realized it was Mr. Lanaghan come to pick up his daughter. He started in on the frappes, hoping the man would not come in. It had been bad enough the other time he came. He'd walked around telling Ron what he would do to improve the place, how they could get old-style lighting fixtures and replace the tottery stools. "They've got diner supply companies now," he said. "You can get new stuff that looks the way this place looked when it was built. You know, originally, diners weren't meant to be shabby. If you really want to be authentic, you should make it as snappy as it was when it opened in nineteen, what was it, thirty-four?" Victor had worried that Ron would get ideas, but later, at home, Ron had reassured him he was only trying to be polite to that asshole. Mary must have been deaf, dumb, and blind to have married him, however stunningly handsome she claimed he was in his younger days.

VI

ON THE SCREENED PORCH, after their swim, they sat down with tall lemonades or, in Dermot's case, a Sam Adams, to play the Chinese checkers game that had come with the cottage. And when they got bored with its obviousness, they attempted Parcheesi, only to find it more boring still. But something told Dermot he did not want to retreat once more to the trailer he had bought for his son on the land he had bought for his former wife, albeit with some help, he reminded himself, from her parents' estate. No, he wanted these two kids of his to stay up here on the porch of his temporary home, his for a few days more. They seldom came to stay in Newton more than one at a time. When Martin had lived with him briefly, Rosa had visited, but she and Nat had gone on to the Speradakises' in Portsmouth for the night. Shirley came, dutifully, for Dermot's birthdays and for Christmas or Thanksgiving alternately, but Bayard did not come at all; Dermot only saw him at his office downtown, and then briefly. And, briefly, they would go visit their grandfather with him when they were in Boston. Briefly.

Dermot looked across the card table and saw himself in Martin's features but did not own the sad droop, the occasional nervous flutter of a hand, the inwardness, which had come from Mary. He saw more of himself in Shirley, her alert eyes and that dismissive gesture she had learned from him, which with a flash of the palm and a squint said, "Enough! Get on with it!" All the lake's coolness had evaporated from his skin. It was, even on this shady breezy porch, a very hot day, but Dermot did not miss his cool house, even less his overcool office with its view of planes landing across Boston harbor. This week had shifted something inside him, slowed him down, made him count up the years he could have had with these two, and the other two, and if not exactly with Mary then some one person to thread it all together with. Enid, Andrea, Julie — a shiver ran up his calves to his knees and circled there, tickling him so that he had to rub his kneecaps hard and then stretch out his legs to make the feeling pass.

"Arthritis, Dad?" Shirley asked.

"Football knees," he said. "So, if we're not going to play another game, want to have a swim before I start the grill?"

"How about the rowboat?" asked Shirley. They had found it under the porch. Dermot was sure it was a sieve but had tied it to the dock, and it was still dry inside.

They brought along their towels and a coffee can for bailing and arranged themselves, with Shirley in the bow and Martin in the stern; Dermot was going to row his kids about as if they were little again and he their full-time father thinking up fun things to do. The gunwales had only two inches to spare, but off they went up the cove, past the boathouse with those guys' skimpy black bathing suits and fluorescent beach towels drying on the wooden railings, into a sea of lily pads with waxy yellow flowers and water bugs skimming about, all the way to the swamp maples along the shore, where in the great shade Dermot shipped the oars because he thought he saw a large turtle in the shallows by a fallen bough. "Probably a snapper," he said.

Martin looked dreamily into the water. "I guess I won't risk swimming," he said.

"They're as afraid of you as you are of them," Dermot said, scooping up a slim floating branch to prod the sandy bottom. Minnows shot away from him.

"It's cool in here," said Shirley. "Hey, Dad, so aren't you glad you accepted our invitation?"

"What, to the five-hundred-dollar rat-hole?"

"Yeah, aren't you glad?"

Dermot used the code they all understood: "I've accepted worse." Shirley planted her bare feet on his back and wiggled her toenails to tickle him. "All right, all right," he said. She was the only one of them who could touch him easily like that. Bayard would not touch him at all.

"Tell your little sister to cut it out," he told Martin, but she only rested her toes against his sweaty back and used him for leverage to arch out over the bow upside down. "So now I'm a footstool?"

"It's so cool in here," she said in blissful tones.

Dreaminess settled over the three of them. Father and son watched the water on opposite sides. There was nothing to see, a minnow, a bug on the surface. Why had they asked him here? Dermot wondered. Why here, in their mother's private place, the place he had always dashed in and out of, reluctantly, dutifully, and not so dutifully at last?

"We simply want to see something of you, Dad," Shirley had said when they called. He had not believed her. He had feared what any sensible observer would suspect, that these two had an unrealistic hope that their parents would come back together, or at least come to like each other more, so that there could be a few times ahead when they would all feel like a single family. It was possible. He had not remarried. Their mother had not. It was unfinished, their family, hanging there limp like a bedsheet torn in two, ragged, fraying, flapping sadly when a wind came up. Julie, Andrea, Enid only led backwards through his life to Mary Blakey, the girl at college who had seemed in one sure moment of youth to offer all he would ever need.

"Dad, I've been meaning to discuss, to talk with you — about the fall," Martin said in a low voice, not looking up from a dragonfly swooping above the lily pads.

"Well, you won't be able to stay in the trailer when the weather turns," Dermot said. He had been worrying about it. "Even if you find a job out here."

"I think I might want to try Santa Fe," Martin said. Shirley said nothing, which convinced Dermot she had already heard this plan. "My friend Suzanne sends me job listings. It's a whole other world. I've never been that far from home."

It immediately sounded like a good idea to Dermot. He realized he wanted his son to be able to go. It had never occurred to him Martin might choose to do something like that on his own. "Have you discussed it with your mother?"

"I was going to talk to you first," Martin said.

"Because I'm the moneyman," Dermot said, a reflex he regretted. He looked down at his stomach hanging above the green plaid of his bathing trunks, not quite a pot but wider and thicker and looser than he liked to remember it.

"It's only for getting out there. I'll have a job lined up. They need tech people."

Is this possible, Dermot was thinking, Martin a tech person, not a store clerk? "You're catching me way off guard, Martin," he said. His son looked up, the nervous flutter in his hands. "No, I'm ribbing you," Dermot said quickly, laughing to change the mood. "Of course I want you to have plans. But I want you to feel," he said slowly, sensing the old guilt rising up through his vitals to his throat so he could not help from saying, "that you don't have to do anything you don't want to. Your mother and I want you to find what you truly want to do, and we'll do whatever we can to help."

"Dad," came Shirley's voice, "get off it!" And she dug her toenails in again. What was this about? Dermot had to turn around and grab her ankles, but before he could start tickling, she said, "You talk like you and Mom are still a *we* when it comes to dealing with us."

"But we are," he said, "when it comes to you, we are a *we.*"

"But you're not, Dad. You both want the same thing maybe, but you're not a *we* anymore. You never were much of a *we.*"

"Honey," Dermot said, holding her ankles tight, but tenderly, insistently, "we can't help being what you call a *we* when it comes to the four of you."

"Dad, what I'm saying," said Shirley, "is that we think of you and Mom as entirely separate people. That's why we asked you to come visit us. Didn't you get what I said: we wanted to see something of you. Separate from Mom. Mom's got her own thing going."

A fresh thought fell suddenly into place: Dermot's kids were afraid they were losing their mother, so they had called for him. That was what it was about. Maybe it would make her jealous. Could he say that? "Honey," he said softly, "your mom's not going away."

Shirley was shaking her head at him. "Dad, I wish you could get it through your thick skull. This has nothing to do with Mom. Martin and I made a resolution, didn't we, Martin?" From Martin's silence, Dermot could tell he was glad Shirley was handling this. "We decided we were old enough to take a little charge. We don't have much of a relationship with our father. So we get him to come out and play stupid games with us and go rowing. There's no mystery."

"But your mother —"

"That's you guys' problem."

Dermot let Shirley's ankles go and massaged her knees when she sat up again in the bow and stared at him till he turned back around and took the oars. "Okay, kids. You're right. It's just you two and me. Gotcha." He pivoted the boat with one urgent pull of his left arm, and they headed out into the sun. "Let's rip," he said.

The film of water that had crept into the boat through its fragile seams felt cool on his feet. Martin was dragging a finger through the water and tapping at lily pads they passed. Shirley, he could see over his shoulder, was now on her stomach leaning over the bow. Dermot swept them along, past the boathouse, past the cottage, aiming for a boulder near the point. He knew not to risk the wider lake, but he wanted to reach some destination. Working his muscles always made him feel better. A bike ride with Julie, swimming at Andrea's health club — he thrived on exercise, he told himself, activity. But it scared him. What did he have to offer these kids of his, what insubstantial, impractical, indefinable thing they needed — that was what he had not arrived at.

"Don't bust a gut, Dad," Shirley said to the parting water beneath her.

Back over Martin's bowed head, Dermot descried the roofline of Mary's house among the trees, high up above the trailer by the shore. It was very hot staring into the afternoon sun, but he had almost made it. They would swim again. They would sit up on the boulder to dry off. Dermot felt nervous as he slowed his strokes. He was better at giving directions. He suspected he did not know how to talk interestingly to his own children.

VII

HE HAD COME UP to see her after his barbecue with the kids. It was a good time to talk because tomorrow he was taking them to see *Apollo 13* and she would be with Bryce, who tonight had a late meeting.

They were sitting on the balcony watching the light fade all around them. Birdsongs ceased, there was no wind, mosquitoes found their way beyond the bug candles burning low in tin buckets. It was time to go in.

Dermot had scarcely ever been inside her house. He had made an initial inspection, she remembered, when she bought the place, but since then he might have stepped in no farther than the doormat to get out of a rainstorm while he waited for Shirley and Bayard to pack their weekend gear; perhaps once he had asked if he could use the bathroom. Those encounters had been gingerly and proper. She had preferred not to be there at all, to go on a dog walk or make chat with Ray Berrouet, the previous tenant in Drew's boathouse, a young police officer in Parshallville, friendly but busy with his own affairs, who knew Drew Hale through the gun club. She would talk to him about weather and the dog and his guns and avoid Dermot.

Strange how many blank years stretched back now, and how since Ron and Victor — and now since Bryce — she was at last part of a neighborhood. For nearly ten years, she recognized now, she had hovered about her woodland refuge as though it might, at any moment, be swept away from under her. She had tried to garden. She had painted and repainted walls, tiled the bathroom, sewn cushions, signed up for classes, volunteered, raked, and shoveled. It had taken a long time truly to put foot to ground.

And now she could invite her former husband into her house. Blustery as he always was in the open air, something in him hushed when she swung open the screen door and he stepped across her threshold. "It hasn't changed much," he said. "Wasn't the still life over there?" It was true she had moved it from above the woodstove to the wall behind the long bench, where the kids all used to sit in a row on winter mornings pulling on their extra socks and boots and parkas before school. She and Dermot had bought the painting as a tenth anniversary present to each other because she had loved it at the community art show and he had wanted to put something original and particularly theirs over their mantel: within a plain whitewashed frame, a sunny tabletop with an empty red glass bowl, a half-full blue glass beaker, and behind them a dark blue pitcher that looked like Chinese porcelain; in the foreground the remains of a bunch of grapes, now a forest of little stems with only a few deep purple grapes left, a rind of yellow cheese, an encrusted knife, a heel of bread. She had loved it because it was so bright and warm and seemed to imply happy well-fed people somewhere. Last spring, though, whenever she looked at it, it had told her that the feast was over and there was nothing more to come, so she had moved it where her eye would not fall on it from her usual stool at the table, which she now pulled out for herself, and pointed Dermot to the one opposite.

"I think you should upgrade to chairs, Mary," he said. "We're old enough to want to lean back occasionally."

"I tend to perch in here," she said. "If I need to settle, I pull the rocker up to the woodstove. When I'm by myself."

"This house has worked out pretty well for you," Dermot said, glancing about with an approving if condescending eye. But he added, in his needling tone, "I don't know how you survive out here in the boonies."

"Tell me one thing, Dermot," she said. "Do you still have questions whether the way we worked it out was damaging to the kids?"

"Anything, by definition," he said in his accountant voice, "would have been damaging. Staying together would have been damaging. There's nothing we could have done that wouldn't have been damaging. Except to transform ourselves into young lovers and start over."

She squinted at him; like an apparition, the young Dermot fleshed himself in around that small boyish nose, and she was picturing the two of them, at a frat party after a game, snuggling peacefully on a saggy couch, not drunk like the rest, not loud, not moving at all, but wholly each other's, alone together in a whirl of festivity, and somehow even beyond the pull of sex, beyond the finitude of separate personalities — afloat in some new bliss. She had felt it, he had felt it, the fulfillment of the promise they had been instructed in, the sacrament, the right resting place of their yearnings. Such a moment, when the universe opened itself up to her like that, would probably not come again until she was facing her own death.

Across the table, Dermot looked somber. His black hair — she wondered if he might be dyeing it — was flopped over his brow, thinner, sadder somehow. "The kids are all right," he said. "Even Martin. Has he talked to you about his plans?"

"His space heater's not going to be enough for deep winter," she said; she had been worrying about it. "He's remembering his last time, but it was March, almost, before he moved in."

Then Dermot mentioned, casually, that Martin had an idea about going to Santa Fe, and she felt hurt, then annoyed he had not told her first. But soon, curiously, she began to sense some relief, not for the plan itself or for it lifting the burden of how to make Martin do anything at all, but that Martin *had* told his father of it first. She could not understand why that felt better, she was not sure she liked it, but it was a relief nonetheless.

"I've certainly heard all about Suzanne," she said to reclaim the greater intimacy with her son. "He showed me a so-called novel she wrote. It's meant to be the spiritual quest of some princess in the desert in an ancient Aztec land. Pretty hard to plow through. I don't think Martin managed to finish it either, but I'm sure she's as reasonable as any of them has been."

She went on down the string of Martin's hapless loves, assessing them, and even alluding to Peggy Hale as if she had known all along, but she refrained from offering details because Louise had not supplied her with them. Dermot had his own ideas about Rachel in Newton; he said she was a prize bitch, and his words made her shiver, though she said nothing. Instead she continued, on through the other kids — Rosa, Bayard, Shirley — as she used to in the old days, lying side by side with him in bed with the lights off, absorbed in the accomplishments and agonies of her children, losing herself. She would prime Dermot for Rosa's flute recital, would interpret Bayard's English paper for him. She was the children's ambassador, the one who told him how to take them, except perhaps for sports, where he tended to tell her.

"Iced tea?" she asked. "A beer?"

"No, I've had enough," Dermot said. "I didn't mean to invade your evening. I just thought I should check in. It's been all right for you, hasn't it, me being here for the week?"

"Sure," she said, for it truly had been. It was the first time since the divorce that she experienced no jumpiness when she caught sight of Dermot or heard his voice at a distance. At last, he had gone out of her.

"It's been relatively painless for me, too," he said. "It was a cheap deal, considering summer rentals."

"It's been good for Shirley and Martin," she said. "I'm glad you got all that Windows stuff figured out. Martin was getting anxious about it." She had run out of things to say, and Dermot would not have anything more to drink. "Want a cookie?" she asked.

He shook his head and then looked up to the loft curtains above their heads. "Boys' side," he said, pointing to the orange one, and "girls' side," pointing to the yellow. "Got it right?" She nodded. "Funny," he said, "how at my house I have two comfy third-floor guest rooms ready for them anytime, but they never come and stay for long. I guess they prefer camping out like this."

It was an acknowledgment, she realized, or closer than he had yet come. "Give them a few more years," she said to ease him past her moment of gentle triumph.

"I suppose," said Dermot, stretching now in the way he had of filling up all the space around him, a vigorous punching out of his limbs and a tossing back of his head with a final yawning hoot. But he was not tired. He was not ready to leave. He kept looking about, attending to details, as if he might never be allowed to see this room again, as if it might hold the secret to understanding his children, finally. He turned to the closed door behind him under the girls' loft. From his eyes she realized he did not know what was inside there.

"We used to call it the free-for-all," she said. "I'll show you."

Dermot got up to follow, and when she opened the door and flicked the light switch, she hoped she had caught on his face a fleeting regretfulness before he said, "Good Lord, it's a disaster area." Drooping deflated balloons were still taped to the ceiling, and the duct tape on Rosa's yellow beanbag chair had split again and spilled Styrofoam beans across the linoleum. Gus Ostermann and Shirley had collaborated on the most recent mural, half-finished cartoons of each other. "What's that, Beavis and Butthead?" said Dermot.

"The one on the left is your younger daughter."

"It looks like Butthead. Or Beavis. I only know about such crap through Julie's twelve-year-old."

"Has Julie moved in with you?"

"No, no, no, no, no," said Dermot rapidly and humorously. He wanted her to know he was quite happy the way he was, and to a point she believed it. "So this is the free-for-all."

"This is the free-for-all."

He was looking at gouges in the plasterboard where one object or another had been nailed in and ripped out. "You're going to have to spackle and sand and then skim-coat this whole room before you paint it again."

"It doesn't bother me," she said. "This is their room."

"I mean, if you ever want to sell." He was fiddling with the sticky knobs on the Foosball game, dented up from all the abuse it had taken. "You might rather be closer into town someday. Martin and Shirley worry about you out here alone."

"I thought they worried about me out here *not* alone," she said. She had not discussed Bryce with Dermot, but she assumed he had heard plenty. Since he had mentioned Julie, she wanted to mention Bryce, and now she sort of had, but it had not satisfied her.

Before she could elaborate, Dermot said, "That, too!" and smiled as if to say it didn't bother him, of course, and aren't kids funny! Now he was inspecting the Nerf ball net, which had never offered much of a challenge to anyone but Shirley ten years ago, but there it still hung on the wall. She could picture Bayard sprawled on his beanbag watching TV and tossing the fuzzy green ball up and in, up and in, for a half hour at a time. The TV's vertical hold had gone out of whack a year ago, but she relied on the portable in the kitchen anyway for what little she watched, the news, the nature shows, sometimes *Oprah* when she was feeling depressed.

"I'm glad there's some soft place to sit down in this house," Dermot said, nudging Martin's brown beanbag with his sandal. "You mind?" And down he sat.

"That's Martin's," she said. "The red is Bayard's, the blue is Shirley's, Rosa's is falling apart; I think Gus was playing rough with it."

"Where's yours?"

"I used to pull in the rocker when we watched TV," she said, but she also remembered them putting all the bags close together in a lump and all five of them leaning and sprawling across them, or sometimes teaming up, little

Shirley and herself in the blue one, Hilda and Bayard nuzzling each other in the red. Where *was* Hilda? She must have been sleeping on her dog bed by the bathroom, where she spent most of her indoor time of late.

"You can't exactly have adult company over and sit around comfortably after dinner, Mary," Dermot remarked.

"What you're wondering," she said, "is do I have adult company over at all."

"No, no, no, I gather you do. Your hospital people, those neighbors of yours, this new fellow down the road." Her sparse furnishings were one reason Bryce preferred to spend their evenings at his house, even when Shirley was out, but she could not tell Dermot that. And the subject of Bryce must have been touchy for Dermot, too, because he turned away back to the neighbors and asked about Ron, the one on the bike, the one he'd had a nice chat with that morning.

"He's a good friend," she said. "I've learned something, Dermot. It's something I actually knew as a kid but forgot. It's that I often prefer the company of plain folks. It's what I grew up around, even if my poor parents were too uppity for their surroundings. But I don't think I was. I mean, they were older than my friends' parents, they'd seen things decline, to their way of thinking, but I took my neighborhood for granted. I always wished I could have some of those kids over."

"Kids like this Ron."

"Like Ron, or even the black kids down my street. I'd talk with them on the corner sometimes." She had decided to settle down on a beanbag, too; the conversation was going somewhere, she did not know where, but it might take some time, and she did not want it to end before it got there. She chose Bayard's red beanbag because somehow Bayard was her staunchest ally and she felt safest there.

"What were their names? Marian Anderson Jefferson and Paul Robeson Jones?" He was trying to be amusing about the sources of their kids' names, which had pissed him off when she explained them during the divorce.

She decided to let it pass now. "No, their names — I can remember — were Sarah Catherine and Gwen. They were cousins. They had all sorts of funny ideas about me being a Catholic. They thought I needed to be saved."

"By the way, don't you find Gus Ostermann a bit weird?" Dermot asked in a typical redirection of conversation. "Julie's older daughter's in the high school with him. I think Kurt and Christina are way too laissez-faire."

"He had a tremendous crush on Shirley last month, I know, which you may not be able to perceive from those portraits."

"He's made her look like an ugly boy."

"Well, she's made him look practically like a fish."

Dermot stretched again, way back, taking in a great breath. His hairy knees were sweaty, and so was his forehead; the sleeves of his polo shirt were wet under the arms. "A week without AC," he said. "I don't know how you do it."

Where had their talk been going a minute ago? She felt dizzy. She should have had a cookie herself, even if he had not wanted one. Then she remembered: they had been talking about her childhood. "Dermot," she said, "I spent most of those Dorchester years pretty much alone. You were always on teams, and you had so many cousins. We were quite different from the start. You seemed to have so much that I wanted."

He was looking at her with a certain apprehension, maybe even fear. He set his dark eyebrows low and tight over his black eyes. "We're not going to start in again about why it didn't work out, Mary," he said with a perceptible tremor in his voice.

That was *not* what she wanted. She did not want to have those ten-year-old talks again, either. She wanted to make this talk different and new. "I'm not accusing you of anything," she said. "I'm sorting something out."

Did he relax? It did not seem so. "Sorting what out?"

"Sorting out," she said, and added with a small quiver of pride, "how I've been rather comfortable most of my life being alone, and how there have been small moments when I've wished not to be, and how these past ten years have been happy ones with both the stretches alone and the stretches with the kids here. These ten years have been very beautiful. But now they're over."

And instead of feeling like an admission of failure, which is how such a speech would have sounded in Mary's ears a mere half hour ago, her words felt like a declaration, a warning, a claim. She had told Dermot something he might not be willing to hear. She had told him she would have her own life now. She would no longer finish up his unfinished business. He would now be the one alone, she felt, because Julie was as passing as Enid and whatever the other one's name was, because the children would not come home to him despite her kind encouragement. They would tolerate him. She would tolerate him. Dermot would go through the rest of his life being tolerated. She knew it at last.

They heard a soft padding and an old brown nose stuck itself into the room, then a big shaggy achy body on four creaking legs.

"Come here, Hilda, you old beast," said Dermot. "You've been through it all, too, haven't you!"

Hilda, the all-forgiving, nuzzled up to her old master the way she always had and would, to all of them, all six, till she died. They were her family, and to the long memories locked into her great nose, her reader of life's messages, the passage of ten years was as the passage of a day.

A SEPTEMBER FRIDAY

I

IT WAS THE LULL between Labor Day and leaf season. Rosa and Nat had asked for a week off. First, they'd visited Nat's family in Portsmouth, then stopped to see Rosa's dad, and by Thursday had circled around to Umbachaug. Nat had not driven down with Rosa since January. In Newton, the mood had been brittle. Her father had been cautious with Rosa ever since she renamed herself Blakey, and his doubts about Nat showed in his overhearty manner and his straining for uncontroversial topics to discuss. Nat kept his crooked-toothed smile on the whole time; one night of that was enough for Rosa. When they drove off, Nat had to play the radio loud and scream along with John Mellencamp to let off steam.

At the cove, Nat was immediately at home, as always. He and Rosa took over the girls' loft. Shirley's bed was still piled with the unwashed clothes she had not taken back to college. Her laundry would have to wait for a long weekend home because Mom was not going to do it. Nat transferred the piles to the floor, and they pushed the beds together and remade them with double sheets so they could be next to each other all night the way there were used to. That was important to Rosa, especially in her mother's house. Her father had pointed them to his third floor, where he seldom set foot, and said to take whichever room they liked, meaning twin beds or double, only the cleaning lady would know. But bringing your boyfriend to Umbachaug, Rosa realized long ago, was rather restricting because there was no door to close. The place was still a bunkhouse for adolescents. And where would they ever put Mom's grand-kids someday? The free-for-all would have to become the guest room, and Rosa and Nat would claim it because they were the first ones likely to start the next generation.

Rosa had put herself to sleep last night planning such a renovation, but her delectable fantasy — including queen-size bed and baby's crib in the alcove — had been spoiled by worries of Shirley and Martin complaining about changes of any sort and Bayard demanding equal space for him and his latest girlfriend. And the old worry about her and Nat. It was hard to imagine her family adapting to the future because they were all so stuck in their ruts. But time moves very slowly, Rose reminded herself. Maybe she did not have to perceive changes for them to be already under way. So she had run her fingers along where the mattresses joined, and her hand had ventured across to touch the gently snoring Nat but not to wake him. He is there, Rosa had told herself, right beside me.

And in the morning sun, dappling onto their upturned faces through the maple leaves beyond the skylight, they were at last able to have the peaceful talk Rosa had been hoping for all week.

"This house always does it for me," Nat said.

"Does what?"

"Calms me down."

"Good," Rosa said. "Your own parents' house didn't."

"I hate us sleeping in the room I grew up in," Nat said. "I can't throw out any of that crap, so there it is, whenever we go home, my whole stupid kid self." His room was a gallery of skiing and sailing posters and trophies, a library of nature books and magazines, a museum of toy sailboats and miniature birchbark canoes and his collection of snow globes, which included some valuable oddities, like a Fort Lauderdale blizzard.

"I wish I'd known your stupid kid self," Rosa said, and she reached up to stroke his rough chin with its signs of incipient jowliness.

"You wouldn't have noticed me." It was his usual line; he claimed girls didn't think much of him back then.

"I would have."

"No, you aspired to be cool." Rosa had to think about it. She told him she had had no idea in high school what the right sort of guy for her would have been. The crowd she hung out with after dark at the landfill had its own standards of coolness, she admitted, but how cool was any of them now? "Luckily, coolness is no longer the point," said Nat.

They talked on, quietly, not wanting to wake Mom because it was not even seven. At the lodge, they were up at five, so to them this was slugabed time, maybe even time to make love. But instead, Nat turned to look Rosa close in the eyes and said, as if it had only now occurred to him and seemed a neat idea, "Why don't we go ahead and get married before another winter comes?"

Rosa was used to this. "Why don't we? There must be a good reason."

"I can't think of one anymore," Nat said, and he rolled onto his back and looked above the curtain at the skylight. The whites of his eyes sparkled, verging on tears.

"What's happening, Nat?" Rosa asked, almost scared.

And he said, "I can't tell if the juice is going out of me or if I'm only just revving up. Something's different. This summer was different."

"How?" Rosa asked, up on her elbow, inspecting his squinched-up face for a sign. "How?" she asked again.

"It felt different. You notice we haven't had this discussion since May."

"We've tried not to," Rosa said.

"And?"

"And?"

"Summer was great," said Nat, "us letting it slide. We were in a rhythm, don't you think? All those people, week by week — the horrible Frost family and that blowhard Bill Armitage and old Balthazar; people come back each year now expecting to see us there."

Rosa liked to think about Balthazar, the aging hippie cook in his hairnet with all his rings lined up on the shelf above the chopping block. "But, Nat —" she began, her automatic resistance to any move of his. He did the same thing. Still, something was tingling in her belly.

"I don't think we should say anything to anyone. I think we should quietly decide for ourselves. Why involve families?"

"Wait a minute," said Rosa. "Are you already at the planning stage?"

He lay still on his back, but his pale eyes turned toward her, dry now, wide and sure. "It calms me down, being here," he said again. "Your mom calms me down. She's so much like you, Rosie. You're the one of you guys who's most like her."

"And that's good?"

"Well, I can see what you'll be like when you're forty-nine."

"And that's good?" Rosa said again, knowing she was

being funny because she did know her mother seemed awfully youthful. Nat reached for her, and they hugged, and she rested her head on his chest, tracing the sidewise letters on his T-shirt: FIRST LAKE LODGE. "You love my mother," she said.

"Your mother —" Nat began, but she shushed him, so he whispered: "Your mother is a lovely person." They turned on their sides, face to face, and stared awhile. "Some say you're better off marrying someone who's enough different from you," said Nat. "We're pretty much like each other. But this summer — that's what happened — I got past minding. I was happier with us two. I don't think we squabbled, did we?"

"Didn't seem like it."

"There," Nat said, "see?"

On the whole, Rosa had been happier, too. Or she had not been at all sad, not more than a day. After her visit home in May, she had found herself, already, free of something. That picture of her mom leaping up and swinging on the branch, the thing Ron had seen her do, that simple picture in Rosa's head that she kept seeing as if she had witnessed it herself, had tipped her past something. She had not pulled off her little hoax because the vision had already begun to haunt her: her mother in her own secret ecstatic life.

"It would be a simple legal formality, we wouldn't have to make anything of it, Rosa," Nat said.

"You're so romantic!" she said, too loud, so Nat put a finger to his lips and with his other hand pointed across to the room below. They lay in silence, and no sounds arose, not even from the dog; there was a time when the slightest early morning creaking in the loft set Hilda pacing and panting and even squealing in anticipation of breakfast, but now she heard only the sharp bang of the screen door and saw only big shapes in bright light. This might be a time to make very quiet love. In the privacy of her dad's third floor, the mood had been too tense for it.

"Let's give it a shot, Rosie," he said. He must have meant marriage, not sex. But start with sex, Rosa told herself, yes, start with sex. Maybe it would allow her to feel her way to a decision. Sometimes it was like that, especially when they had to be quiet, and intensely focused, and quick.

And they made it down to breakfast before her mother woke up.

Rosa fed the dog and remembered to embed an ibuprofen in a moist chunk of the health-diet dog food Mom bought faithfully once a month over in Dowland. Hilda's collar clanking against her food dish must have served as an alarm clock, for Mom finally emerged sleepily in her robe, heading straight for the bathroom. Nat and Rosa took their coffee cups out to the balcony to sit in the sun.

And so the day went: lie back and soak it in, stroll off into the woods, muck around the lakeshore, stop in to see Martin once he woke up, go for a real run out the railroad bed, take one last shivery September plunge into the cove, change into fresh jeans and sweatshirts, head off to Haviland for toiletries and new windshield wipers for their beat-up old Wagoneer, and then try the Original 108 for lunch. Nat had heard a lot about the place.

Rosa knew why she took Nat to the diner. She had a strange hope that Ron would say something important again to nudge her in one sure direction. But she did not get it from him this time. He was dancing around doing ten things at once. Glad to see her, of course, and very interested to meet Nat. Hoping to catch them later at the lake. The diner was jammed. It was Victor, actually, who made time for them. He stood at the end of the counter, where they had sat down after Mr. Zart and the Parshallville cop who used to rent from Drew Hale got up to leave. "Hey, little Rosa," said Officer Berrouet, "it's been a while." What with having met Watertank Thibault in the convenient mart earlier, Nat was getting the impression that everyone around here knew Rosa. Then Victor leaned in close. "Ron's glad you're down," he said. "Your mother missed you all summer." This did not feel like a reproach, just meaningful information. "Ron worries about her," Victor said, and then he explained to Nat, in case he felt excluded, that Mary was going through a lot of new stuff: Ron had put the bee in her bonnet about getting a job, and Bryce Murtagh was still in the picture, and Martin was going to be leaving for the West, and then Rosa's dad had been there and Ron had taken a fit about that. It was as though Victor wanted to let them know only what Ron thought, not what he thought. But it was sweet of him. He was shy about it. Nat had liked him.

"I get the feeling," Nat said now as he drove them back to the cove, "that Victor considers me your husband already. From the way he was clueing me in. As though I had a stake in your family. Which I do." Rosa was not ready to say anything, so he went on. "I do have a stake in your family. I have more of a stake in your family than I do in mine."

"Guess what, Natty," Rosa said, watching him watch the curving road. "I have a stake in your crazy family despite you."

"Right through the heart," said Nat.

"Yuck-yuck-yuck," Rosa said and then, "No, I happen to love your mom and dad and I don't mind your sisters as much as you do. I do love your dad, and I love your mom, sitting on the porch swing with her and talking about how much toilet paper you can go through in a week or watching stupid TV with your dad."

"You and Dad and *Funniest Home Videos.*"

Rather than think of a comeback, Rosa threw in, out of nowhere, "So now what's this about us getting married?"

"Hey, great idea!" said Nat.

"Whose idea was it?"

"The collective unconscious's," he said.

Another mile and they were at last on the gravel road out to Hale's Cove. Nat slowed way down and then stopped in the middle of the woods. He gave Rosa a kiss on the cheek and then sat back. "Okay," he said, "here's the deal. We get through leaf season and the last hunters, and, I guess, Thanksgiving. Then, before it's officially winter, we'll go and do it. You and me and Balthazar and Aggie. And then if they want to give us a party someday, our families, I mean if they think we deserve it — oh, maybe five years down the line —"

It made strange quiet unwavering sense to Rosa. They could keep it their secret wish and not know exactly what day it would come true, but now she imagined it finally would.

11

MARY LANAGHAN had been offered a job at the retirement community of Basswood in neighboring Fraddboro, coordinating social events and recreational activities. The administrators might have preferred a more experienced person, but the money was not there, and the warm recommendation from Ara Zeytoundjian, so they told Mary, had convinced them they were making a wise choice. Thirty-five hours, twenty-six thousand a year with health benefits and four weeks off.

She had told no one in the family. Christina had counseled her by phone, Ara had been terribly kind, in principle Bryce was all for it, Ron took full credit, and only Louise Thibault, when she emerged from one of her training sessions at the hospital in a foul mood, had made the prospect sound dreary. "Oh, Mrs. Lanaghan," she had said, "I mean, Mary — I don't know. It can get you down, all those old people. Especially the rich ones." Mary could still hear her words drooping out of her exhausted mouth, which had to breathe for so much flesh and blood and had a hard time keeping up.

The job would start in ten days. Mary had been reading library books on gerontology, occupational therapy, card games, quilting, bingo, all sorts of things. Her predecessor would overlap a week to work her into things. There were some three hundred old people waiting to test her out. It was intimidating.

This morning, with Rosa and Nat out of the house, Mary had sat down to compose a letter to Dermot announcing her news in businesslike fashion and, following Kurt Ostermann's advice, agreeing to forgo alimony for as long as she should remain employed. Their lawyers would sort it out. For her, it would mean, taking taxes into account, a slight loss, but Dermot would be legally bound to resume payments should she fail to keep the job.

Mary put the letter in an envelope but did not seal it yet and took Hilda on a walk to mull it all over one more time. She would call Kurt at work in Boston and read him what she had written. She would not show it to Bryce, though; she did not want to draw him in, and while she almost wanted to call Bayard in New Haven and run it past him, she knew she could not consult Martin or Rosa, and so she would keep it from the kids entirely until it was a done deal. She would still have enough extra to help them out, modestly, as she always had. Besides, she suspected Dermot was gearing up to buy back his children's affections.

Out the railroad bed, Mary and Hilda came to where, in July, Christina had veered into the woods and found that mossy spot to sit on. Hilda was reluctant to ascend the path, so Mary scampered up alone and found the flat rock where the dog had napped; it looked like a pagan altar set upon a velvet cloth of green. Mary wanted to lie on that great slab and make of herself an offering, to something she was not sure of, something so serious she could only laugh at herself for having such a pretentious thought. She reached down to touch the granite, smooth along the top, rough at the sides, and to run her fingers gently across the soft moss, and then, with a final glance back, she returned to Hilda, who was staring blankly toward her, hardly seeing, hardly knowing. Hilda lived in timeless gray space, made interesting by smells.

When they passed the boathouse there was no sign of activity and no sign at the cottage either. Drew's last renters, weekenders only, from Worcester, would be coming up through Columbus Day; Mary had not yet caught sight of them. The dog was moseying along the water toward Martin's trailer, where she expected a biscuit or cookie.

Mary stopped still and listened for music, but all she heard was the quack of a duck down the cove. She took a few steps and stopped again. These were Martin's last days here, and the two of them had not been getting along. In a week, she would be saying good-bye to him. His depression, if that was what it was, had allowed him no fresh summer start; it had proved a false hope that relaxing for a season could heal anything, and Mary knew she had missed her chance to help her son make some headway. She had told herself not to be the meddlesome mother, and after some initial suggestions, she had dropped the idea of his working at the day camp, of finding out if they needed anyone at the Old Fraddboro Store. She had also tried only twice to interest Martin in the young adults' support group at the hospital. It was clear that anything she said struck him wrong and so she had followed Rosa's advice and let him be. He simply needed time off, even though the daily evidence was that he slept too much, read tons of sci-fi paperbacks, played CDs and CD-ROMs and computer games, kept up his e-mail and the Internet, and hardly saw anyone his age at all. There had been Peggy, briefly, whatever that meant, and Shirley had kept him from being a complete hermit, but now it was too late, the summer was gone. Mary felt guilty for having backed away from him, for having talked herself out of attending to the quiet crisis he was in. She had been too involved in Bryce and had ignored her son.

"Hey, pup," came his voice. Hilda had sniffed her way to Martin, and now Mary had to follow. She found them, son and dog, sitting face to face, Martin popping grape after grape into Hilda's mouth. The old girl would eat anything now, raw carrots, pieces of banana, even brussels sprouts. Cross-legged in his cutoffs, Martin looked like a fuller version of his sixteen-year-old self when they first came to the cove. Now he would drift off to New Mexico as he had drifted off then to college.

"Hi, Mom," he said.

"May I join you two?" Mary settled on the step of the trailer. "You'll have warm dry days like this all the time in Santa Fe," she said.

"It gets cold there, too," said Martin.

"But there'll be so much more light and all be so clear."

"We'll see. Hey, Mom, look, Hilda ate the whole bunch." He was stroking the gray muzzle and rubbing the wet nose. These might be his very last days with the dog of his youth.

"Have you had a good talk with your sister?"

"Nat was there," Martin said.

"You approve of Nat essentially, though."

"He's too much of a woodsy type — folky, grainy, low tech."

"Oh, come on," Mary said. She was not up on Martin's fine distinctions. From what she could tell, that girl Suzanne in Santa Fe was folky and grainy; there must be a subtle difference. Mary supposed Suzanne was mystical and spiritual where Rosa and Nat were plain earthy. Perhaps it was time to tell Martin her own news. She had not intended to, because he would be safely gone the weekend before she started at Basswood, but it suddenly seemed unfair of her to save it for a phone call.

"Here, Hilda, fetch." Martin threw the cluster of stems into the cove to tease the dog, who did not fall for it. It floated light as thistledown on the lapping water like a tiny tree.

"I've been looking into getting a job when you're gone, Martin," Mary said.

"No way," he said.

"I have. I've actually been offered one."

"No *way!*" He seemed truly astonished. She went on to tell him about seeing the ad in the *Vigilant* and applying on a whim, but she did not admit she had already said yes; she wanted him to feel consulted first. "But wait a minute," he said. "What does this do to alimony?"

"It doesn't change college support for Shirley, and obviously you kids will still get your special allowances from your dad, and I'll have enough to help you out when you need it."

"But for you?" said Martin.

"I'll be making a salary with health benefits. We'll get it spelled out, don't worry."

Martin looked disapproving. He used his T-shirt to wipe his arm where Hilda had slobbered. "Mom, you don't know what it's like having a job," he said. "It's not like bopping into the hospital for a couple of hours. You'll have some nasty supervisor getting on your case. You won't even be able to go to the bathroom when you want to."

"I doubt that."

Martin was staring intently into her eyes. "But you've never worked for somebody before. Couldn't you go for part-time?"

That had been Mary's own first thought, but Ron had shamed her out of it. He had said if she wanted to feel herself in the adult world, she would have to work like an adult the way he did. Her other work was done, her kids were grown, but that did not mean she now got a break. "You're not even fifty," he said. "Life goes on, girl." So Mary tried to convince Martin she was eager to work, to get something back of her own self, but as she heard her words she realized how they could seem a reproach to her son. His face was falling, and he was poking pine needles into the sand, constructing a bare little forest.

"What does Bryce say?" he asked.

"He's for it."

"I thought so." Martin looked up and flipped his black

hair out of his eyes so he could shoot an angry look at Mary.

"So?" she said. Her heart fluttered. She wished she had waited. Now she would have to tell Rosa, too, and the peaceful family weekend would turn to bickering.

"He wants you to work so you'll lose alimony and Dad won't be involved anymore. You know, Mom, when Dad was here, we saw Bryce once out mowing his lawn on his ridiculous tractor. Dad thought he was a total turkey."

"Well, thank you, Martin, for telling me. That's very helpful of you," Mary said. Hilda had sensed the tension and slipped off beyond the trailer. Mary felt horrible small tears creeping up in her eyes. They embarrassed her because they discounted the force she felt inside, but Martin was watching the cove and facing away. Maybe, he heard them in her voice. He was angry, too, but he was her son, so she had to worry about his anger as something she needed to help him fix; he did not have to worry about her anger, he did not have to worry about her — she was his mother.

"It's only what Dad said," he replied sullenly. "For once, I agreed with him. It shouldn't matter to you. You can suit yourself."

Mary sat in silence. She had been trying to suit herself, but for too short a time to have the hang of it. The idea of Bryce on his mower did not particularly please her, either. The idea of his close-cropped lawn in the woods did not please her. But something in him pleased her. She had to defend it, not against Martin or Dermot but against that cold part of herself she had so much trouble with.

"Well," said Mary, forcing out the word, "you won't be here to worry about all this. You'll be on your own where you should be. I think it's been bad for us, honey, to slob about in these backwoods of ours together all summer. I didn't suppose it was a good idea, but your sister drove down from New Hampshire and convinced me. Oh, I guess it's my fault. I haven't known what to do with myself without my kids around. I've had you guys since I was younger than you." A smile slipped up Martin's cheek, Mary could see from one side. "Rosa is behind you, honey," she said. "Do you know what a devoted sister you've got? And you can cope with Nat. Get him talking about animal life up there."

"That place is a hunting lodge, Mom," Martin said.

"Only in hunting season."

"Duh!" Martin retorted.

"But Nat doesn't hunt. It's just a living."

"And he goes on about how hard he and Rosa have to work up there like they're making such a noble contribution to preserving the wilderness."

"They don't know what they're going to do with their lives yet, Martin."

"But what if Rosa gets married to the guy?"

It was a possibility Mary could entertain only in some distant time, when all of them would have found their perfect whole selves, have fallen into their proper places, harmonized, turned bright new true beautiful colors. It did not yet seem a possibility for the present world, which crept along day to day with its weight of timid sorrow and of which she was growing tired.

"We're not getting through to each other today, Martin," Mary said. "I think we're both nervous about things. Are you really sure about going off to New Mexico?"

III

"THAT DOG OF YOURS is deaf, dumb, and blind," said Drew, when he came in sight of Mary Lanaghan and her oldest kid talking in front of their junky-looking trailer by the cove. "Didn't even see me coming down the path. Kept on nosing around."

"Good afternoon, Drew," said Mary. "I didn't hear your car."

"Hello, son," Drew said to the kid, who looked up at him and nodded. Oddball, Drew thought. "No, I parked behind your house. I was going to ask if you had any trouble from those new renters. Figured you might be down here."

"Beautiful day," said Mary.

"The weekend's going to rain again," Drew said. "Those people haven't had much luck with their weekends."

"You know, I haven't seen them once," said Mary.

"Well, here's a hint," Drew said, putting a glint in his eye; he had been hoping he could surprise her like this with the information. "They're black. They called me up, so I had no idea when I said yes. Then they drove up to Leominster with a deposit, and I was as friendly as I would be to anyone because I know the kind of trouble they can get you in."

"Ah, Drew," said Mary, smiling up from her seat by the trailer door. She would have resembled a redneck welfare mom from Sewall if she only had a cigarette in her mouth and spoke worse. Her wool sweater full of holes and her hair pulled back in a ponytail and her milky freckly face made her look almost like the country girls of Drew's youth. "I'm sure they didn't suspect," she said.

"They come up weekends."

"I'll be on the lookout."

"You be nice to them, Mary. They're supposed to be your kind of people, aren't they? All I care is I get my rent check."

"How's Peggy doing?" Mary asked. She always changed the subject on him. Drew was hoping to get an argument going, but Mary seemed to know he could not resist telling her about his daughter.

"For one thing," he said, "she isn't divorced yet. It was in the works, and then they tell the lawyer to hold off. You hear from her?"

"Not since she moved out on her own."

"Hey, son," said Drew to silent Martin, "you tell me what you made of her. Do you guess she's got a screw loose?"

The kid had been sticking rows of pine needles in the sand. Drew knew he had problems. He must be twenty-six by now. "Mostly, she's lonely," he said. "You can't put the blame on her."

"She has no call to be lonely. I never saw a girl with so many friends. See, Mary, she's the extremely social type. She'd never want to live out here in the woods. A couple of weeks was enough for her. Of course, way back she was a kid here. I could've hoped it'd be in her blood." Drew felt sheepish admitting disappointment, but he knew Mary Lanaghan saw through him anyway, so he generally tried to ease up on his bluster around her. This year he had begun to approach her differently. In ways, it was more her cove than his. By now she had come to know it better; he only made it up about seven times a year. "Well, don't let those black people scare you," he said with a twinkle. "They seemed decent enough. You couldn't tell on the phone. I'll maybe go over and check on the place before they show up. Hey, son, Peggy told me you're heading out West. Then I might convince your mother to move this eyesore trailer up further in the woods. I like to keep the cove pristine. This is a sacred lake, remember? I told you about that, didn't I? You people are junking it up."

Martin was looking nervous, as if Drew was serious, but Mary knew him well enough. "Private property, Drew," she said and pointed to an orange ribbon around a tree: "That's your line right there."

Drew did a little hop and skip and landed on his own domain. He stuck out his forefinger at her and said, "You got me on that one," and Martin's face relaxed. Drew could remember him as a teenager, the same lost slow look about him. He probably took the divorce the hardest. Drew could not feel total disdain for the kid because the world was full of his sort now. There was not much they had to do or many places they wanted to go. They belonged to the great anonymity. Plastic chairs, Drew thought, aluminum combination screen doors, Toyotas . . .

As he turned, Mary called after him, "Have fun snooping, Drew."

"That's me, the old snoop," he called back, making his way along the water's edge till the cottage came into view. It sat on its sandy hillock, on its carpet of pine needles, shaded mightily from way above but, at ground level, attended only by bare solid tree trunks, a restful situation. Drew paused and waited awhile. Nothing stirred. The old life of the house was suspended in his memory, filling it invisibly full, and these blacks would be moving about inside like mere shadows, permeating, passing through the old white woman scrubbing pots and pans at the sink, the old white man stoking the potbelly stove, the little scruffy boy playing red, white, and blue tiddlywinks on the musty green-gray rug, itself a magic forest of patterns he would remember perfectly even into his sixties.

The big decision had been long in coming, years really. Elizabeth would have nothing to say on the subject. It was his house, his whole life; she had only aspired to get beyond it, to a tidy house in Leominster. Peggy would have nothing to say. There was something too sad about the place for her now, the sadness of her separation, of what Drew felt was her last hope of rescue even if she did not see it that way. The Lanaghan kid, he had been some strange sort of melancholy companion for her in those weeks, but she had left melancholy behind now. She would not return here.

Drew had discussed his decision with Albert Thibault, who had cut all cords himself, vehemently, though he could not dislodge Charles and Louise. Albert spoke of Florida as his refuge from years of battling cold and rust and rot. He did not miss Umbachaug, only his kiddies. But Drew would miss Umbachaug. He would miss this sight. He felt suddenly like a spy, nestled in a blueberry bush, veiled by a bough of hemlock. He was only glimpsing the place. A few swipes of a bulldozer would knock it to kindling. It was already a memory.

He put out a foot, then another, and found himself walking up the sandy slope into the clearing, touching each tree trunk he passed. He had forgotten Mary and her son a hundred yards behind. He had also forgotten Mr. and Mrs. Pingree, who would be driving up from Worcester. Drew was telling himself that he must spend one more night here, when the leaves had turned and fallen, before the cove froze over, with a wood fire, with all the ancient quilts piled high on top of him, and he would stay up late and reread, perhaps, *Drums Along the Mohawk* from the high shelf and hear the familiar creaks and moans the wind drew from the house, smell the moldering, the wood smells, the dead mouse under the floor. It would be enough.

He peered in at a window. Nothing was out of place, but there was a huge blue-green beach ball resting on the dining table. He had never seen it before. A black man's idea of what you brought to a lake? It was hardly even official summer anymore. There it sat like the globe of the earth, placid, at rest, having spun its last.

Drew moved on. He did not need to go in. He was even privately embarrassed he had come up at all. Perhaps, his decision had required it, one more look before he could make it. The place had been haunting him ever since Peggy had left — well, ever since he had got those Serbo-Croats in and moved her out. The place had haunted him.

He walked back slowly along the road and was just as glad not to find Mary Lanaghan at her house, only the half-dead dog asleep on the balcony. He got in his Chevy and headed out. Halfway down the cove road, he came up against a sort of big Jeep stopped in the middle of his right of way. New Hampshire license. Two kids were smooching in the front seat, so Drew let out a blast of his horn, scared the pants off them. The boy hurried to wheel onto the shoulder and waved apologetically as Drew barreled past. He needed to get back to Elizabeth.

IV

MARTIN DID NOT KNOW what to do after his mother strolled up the path and left him by the cove with the miniature forest he had constructed of pine needles. Their argument was over; Drew Hale's visit had broken it off. When he was gone, Mom had begun reminiscing about crotchety old Drew ten years ago and how Bayard had followed him around that first summer and how sad he got when Drew moved his gun shop to Leominster and turned the boathouse into another rental. She remembered when that policeman Ray Berrouet first moved in and what a shine Rosa took to him, though he never knew it and she denied it now, remembered Mr. and Mrs. Hale in the cottage two weeks each spring and all their many renters, remembered the cottage boarded up November to May. She talked of the winters past, the kids shivering at the school bus stop after their long snowy walk down the road before Bryce Murtagh's house or anything else had gone up there, Shirley always bounding ahead. Did Martin remember? He tried to sound nostalgic, too, to make up for having been mad at her all week. He reminded himself that the dream Mom had once dreamed for her life had proved a phantasm: without much thought, his father had gone and had sex with someone from his firm named Enid Perlman. It was strange to Martin that he, the son, must have spent a great deal more time thinking about what his father had done to his mother than his father had himself. Now he was training himself not to think about it so much, not to think much about the past at all. He was not even thinking of Astrid or Rachel anymore; he was hardly thinking of Peggy Hale. He was trying to think only of his future in New Mexico. But when he thought of Suzanne, he feared how it would be to meet her at last because, as he had warned her once more in his latest e-mail, he would not be at all what she expected him to be. And she would be, in the flesh, more — he knew — than he could ever now imagine. So when Mom left and went up to the house and Martin was stuck thinking of where he was about to go and not wanting to think of his past anymore, not even of the sad quiet summer he had had, loafing about and aimless, he did not know what to do at all. He had been poking pine needles in the sand merely for something to focus on while they talked; his hands were nervous that way. Now he stared at the delicate landscape he had made. He could mow it down with one swipe of his foot, but he could not decide to do even that. If only Mom had stayed and kept talking, and if he had kept sticking the endless supply of needles into the ground —

There was one voice he could get to speak to him. He stepped up into the trailer, pushed a few buttons, and Elmer Fudd said, "You have mail." Every day, Martin waited till the moment when he most needed to hear from Suzanne, and then he checked. It was like saving the bite with the thickest frosting for last.

It turned out he had two letters, the first from his father. Subject: Money Matters.

> Martin: I've decided to get you a credit card, at least for now. You can't be setting yourself up in Santa Fe on traveler's checks. You'll need a lot of things for starters. I know you'll use it wisely and fairly, and once you're on your feet you can get one in your own name. Bayard got his Ireland trip and I'm getting Shirley a used car when she graduates, so I think it's fair. Your mother approves. I'll go over it in Boston with you before you leave. We should also talk about trading in for a laptop, don't you think? Or are you planning to carry the old clunker on the plane?
>
> Love, Dad

Martin read it through a second time to hear his father's voice in his head. He was glad, of course, relieved, eased, but it had also turned him somehow softer inside, so he went right away to the next letter. Subject: Me and You.

Dear New Martin!

It's true you are "new" already. When I came out here from Emporia I discovered I had already become new or I wouldn't have done it. Our bodies know things ahead of us. I know you think it will be our dry sun and our vistas and the sudden storms that rush passed that will make you new. But it is mostly time and time happens everywhere. This place is only a sign of the change in you. I could have gone east and found mine in your ancient lake as well as here. I could have found it in Emporia. All we need is to close our eyes and look within. Your landscape within is as vast as my desert. The "me" you will meet and the "you" I will meet have met already. When our skins finally touch they will recognize one another. Never fear.

Suzanne

Martin's worried letter the night before had tried to get beyond this sort of philosophizing to the specifics: his hair was not as long as she was picturing it, his skin not nearly as dark; he was shyer than he seemed in letters; all their talk about books and music had been real, had been honest, but even so, he confessed, he had written her less about the science fiction he loved and more about fantasy, which he was only just getting into; he had undersold his They Might Be Giants side, his Tom Waits side, his irreverent, alternative, maybe even cynical side and tried to open himself more, to let her lead him. Their first link, the Peter Gabriel news group, which he had approached from rock and she from world music, that link had led him to discover the Musicians of the Nile and Rossy's Madagascan pop and Deep Forest with its real pygmies, and on to the throat singers of Tuva and Hector Zazou and R. Carlos Nakai — he had listed them faithfully. But, he also admitted, he still played the Cramps and Siouxsie and the Banshees, and he had a soft spot for goofy Jonathan Richman and the Modern Lovers, whose songs Louise Thibault used to kid him for liking. What had Suzanne made of his confession? Her letter referred to none of it.

Martin sat back and stared at the words glowing at him. "The 'you' I will meet . . ." Did he have an idea who this "you" was that she saw him as? Did the parts make sense together? Maybe, he liked everything — anything. He had no specialties like Bayard, who had moved away from rock and was only serious about classic jazz and German chamber music, indifferent to the CDs Martin spent money on. Suzanne had not put in a word for Tom Waits, or the *Dune* trilogy; she had only said she and he had already met but their skins had not yet touched. Was that bullshit? Martin wondered, honestly, in his most private thought. Quickly, he went into his saved mail and found the more forthcoming Suzanne, the easygoing confidante of his last seven months.

> . . . off on a trail ride so I want to finish my chapter about the 8th Mystery. She has to learn how the Great Spirit can call up sudden rain from the dry earth . . .

No, somewhere else.

> . . . I agree with you about Enya. I didn't use to give her a chance because she seemed so Top 40, the Orinoco Flow song. Of course I liked it but you know, it's smooth, right? But in her Gaelic tracks yes, I'm beginning to go with it. Thank you for giving her to me again. Maybe now that you're coming we'll . . .

Martin signed off. He was too nervous. When the screen saver came up, it was in its sunset phase, the light fading gradually until stars came out. He was already putting on his sneakers. He had to move.

Outside, sparkling Umbachaug caused him to squint. He

began walking, not toward the house but picking his way awkwardly between blueberry bushes and dying ferns until he was well down the shore. He had the sudden idea to circle the cove, go all the way to the public landing on the main lake, then out the path to the piney point, where he would take off his sneakers, toss them across, and — why not, Rosa and Nat had gone in that morning — swim over to the day camp land and make his way through the woods to the railroad bed and then back to the loop in the road and to his mother's back door. He had never taken such a walk. Martin had not been interested in exploring the land about him. Perhaps, Drew Hale had scared him off it from the start with his quizzes about geology and history, perhaps Bayard had laid too strong a claim to it. Now, aside from the occasional walk with Hilda and Mom, Martin stuck to the small clearing where his trailer sat. And soon he would be in immense New Mexico.

Again, he was too nervous to think anything at all further. When he came to the marshy lower end of the cove, he had to veer away from the water and head up among a stand of pines. Something flashed in his right eye. It was a second-story window on Bryce Murtagh's house, which sat in the middle of its unnatural square of lawn right there through the trees. Martin stopped still. The rear of the house was even uglier than what faced the road. There was a broad deck on spindly uprights and a huge gas grill that looked like something in *Apollo 13*. Those first-floor plate-glass sliders had their curtains closed. Only that one bedroom window on the corner upstairs had its curtain pulled open. Martin stared at it. He wrapped his elbow around a tree trunk and stood leaning, staring. Mom was at her house, Bryce was off at work; they were not inside. Nor were the children who had once lived there. Nor the wife.

Martin had no idea what the house made him want to do, but he felt its one eye staring back at him and, for ten minutes, could not budge.

When he finally did, he found he had given up the idea of circling the cove. He turned away from the ugly sight and threaded his way through the pines to the road so he could walk more comfortably back to the trailer for a nap.

V

CHARLES HAD BEEN UP and stomping around the house ever since Louise got back from Mrs. Germaine's. The old lady was full of her usual gibberish today, convinced that Campbell's Healthy Request soups were the answer. The convenient mart did not stock them, so Louise had to go to the Grand Union in North Haviland, which did allow her to check out some goodies she was not accustomed to, including the chocolate-and-cream-cheese bundt cake she brought home for her brother's wake-up snack.

Now he was doing something in his room. It sounded like putting up a shelf. He would hammer a few times and then say, "Oh shit," and then saw on something. Louise had cleaned up after his coffee and cake and was trying to figure what to make for dinner that would do for Charles and also for leftovers when Dave Paasivirta came by later. She would make a meat loaf, she decided, and pulled out the family pack of three ground meats she should have cooked up yesterday because it was on the verge of going bad, but that was what Worcestershire sauce was for, she told herself, and that jar of herb mix.

Louise could always dig her fingers into ground meat and feel calmer. Mushing the pork in with the beef and the lamb in with the pork, and vice versa, was a slow delightful process. She stared out the little window and noticed the maple in the low spot behind the house was beginning to turn. This meat loaf making was better than the meditation technique they tried to teach her in class. She had not been going so regularly lately and had begun to doubt if she would sign up for the final session. Her heart was not in it so much anymore. Even Mrs. Germaine was cheerier than the case studies they had, the hospital visits, the house calls. Her classmates, by now, had become so confident and what she would call chipper, Louise decided. They had developed that way the teachers kept talking about of looking you in the eye. It did not come naturally to Louise; she would rather shuffle around off to one side. And the inner calm she was supposed to be cultivating was hard to stick with. She would get it for a bit, and then some elder would start coughing up and hacking and be waving their arms like a crazy person and Louise would get jittery inside and have to sit down and let another student take over. Felicia Torbone was great at it. She could soothe the brow of any old codger that came her way. She seemed full of love for them all, and it was real. Louise admitted she herself could sometimes care less.

After she had mixed in the garlic croutons, she got the larger loaf pan and lovingly patted in the meat, layer by layer, with sprinkles of Worcestershire in between. Cooking did her good. Death and dying was more than she had imagined it would be. She had hoped that kind of work would make her happy, give her something, like her poppa's work with cars. But it was clear to her now. These stages they taught her were not about keeping things going but about letting them go. Felicia Torbone was like the

Angel of Death swooping about, but serene and accepting, as they said in class. She had been the biggest slut back in high school, Louise remembered. When Felicia was a senior she was having intercourse with tenth-grade boys and even after she graduated, too. But she had got religion since. It was freaky to see her so steady and concerned now. To her, death was no big hairy deal, just the next beautiful stage.

When the meat loaf joined the potatoes in the oven and its aroma began to fill the kitchen and Charles started hammering again and cursing, Louise turned to fixing the salad with more croutons from the box and loads of creamy Italian the way Charles preferred. Then she got out the butter and sour cream and set a dinner plate down on the blue-and-white-checked oilcloth. She would wait to eat when Dave got there, but she could snack some with Charles, so she put a plate out for herself on the counter, then went into her own room to freshen up. Ricki Lake was on with her usual contingent of overweight black people hollering at each other. Louise scarcely paid attention anymore.

She sat down on the edge of her bed, then decided she could use a brief lie-down, having been on her feet all afternoon. She did not like to nap in daylight because it made her feel like Mrs. Germaine, lying there in her clothes, waiting for something. Mrs. Germaine did not appear to be moving through any stages. She was stuck in the chatty confused stage. Maybe she was a mite feebler, but Louise could hardly tell. Every day she seemed mostly as she was the day before. Actually, that made Louise feel better. She no longer looked for spiritual messages in what the old lady said because all she got were the same stories over again: "I have lived in this house for more than sixty years, Louise, since I married Mr. Germaine in nineteen thirty-four," she had said for the seventeenth time this month. "We never had children, thank the good Lord. It's all mine!" "You must have got lonesome rattling around in this big house by yourself, though," Louise said. "Oh, I don't know what lonesome is," came the reply. It was one of her usual lines. "I don't know what absentminded is," she had said last week when Louise wondered wherever she had mislaid the hairbrush.

So as not to waste her thoughts on Mrs. Germaine, Louise lay there and thought instead of skinny Dave. This was the bed they fooled around on. Louise would lie back and Dave would get naked and bony and climb up and have his way, as he put it. It was not too bad. It sent little thrills through Louise and even occasionally something deeper when it hit her just right. Mostly, she liked watching him at it. He got so red on his back and across his pimply shoulders, all heated and sweaty. Charles suspected what might be going on, but he never said more than "Was your gentleman over last night?"

"So get real no way am I puttin' out for no jive turkey," said the television. Louise was drifting off, and it took Charles pounding on her door to wake her up.

"I'd say it's about dinnertime," he yelled.

"Hold your horses," said Louise.

She found him down the hall in the kitchen, dressed for work, knife and fork in hand. This was one of his favorite meals. "I can smell it all over the house," he said. "Got the grated Parm?"

Louise nibbled up at the counter while he hurried on toward seconds. "What was all that hammering?" she asked him.

"Knickknack shelf," he said between bites. "It kept going lopsided on me . . . I want to get all the souvenir mugs

Momma sent . . . and make a nice display of Grandmère's frog figurines . . . and my marble statuettes . . . Varnish it first."

"Maybe we should see if Mr. Hale would help fix up the attic this fall," Louise proposed.

"We should've had Poppa ask. But, you know, Mr. Hale's too old for that kind of work now. Say, how about your pal Dave? He's sort of a carpenter."

"He's going to Idaho."

"He's not going to Idaho," said Charles, fork in air. "He just dreams he's going to Idaho. These potatoes will get back to Idaho before he ever gets to Idaho. Or are these Maines?" Charles asked, looking at his forkful.

"He's saving up," said Louise.

"He's not saving up. Not with that wife he ain't."

"She isn't going."

"Yeah, but she spends every penny he makes, sis. You should see her at the mart loading up. And the lottery tickets she buys! Hey, she'll run out on him first. Dave's a loser, get used to it."

"Well," Louise said, "I'd just as soon he stuck around."

"I bet you would," said Charles, scraping at his plate.

So she went to serve him up seconds. "Aw, what do you know, bigmouth?" she said. "Just save me and Dave a little supper, if you please."

"Heap it on me," Charles was saying.

The two of them got along, she had to admit. For most brothers and sisters, living together would get nasty, but they had a lot of fun with each other. He perked her up when she had too much of terminal home care. She made him nice meals. Mostly, they had their own rooms and she did not have to look at his mess. She bet his knickknack shelf was a disaster with sawdust all over the bedclothes and holes in the wall. That room! Louise knew he had a stash of swingers' club magazines under his mattress, and sometimes he got weird letters with what felt like photos inside.

When his plate was clean again, Charles asked for one more slice of bundt cake to top off the meal and then went into the bathroom, leaving her to clean up and set the table for two. Charles was gone to work and it was nearly dark by the time Dave showed up. Louise stepped outside when she heard his pickup and saw the evening star, or some bright star anyway, up above the apartments across the road.

"Hi, Corncrib," Dave said. The white paint splotches all over his jeans shone in the twilight.

"Hi, Stick." She always called him some variation of skinny — Bone, String, Pole. He was six-foot-three and had pocky skin, which made him feel bad about his looks.

She let Dave go into her room ahead of her and get himself settled. She had already drawn the shades and lit the one lamp on her grandmother's bureau. Usually, they started off in there and ate afterwards.

VI

WHEN HE FOUND HER at his door, Ron asked Mary Lanaghan if she had seen the black people over in the cottage. He saw them sitting on the screened porch when he was charging along in just his URHS shorts. "They looked at me like who are you, fella?" Ron told her.

"They came up for peace and quiet," said Mary, stepping inside.

"I'm peaceful, I'm quiet," Ron said. But he admitted he had been singing along to the Artist Formerly Known as Prince, and Mary pointed out that he did not know how loud he was when he had earphones on. "I don't know what you're hearing in your head," she said, "but it sure sounds odd on its own."

Ron pretended to wince and grabbed the remote to mute *Entertainment Tonight.* Anyone else and he would have turned the sound up, but Mary came over so seldom, and it was clear she had something on her mind. Victor was closing up at the diner with Kevin, and Ron had already done his workout and shower and now was tidy in clean white sweats. He spied the bowl of carrots and pretzels on the coffee table from last night's TV time, so he left the cheese sticks in the fridge, took a protein shake for himself, and handed Mary a Rolling Rock whether she wanted it or not. She took the cold can in both hands and settled back on the couch. She did not look as happy as last week when she had heard about her job. Ron knew he would have to do some pep-talking.

She was gazing around his place as if she had never seen it before. It was dark and cluttered compared with hers; it was carpeted. He knew Mary liked bare floors and frayed old rugs and real paintings on the walls, not three years of Bruce Weber calendars and the framed glossy autographed photo of Ron's ideal physical specimen, Mark Wahlberg.

"Rosa gone back up north with the lumberjack?" he asked.

"I thought Martin should have an evening alone with her. I probably should've asked Nat to walk over here with me," Mary said. She did not look at all happy.

"Nah," said Ron, plopping beside her as close as if she were Victor, and stretched his arm tight around her shoulders so she could feel all the strength of that bicep bracing her. With her sad face, she put him in mind of Sarah, his oldest sister, the one who left town with a motorcycle gang and scared the rest of his sisters into staying home forever. Ron had been ten. Sarah had never made much time for him. Her biker friends used to call him Babydoll and one had even asked him for a blow job. Before Sarah left, she was sitting on their front porch in the dark playing the radio so loud no one would hear her sobbing. Ron had snuck out and given her a squeeze, and she had let him hug her right through the Supremes singing "Reflections." Mary Lanaghan was not crying and Ron was so much stronger than when he was a wimpy kid, but it all came back to him. He must have wanted to have this much strength to comfort Sarah. Soon after, she had gone and got lost in California. She would be almost Mary's age now.

When Ron looked at Mary, her eyes were glistening in the TV light. *E.T.* was running a report on Heather Locklear he did not mind missing. "When someone hugs me lately, I feel like I'm going to cry," Mary said, dabbing one little finger at the four corners of her eyes.

Ron watched her closely. He thought she was beautiful. She had swirled her hair up in a pile held by a tortoiseshell comb; how that worked he did not know. Her delicate eyelids kept blinking so no tear would escape.

"In a week Martin goes off and you're on your job," Ron said. "It's a transition time, Mary." She nodded. Transition was a big concept in his group at the hospital. Ron had decided to start by doing some talking himself, to ease her up. "It's okay," he said, "I'll look in on the dog, and the weather's changing so she'll sleep a lot. It'll go great."

"Martin's mad at me," Mary said.

Ron could have predicted that. The kid was a self-centered little prick. "That's what mothers are for," he said. "I'm set to kill mine. But you got off easy because your kids are basically pro-Mom."

He could tell the talk and the hug were helping. Peggy and Stewart dumped their troubles on Ron, his pal Eddie was forever bitching about life, and Kevin was such a whiner. Victor was the only other one who mostly kept it to himself. For all Ron loved to meddle, he knew that was the reason they stuck together. And because Mary Lanaghan was also reluctant to let him help, he had come to love her as well.

"I failed Martin this summer," she said. "I got tired of him and his helplessness. He could tell. It hurt his feelings. I keep trying to make up for it. I thought I wanted him to come home, I was going to insist he get a job, but I didn't do anything. And I didn't push therapy. I got tired, not of him but his helplessness or whatever you'd call it."

"You have a right," said Ron.

"When Christina was here it was better. He was happier with the old neighbors around."

Ron wanted to tell her, the way he did in group, that it was not so bad making people mad; he was used to it, he almost liked it. But now he kept listening.

"He's going to go out to New Mexico and come to another halt. Everywhere he goes it happens. He can't stand his boss, or someone thinks he's weird. He's always got an excuse so it's not his fault. When he was in Northampton, he caught a kid shoplifting and the record store owner defended the kid — that's what Martin says. Martin wasn't handling it right, so the boss got mad at Martin; the kid said he meant to pay, he was just holding the CD under his coat. Martin quits jobs in a moral outrage, and then he's lost again. Why does it keep happening?"

Ron had no answer. "The point is, Mary, he's a grown-up," he said, the sort of thing they said in group. "This summer it was good you let him be. Look, you've your own thing going now, you've got Bryce down the road." This was the subject Ron had more to say on. He intended to get her talking about her love life, instead.

Mary loosed herself from his arm and sat up. Finally, she took a sip of beer. There was the Joe Isuzu commercial that Ron knew by heart silent on the TV. "I think I'm letting Bryce fade, Ron," Mary said in a voice he could barely hear, even without the sound on. She stared at the TV awhile, but blankly, as if she saw nothing.

"I'll bet it's his wife and kids, and you don't want to get your hopes up," he said because Mary had not said anything else yet.

"Bryce is a sweet man," she said. "There's no reason not to keep going. I tried thinking of how *you* would handle it, Ron — well, I mean, to a point, but —" She was rotating the green can between her fingers, round and round, and shook her head in the perplexed way Ron expected when anyone referred to his behavior.

Then, looking more closely, he realized that with Mary it was not quite the same. Straight people thought two men together or two women was weird, yet they kept complaining about the differences between men and women like it was some big gyp. But Mary felt worse about herself than other women because she did *not* know how to blame it all on men. If she found something lacking in Bryce, she would never say it was because he was a man. She did not understand yet that men tended to lack things.

"But you've been going along easy enough, Mary, haven't you?" Ron asked.

"We sit around and watch TV in our underwear. We have good sex. Am I expecting too much?"

"Nothing like good sex for a relationship," said Ron. "And some extra on the side, too," he added to keep it light.

"Nevertheless, it's fading," Mary said. "You don't realize the value of what you and Victor have. You two know each other. You've known each other so long. How can I find someone to know that well at this stage of my life?"

"Being straight sure must be aggravating," Ron said. "You screw three people and think you've seen what's out there." Mary smiled and sank back, rubbing her neck against Ron's arm. "Martin will be glad you're dumping Bryce," he said.

"I'm not dumping him."

"You hoping he dumps you?"

"We're going along as we have been," she said. "I don't know what else to do. It's that with Bryce it feels like I'm twenty-two and don't know enough to take it where it's going. I've had four kids and got them almost all through college, but I still don't know what I didn't know back then."

Ron got to thinking again, sitting there holding her. He was going to be godfather to his sister Alice's baby when it was born. After a dozen other nieces and nephews, someone finally had to ask him, or maybe it was only to spite their ma.

"Can we turn off the picture, too?" Mary asked. "I'm sorry, it keeps distracting me. I know it's your regular show . . ." Ron aimed and punched the power button. "I didn't mean to insist."

"Mary, don't be so unpushy. After all, you're the mom."

"I know. I'm the mom. It's sunk in finally. Maybe because of seeing Dermot here."

This was something Ron had not heard from her before, and it had popped out as if it did not count for much. "Hey, face it, you won," he said.

"I probably won long ago and didn't realize," Mary said. "I had to hide out here for ten years. I used to think this whole thing was my personal collapse. But Dermot himself being out here in my world," she said softly, "and the way Shirley and Martin tried to take care of him and make him feel part of their lives —" She started going teary again.

Ron tightened his hold and reached farther around and down her slim arm, which was all goose bumps. "Hey, girl," he said.

She did begin to cry in short choking gulps. Ron had been hoping for it. Mary could not have been sitting beside him all this time talking the way she was and not have needed to cry. Victor would have held it in, of course, but then he would have said, "Let's go downstairs and get naked," which, Ron sometimes thought, was Victor's own way of crying.

"It was so sad for Dermot," Mary was trying to say, but her sobs caught up the words so she had to try several times to get them out.

"You're weird, Mary," Ron said after a while, "crying on behalf of that Dermot Lanaghan. You don't fit my picture of a normal human being."

"You don't fit my picture either, so there," Mary said.

He passed her a carrot. No? Then a pretzel. She took it. She had scrunched the beer can down between the couch pillows.

"Shouldn't Victor be home?"

"Eight-thirty is when I start getting suspicious," Ron said, looking at the cuckoo clock Mr. Zart had given the Bardonecchias for their twenty-fifth anniversary. "It's only eight. You stick around and watch a video with us."

Ron stood up and got himself a beer this time and asked if Mary wanted a cold one. She shook her head. He thought he heard, in this evening silence he was unaccustomed to, a radio playing Motown. When he was little, there was always something black on a station from Worcester. His father had adopted that music to bug the neighbors. All the Finns in Sewall tuned in inspirational programs, and the Baptists and Catholics listened to country, but the Starkses were Episcopalians, and so they had to distinguish themselves. And even if they sat in the last pews of their church so as not to crowd the Quidnapunxet River families, they had been going to Saint George's long before most of those transplants, and their name was on more tombstones in the churchyard than any other name in Sewall. Ron was proud of that, though he did not think much of religion itself. He did look forward to being a godfather, however, to taking on some responsibility for a kid, just not too much.

"Hey, what happened to that rich boyfriend of yours, what's his name?" Ron asked.

"Ara?"

"He goes to our church, you know, but Aunt Ellie says he wasn't born into it like us."

"It was his recommendation that got me my job," Mary said. "I feel guilty about that."

"Mary," Ron said, "because a rich guy helps you out doesn't mean you have to let him fuck you."

"Ron Starks!"

"Well, I probably would, but that's because I'd be into it."

"Explain one simple thing, Ron," Mary said. He had obviously cheered her up. "How do you and Victor ever work it out when you can be so bad?"

VII

NAT MADE THE FIRE in a ring of stones he arranged on a sandy patch behind the trailer. For seats, he pulled three heavy pine logs out of Drew Hale's woods. He broiled the Greek sausage Mrs. Speradakis had sent along from Portsmouth, and the three of them nearly finished off the two six-packs of Sam Adams they had picked up that afternoon. Rosa had never before known her brother to drink more than one bottle. She was glad to see him loosening up, but by his fourth she began to worry even though it made her mad to worry over Martin. She was slightly drunk herself by then, so it took a while to remember she no longer had such cause for resentment: she and Nat were going to be all right after all. She had not felt this safely rooted since her flute-playing days before her parents broke up.

Rosa wished she had her flute now. Would she remember the fingerings? She could sit in those darkening woods by the fire with her boyfriend and her brother and play something by Handel, and it would feel truly serene at last, not nervous the way it had with her dad across the living room noting each flub with an almost undetectable grimace.

Nat was telling him about the canoe trip they had led on the Allagash, about the moose wading in Lake Chesuncook, and their climb up Katahdin and how much quicker you got drunk after coming down off a mountain, and Martin was telling him about an ancient Spanish church in the desert where crippled people hung up their crutches after sitting in a sacred mud bath. Neither one was listening to the other, just trading airspace. Nat had retold their canoe trip stories to his parents, to her dad, and to her mom, so Rosa hardly had to pay attention, and Martin's New Mexico lore was nothing but more Suzanne obsession. Now that her brother was finally doing what Rosa had recommended, she had developed doubts, but he was not setting out adventurously on any old bus west, leaving e-mail and Windows 95 behind; he had a plane ticket. As usual, the parents had stepped in. It was not worth arguing over. I'll leave all of them be, she told herself, and keep my secret to myself so they will not try to make me adjust it.

Martin declared he had to pee. He staggered when he got up and crossed Drew Hale's property line into the trees. Faint music was coming from the cottage, a nice slow bass line.

"He's plastered," Nat said. They could hear him pissing against a tree. "I'm not sure how he's doing, Rosa. Don't give him that last one."

"I got it. It's mine," she said, but she opened it and then decided not to take a drink. "Want it?"

Nat reached over from his log-seat and took a long swallow, belched, and handed the bottle back. "Douse the fire with it," he said.

"Wait till he finds his way back."

Nat slipped over to her log and gave her cheek a kiss, then returned to his own log, toppled backward, and had trouble pulling himself up to a sit. "Beer's good for him," he said, laughing. "Hey, you want me to let you guys talk?"

Rosa shook her head. A year ago she would have expected Nat to sneak back to the house, but her loyalties had shifted. Martin himself had shifted, she perceived as he reemerged from darkness into the red glow of the embers. He was not protecting his body as much. He used to walk as if he might get kicked — or merely touched — in the chest, in the groin; he used to hold his arms ready to block an approach and hunched slightly to obscure his midsection, which now stood there, open.

He lowered himself to the third log. "It's been strange with Mom," he said. Nat shot a glance at Rosa, who was aware of her own eyes widening. "She and I steered pretty clear of each other all summer," Martin went on, louder than usual. "Rosa, you said this was going to be major regression. You thought Mom and I were going to hang out. You said it would be a grave mistake, quote, unquote."

"I'm glad to be wrong," said Rosa.

"Shirley wanted to hang out with her a lot more than I did. Shirley was hoping for some mom-daughter bonding this summer. Her last real home summer. And what does Mom do? It was so unfair. Can you believe this summer we actually had more fun with Dad than Mom?"

"Oh, come off it, Martin," Nat said, "no one has more fun with your father — we just visited him."

Martin looked hard at Nat. The oddness of it made Rosa realize how he seldom looked at Nat at all.

"Shirley got a raw deal," Martin began again. "She was working days at the diner, and at night where was Mom?"

"Let me ask you a question, Martin," said Nat. Rosa was wishing she had sent him back to the house. He never entered family arguments, which was why everyone thought he was so nice; they never saw him difficult the way Rosa did. She looked into the glowing coals and hoped it would not get awkward. But what Nat said was: "Would you like another beer?" Martin looked up. "There it is. Rosa can't finish it."

"Wait a second," Rosa said and took a quick gulp from the bottle by her foot. "He's had his four." And she glared at Nat.

"Oh, give it to him. He's not ready yet to tell us what's on his mind."

"Nat, why are you being such an asshole?" Rosa said, clutching the bottle.

"I've had exactly four," Martin said.

Nat kept gesturing to Rosa to pass Martin her bottle. Nat could act so arbitrary. But she handed it over, half empty, to Martin, who took it and shrugged but did not take a sip as yet. He sat with his elbows on his knees and swung the bottle between thumbs and forefingers, up and down in the soft firelight. Nat chuckled and made the hoot he made when coming through the woods to their cabin up north.

"All right," said Martin, "you're an owl, Speradakis."

"Drink up," said Nat. Martin shrugged again.

Maybe Nat had a plan in mind, but maybe he was drunk. Rosa felt pretty drunk. She wanted to get something out of her brother, too, but she did not know what it was. The way he sat there now, he looked like one of the guys for once, swinging the beer bottle up and down. Peggy Hale had taught Martin something; Rosa could see it in all his limbs. He raised the bottle to his mouth. Nat gave his owl hoot again. The electronic bass was thumping nice and sweet through the trees. Suddenly, Rosa felt they were safe, leaning close in around the little ring of fire on three old logs in the bugless cool woods of September. Alcohol had a way of shifting the mood. If it was dangerous that way, it could also be a blessing.

"I can't stay in the trailer once it's winter," Martin said. "And I don't want to be back in Newton."

"'Cause it's too much fun being with Dad," said Nat.

"Asshole," said Rosa.

"All right, so don't go back to Newton," Nat said.

"Or Northampton. I want to be where no one knows what my life was like."

"Excellent choice," said Nat.

"But Suzanne knows you inside out, I thought." Rosa had not stopped herself from saying it despite her mellow frame of mind.

"Suzanne believes in quests," Martin told Nat. "Past doesn't mean anything to her."

"Sweet," said Nat, who hated New Age bullshit; he must be drunk, Rosa thought.

Martin started in again about New Mexico and the sacred healing mud bath and those dozens of crutches hanging on the wall, but this time Nat looked like he was actually interested; he even said "Cool!" occasionally.

Rosa was only attentive to the way her brother's voice seemed now to mirror the bass line in the distance, rising in pitch when the other went lowest and one step behind the beat. Everything was mesmerizing her, these sounds, the fierce embers, the white pine branches gently brushing at the air.

"Healing is a matter of faith," Martin was saying, and Rosa began to listen again. "I don't mean religious," he said. "It's not broken limbs I'm talking about, it's everything else. The problem with Mom is she's never healed. She lost her religious faith before we were born but didn't get any other. She thought she had family faith, maybe. Then she lost that. Our parents never gave us the religion they grew up with. They didn't want us having to deal with it. There's lots of fallen-away Catholics out there like them, I promise you. But what they have is bad residue, none of the beauty. That's our parents, you've got to face it, Rosa. See, I want to go to that little church in New Mexico and feel something. Suzanne felt it, and she's brought up Methodist. But I'm not talking about religion. A mud bath in a dry desert. Isn't that all you need to feel it?"

"You're drunk," said Nat.

Good, thought Rosa, Nat's not getting too suckered.

"You don't care about spiritual things," Martin said. "Neither does my sister. That sister there. The other one, Shirley, has her spiritual side. Rosa and my fucking brother are secular people. That's why everyone thinks they're so normal."

"Who thinks I'm normal?" asked Rosa.

"My problem is I keep coming across the wrong types," Martin went on, but Nat interrupted him.

"Hey, let's go see where that music's coming from," he said.

"It's coming from there," Martin pointed slowly, full of memory, Rosa could tell.

"It's just the renters," she said.

"Not those diner guys?" Nat asked.

"No, the cottage, get it, the cottage."

"Who's having the party?"

Martin looked at Nat. "They're black people," he said. "Drew Hale rented to them by mistake." And he laughed.

"It's a radio," said Rosa.

"Let's go see," Nat said.

Martin belted the rest of his beer and stood up, swaying to one side. This could be bad, Rosa thought. "Hey, let's go back in the trailer and have ice cream," she said.

"Let's go see what they're doing," Nat said.

"Come on, Nat, you're being an asshole."

"Do the owl, Speradakis," Martin said. Nat had trouble doing it. "No, do the owl, the real owl."

"I can do the loon, that'll scare 'em."

"We're not scaring the renters," Rosa said.

"They're blasting their fucking radio," Martin said.

"They're not blasting it. You blast *your* music, Martin. This is not blasting."

"It's not because they're black, Rosa," Nat said.

"I know it's not because they're black."

"There were those guys last year who drove your mom crazy."

"They were a lot louder."

"I snuck over when Peggy Hale was living there," Martin said.

"I bet you did," said Rosa.

"All right, all right, enough. Come on." Nat had stumbled into the trees, and only the dark branches waving behind him marked his path. Martin was following, and Rosa did not know what to do. There was no beer left to douse the fire with. She heaped some sand on it, and then it was entirely dark except for the moon somewhere. She heard underbrush crackling. So she followed until in vague light she came upon two male shadows before her. They had stopped to wait. Now, the music had a slower beat, really mellow — lovemaking music, Rosa thought.

"We have to be dead quiet," Nat said.

"What's the point?" she asked.

"To get close."

"Why?"

"Fuck. Shut up. Come on."

But Nat tripped on something and fell and started giggling, and Martin was giggling, too. Rosa shushed them. It was not funny. It could only get embarrassing. Mom would be upset. She used to be upset when Rosa would merely walk by the boathouse hoping to bump into Officer Berrouet when he lived there. She used to be upset over any intrusion on people's privacy. Mom was the privatest person she had ever known.

Martin and Nat were creeping ahead of her, but they were much louder than they realized. Rosa was annoyed at

Nat for egging Martin on. Nat would never have done this sort of thing at the lodge. He was truly pissing her off. "Nat!" she called. From what she could see through the trees, there seemed to be two people dancing on the screened porch, a nice slow close dance. And there were Nat and Martin crouching ahead of her like lumbering bears. Rosa wanted to scream at them. She camouflaged herself against a tree and waited. Then the boys suddenly charged out into the clearing and darted down the road, kicking up gravel with their sneakers, and Rosa heard Nat's loon call in the distance.

The music stopped.

"I told you," the woman's voice said.

"It's possums," said the man.

"This isn't a safe place for us."

"It's possums." He was peeking out the screen.

"It's kids. I know it's kids," the woman said. "And who are we to call? What are we doing out in these woods in the first place?"

"It's our cabin," the man said.

"One weekend on the Vineyard would've been preferable," said his wife.

Rosa had to stand stock-still until they turned the radio back on. She was furious at Nat now. She no longer felt like sleeping next to him tonight. It always happened when they got close to setting a date: Nat acted like a shit.

Mom would forgive him, though. She would make an excuse and tell Rosa to forget it. As embarrassed as Mom might be, it would be Rosa she was mad at. That was the essence of it. Mom had so much wanted Rosa never to be angry at the man in her life. She had not approved when Rosa changed her name to Blakey. Oh no, she would never go back to Blakey herself. Her kids were Lanaghans, and so was she. By kids, of course, she meant the boys.

AN OCTOBER SATURDAY

I

THE MAPLES WERE giving up their leaves, and now the cove mirrored the yellow, red, and orange only in scattered patches. The lily pads in the shallow spots had gone limp and brown beside the stubs of their dead flowers. A gray sheen was on the deeper water; out to the piney point it was dead still. Bayard Lanaghan watched a bright leaf fall from its real tree to float among reflections.

He had come up for his birthday weekend. His mother had planned a dinner with the Ostermanns and Bryce, and she had suggested he bring a girlfriend, ideally one with a car, but he had not wanted to. For weeks, he had been cramming for Grad Recs and studying catalogs, filling out applications, and asking his old professors for letters; there was no time for going out. All the way up on the bus yesterday, he had skimmed the Colonial section of his American lit anthology; between Governor Bradford and Phillis Wheatley it was pretty much of a blur. His mother had picked him up in Leominster after her work.

Another leaf fell, bright onto the dimmer colors within the water. Bayard realized he had been staring stupidly. He shook his head hard so his hair flopped. Running out the railroad bed with Ron earlier that morning, he had begun feeling a little spacey. He was used to Ron calling him "gorgeous," and he had called Ron "studmuffin" back because Michael at the bookstore referred to the college boys as studmuffins and Bayard assumed it was standard gay terminology. But it must have sounded like he was flirting because Ron said, with a suggestive smirk, "Hey, you're looking eligible for a very special birthday treat, young man," and Bayard was not sure how to interpret that.

When they made it back to the boathouse, Ron had asked him in for some ice water and offered a shower. It was easy enough to say no thanks, but they had sat on the kitchen chairs, sweaty and still out of breath, and talked awhile. Ron poured himself a glass of a diet supplement he took to strengthen his immunes. He was not surprised that Bayard already knew he had tested positive. "Your mother's worried about the way you run around down in New Haven, fella," he said, "so I told her she should make sure you know it could happen to anyone so you'd be careful. Of course, there's no real risk if you're the one getting blown," he added with that smirk again. "And with a rubber, hey, you're safe fucking just about anything. It's the other party that ought to watch it."

"I'm totally safe," Bayard had said quickly. He worried his mom had been freaking about him more than he knew; she mentioned things so casually, he could hardly tell. "You know how lucky I am," Ron said. "I mean, for getting it so late. If I'd got it in the eighties, I'd be long gone. My doc says there's amazing new therapies coming up soon. So far, so good." He chugged his supplement then gave Bayard a close-up look. "So when are you gonna get serious about someone, babe?"

Bayard explained that now he was only thinking about grad school, after which all sorts of things would settle in his life. Ron kept his eyes on him, not aggressively, really, but enough to make him conscious of the scrutiny. It was the same way Bayard himself tended to look at women — eagerly, interestedly, but no heavy threat. "Besides," he said with a laugh, "neither of the new clerks at the bookstore where I work is particularly hot." It sounded like a sexist remark, but Ron just said, "You must be horny. Myself, I couldn't go for that long without." Then he changed the subject to the dock Drew Hale wanted him to help take up that afternoon. "On the phone I told him I'd do it, but the old bastard's got to come up and supervise. Hey, and check it out, your mom gave me the key to Martin's trailer if I needed a place to hang out sometimes on my own."

So there were no more innuendos about sex, except that after Ron said he had to shower and bike to work and Bayard said he had to go help his mom, Ron reminded him, offhand, that he was definitely still eligible for that special treat, and Bayard said something stupid like, "Wow, it must be my lucky day." It was just flirting — if anyone should know that, it was Bayard — and he did relax about it as he walked back to the house, but Mom was not quite ready to head to Old Fraddboro, where they had to pick up dinner stuff and then make sure the videos were set for Film Classics Night at Basswood, so he walked down the shore to the swimming spot and found he was not nearly as relaxed as he had thought; he stared out at the cove and watched the leaves falling.

The image of Ron blowing him kept imposing itself on the gray water out there. And then it blurred into some approximation of him fucking Ron, but he totally spaced on that one and focused again on the dead leaves drifting closer in to shore. This was messing with his birthday mood. He was here to visit Mom and Bryce and see the Ostermanns and let off the pressure he had been putting on. He had always liked Ron, he'd been pleased when Ron had caught up to him on his run, even the flirting was kind of a kick, but now it had followed him here. In all his sexual adventures, Bayard had never before had an older guy come on to him.

He blinked a few times to wake up, yawned, stretched, and wondered why he could not shake it out of his head completely. He tried considering the intellectual context. Homosexuality was definitely big in literary theory. Bayard had written his paper "Macho Kinkiness in Mailer and Hemingway" and discussed it late into the night with Shirley until she admitted he was pretty open-minded for an intimacy-impaired straight male. But he had never given the subject any thought in relation to himself. He was rather indifferent to men's bodies as such, though he was quite aware of his own, keeping it in shape, testing it out. Maybe it was the flattery. Women did not quite put it into words to his face, though he was excellent at making *them* feel admired because it was for real, he did admire them, and he managed to stay friends with most of them after he cooled off. He had more women friends than men. Did that mean he had missed something? He had certainly never gotten much admiration from his dad.

But there was a problem here, Bayard told himself. He definitely had no hang-up that it would make him gay, but he kept thinking over what Ron said about who was the one at risk. That meant Ron would be. Ron must have put himself at risk lots of times. Obviously. And it had finally caught him. What would it feel like to be with someone like that? Actually, something in it excited Bayard, not sexually, but some other way. It was that he, Bayard, would be the dangerous one, or acting like it. The whole encounter, in fact, would seem like an act. It would be all Bayard; Ron would not matter. Bayard could never treat a woman that way.

Well, he could ponder it. He did not have to do anything at all. And if he saw Ron later, he would let him joke some more, see where he took it. Bayard wondered if he could even keep a hard-on in a situation like that. When he woke up that morning, having turned twenty-three, he had no idea he would soon be obsessing over any such possibility. All right, so he would be sort of nervous all day. He could cope with that.

II

ERIC PFLUEGER HAD to make a personal inspection of the pasture across the road. There were fluorescent orange ribbons on stubby stakes marking off lot lines and driveways and six eventual foundations in a ragged semi-circle. Instead of clustering the houses and leaving some open land, they had to create useless strips of lawn good for nothing but mowing. Americans are so stupid, Eric thought.

He walked to the edge of the woods and turned to look back at the little gray house. All summer his dad had put off painting it. The threatened development must have disheartened him, but if he was going to sell, he would have to spruce it up first. Maybe, he preferred it to be a hovel now. It was hard to figure him out. Chucky was blatant, but his dad was mysterious. In high school, Eric had looked down on his eccentric ways. "The man has no ambition," he would say to Monica. She defended Dad halfheartedly because she had a sentimental attachment to the simple life and did not realize how hard it would be for anyone to live like that in the future. Dad barely kept up with the technology in his own field. What would he ever do when he started losing contracts, which he surely would the way it was going? "My dad's a preserver of standards," Eric had explained to his girlfriend Kayla. But he was not even preserving much lately. House painting was the sort of task he always used to do. It was Aunt Anne's cancer that had got him down, more than the development, more than breaking up with that woman. It must be terrible to have a sister dying.

Eric tried to envision the pasture in its next incarnation. The stone wall was already breached for driveways, and soon there would rise two-story houses in all their solid tidiness with decks and enormous garages and mulched gardens and pathetic saplings at regular intervals. Architecturally, his dad's house had considerable integrity and might even be of some historical significance, but Dowland had no planning commission like Fraddboro's, so who cared? In a few decades, there will be no such houses left, Eric thought, they will all have tumbled down.

His dad had just stepped out on the front porch with a tray of lunch stuff, and now he gave a broad wave, so Eric waved, too, and headed back down the course of a future driveway. His Tercel was shining white next to his dad's pale green Rambler. He had forgotten, once again, to bring a Williams decal for him to stick above Monica's Smith one, darn it.

"Lunch!"

"Great, Dad." Eric saw he had dutifully put on his Softram T-shirt over his frayed blue oxford. "Getting set to paint?" he asked as he came up the warped steps. "That's a good painting shirt."

"I think it'll wait till spring."

"We could like start scraping this afternoon, Dad. Veterans Day weekend I'll get Kayla to come along and help us finish the job."

"I'd like to see something of this Kayla, Eric."

"She was on our canoe trip. You met her."

"I know, but you were all a big bunch passing through. I didn't get to know her." He poured Squirt from the big bottle into a tall glass filled with ice and passed it to Eric, who settled into the other chair. There were deviled ham and tomato sandwiches piled on the tray, so Eric grabbed one, sat back, and launched into a diatribe about land use and American concepts of privacy. He relied on the topics he had been studying to make sure his dad was not too out of touch with the real world. That morning, though, he had been sure to ask about his recent trip to San Diego to see Aunt Anne, but he could not tell if his dad had wanted to say any more about it now, so land use was safer.

Privacy, Eric maintained, was relative. If people knew how to live, in one sense, closer to each other, they would have a greater sense of the territory around them and live in a healthier proportion to nature. It had to do with the known and the unknown. Americans (his professor was from Finland) thought privacy resided walled up in the known instead of in the remnants of wilderness. And forget about the old myth of wide open spaces — we don't really want them.

"No stopping progress," Dad finally interjected.

"But what's progress, Dad? We have to redefine it. Think on the micro level: that development over there. It's an ecological nightmare."

"You've been giving this a bit of thought."

"It's the world we're going to be living in." And that was when a hint of resentment always crept in. His dad should have made more of a stink in town meeting. He should have come up with an alternative proposal. The MIT professor up the road would have thrown some weight. But for his dad it was all or nothing. The vote went through, and that was that. "My dad is a fatalist," Eric had tried to explain to Kayla. "He decided he simply wasn't what Mom wanted him to be, and since Kathleen Whozits seemed to take him as is, he closed his eyes and went for it, and there he was, divorced before he knew it." Kayla's impression of his dad from that one weekend they all stopped by after the canoe trip was different, though. She had actually had a talk with him about poetry. Since when had Dad given a thought to poetry? But Kayla could draw the most unexpected things out of people.

Dad stuck his shoes up on the railing, tipped his chair back on its hind legs, and said, sadly, "I guess I haven't been thinking much about the world we're going to be living in since Anne's not likely to be here to see it."

"Bad attitude, Dad. Aunt Anne would not approve."

"I know. She amazes me. She plans on making it through another year."

"Are you going out there again?"

Dad thought a second and then suddenly said, "Why don't we all three go out over Christmas? What would your mother say to that?"

"She might let us," Eric said. "It's her year, though."

"I'll give her the next two Christmases and all the Thanksgivings."

"But like could you afford to take us?"

"Anne would help out. Let's call her right now."

"Dad, calm down," Eric said.

His dad looked wistfully at him. Lately, Eric had found himself defending him to his mom and Chuck E. Cheese despite the sly pleasure he sometimes still took in hearing them dump on him. He put this new loyalty in terms of

Aunt Anne's cancer and the therapy Dad was in, but it stemmed from something more elementally filial. He had talked to Kayla about it, not really to Monica. Monica expected cynicism from Eric. She liked thinking of him as the hard-boiled proto-yup. But when his mom called his dad "that teenager" and, worse, "that crackpot," he found himself telling her to lay off. She meant it humorously, she said. "I know," Eric said, "but it ain't funny, Mom." Now he told his dad they had better wait to check with Monica and Mom before they called San Diego.

"Then call Mom," Dad said. "Feel her out."

The Cheeseburger was planning on taking them all skiing in Maine for New Year's, Kayla, too, and Monica's Tommy if he was still in the picture, but Eric had decided he could at least call and see what his mom could do to rearrange Christmas itself. Eric was the only one she would listen to. Monica tended to overanalyze and ended up arguing point by point, and losing, but their mother knew that Eric did not ask for things he did not have deep reasons for wanting.

"On one condition," Eric said. "We're going to start scraping paint as soon as we finish these sandwiches."

"I don't think I have the heart for it," his dad said.

III

On saturdays, Mr. Zart took a later lunch and tended to linger. It was one o'clock, time to close for the weekend. Ron was cleaning up in back, so Victor was stuck listening to the old guy ramble on. It was giving him a sad feeling, not for Zart himself — he was as happy as he ever was — but for the whole town of Parshallville. The old stores were closing down, but that was not it quite; Victor felt something larger happening. It showed in his accounts. Ron was upbeat, always, but it cost more each year to run a diner and you could only raise your prices so far before people started coming by less often. Mary Lanaghan's ex-husband had his idea of how to make a go of it: send off for authentic fixtures and doll the place up. But then it would no longer be the Original 108, it would be a newcomer's idea of it. The fact was, old things were old, they got shabby, like Zart, like the dusty racks of yarn and thread and bolts of fabric in his store, the cards of ribbons and laces and buttons. When people tried to make old things new, they made them young instead. People said they loved the old, but they loved only the idea of the old.

Victor looked at his row of stools, with Zart on the ninth. The fourth had permanently tilted, the eighth wobbled when it turned, there were patches on the rips of the second and sixth. Combine all this with smudges and dents and Victor would know which number stool it was if he met it on the street. He had grown up with those stools, those booths, had watched the cracks emerge from the linoleum like fissures in parched earth. In his youth, he had mopped over every corner of the place as they had Kevin do now. The difference was, Kevin took no particular notice of anything unless it was big and male and out of reach. Why had Victor watched everything so closely, counted everything, the plates, the forks, the coffee cups — all his life? Mr. Zart counted things, too. As his stock dwindled, he deducted each departing item, lifeblood leaving his old body. He knew where everything was he had left, but he did not understand his taxes anymore, or his insurance rates, or depreciation; that was where he got help.

Ron was politely waiting for the old guy to leave before putting on the last blasting song of the week, but Victor could tell he was eager to lock up. He was clattering pots and silverware and humming something unrecognizable.

"But Ugo was a fine cardplayer," Zart said. "He played by the rules. He was too good for some of us, lost him a friendship or two. That horse's ass Albert Thibault — used to drive the plow for Haviland — he was one of us once. Well, here's your two-fifty, I guess. I've outstayed my welcome."

Victor sauntered down to the other end of the counter and took the bills and a pile of nickels that turned out one short, but he said nothing.

"They finished the roadwork down there in Haviland Center yet?"

"I think so," Victor said. "I don't go in there much."

"Yep, you're a Parshallville man. Maybe you live over the Haviland line now, but that don't make no difference."

"I'm a Sewall man," said Ron from the back room, and then it must have struck him funny, so he sang it to the tune of "Soul Man." He thought he was so clever.

"Sewall's all right," said Zart, "except the river people. It's Fraddboro I got no use for. I remember when it was mostly farms over there. I bet there ain't one real farm left. Who lives in that town anyway?"

Victor shrugged, his usual response to Zart's palaver.

"Well, excuse me for sitting here talking like a sausage," the old guy said, and then he shook his head as though that was not quite what he had meant to say. It had happened several times, Victor had noticed, in recent weeks. He came around the counter to make sure his father's friend got off the stool safely, but Zart would not take his arm; he held on to the end of the counter instead.

When he was out the door, Ron took the mop, flipped the "Sorry, We're Closed" sign around, locked the front, and put on "Soul Man" for real at high volume. Victor did not want to hear it. His mood was for silence. He came up to Ron, from behind, and gave him a sharp spank, which Ron liked, and said, "You lock up back. And why don't you take the car?"

"I can't hear you!" Ron shouted.

"You take the car! I'm walking home."

"What now?" Ron shouted, so Victor handed him the keys and put his hands over his own ears, then blew a quick kiss, so Ron would smile at him before he slunk out the back door.

It was a dreary day. Victor remembered it was the night to set the clocks back to true time. This was a source of his sadness, too, he decided, the coming jolt, the apparent loss of light. It was an illusion. Time as it was counted was man's, but time as it was felt was God's, and Victor felt time just as he felt the stools he also counted.

He did not look behind him to see the tattered green awning of Zart's Dry Goods or the blistered sign of Dill's, his father's competition, long since boarded up. He set his course to cross the weedy grammar school playground toward the path leading to the railroad. Victor seldom walked home. He did not know why today he had to. It was not to use up the extra hour ahead of time. It was for the silence, that was all it was for, silence, being silent in silence. Soon he was beyond the whirring of tires on 108 and the gasping of trucks. He passed a swampy place where Ron claimed men went to butt-fuck in the mud. What Ron said was his own illusion, Victor knew. Ron made excitement out of passing meaninglessness. Ron had to turn up the volume, to mop and dance. How had they come to live together? All love was God's, that was how. It was not simple man's or it would not hold for so long. But excitement was man's. Excitement was an illusion. The thought of Mary Lanaghan's second son was Ron's excitement of the day. Ron had told Victor about their morning run, so he imagined seeing the two of them, meaty Ron and that sinewy boy, far ahead pounding along toward him through the trees. What he really saw, though, was an all-terrain vehicle roaring along on its huge tires; then it swerved crazily and disappeared over the lip of the railroad bed in the direction of the landfill. When the sound died, Victor heard the usual gunshot cracks of a fall weekend, and then he did not hear them anymore because he had heard them all his life and did not need to notice.

He preferred the silence that resumed in his head. He began to perceive that the woods he walked through were old and young at the same time. They were not like the diner he had inherited from his father and shared now with his lover. A single tree might be the same tree that had grown there before they put the tracks through, and now, long after they had been taken up, it was at the same stage of growth, not precisely the same tree, Victor acknowledged, but as young or as old as any tree had ever been. It and its fellows would always be original. They renewed their living souls through time. But things without souls had to attach themselves to people. Some, like the famous statue of David that had stood on a shelf in his father's den and that his sister Antonietta had insisted on keeping though Victor coveted it, some things like that attached themselves to people for very long. Some felt almost like nature — the towers of the cathedral in Cologne, which Victor had climbed with two buddies from his unit — but even that high pile of stones could not renew its soul the way Monadnock up the river in New Hampshire could, for though weather wore it down it was still a mountain, as old and as young as it had ever eternally been.

He had passed the Haviland marker. There was a path off to one side, which impulse caused Victor to venture on. It led him steeply up a hill to a flat slab of granite beside a bed of deep moss scattered over with red leaves. Victor's thoughts had exhausted him. He had worked hard, up at five, on his feet all morning, but he was used to that; it was this burden of thinking that caused him to stretch out on the moss and fall almost instantly asleep until he heard a high buzzing motorbike, which in his dream he imagined as a great mosquito and then, for a second of waking, a biplane at the air show in South Fraddboro last summer. When he knew where he was and who he was exactly — because at first he had been a younger Victor, and then not quite Victor at all — he sat up and saw that the light had brightened. It made its way down to him through the unleaving trees from a bluer sky. He began to think of his mother, and of his sister, of how they held him when he was little and how he now would hold Ron after he had made love to him and tired him out at last. The holding was the best of it. As fine as all the rest was, it was the holding, slowing it way down, stopping the time for a quarter of an hour — Ron needed that before he stirred himself up again in his usual way. What he was pushing for these days was a satellite dish, the small size he saw on a special deal in Haviland Center, so they could get the cable stations out in the woods. Either that, Ron had insisted, or they were going to have to think about moving back into town.

IV

THE EDGE OF COLOR that swept down the map every fall had reached Umbachaug long before Newton. At last, it was at its height around Crystal Lake, and the Ostermanns were somewhat sorry, driving off north and west, to see how quickly the display faded. Gus had stayed at home because Shirley was not coming, and he saw no point in celebrating her brother Bayard's birthday without her. On their Sunday calls, Christina had kept Mary abreast of Gus's mounting obsession, begun idly enough last summer but now all-consuming. Kurt saw it as a means to put a hold on romantic involvements at Newton South. Gus was only fifteen. His crush on an elusive college senior gave him plenty to talk about but little to act on. He e-mailed Shirley daily; they discussed sexuality in all its ramifications, and she sent him drafts of portions of her thesis, which he brought to Alliance meetings to prove to his friends that he was on the cutting edge of the gender revolution. "Sound familiar?" Christina had asked Mary, but Mary reminded her that, unlike her and Kurt, she and Dermot had never quite managed to challenge the status quo. They had upped and gotten married one Sunday in May without any notion of changing the world at all.

Kurt thought 108 would be pleasanter than zooming out Route 2 and cutting north. When they recognized Mary's dog food outlet in Dowland, they knew they were again in familiar territory. Passing the sign for Basswood, Mary's place of employment, Kurt had occasion to remark on what a new life she was leading these days, but Christina decided she had better forewarn him; what Mary presented as doubts about her adequacy on the job, Christina heard as plain discontent. "The truth is, it's not the right place for her," she said flatly, and her husband glanced over in dismay, then quickly turned his eyes back to the road. "No, let me explain," she said. "You know what Mary's like. It has something to do with their sense of privilege, the Basswood people. It's not exactly an old folks' home, Kurt. It takes years on waiting lists to get in. Mary doesn't enjoy taking care of such fancy people, that's all." Kurt was still puzzling. "But, of course, she turns it into her own ineptitude. I'm sure they think she's wonderful, but one instance of failure can crush her, such as if no one signs up for her quilting bee."

"Well then, let me ask you this, Liebchen," Kurt said, "how do you want me to talk about her job with her? Hmp? I mean, I'm the one who worked the whole damn deal out with Dermot."

"I'm only saying she hasn't yet found the right job," Christina said.

They slowed down through Old Fraddboro and admired its distilled essence of New England village. "Mary's favorite store," Christina pointed out.

"Talk about fancy," said Kurt.

"Oh, how can I explain Mary to you?" Christina sighed.

"Mary falls between two stools," Kurt said.

Christina thought about it. Kurt was right. "Poor Mary," she said.

"That dreadful year, Liebchen, when she was practically our big messed-up teenage daughter — I learned something from that. It was my first example of a friend — Dermot, I mean — turning out to be a shit. Hmp. I didn't think it happened in people our age."

Christina told him to take the road around the bottom of

the lake instead of 108 to Parshallville. As he waited cautiously for a set of straggling motorcycles to whip by, one by one, she saw the Kurt she had married in a New Hampshire meadow of wildflowers that set off his hay fever and gave him that same pained expression through the whole ceremony.

On the Haviland Road, she began to think again about Gus's Shirley thing. Kurt was convinced there was no harm in letting it ride, but the sense Christina had of her own good luck made her, superstitiously, want to warn her son of love's difficulties. She thought of her front porch talks with Rosa Lanaghan during the rough time. She had told Rosa that no one found perfection, that all parents could do was struggle with what they had, and sometimes the struggle proved too tough. Platitudes, Christina knew, but she had hoped through her peaceful voice to counterbalance the shy loneliness in the girl. Yet what Rosa may have taken away from her was, perhaps, something fearsome: the thought, grim to a teenager, that she would never find the right boy. Okay then, let Gus discover his own disappointment. Christina was determined to do it right with her only child. Mary and Dermot had been instructive to her. She might not have had the strength of her convictions without their mistakes.

They passed the sign for the public landing at Umbachaug, and Kurt slowed down for the switch from pavement to the gravel road to Hale's Cove. Christina felt a breath of the calm that had enveloped her here last summer, the atmosphere for wasting time, which she never found in Newton, what with the whole miserable world pressing against her conscience. She found she could put the religious parent organization, which was threatening the school curriculum, entirely out of her mind.

Mary had heard their car and was coming to greet them down the stairs from the balcony. She was sorry not to find Gus with them, but Christina made homework his excuse and reported he practically had a full head of hair again, and his intention was to let it grow as long as the hippies used to and then shave off all but one fabulous ponytail. Mary said Bayard was over helping Drew Hale take in the dock, but Bryce was here, and so they came up the stairs to find the man who had made such a slight impression on Christina in July sitting on the balcony with the big old dog at his feet.

Mary went to make tea; Christina could have abandoned Kurt, who had not met Bryce before, to work through their pleasantries, but she was curious to see how they managed. Kurt was good at seeming interested in what other people did; in fact, he *was* interested. But Christina paid more attention to the way Bryce presented himself. There came a spew of information about new software, as though he was favoring them with top secrets of the computerized world. Kurt understood these things, to a point. "And how are your kids?" she finally asked, so Bryce shifted modes and went on with other sorts of details that Christina was obliged to pay more attention to. But he was affable, even oddly appealing; he lacked Kurt's rugged nature, Kurt's solidity, was more of a superannuated college kid, the way Dermot used to seem at times. Aside from his basic boringness, Christina could not locate an offensive element in him yet.

She suggested pulling the plastic chairs to the balcony's southwest corner to catch the declining sun. It would shortly be too chilly to sit comfortably outside. Mary set up a low table with the tea things and an array of cookies, which she told them to eat before Bayard got back and demolished them.

"Kurt picked out some CDs for his birthday," Christina said. "I hope he has a player."

"Everybody has," said Bryce. "Except Mary, that is. She's my nature girl."

"I have a cassette player," Mary said, but Bryce did not think that counted.

"And she doesn't have a dish, so out here in the woods she barely gets three channels."

"You should see Bryce when he has to spend the night over here," Mary said.

"I'm okay as long as I bring my laptop."

"But then I can't make phone calls."

"I have two lines at home, one for the net," Bryce explained, and Kurt said they had to have three. Mary asked what the CDs were of: reissues from the thirties of Schnabel playing Schubert and some early Count Basie. Bryce said, "Oh, Schubert, good," and nodded, "Mmm, Count Basie," and Kurt assumed Bryce knew precisely what he was talking about. If Kurt loved something good, he imagined his friends loved it, too, a quality Christina had long ago decided was more endearing than maddening.

"We didn't want to get him books since he works in a bookstore," she said.

"Busman's holiday," said Bryce.

"It's all he's been doing lately," Mary said, "reading for grad school. Not one girlfriend in the picture that I can see."

"He's applying to some good schools," Bryce announced. "I can't imagine what it would be like to have a kid going to grad school."

"Especially in English," said Mary as if it were a dig at Bryce.

"We just want to get our kid through high school," said Kurt modestly. He was entering at the right level; Christina knew she had a harder time being as generous.

Christina had been in favor of Bryce at first — anyone, really, to get Mary into the world — but today she had seen instantly how nothing fundamental had been built on since July. If there was anyone here Mary was in love with, she thought perversely, it was her son. Mary was still amazed she had produced a boy like that, so handsome and popular and vigorous. "You idealize him, Mary," Christina had once told her, "and that's not good for a kid." They were sitting about the pool the week before Mary found out about Enid Perlman. Later, Martin had tried so hard to become the man in her life, but from age twelve it was already Bayard who embodied for Mary all that was wonderful in men. Poor Martin.

Bryce now brought the conversation around to the differences between Newton and out here. He had heard they had an excellent school system. Kurt went into some detail, even mentioned the Gay-Straight Alliance, which Bryce took note of with a slightly furrowed brow, and after Kurt further described the sports programs and music and art, Bryce said, as somewhat of a non sequitur, "Well, we wouldn't have anything like that around here."

Christina knew exactly what he meant even if Kurt did not. She could leave the men safely together, she decided, so she proposed a dog walk, herself and Mary; they needed a time alone. "But let's not go by the cottage and have to deal with Drew Hale," Mary said.

"Then, we'll go the other way."

"Let's go sit at my private swimming spot," Mary said. "I don't think Hilda's up for another stroll."

"She'll stay here with me," said Bryce firmly. He reached down and patted the dog, who had repositioned herself beside him when they moved the chairs down the balcony. Christina knew enough about dogs to understand that Hilda was protecting her place in the pack between Mary and Bryce. She was number two and, even blind, she had to keep Bryce in line.

"Are Ron and Victor joining us for dinner?" Christina asked, still in earshot of the balcony.

"Do you think I should've invited them?"

"I don't know. Bayard likes them."

"It didn't even occur to me. Oh dear."

And when they were farther down the path, Christina said quietly, "Well, Bryce would probably be uncomfortable."

"You think he's such a conservative, Christina," Mary sputtered. "Well, maybe, but he's very relaxed about sex. He isn't threatened by gay men. I just didn't think of it. I was thinking Bayard might bring a girlfriend or Gus would come. I should've. I could ask them now."

"You're so funny, Mary," Christina said.

When they got to the gap between blueberry bushes with its small patch of smooth sand wide enough for the two of them to sit tightly side by side, Mary said in a serious voice, "But Bryce and I did have a talk about breaking up. Before you got here. I don't know why it had to come to this on Bayard's birthday. I hope Kurt isn't talking about Bosnian relief up there. That's how it started. I was telling Bryce about the committee you're on, and we ended up squabbling. How's old Bubbie Friedenheimer, by the way?"

Christina knew they had a lot of talking to do if she was going to bring Mary around to what was truly on her mind. Maybe the smooth cove itself would calm her down, the gray still water. At home, Christina would yearn for stillness like that. Look at it, Mary, she thought, think about it, be like it. It's a way to find out who you are. And then Christina smiled at herself and began to catch Mary up on the old neighborhood, before easing her back to the troubling subject of Bryce.

V

ELIZABETH HAD NOT even wanted to get out of the car. She had her paperback and could watch them heaving and hauling perfectly well from where she sat, dry and warm. She had wanted to come along. She was not a sentimentalist, but visiting the cottage did mean something to her, Drew was sure, if only that it reminded her of the hardships of their earlier years together. She had wanted to see it one last time with him; she understood that the *very* last time it would have to be he, Drew, alone.

He stood on the shore watching two young men do the job he used to do by himself. He could have left the old dock extension to freeze and crack apart, but last summer he had put on those new planks, as if he intended it to last another fifty years; something in Drew, the curious artificer, could not let a thing uselessly break. And he might be able to sell the dock to some summer home owner across the lake. There would be much to dismantle and sell off next spring before letting loose the bulldozers, but for now, let him proceed as though no spring would ever come, as though the cottage, the gun shop, the road, the trees themselves would remain here forever.

The muscleman was in the water up to his shorts and swearing like a trooper except that his voice had a perceptible swoop to it. Drew could spot fairies. Mary's son, the one he had always liked, was doing his best up top. Finally, they got the dock up off the poles, and Ron — that was his name, although Drew tried hard to forget it — heaved his end above his head, and Bayard Lanaghan pulled hard, and up from the water they came, Ron's legs dripping and all goose-bumped and red. They set the dock down on the stone patio, which was Drew's one vain attempt at beating the competition on the Fraddboro side. "Thanks, fellas," he said.

"No problem, Mr. Hale," said Bayard.

"Fuck! That thing was a load," said Ron. "What would you do without me, Drew?"

Drew smiled wryly. He knew much more than he intended to say; this man would be out of his life soon enough. "Now how about moving that trailer of theirs into the woods?" he suggested with a chuckle.

"Are you shitting me?" said Ron.

"We'll lift it off the blocks. Those wheels will still roll."

"Yeah, right," Ron said. "Besides, I like sitting down there in the evening and kicking back. Mary gave me the key, you know."

"Is that so? Well, someday you and your pal may be shacked up there permanently, the least I know."

"After all I do for you?" said Ron. Young Bayard was looking unsure of this joshing. Drew loved bamboozling people. The fag saw through him, of course; he was from Sewall, a town where no one ever told it straight. Those swamp Yankees lived to outfox each other. Hell, they all were on welfare, which was proof enough. "Hey, Drew," said Ron, "you aren't going to raise the rent on us, are you?"

"Might *raze* the whole damn place."

"Aw, you talk," said Ron. "Hey, Bayard, you coming by?"

"My mom's got company. The Ostermanns."

"Those Serbo-Croats again?" said Drew.

"It's the boy's birthday," Ron told him. "Anyway, Bayard, you come by later. Check out the trailer, man."

Bayard said sure he might, and off he went up past the Chevy, where he said something polite to Elizabeth on his way. Drew did not feature sticking around talking to his tenant, but Ron said he had something for him and jogged off to the old gun shop in his squishy boat shoes to get it. Drew found his knees stiff hiking up to the car. A man barely in his sixties should be capable of more than this, he said to himself. He sat around too much, fussing over some ugly old piece of furniture, or stood bent over his lathe or fiddling with the tiny mechanism inside some damn clock. His father had had bad joints, too.

"Nice boy," Elizabeth said. "Why couldn't Peggy find one like that?"

"Too rich," said Drew. "Lanaghans make Tomaszewskis look like poor folk."

"They could all of them do a lot worse than Peggy."

"She'll always be your little girl, dear," said Drew. Even Elizabeth was not always sure if he meant something sincerely, so she raised an eyebrow at him as enigmatically as she could. It was a game they had played for years.

Ron hustled back over with the old sign in his hands: D. HALE REPAIRS ALL.

"I'll be damned," said Drew. "I thought I threw that out."

"Don't you want it?"

"Hello," said Elizabeth. "You're Peggy's friend, aren't you?"

"Hey, Mrs. Hale," said Ron. "How's she doing? Why doesn't she come by and see me? Her and that Stewart are way too thick lately."

Drew interrupted: "Now tell me what happened to that other one, the oddball. I didn't want to ask in front of his brother. He went off somewhere?"

"Martin? That's a great story," said Ron. "He gets out there — Santa Fe, New Mexico — and it seems his pen pal, the one he went to meet, she's a wee bit older than she let on by computer. She's like my age. Mary's all agitated about it, but the kid, he seems okay with it."

Elizabeth was pretending not to listen, but Drew said, "I suppose he's learning a few new tricks then."

"Oh hush," said Elizabeth.

"Nothing like a good older woman," said Drew. "Some might say the same for an older man." Elizabeth was shaking her head at Ron.

"I'm used to your husband, Mrs. Hale," he said. "He's not so bad as landlords go."

"He's all mouth," Elizabeth said.

"Here, dear, you want this piece of wood for your memories?"

She obviously did. "I don't know why you'd want to throw that out."

"I got a classy new sign in Leominster. What do I need that rotting old thing for?" He made like he would toss it into the trees, but as soon as she gasped, he slipped it in the car window to her. "See you, my friend," he said to Ron. "Those black people didn't bother you, did they?"

"I swam out and got their beach ball when it blew up the cove by us. That was about it."

"Blacks don't really swim, you see," Drew said, "not that I've ever heard of." He got in and revved the engine so he would not have to stand around chatting. Ron shut right up and watched him maneuver until he was pointed back south. On their way out, Drew noted with a sneer the Serbians' Volvo station wagon behind Mary's house.

Elizabeth wanted to stop in on the Thibault kids, and so did Drew, but he made it seem at her insistence. The new pavement through Haviland met his tires with a soothing murmur, but the center looked different because of it, polished up in a way that did not entirely please Drew. "Sure is an improvement," he told his wife.

They passed the crossing, where the pitted concrete resumed, and soon made the turn into the space by the cross-eyed house, famous to all in town as the home of the enormous ones. The white Lark was not out back, so Louise must have been at Mrs. Germaine's, even on a Saturday, but Drew knew Charles required she have the car back in time for his shift at the convenient mart a half mile up the road; he was not keen on walking anywhere.

Elizabeth had brought her butterscotch pie for the kiddies. Pauline had asked her to, if she ever got up that way. In Florida, she fretted over those two fending for themselves, though keeping food in the house hardly seemed their difficulty; it was laundry and sweeping up Elizabeth would have fretted over. Drew let his wife go up and ring the bell.

It took a while. Charles eventually opened the door blinking his eyes, but he woke right up and gave Elizabeth a wide hug. Drew decided he had better get out of the car. He followed them down the short hallway to the kitchen, where Charles set about making coffee and Elizabeth put the pie on the table. "It's the same tablecloth your grandmother had," she said.

"Everything's the same as Grandmère had it," said Charles.

"When your parents were up visiting, Charles, it was all I could do to remind myself this wasn't still her home."

"She'd have made ninety-six next month," said Charles.

Drew asked, "So where's that sister of yours?"

"She'd better get here or there won't be any pie left," Charles said. He was putting out plates and forks. "Have a seat, have a seat."

They sat against the wall and left him his pullout bench with the green vinyl cushion. Elizabeth had been deputized by Pauline to get a clearer sense of Louise's plans, but Drew was not convinced they would learn much from Charles, who was more liable to go on about himself. "She still with Mrs. Germaine?" Elizabeth asked, a question she full well knew the answer to.

"And old Mrs. Bulmer, too. That one's been in a coma for a month now, but her family pays Sis to go set by her so she won't feel neglected. I tell you, Mrs. Hale, I don't know about you, but I can sure see why Louise quit with that terminal business. It got her way down. These two old ladies she's got are bad enough, and she's got some spryer ones up in Basswood now. I tell her she should look for a kitchen job at the hospital if she wants to be around sick people. Remember I used to work there? And as you know, Sis is some cook. I bet Mrs. Lanaghan could help her get in there. Or that teacher of hers, except they were disappointed with her for quitting after putting so much effort into it. And then, of course, there's the other big tragedy, but I'm not supposed to mention it, so don't let on you know. You probably never heard of Dave Paasivirta. I can't believe it, but he's actually gone off to Iowa or wherever he was going. So Sis is broken up about that. I maintain he'll be back as soon as he sees what winter's like out west. We think we've got it hard. Hey, it cleared up nice today, though." Drew glanced out the little window at the straggly forsythia bush. Charles had poured them all coffee and was slicing the pie. "Come home, little sister, it's going fast," he said.

Elizabeth never minded the way that one went on, but Drew ate his slice without a word so as not to encourage him. It was the idea of looking in on his old friend's kids that appealed to him more than actually doing so. He forgot that, every time. Albert was a quiet man. He had let Drew do most of the talking. And Albert had a great poker face. He was the master. Drew only aspired to Albert's ability to pull the wool over the sharpest eyes in all five towns.

VI

"BUT, MY DARLINGS," Christina was saying, slightly under the spell of the nice wine she and Kurt had brought. "We're all safe and we're all healthy, and there's nothing much else to ask for that I can think of."

But Mary thought of Ron and, despite the hope of new treatments, wished he was healthy, entirely healthy, the way he had been before she knew him. She had told Christina last summer, but, naturally, Christina did not imagine Ron included in her "we're all safe." Mary should have invited him and Victor tonight. Without Bryce, she would have. Mary had not told him about Ron's virus, maybe because Bryce was paranoid about his kids and she did not want it to become a problem between them. But Ron was her friend, and Victor was his partner. Kurt would have asked them how you ran a diner. He made good conversation with strangers, never did all the talking like Dermot, and he was the only man in her Newton days who did not think Dermot was such a prince. She turned to her right and, also partially under the spell of the wine, patted the back of his hand. "I wish Gus were here, too," she said.

"He's probably blasting the neighborhood with Nine Inch Nails," Kurt said. "We have volume control issues, hmp."

"He'll be deaf by twenty," said Christina. "How's our twenty-three-year-old's hearing?"

Kurt said, "This is the man I introduced to the Schumann Piano Quintet when he turned twelve. That was how you started, wasn't it?"

"Mmm, Schumann," said Bryce.

"It was Schumann, then Brahms clarinet sonatas with Benny Goodman," Bayard said. "That was before CDs."

"You saved my son's ears," said Mary.

"He saved more than my ears," Bayard said. "Mr. Ostermann got me through that whole next year, Mom."

She felt good hearing him put it in words. Kurt knew how grateful Bayard was, but this set them on a new footing, Mary thought. Bayard was no longer the child who simply took.

"Why is it easier to bring up other people's children than your own?" Kurt asked, and Mary had to pat his hand again. Then she turned to her left and saw Bryce was looking briefly sad, missing his kids, she knew, so she patted his hand, too, and he seemed startled. It was the first move she had made back toward him since their afternoon scrap.

There were seconds on cake and ice cream, and Bryce did all the serving to show, Mary deduced, that he belonged in this house even though, when it was just the two of them, he said he felt like he was camping out there.

"Have some more, sweetie," Mary told Bayard, but he tapped his quite flat stomach and shook his head. She worried about him in this monkish phase, reading and thinking and exercising and eating sparely. She could not tell what it meant to him. "I do wish you two would sleep over," she reiterated to the Ostermanns. "You can have my room and I'll take the girls' loft." She did not offer to go to Bryce's because tonight, after her talk with Christina, she did not want to. He was putting the butter pecan back in the freezer and not listening.

"Gus would be too delighted if we stayed," said Christina.

"It's only an hour if we take Route 2," said Kurt.

"Damn," Mary said, "we should have planned this better."

Bryce had made coffee Mary's old-fashioned way, as he put it, and poured for everyone but Bayard, who said he needed his sleep. He had been subdued this evening, happy with the presents and the company, but not glowing as Mary had hoped he would be. She counted on him to be the cheer spreader.

The only halfway comfortable place for them to sit after coffee was the free-for-all, so Bryce suggested instead an evening walk to his place. He had never invited anyone over before; none of Mary's kids had seen inside his house. "That sounds good," Kurt said, "before we hit the road."

"Oh, don't hit the road!" Mary pleaded one last time, though she knew they were about to. For some weeks, she had been counting on Bayard's birthday to keep her on course, and now it was almost over.

"Mom," said her son, "you've still got to tell Mr. and Mrs. Ostermann about what's happening at your job. You know you want to talk about it, and all you've done is tell funny stories about snotty old dames."

"Oh, it's the same stuff Christina's heard me say already. She knows I don't feel right over there."

"We went over there this afternoon to set up videos," Bayard reported. "Three hours ahead of time, everything has to be set up. They're all so polite and nervous about it. Mom, you're not explaining yourself," he said, glowering at her across the table.

"It's my first real job ever," Mary said and felt shaky for a second, wine and coffee working against each other inside her. Bryce would not understand what she was talking about, and that also provided some of the tumult. He was watching her with the innocent eagerness she used to welcome. "Oh, I never imagined myself ending up in that sort of world," she said, almost fiercely. "I've always wanted to help people, but I'm too easily intimidated."

"You weren't at the high school or the hospital, Mom."

"But I wasn't being paid there. I explained that."

Bryce had extended his arm to her shoulders, cautiously, but in front of the others she did not shake it off. "That Basswood's a beautiful place," he said. "Very hard to get into. That's the way those people are. It takes a while to get used to being worth something, hon."

"He's right," said Christina. "Or maybe you haven't found the right job yet."

"But when I moved out here," Mary said, because the thought had been maturing in her head, "there was something I wanted to get closer to."

"It doesn't matter where you work if you feel valuable in yourself," Bryce went on. "That's all I'm trying to tell you."

"But wait," said Kurt, "what did you want to get closer to?"

It was hard to say. What came out of Mary's mouth surprised her: "I wanted to get closer to my parents." Christina purred with amusement, and so Mary smiled at herself and tried to think for a moment before she said anything more. Again, she did not expect Bryce to understand what she was about to say. "Well, my parents were self-contained. It was just the three of us. They didn't go out or have many friends. They didn't like me playing with the black girls moving in down the street. It was an old neighborhood. My father was a bank clerk, as you know; my mother was devoted to the church and the branch library. I didn't mean I wanted to be like them."

"You wanted to get closer," said Kurt.

"I wanted to get closer to them in spirit."

"But," Bayard protested, "if they hated black people, for instance, why would you want to get closer to them in spirit? I know they're your parents, but you named us after black people. You named me after Bayard Rustin."

"What you have to understand," Mary said, feeling like his mother again, "is that each generation learns something we had no idea we were wrong about before. I truly believe I picked your names in the spirit of my father. He hated his bosses. He wanted things to change. He was a rather bitter person. Sometimes, he was hopeless, when he handled other people's money. He retreated. But if he'd had power in him to protest, he would have. When I got married he was suspicious of all the money Dermot claimed he was going to make. He thought Dermot had no idea how hard it was going to be. They both died before we really got settled, but already they didn't think much of Dermot's success. The Lanaghans were proud of it, not the Blakeys. Money — that was not what they'd sent me to Boston College for. They expected me to become a teacher."

"You never told me that, Mom."

"They didn't like seeing me swept away by Dermot Lanaghan."

"Mom, but you always talked about how tight and claustrophobic it was when you were young. I didn't know they wanted you to be a teacher. You would've been a great teacher. Why didn't you do what they wanted?"

"I don't know how to explain it to you," Mary said, leaning forward on her elbows and looking at the Ostermanns on either side of Bayard. "You guys explain it to him."

"Was your father a Socialist?" asked Bryce.

"He wasn't a Socialist. Just a failure. Maybe he had a sort

of socialist soul and didn't know it. But he was a Catholic. He didn't think much of the princes of this earth."

"I'm as Catholic as he was," said Bryce.

"No, you really aren't, Bryce. None of us is. My parents were the last generation. I was a late child, and they were a lot older than most. They were more like the generation before the last."

"Mom, what's with this Catholicism and Socialism? I'm talking about you being a teacher."

"I didn't mean the doctrines, Bayard, I meant the spirit of things."

"Sometimes, I don't know what to make of Mary," Bryce said across to Kurt. "But these stools are killing me. Let's take that walk."

Mary knew that was the end of it as far as Bryce went, but she could not stop herself from adding, "Oh pooh, you don't even try to figure me out."

"Honey?"

"Well, you don't. You might learn something."

"I'm sorry, hon. You know what I meant."

"No squabbles on the birthday," said Kurt helpfully.

Mary put her left hand on Bryce's, mostly for Kurt's sake. "Don't pay attention to us," she said. "Let's go see the Murtagh estate."

Bryce tried again. "I only meant you have this notion about not wanting to make money."

"Leave the glasses, sweetie," Mary told Bayard, who looked embarrassed or angry, probably both.

"It's not that I disapprove, hon," Bryce said as they filed out the door after the Ostermanns. Christina had not caught Mary's eye. Bryce was doing the exact thing Mary had told her about down by the cove, so Christina did not have to make a point of it; it was made.

The dog worked her way to the bottom of the stairs, gingerly reaching out one paw after another, testing the space in her blindness. It made Mary feel like laughing and crying together. But Hilda would not budge farther into the darkness. She squatted on some leaves, piddled and sniffed a bit, then went back to the stairs and sat.

The humans, as Mary saw them, ventured on. There was enough moonlight to see the way once your eyes adjusted. Christina was reminding Kurt of the lovely walks they took in July and how she missed this feeling of being enclosed by nature, not just glimpsing patches of it.

"That's why I moved here," Bryce said. "The same home in the suburbs, we'd have fences to keep out the neighbors instead of trees. Taxes are lower, besides. Of course, I thought we'd found our dream house and expected it to solve all our problems, but what else is new?"

"I thought this place would solve all my problems, too," said Mary quietly.

"We'd better stick to Newton then," said Kurt with the *hmp* that often followed his pronouncements.

"Only if we come here more often to visit Mary," Christina said. "Maybe, Drew Hale would sell us the cottage. We could fix it up, Kurt."

"There are financial considerations, Liebchen," Kurt said.

"We could think of it as a second child," said Christina.

"Hmp. It's a possibility."

Mary was afraid they would get too serious about this drunken idea and then it would fall through, Drew would have other plans for the land, or Kurt would stop indulging the fantasy. The idea made it seem more possible for Mary to continue with Bryce, though; she would have her friends on weekends and in the summer, the real life that somehow mattered more. But Christina and Bryce would eventually get into a terrible fight about how to handle the former Yugoslavia.

"If the Ostermanns moved back next door, Mom, you'd have pulled off quite the coup," Bayard said. "Dad would be ripshit."

"Let's not do it for *that* reason," said Mary.

"It could be a wise investment," said Bryce. "I got in on the beginning of the development. They put the model in first to attract buyers with the woodland setting, and we got it before the big jump in prices."

Now it only amused Mary that he was still talking about money. Maybe he could not help it. What else did he have? Bryce seemed to be floating through these dark woods alone, making useful remarks, believing he was making friends. She was sorry for him and feared the feeling. Alone with her, he was strong and sure and when he picked her up in his arms it still gave her the sense of safety she had not had in so long, but it was not love. Part of Mary wanted to go back to being the dog lady in his life.

"They could bring the gas line out farther so you wouldn't be stuck like Mary with tanks. You'd get your electric upgraded. Extra phone line. I don't know, maybe there's rot under that cottage. The diner guys' needs jacking up and getting some concrete pilings poured. The trouble with these old structures is it may not be cost-effective. Mary's house was built in the seventies, and they did it right."

"Nice to dream about, isn't it, Mary?" Christina said, taking hold of her elbow with a squeeze. "Who knows? We'll look into it."

Across the sudden gap in the woods, Bryce's kitchen windows were shining brightly. He had his lights on a complex set of timers to confuse potential thieves. Mary saw an upstairs lamp snap on as they walked up.

Bryce gave the complete tour, and Kurt was friendly about it. Maybe, he was even interested in the place, as a specimen of what he had never before experienced on so intimate a level. Christina kept her mouth shut but nodded appreciatively; Bayard rolled his sparkly eyes at his mom when they had lagged behind the others. He picked up a kitschy porcelain farmhouse with sheep grazing in its porcelain garden and shook his head. Mary put a finger to her lips and tried to look annoyed, but her son was too much like her; she always had the most fun with him. His humor had that familiar edge of irony in it. But, hearing Bryce up ahead extolling his pulsating showerhead and whirlpool bath, she realized she would be sleeping down here tonight. Bryce was going to need her after his evening of trying so hard, after their period of such disagreement. He was more afraid than she was.

"Are these your kids?" she heard Christina ask him. "They're darling."

"Fiona and Sean," said Bryce. "Eight and six."

VII

BAYARD WALKED the Ostermanns back up the dark road. He felt bad his mom was staying with Bryce Murtagh, whom he did not want to become part of his family, and he felt jumpy remembering that Ron Starks was possibly waiting in Martin's trailer in case he came by. Mrs. Ostermann was being amusing about Bryce. And then she actually apologized for having tried to convince Bayard that Bryce was good for his mom. "But maybe he was," Bayard said. "It's that she doesn't know how to get out of it now."

"She feels obligated," Mrs. Ostermann said.

"Bayard, if your mother could say for sure what she truly wanted," said Mr. Ostermann, "I have a feeling she'd soon have it. She did it once before when she brought the four of you out here. It was a tremendous effort of will, hmp, but she did it."

"I believe in cycles," said Mrs. Ostermann. "Ten years is about right. Mary's ready to slough off the old skin."

"Would you really think of buying Drew Hale's cottage from him?" Bayard asked, not sure yet what he thought of the plan.

"I'm sure he'd drive a hard bargain," said Mr. Ostermann, "but we could speak with him. Friends of ours had been talking about the Vineyard."

"But isn't that a lot more expensive?" asked Bayard.

"Cost isn't really the issue," said Mrs. Ostermann. "Don't listen when a lawyer complains about cost. It's an expensive world we live in, Bayard. Your father lives in it, too. I'm afraid you kids have no idea what you'd need to live in that world and that someday you'll want to."

"We've spoiled you," said Mr. Ostermann.

"I don't even have a car," said Bayard. "I won't need one in grad school if I go to Penn or Brown. I'm like Mom about money. It's one thing that keeps girls from getting too interested."

Mrs. Ostermann laughed, but Mr. Ostermann did a run of hmps and then said, "But you've got to get serious about love sometime. Love comes first. Then you'll get serious about money."

"It's hard for me to get serious at all," said Bayard. It was awfully dark along the road with the hemlocks and pines on each side, but he knew the way better than his old Newton neighbors, so he walked slowly ahead of them; they could follow his white shirt.

"You're serious about music and books," came the voice from behind him. "You're serious about your family. You know what seriousness is. It's only a matter of time."

"Kurt's right," came the other voice.

It was a sad moment, saying good-bye to them with tight hugs from each and promises to see him soon. "E-mail me," Mr. Ostermann said. "You have my address." Bayard was not the best e-mail correspondent, but he said he would and for a second imagined spinning out long confiding letters to Mr. Ostermann, who would put him back on track again as he had once before, but he knew, at best, he would write to thank him for the CDs when he had listened to them thoroughly down in New Haven.

When their red taillights had turned away into the darkness, Bayard stood awhile, aware of being entirely alone, until he felt the cold nose of the dog touch his hand. He led her painstakingly up the stairs to the balcony, in the kitchen made sure she had water, and ascended the ladder to his bed in the loft. Because he had not gone to the bathroom, he knew he would be down again, and then he would face the possibility of walking back out into the woods. Now, he lay on his bed and looked at the black skylight above the curtain, finally perceiving a vague sprinkling of stars. He thought of sex with Felicia, whom he had not thought of in years. She had taught him a lot, too much even, he thought, or at least too much too young. She was four years older and had tried everything. He had never forgotten that she said he nibbled her clit as good as her dyke friend Beth. And she taught him how to use his finger at the same time as his cock, and once he was sure his mom had heard Felicia moaning from across the cove because he saw her bedroom light come on and it was after midnight.

Now, Bayard found his heartbeat quickening in his chest. He pictured it, in the black and white of those wild dark times on the point: Felicia wrapped all around him and rocking and squeezing while he thrust and danced his hands over her hot skin. There had never been any danger of Felicia wanting more than that, so he would go farther, give more than he gave to anyone else. He could jerk off now, thinking of it, and he would not have to think anymore of going looking for Ron. Bayard feared what he could convince himself of up until he came.

But he kept holding it back, thinking he could take another walk, and if Ron was in the trailer, they could talk some more but he would not have to do anything. In fact, it would be polite to make it clear, not leave it hanging over them.

Descending the ladder, Bayard felt it in his whole body, the physical memory of years ago slipping out at night, silently down the rungs until he could pad silently across the linoleum and out the screen door, leaving Martin asleep above him. It was convenient that the stairs were on the free-for-all side, not by Mom's bedroom. But if she had declared her room her private territory, as part of the new regime at the cove, then, Bayard had felt, he could declare his own secret territory in the night. Mom probably had known and not wanted to talk about it with him, just as he knew now of her staying with Bryce Murtagh and did not want to talk about it with her. The only difficulty in his teens had been Hilda. She would stir and want to come along, so he always had a large Milk-Bone ready as consolation. Tonight, she barely seemed to be breathing as he stepped past her and flipped off the balcony light.

It was colder, truly fall, still and silent. His entire birthday had felt suspended like this, the space between two moods, neither of which he could accept as his own. A birthday should be a time to assess what you have become, but Bayard, the person, was a vague outline now in his own mind. He was aware of his innards, though, his pounding heart and a shaky feeling in his knees. He felt drawn toward exploration, as if he had explored everything behind him by now and had only one unknown ahead.

There was no light at all in the trailer, and he sensed a sudden shift inside, not toward calm but a new imbalance, almost a panic. Then he saw the door was open, so he called out, cheerfully, "Ron?"

"Hey," came a voice from inside.

"I wanted to come down and just say hi," Bayard said. "I didn't know if you'd be here."

"You can come in," Ron said. "Don't worry, babe."

So Bayard stepped in and could tell Ron had his sweats on. He was not naked as Bayard had somehow imagined he would be, like an ancient statue, muscular, smooth, cool as stone. "Have a beer?" Ron offered.

"Well, we had too much wine with dinner," Bayard said. "The Ostermanns just drove home."

"I heard them half an hour ago. I was about to figure you weren't going to come by and I'd head home to my water bed. This bunk of your brother's sucks. No wonder Peggy stopped coming back for more. No beer?"

"No, thanks, Ron." Bayard knew what he had to say but was on the verge of not saying it. Then he said it, seriously, before he could think more: "I felt I should say thanks for your offer, of the special treat, I mean. It's sort of tempting, really, it is. I mean, hey, why not try it? This is just sort of a bad time for me. Wondering about my future. I feel all scattered, like I'm not sure who I am lately. It's weird."

"That's okay, gorgeous. You'll be okay."

"I know, I'm sure. I've always been okay. But I don't want to do anything that might, you know, add to this scattered feeling right now."

"No problem," said Ron.

Bayard could not tell if he was really as casual as he sounded. He could hardly see him amidst the gray edges of shapes and depths. Bayard felt all sweaty and faint. "It's not that I don't think you're a sex god," he said to regain that flirty feeling of the morning.

"Hey," said Ron, a wonderful slow sound of understanding in that small word.

"And it's not because of, you know, worrying about safety. I know it'd be safe. I mean, that's not why."

Neither of them said anything until Ron finally said, out of the dimness, "I'll tell you what, so as I don't have to go home totally disappointed." It was not scary when he said it. Bayard's heart had not stopped pounding hard, but he did not feel scared. "Forget sex," Ron said. "How about instead you let me give you one nice long kiss?"

"Really?" said Bayard. Ron had stood up, he could tell, and was standing near him, shorter, solider, but shy now.

"Because you have such a beautiful face and that's the best part of all," Ron said softly.

So before Bayard knew it, he felt himself held close, strongly by very strong arms, and he inclined his head enough to meet Ron's lips that smelled beery but were soft and warm. It was not for long, then Ron rested his head on Bayard's shoulder and said he had always wanted to do that. Bayard held on for a while and he only barely sensed a hard-on pressing against him as he had imagined he might, but it was all right.

And then they talked about nothing much — the cool weather, taking in the dock for Drew Hale, the old sign

Ron had found — but on his slow way home to bed in his mother's house, Bayard thought back to that sudden shyness of Ron's. It was as if he knew Bayard had something to give him. But what was it he had managed to give Ron with that kiss?

A NOVEMBER SUNDAY

I

THEY HAD ALL come home but Martin, and they had stayed through the long weekend, but now it was Sunday and they were having their last breakfast with Mary for a while. With Nat there, it was almost like having four of them again, though Nat was no substitute, as fond as Mary was of him. She had come to feel he was right for Rosa, if only Rosa would relax into the way they depended on each other and not get prickly when things went wrong; Rosa did not know how wrong things could go in this world. But Mary had been telling herself all weekend they did appear calmer, Rosa and Nat, more settled, as if a decision had been reached unconsciously they had yet to discover. The prickliness went by more quickly, and the warm glances, which Mary was on the lookout for, lingered.

So she had hope that someone in this family might recognize one true happiness before the year was out. She looked at the oatmeal eaters, miraculously all awakened at the same late hour, ready to be fed at once but too late to come pile on Mary's bed the way Sundays had been in the old days. She passed the bowl of brown sugar and the tin of maple syrup, which Nat had brought her in September from the north. He was telling the story of the Republic of

Indian Stream, as the very tip of New Hampshire had declared itself to be for a couple of rebellious years in the early 1800s. Nat thought they ought to try it again.

"So where you guys live," Shirley asked, "claimed it wasn't part of the United States; it was its own country?"

"I don't think anyone particularly cared," Nat said. "But it lasted a short while. Every place has its history."

The toast kept popping up, and Mary, who had eaten earlier, would spread them with margarine, choose among the jams from the Old Fraddboro Store, and offer them round to the kids. She knew Bayard was waiting for lemon-rhubarb, so she obliged him every time; Nat seemed to have no preference, and the girls had each stopped at two slices. Mary, in a submerged mood, kept mostly quiet and listened to them talk, made another pot of coffee, even heated up the milk as Bayard had prompted her to do (his bookstore had a coffee bar in one corner), and then sat admiringly on her stool. She told herself not to be sad anymore, this was what it was all for, but still she felt somewhat drowned. She kept that to herself.

"Mom," said Shirley, "how about it?"

"It's your turn now," Rosa said. "You're too quiet."

"I'm enjoying you guys talking."

"But you have to reveal what's been on your mind. Nat and I aren't heading off until you come clean. We won't see you again before Christmas, and by then all sorts of changes may have occurred."

"Let's wait and see what they are," Mary said trying to put a spark in her eye.

"Come on, Mom," said Shirley.

"I'll say one thing then. I wish Martin was here."

"I predict he'll be back by New Year's," Bayard said.

Shirley said, "No way."

"Bet."

"Five bucks." They shook on it.

"Dad'll send him the money, you wait."

"You're such a cynic, Bayard."

"What's cynical about your father sending him money?" Mary asked.

"Bayard's cynical because he does not believe our big brother will ever grow up," Shirley explained. She had her baseball cap on, frontwards, and looked adorable, but Mary affected an impatient attitude, eyebrow raised.

"I would like to figure out this Suzanne," Rosa said. "Is she the earth mother type —"

"Like you," Bayard put it.

"— or the wispy moon child type? Fuck off, I am not the earth mother type."

"Children —" said Mary.

"Whatever, Martin's clearly getting it on," Shirley said, "so let's not knock it. Everyone in this family's getting it on but me."

"Because you're the baby," said Bayard.

"Children!" said Mary with more force.

"Okay, Mom, then *you* talk," Shirley said.

"Seriously, Mom, I meant it," said Rosa. "It's not the same on the phone. Here's your last chance to tell us all at once — all but Martin, I mean — about your future."

"How can I tell you about my future?"

"Does all this silence mean you're content? It's hard to read you, Mom. Is the job wearing you down?"

Four pairs of eyes were watching her, but then Nat lowered his and went back to scraping the drying scraps of oatmeal from the sides of his bowl to seem busy, not to be one of the inquisitors.

"You're asking what part Bryce plays in my life, aren't you?"

"It's up to you, Mom. You tell us," said Rosa.

"I hadn't realized I'd seemed so quiet."

"You realized, Mom," said Shirley.

Mary looked across the room at the still life. Now it was only a painting. In her flood of sadness, the remnants of the past had lost poignancy, and so, although she in her body felt drowned, there was also an empty place in the back of her head now where, she imagined, all the sentiments of her youth once lodged, the sacred reservoir — it was gone. But she could not confess it to her offspring, perched there, staring at her.

"I don't believe you should worry yourselves much about Bryce," she told them. "We enjoy each other's company," she said, but it was barely true on her part now, "and we're good friends. We're grown-up people with families. I'm certainly not going to take on two little stepchildren I've hardly met. This year has been, at best, a period of transition for me. And I don't know precisely where I'm headed, emotionally speaking, that is. It's not like driving along a highway."

"More like the woods," said Bayard in sympathy.

"But he's so boring," Shirley said. "I'm sorry, Mom. We've each said it privately, so you might as well know."

Mary tried to stiffen, but she could not make herself feel hurt; instead, she let herself laugh.

The phone rang, to her relief, and to her greater relief it was Gus Ostermann for Shirley. "Talk about boring," said Bayard, but Shirley shushed him angrily and pulled the kitchen phone into the bathroom and shut the door. "You should get a cordless, Mom," Bayard said.

"At least she's got a Touch-Tone," said Rosa.

"I'd never know where it was if it was cordless," said Mary.

Then Rosa prodded her: "So that's the end of our discussion?"

"Is this something you really want to know, sweetie?"

Mary asked. Rosa was so pretty in her thick gray wool turtleneck and her tumbling dark hair, so substantial next to substantial Nat in his flannel plaid and insulated undershirt, that Mary saw it for sure: they will be married, and Rosa will be safe — and so will Nat, she reminded herself. Being with Bryce had helped her with the man's point of view. Mary had never before believed that men also wanted to be safe or that she had safety in her to give, but look what it had gotten her into.

"Mainly, I want to know," Rosa said slowly, "if you're going to be all right when we head off today. That's all I want to know."

"And I want to know if Mr. Zeytoundjian stands a remote chance," said Bayard. Mary could see he was annoyed Rosa was horning in on his role as comforter and ally, so he was taking another tack.

"Mr. Zeytoundjian," she replied, "is a very kind man. No jokes about Mr. Zeytoundjian."

"Shut up, Bayard, let Mom talk."

"Of course, I'll be all right when you head off. This is where I live. Mostly, you're not here. I've accustomed myself to that. One by one, you've left. It's been gradual. I've hardly noticed it happening."

"I have an idea you've noticed it this year," Rosa said with a strong pull in her voice.

"Do you remember last spring, honey," Mary asked, "when you wondered if I ever jumped up and swung on tree branches on my walks? I don't remember what I said, but I remember you asking me. Did I tell you that I did, that I felt at home in these woods?" She wanted to reassure her daughter and kept her eyes from welling with tears as they had then.

"You're a different person now, Mom," Rosa concluded.

"Maybe I'm stronger," Mary said.

"You don't seem stronger. Really, you don't, Mom. Does she, Bayard?" He shook his head, but he was leaving this one to his sister, and Nat was looking sternly into his empty bowl, so Rosa went on: "I'd say you're more vulnerable now. I'd even say that's maybe good. But, Mom, that's why I'm trying to say I worry."

Mary must have always wanted her children to worry about her, because what Rosa said was familiar in an odd way. She had known for some time, even ten years ago, that they worried, but she tried to think of it as worry for themselves and now this was worry for their mother. It was planted deep in their childhoods and only now rose up in this morning light.

"I worry, too, Mom," said Bayard, second, not quite as ready to have said it, Mary knew, but preparing to say it, eventually, for real.

Then Shirley came storming in from the bathroom with the hung-up phone. "That Gus sends me round the bend. He calls every other day just to yak. He's actually a smart kid, it's sort of cute, but basically, Mom, how did I ever get into this? Now he wants to come visit for some suicide and sexuality conference he found out about. He wants to stay over in my dorm room. I actually said okay, but then he says he thinks it'd be cool to try to pass himself off as a Smith girl for an experiment. I'm sure he'll do it, too. But I can't trust that little dude to stick to his sleeping bag. Why did I say yes?"

She heaved herself onto her stool, turned her cap around frontwards — for phoning she seemed to prefer the bill in the back — and asked for a refill. Mary, who had gotten to her feet to start clearing off, came over with the pot and poured the half cup left into Shirley's mug.

"I could strangle him," her daughter fumed. "Hey, so what did he cause me to miss? Did we resolve Mom's relationship?" Mary put her arm on Shirley's shoulders. No one answered her question, so Shirley shrugged and took a sip, then reached her free hand around her mother's waist and gave a quick tug. "This coffee's deadly, Mom."

So Mary went to heat up more milk.

II

STEWART HAD GONE to Mass with his mother and now had come over for his run. Thanksgiving had put on the pounds, he told Ron. He had his URHS sweats on because it was cold out and, he said, "You wouldn't want to see what's under here these days anyway."

"Try me," Ron said; Victor and Stewart exchanged an aggravated look.

Victor had been cranky all morning. Holidays did it to him. They had been with his sister's family Saturday to make up for Thursday with the Starkses, where Victor had spent most of the time in a corner with a magazine, not that anyone noticed. Ron's sister Alice would be having her baby, which they said was a girl, after the new year; Ron had never before looked forward to the birth of a nephew or niece. His brother Henry was loaded by noon and started calling Ron "Godfather" even though Henry had been godfather already three different times. Victor had sat by Grandma at dinner, which did not require much of him but keeping the old lady from slumping over too far. Aunt Ellie had to be out serving that Armenian family, but she had prepared the food ahead of time because Ron's ma was not about to; she would as soon open a few cans.

No one in his family knew about Ron's virus. He had asked his friends — Peggy, Stewart, Mary — not to let on to anyone because he did not need the hassle; they would kick him out of the family again, which might not be all that bad, but why subject himself to their ignorance?

Ron was doing his stretches on the floor, while Victor and Stewart half-watched TV, a panel of Republicans arguing with each other. "You limbered up earlier?" he asked Stewart.

"Enough," Stewart said. He did not look like he had done much exercise lately. It was the Peggy Hale influence, Ron could tell.

"Get your asses out of here so I can watch my program," Victor said.

"Those old farts?" said Ron.

"They run the country in case you haven't noticed," Victor said.

"They're Republicans."

"That's what I mean. They run the country."

"They're a pack of assholes," said Stewart. "Bill Clinton's an asshole, too. Peggy's dad wants Ross Perot again."

"Talk about an asshole," said Victor. "Hey, come on, get out of here."

They did not talk much on their run because it was a cold morning and their breath stung. Stewart got winded, but he claimed he had to slow down because his knee was going bum on him. Ron took off ahead but got lonesome the way he always did after he had been with Stewart, so he turned around and joined up with him already on his way back to the boathouse. They sprinted the last hundred yards, and Stewart had to lean against the maple, panting, but he beat Ron because Ron let him.

"Let's smoke a joint in the car," Stewart said when he got his breath, "so we don't bug Victor."

In the Neon, Stewart turned up the sound — Al Green — and took his stash from under the seat. "High school," Victor would have said if he saw them.

"You need to vacuum this interior," Ron said.

"Fuck," said Stewart, trying to light up. Finally, he had it. "Hey, I see Mary Lanaghan's got the family over. You make it with that son of hers yet, buddy?"

"Still working on it," said Ron, a devilish flash in his eyes.

"Yeah, yeah."

"No, seriously," Ron said. It was something he had mulled over plenty since that kiss, which he had decided not to tell anyone about, not even Victor. "He came by yesterday and mentioned some girl he's been seeing who works at his store. But no commitment, he made sure I knew. Why would he drop that bit of information if he was closing me off? I told you how he calls me a studmuffin."

"That's supposed to be a come-on? Jesus, Ron."

"Well, he's still curious, I can see it in the way he looks at me," Ron said. "You think I can't spot that?"

"Yeah, yeah," Stewart said.

"Fuck off."

"Here, have a toke."

Ron did. He never smoked except with Stewart. The music was warm in his ears, and through the windshield he watched the bare woods standing stiff in the cold, but it was warming up considerably inside. He tried imagining how Stewart would get so stoned he would let Ron blow him right there in the car, but of course all Stewart wanted was to talk about Peggy.

"She's moving back in temporarily," he said.

"The garage apartment?"

"There's no point in her paying rent to her girlfriend."

"Why doesn't fucking Drew let you two winterize the cottage?"

"Yeah, right."

"It'd be a smart investment. What's his objection? You're still married."

"It's *my* objection," Stewart said. "I wouldn't ask that old fuck for a dime. Peggy says he's got plans for that place anyway."

"He's always threatening some bullshit."

"He's an asshole, Ron. Peggy's got to stay away from Leominster."

"So how's business?" Ron asked after another toke.

"It's all right — and Peggy could get herself a job up here."

Ron knew what the real problem would always be, but he did not want to say anything more about Mrs. Tomaszewski; he had said it all. After almost a year of group, Ron had noticed how most people did not alter much. You gave them great advice and they liked hearing it, but that was as far as it went. Then it was not about altering, Ron had decided, it was about finding what was there deep inside and bringing it up and living with it. Mary Lanaghan was the only person he knew who had been doing that, and she did not even have a group. Ron had been watching her closely. She could not see it happening the way he could. She thought she was a lost cause.

Smoking made Stewart lean back and get quiet. Ron could see his gut pressing against his sweatshirt when he stretched, but Ron liked a bit of gut because he was too used to Victor with no gut at all. Stewart really was a married man now. This is it, Ron thought. His last try at bacheloring is over, but he is as sexy as he has ever been. To Ron, he was maybe even more so.

"No, I'd rather we find a place in Parshallville," Stewart said. "Those new condos going in on 108 near the Fraddboro line, there's two-bedrooms for seventy-nine. We could about make it."

"That's big bucks," Ron said.

"Ron, you can't get anything for less than seventy-nine."

"When did the fucking world get so expensive?" Ron asked the woods out there. He was experiencing some confusion over whether he was inside or outside the car.

"You know, somewhere in that world," Stewart said, "there's a fifteen-year-old named Joseph Tomaszewski. He's probably got a new last name. I never hear from his mother anymore. Somewhere out in that fucking world I've got a son. Can you believe it? I let him go, Ron." And after thinking about it for a minute, he said with a harshness in his throat, "Bad news."

"At least you got Peggy back," Ron said, not quite sounding like his own voice.

Stewart was looking at him hard, no fooling around now, and Ron was back inside the car, for sure; he was almost inside Stewart's eyes. "She doesn't care what may or may not have happened in the past," Stewart was saying. "She must have learned forgiveness from her mother because she definitely didn't from Drew. Hey, I don't have to explain Peggy to you. She's just a beautiful person. She knows how to have fun, but that's not what I'm talking about. She's got something I don't. It's almost sort of spiritual. Like in the lake last summer, in her pink bikini — she belonged there. She'd just lay back and float with the sun on her face. I need some of that in my life. Peaceful. You think I'm kidding."

Ron had heard this before, even the part about buying a condo, and the peaceful part was what Stewart came up with when he wanted to fall in love again. The difference this time was that he had fallen in love with Peggy a couple of years ago. Stewart was stoned, but Ron suddenly felt entirely straight again. The windshield formed a perfect seal between them and the woods; he could see through it perfectly and yet hear nothing but Al Green. Songs, he concluded, were either about starting up the romance or breaking it off, never about the middle part. Stewart's windshield was so clean. Ron imagined what it would look like if he crashed through it, how it would crack into thousands of tiny cubes and give way slowly like a breaking wave.

Stewart lit the joint again and passed it over to him.

III

IT WAS NO SUBSTITUTE for Thanksgiving, but it was the deal Jim Pflueger had struck with his ex-wife, Donna. The kids had stopped by on their drives back to college, and Jim had baked vegetarian lasagna because by then they would be sick of turkey. The significant others — how significant, Jim could not tell — were with them. He had become fond of Kayla over their scraping and painting weekend, so he felt he had to try harder now to befriend Tommy for Monica's sake. Luckily, after lunch Eric and Kayla went off for a walk, which the other pair did not feel up for. Tommy was bookish, a nerd by Monica's old standards, but he was also young, and Jim pictured his gawky features filling out into handsomeness; he supposed that, to Monica, he was handsome already. Young women had their own frame of reference: a soft complexion was not necessarily too boyish; it was what most of their boyfriends still had.

While Tommy helped with the dishes, he talked about the Dickinson house in Amherst and the Frost archives — it reminded Jim he had to get a stack of wildflower books back to the library tomorrow. This had become his Monday lunch habit, a sandwich from the general store, mail his weekly long letter to Anne now he had worn out the daily postcard thing, and pick up some new books to read. He must give off a bookish impression himself. Eric was not much into books of the literary sort and Monica seemed to read them mostly for the feminist perspective. Jim had the horrible thought that Tommy and Kayla might be better suited to each other. Then he wondered if he wanted them to be, so he could keep Monica and Eric to himself.

Tommy had applied to several schools in geology but first wanted to go to the University of Montana in poetry writing. Monica had explained privately, with worldly resignation, that his family had enough money to let him give it a try before he figured out what to do for a living. She was in the midst of her own applications but assured her father that, in psychology, loans and scholarships were the rule. The days of his helping with her tuition were over.

Jim watched her in the front room folding the napkins and wiping off the place mats. She had told him she liked his simple life; she would never want to live with as much stuff as her mother did. Her own generation, she said — and it had launched a big discussion — was the generation of stuff. Kids have always had stuff, she conceded, but stuff has been accumulating exponentially, and if we choose not to let it pile up and smother us then we seem to throw it out as often as we can and replace it with more. Eric had a complementary take on the subject: he called it the battle of plastic, the plastic that proliferates and the plastic that miniaturizes. He stressed the economics — the streamlining of corporations and information transmission versus the expanding production of throwaway goods — while Monica spoke for the individual psyche lost in barrages of stuff, and by stuff she also meant the electronic impulses in every cubic foot of our air.

Kayla and Tommy kept quiet through most of this performance, perhaps not wanting to offend Mr. Pflueger, who, for all they knew, was a Republican, or perhaps they did not come from families that hashed through issues at the dining table. Jim wondered how his replacement, Charles O'Keefe, dealt with these grandstanding kids of his. Donna used to enjoy egging them on, but Charles was more of a stifler, one of those damn Harvard liberals who valued discussion with no one but experts. Jim hoped the two of them drove him nuts.

"While it's still halfway sunny, shall we hike down the road and catch Eric and Kayla walking back?" he suggested.

"Oh all right," said Monica. She had pushed in the two chairs that belonged at the table and was returning the others to the desk by the window, the spot by the woodstove, and then the stool to the kitchen, where Tommy was drying his hands at the sink.

"Unless you're still pooped," Jim said.

"I'm pooped, but it'll wake me up before we head on."

"I could use a walk, Mr. Pflueger," said Tommy, pronouncing the *P,* which most people did not.

"What way did they go?" Monica asked, peering out front, but Jim had not noticed. "Let's walk to the dead end, Dad. It's the only way that doesn't bum me out."

It was not quite parka weather, so Jim took his blue-jean jacket with the woolly lining and followed his daughter and her boyfriend down the fresh gray steps out onto the gravel. No one commented further on the barren, leveled pasture with its lot line stakes and muddy driveways waiting for the backhoe next spring. Soon they were beyond it, with woods on either side and the sun at their backs.

Monica was telling Tommy the stories Jim had heard about the hippie commune in the old farmhouse long before he moved here. To her they made a great lovely myth. Jim knew he would never have managed to live in a commune; he had been brought up to be realistic about the world with the result that he was skeptical. Other people, even old hippies, seemed to know how to plunge in. He had mentioned that to Forest, to excuse himself, maybe, for being so literal-minded, and the doctor had nodded tentatively, as usual, and asked if that was necessarily a bad thing. "How can it not be?" Jim had asked back, on the verge of anger, as he often was in that cinder-block cubicle. "Because 'literal' means 'by the letter' or 'by the word,' and the word is as real and alive as any object or feeling. Some people even say the word is God." It was Dr. Forest being glib, then he further pointed out that Jim liked to call himself a wordsmith and had never felt his trade to be without honor.

But honor was a hell of a troubling concept. What kind of honor had the Kathleen years brought him? Jim thought of how his marriage had crept off into a corner and of the silence in the house that final year, of Donna's rigid silence. He remembered his cluttered desk at home, where he continued the overdue projects he could not leave behind at the office; he remembered the old word processor, the Magnavox VideoWriter, with its orangy light and what seemed now like its prehistoric slowness. After the good front of a boisterous dinner hour, the kids would be up in their rooms studying to get into the best colleges, which they did despite what the huge mechanism of marital failure was doing to them. Donna liked to pin it all on his lack of drive, which to her was more like laziness. Kathleen came only after that, Jim had to keep reminding himself, and she had helped him appreciate his own pace, though in doing so he betrayed all he had sworn himself to. The so-called word went out the window there, Dr. Forest. And then Jim — with Donna, Monica, and Eric three blocks away in the house — was trapped in an airless attic apartment in a city he had not grown up in, his own sister way across the continent. The only honor he could come up with now, as he walked abreast with Tommy and Monica and only half-listening to her stories, had to do with not deserving something for nothing, for he had once let himself come all too close to nothing. But now words, for him, were growing back into their original meanings: *daughter* and *son* and *sister.* There might be more words to come, but these were the ones he had been working on with all his heart. The shabby little Dowland Free Library, he had found, was helping him.

Eric and Kayla had to have taken the other direction because there was the anthropologist's farmhouse, the former commune, curtains drawn closed, and no sign of the kids.

Jim smiled at his enthusiastic daughter's legend making: "Can't you picture the stoned-out hippies with goats tethered all over the lawn? The professor told Dad there was a bathtub on lion's paws out back that they filled up from a heated oil drum and took baths in with goats chomping all around."

"I wonder what they figured the world was going to be like in twenty-five years," Tommy said.

"Young people didn't worry as much about the future in those days," Jim said, as wisely as he could.

IV

IT WAS HARDEST saying good-bye to the dog. Hilda had been Shirley's companion from age seven, had kept her from ever feeling lonesome. Now, when she left Umbachaug, she never knew if she would see Hilda again. She could not contemplate it. When Rosa and Nat had driven off, she had to lie on the floor beside the dog for a full hour talking of doggish things — walks, table scraps, smells, pee and poo, wet noses — until Bayard said he would miss his bus.

They gave their mother long hugs, but the tears in Shirley's eyes were for Hilda. Only a month till Christmas, she told herself, she will make it. The sound of the door shutting behind them jolted Shirley; she held her brother's free hand going down the stairs, and he let her, the way he always did, and did not ask why.

Beside their mother's Cavalier, with its proud Smith College decal, sat the rusted-out Tercel she had convinced her father to let her buy now instead of waiting till graduation. She needed it to get to her internship working with teenage latinas in Holyoke. They had harder lives than Shirley had imagined anyone could have, the way their fathers and brothers and boyfriends treated them, and their mothers were not much better. Shirley had begun to feel an awful gap between herself and so many sadder people in the world.

"When are you going to get a car, Bayard?" she asked as they pulled away from home, so she could set her mind on something she did not care so much about.

"I'm not asking Dad for anything these days," he said. "What about grad school, though?"

"We'll see," said Bayard. "I'd rather not. He can give it all to you and Martin."

"Don't be such a bitch," said Shirley.

"Look, I let him send me to Ireland and I didn't even want to go."

"You liked the pubs."

"I should've gone to England, but no, it had to be Ireland. Dad's idea, Dad's money, what can I say?"

They were quiet passing Bryce Murtagh's house and the other ones with their unknown inhabitants. At the main road, Shirley had to wait for a looming truck, so she said, "Good-bye, woods; good-bye, cove; good-bye, dog; good-bye, Mom." Bayard echoed the last in a faint singsong as Shirley headed for Haviland.

At the end of the long weekend, she felt talked out. Rosa and Nat had stuck close, so she had her private times with Bayard, not her sister. She would have liked to find out how Rosa had coped with lesbian feelings, or if she ever had them, but it was hard to bring up, even in the context of writing her thesis, so they had devoted their only time alone to talking about Bryce. Rosa thought Mom was in a trap she could not get herself out of, being unable to hurt any living creature, but if Bryce got tired of Mom first, then it could all be his doing. "Mom might have ways of making him tired," Shirley suggested, "you know, passive-aggressive," but Rosa said Mom was pure passive, and that had led to an argument. Shirley did not feel close enough to her sister. In their family, girls got along better with boys and boys with girls. Sharing the loft had only made the sisters back off from each other.

"Do you miss Martin?" she asked when the silence had gone on too long.

"I know you do," Bayard said.

"I was thinking how Rosa and I aren't that close and neither are you and Martin. Maybe that's why I keep being drawn to girlfriends."

"So I should be drawn to boyfriends," Bayard said, to be funny.

"But there's something to it," Shirley said. She could always speculate openly with Bayard. He played the mentor too much, but she let him, and he let her say anything she wanted to. It was strange, though, that she was doing the driving and he was sitting there on his way to a bus. He looked tired out. He had been up all night with his reading lamp showing orange behind the curtain while Nat and Rosa lay in their nest of beanbag chairs down in the free-for-all. Shirley had slept restlessly, and the light was shining whenever she turned over and looked up. She worried about Bayard. Everything he had to say about the woman at the bookstore sounded only half there, and he was nervous and skinnier than in the summer. He was studying too hard. So she asked him, "But why don't you have more — I don't mean boyfriends, but I mean male friends? I know you have drinking buddies, but you never talk about them as your friends. I need my women friends so much right now."

"In college I had male friends."

"Is that what happens when college is over?"

"Well, you don't have the ready-made crowd. Maybe, I prefer the company of women," Bayard said.

Shirley remembered trying to explain her brother to Monica Pflueger last summer. Monica had not liked the sound of him. She was one of those really mature people Shirley wanted to hang out with, but they remained in different circles; Shirley's friends had found Monica way too theoretical when she delivered her homophobia paper at the psychology forum this semester. "I prefer the company of women, too," said Shirley, but she was not sure it was true because of how much she loved her brothers. "We each have to make a project of doing better with men," she said.

"Whoa, little sister," Bayard said. It was obvious he was not used to her mentoring him back.

In Haviland Center, she took the Leominster Road southeast, and when they came to the crossing, they looked for Watertank and Corncrib's cross-eyed house, which their mother always pointed out. "One day they won't be able to get out the door," Bayard said, and Shirley imagined two giant people ballooning into every corner of two small rooms and breathing out the little windows until the house burst apart. "Thanks for taking me out of your way," Bayard said. He had softened in just the past minute; Shirley could feel it. "All right, let's talk about it. I should do better with men?"

"I wanted to ask Rosa," Shirley said, "and it isn't the same asking you, but I wanted to ask her what she did with homoerotic feelings — going on the assumption that everyone has them the way everyone has hetero feelings. You're the one who told me to read that Vietnam book by Norman Mailer because it was so homoerotic."

"Sexuality, the hot topic for nineteen ninety-five," said Bayard, but she could see he was thinking. She could not have asked Martin that question without freaking him out. "Gus Ostermann might be a better person to ask," Bayard said.

"Give me a break."

"You're worried about homosexual feelings, and you're worried about heterosexual feelings. Try not worrying about either. Let them find their natural mix."

"Is that what you do? I know it's none of my business, but I told you all about Michelle and Susanna."

"And they sounded extremely hot," said Bayard.

Shirley was getting bored with this. Martin would freak, Rosa would not even start, Bayard evaded, and she was afraid to talk to Mom. She put on a truly disgusted expression and drove. Then she said, "Why can you be so charming to the world and such a turd to me?"

"Sorry for not sharing," he said. Shirley had told him how she hated that phrase: *to share* meant to divide something and give some to someone else, not to confess. Using words for their precise meanings was Monica Pflueger's thing. She had set Shirley straight on *sharing;* her other peeve was with *basically.*

"Anyway," Bayard said, as if he was going to change the subject, "I've experimented, but it didn't do much for me. It was too different from what I want from lovemaking."

"You had gay sex?"

"Let's say I gave it a brief try once," Bayard said.

Shirley always figured he had fooled around in school; anyone as horny as Bayard was bound to have. "But the feelings?" she asked.

"I don't think it's what I want, sis," he answered.

"I can't believe you act so casual about everything, Bayard," Shirley said. They had left Haviland behind, and she felt herself moving back into her college self, the one with the car and the friends of her own, the one she liked better.

"I'm not casual at all," he said. She stared at him coolly then turned back to the road, which was filling with holiday traffic. "I'm not casual about missing my bus." She was not going to respond. He bugged her. It was not like the old days. Something was happening to Bayard she could not recognize.

It was hard for Shirley to keep silent because she did not want to leave it this way with her brother, but she was angry with him; she was angry with her whole family, and that made her honk the horn at the stupid driver who cut right in front of her from the shoulder. "Whoa, sister," said Bayard, and then once again he seemed to soften. "Do you want to talk about Mom?" he asked.

"Not particularly," Shirley said.

"You think we talk about her too much."

"I wish you could for once tell me what you really feel about this woman you're seeing from the bookstore. I told you about Michelle."

"I'm wired about Grad Recs is all," Bayard said. "There's too much you have to know, and everything depends on it, where you get in, how much money they give you."

"So you're not serious about this woman?"

"Helen?"

"Whatever." The Tercel clattered its fenders as Shirley took it up the ramp to Route 2 east. It was a tense merge, no time to be trying to have this talk.

"I can't get serious about anyone right now, Shirl, because I don't know where I'm going to be," Bayard said, staring at the bad traffic ahead of them.

"I'll get you there in time," Shirley said. She slipped into the left lane and floored it to keep from being rear-ended by drivers as angry as she. Everything around them threatened to collide.

"Glad you're doing the driving," Bayard said and seemed to mean it. "Why do people put themselves through Thanksgiving? We're such a frantic country."

A light rain spattered on the windshield. "Damn," said Shirley because her wipers only smeared a bird dropping across her field of vision and the washer fluid would not squirt enough. Civilization was springing up on either side — malls, developments, bright fast food and gas station signs on high poles against the rain clouds. She would have to be edging right for their exit. "But isn't there something calm about being with a woman, Bayard?" she asked now, to see what he would say. He murmured what might have been a yes. "Maybe that's all it is for me," Shirley said. "I feel tense with men. I mean, I sometimes feel excited, but I feel tense, as if there's a war on. I can't handle it. It's Gus Ostermann to the max. I told you how it went with Michelle and how it never really went at all with Susanna — it doesn't always work out with women, but it's like we're on the same side. Do you feel women are on some other side from you?"

"Maybe that's what I like," said Bayard.

"But don't you ever want to be on the same side? That's what I'm trying to write about for Professor Woo, how this new androgyny wants to put an end to the battle our parents fought."

"I guess I'm not into the new androgyny," Bayard said, almost regretfully.

"It's not only how people look, though," Shirley explained. "It's an attitude we can't escape. It's in the air all around us. We're changed by it." Bayard seemed to be seriously considering what she was saying. "I mean our generation," she said. "Because we aren't set yet, we're still figuring ourselves out. Mom's set. I have to accept that. There's no way she's ever going to be a lesbian." She said that to allow her brother to laugh and then slowed down for the backed-up traffic at their exit.

"But you think maybe I still stand a chance?" Bayard asked.

Shirley gave him a nod of not entirely mock encouragement, which he smiled at in his enigmatic Bayardesque way, and she pulled right up to the taillights of the car in front of them. Everyone was honking like the typical Massachusetts drivers they were.

V

HALE'S COVE, backwater of Umbachaug, choked in the shallow places with dead lily pads and blown leaves, was still and quiet. There was perhaps a month before it would freeze over, or this very night it might begin icing up in shady corners, all the life tucked under, drowsily skimming the bottom or burrowed into the sand to sleep and wait for April. The low sun barely made it through the pines on the high ground beyond the railroad bed; it was three in the afternoon, rain clouds flying on. Victor Bardonecchia had no special affection for this spot on earth he now inhabited. He liked the quiet, but the house was moldy and shabby and filled with a sadness because it was where he had learned of his lover's infection — an abstract knowledge, a looming danger, but Victor had felt it lodge within the boathouse walls and there would be no extracting it.

While Ron napped, he had been sitting on the deck off their bedroom, whittling in the cold. He liked the feel of the knife in his cold hand, of the brittle wood. He was making nothing recognizable, only a long shape of elaborate design, cross-hatched and striated, another something without purpose — Ron called them psychic dildos. Victor had carved many such in recent months because he kept dreaming there was a labyrinth in his attic, a forest of decorated beams and posts forming T's about the room. So he began whittling them in miniature as a way of controlling the dream.

When finally no sunlight fell on any corner of the deck, Victor swung himself over the railing and onto dry land, so as not to pass through the bedroom and wake Ron yet, and carried his knife and stump of tree limb up the slope to a sunny patch that spilled down a maple trunk onto a pile of leaves. He sprawled there as he might have as a boy, on his stomach, propped on elbows, holding the weighty object before his eyes, turning it, as if on a lathe, assessing its symmetry, discovering an emerging pattern in the intricate scratches. Mary Lanaghan, on her walk, found him like that. It took Victor a while to return from his small world to her larger one, where a dog was panting and a soft voice said, "It looks like a chrysalis. What is it?"

"Just whittling."

"Imagine, Victor, what butterfly would emerge from that!" And Mary spread her arms in wonder at the idea.

"Kids gone?" he asked.

"I'm alone again," she answered, but not sadly. Indeed, he heard a note of relief in her voice but also judged it a false note. Himself, he was glad to be done for a month with his sister's family and with Ron's, but he knew Mary could not be so glad. Although he had observed her up close only a few times, Victor could see into her. She was like a woman wrapped in nearly transparent flowing silk, revealing, where it clung, her breasts and hips and thighs, not a woman in jeans and jeans jacket with a long gray knit scarf swooped twice around her neck dangling down as she leaned over him to inspect his creation.

"It's a design, that's all," Victor said. "I like patterns that balance out. Seven rows here, seven rows there, see?"

"The wood is white like bone," Mary said. "It looks ancient."

"Bleached in the sun," Victor said. "I collect them. I strip the bark and let them weather."

"Where's Ron?" Mary asked.

"He had a late night. Then Stewart was here this morning and got him stoned. He's passed out."

Mary said it was hibernation weather. Victor felt suddenly cold. She squatted down beside him into the faint sun, but it barely felt warm to him. They talked awhile about Ron's virus, and Mary told him how she had Ron's doctor sending her photocopies of all the latest articles on the new theories of when to begin treatment, and she had Ron showing her his lab reports, which still looked good. From Ron, Victor did not want to know actual numbers because numbers would invade his brain and keep him calculating gains and losses, turning Ron to mathematics, but he was glad for Mary's watchfulness; he never trusted Ron to tell him the full truth.

And then in return, it occurred to Victor he should ask about Mary's own boyfriend. At the mention of his name, Mary sank from her heels back onto her butt, pulled her knees up under her chin and clasped them for warmth. Victor turned onto his side and set his carving like a slender canoe on the brown sea of leaves between them.

They had been talking, Mary said. Bryce Murtagh had told her he had been trying hard. It was possible with her, Bryce said, to feel an easiness he had not felt with his wife, but for the reason that Mary was not his wife, that they had separate houses, that they shopped for themselves and did their own laundry. Bryce feared, Mary said, that he would become an old fussbudget again if they moved in together. He hated it in himself, but he could not help it, he said, he was a control freak and aggravating to live with. He did not dare risk anything beyond their current arrangement. It had nothing to do with Valerie. It had to do with him. Mary was his nature girl, but he could not be like her.

"Valerie is the wife?" Victor asked.

"I suspect she'll be back by spring," Mary said. "I suspect she's been chastened, too."

"And you?"

"I dread a change of any sort, can't you tell, Victor? I've been known to cling," she said.

"You might bump into someone else," Victor told her. "When I came back from the service I bumped into Ron. I knew him from high school, but I never noticed him much. It was when my father was dying, and I was taking over the diner. There we were. And so my life changed."

"I'm almost fifty, Victor," Mary said with her soft lovely lips. "I think I'll be clinging to Bryce for now."

"I could see having separate houses," Victor said.

"Because I don't expect to be starting over at my age," said Mary, and then she told him about the hormones her doctor had started her on to balance her out and make it easier later. Ron would ask her for details, but Victor felt embarrassed to know even this much, and he did not see what Mary meant about being her age because Ron was right about her being beautiful. Did straight men notice or did they only have this idea of younger women? Victor could understand that. Kevin was young. Late after closing up a month ago, he had let Victor have sex with him because he wanted to find out what it was Ron raved about and now he knew and was content to tease and flirt again and go looking for the next excitement he had yet to experience. That was Kevin. Ron thought it was a riot, but Victor hardly recalled it once it was over. Now he imagined Ron asleep and looked at Mary, at the experience in her face, the wisdom that must come from passion. Straight men must see it there if Victor did. Ron saw it everywhere, but Victor saw it rarely. Not in Kevin. He saw none of it in the pleasant face of Bryce Murtagh, whom he had never said more than a good morning to. Mary told Ron that Bryce was wonderful in bed, but it was hard for Victor to see passion in straight men. Stewart Tomaszewski did not show much, either. Sex was not necessarily passion. Both were in Ron, though. Ron had saved Victor, who had resigned himself to lonesomeness forever.

"Your son came by to see us," Victor told Mary. "You know, Ron has a wicked crush on him."

"That's all right," said Mary, "Bayard can handle it."

"And Shirley came by the diner in her new car."

"It's a rattletrap," said Mary. "I worry about her driving it."

"You have decent kids. I'm not really big into kids," Victor said, "but I don't mind yours."

"I'm pretty proud of them," said Mary. "They don't know what they're going to do with their lives, but they're nice people. I did part of my job, anyway."

"No one can do all of a job," Victor told her.

"I do worry less than I used to." A thought seemed to be moving across Mary's face. "Instead, I feel flooded inside and everything's blurrier, watery, like wading waist-deep in water and you can't move your legs fast enough."

"I have nightmares, too," Victor said, and he picked up the white bonelike post he kept seeing, large, in his sleep. "Like this," he said and handed it to her.

"I still say it's a chrysalis," she said, turning it over in her reddish hands. "Something is waiting in there."

"I have a stack of them upstairs. These are only models from my nightmares."

Mary's face was fading from curiosity to puzzlement. He had said something too private, he realized. Ron did not even know about those dreams; when he woke up, Victor would say, "You're awake now," and seal it back into his lips with a morning kiss.

"I mean it's abstract art," Victor said quickly and brushed leaves off himself as he started to get up. "I'll go find out how Sleeping Beauty's doing," he said. "You want to see him?"

"Let him sleep. I'll see him later in the week. It could snow, couldn't it?" She was trying to keep Victor there.

"It's not going to snow," he said as a charm against his dread of winter.

"But you two keep safe," Mary was saying as Victor began backing off away from her toward the boathouse with a slight wave.

"Have a good dog walk."

"Oh, this is about as far as we get these days."

Victor did not turn to see her go but went straight in and up to his attic and flung himself on the pillows, not even taking off his jacket. He felt chills in his ankles and wrists as if they might freeze up and kill off his hands and feet. But his fingers came back to him, and so he spent the next half hour carefully tabulating the week's accounts. Then he stuffed the papers into their respective milk crates and would have resumed whittling, but he heard a stretching groan from two floors below. Victor had been hoping for this. It was perfect timing. He could tell that Bayard Lanaghan and Stewart Tomaszewski had left Ron in a high state, and now Victor could work it out of him. It was what each of them needed, and it would last a good hour. He came down the ladder and then started for the stairs with a heavy tread so Ron would know what he was in for.

VI

LOUISE HAD TAKEN on Sundays as well. She needed the money, and the easiest and highest-paying client she had was Mrs. Germaine, who had no one to leave it to and was spending it on herself. Why not? thought Louise, I would, too. That was what she liked about the old lady — no apologies.

But she did have to listen to her babble. Now that she did not have to think of it in terms of death and dying, of clues to the hereafter, the way she did at first, Louise found some of it funny but most of it tedious. People only care about themselves, she decided, and that was why so few of them went into the helping professions where they were needed. She told herself she was doing good for the world. She had a good soul. Her brother Charles often told her so.

The Sunday crossword in *The New York Times* — Louise did not see why the old lady bought a whole Sunday paper from a far-off city for a puzzle — took up most of the afternoon. Mrs. Germaine had struggled with it more than usual but was highly amused when the chief export of Nauru turned out to be guano. "Birdshit," she howled, "they export birdshit!" Louise had never heard of Nauru or guano. She learned things at Mrs. Germaine's, but they did not add up to useful information. Pfitzner was a German composer named Hans. So what? And Louise did not believe you could begin a name with *pf* until she remembered Michelle Pfeiffer.

She did enjoy the music Mrs. Germaine listened to. That afternoon it was not by Pfitzner but some other German-sounding name. Louise tapped her feet along to it as she sat on the chaise in her muumuu and looked out the window at the clouds filling up the sky all over again. Mostly, Mrs. Germaine talked to herself and did not expect answers, but Louise was ready with an "umm" and a "really" when it was expected. Sometimes, when Mrs. Germaine was feeling more debilitated, she would ask Louise to entertain her, and Louise had the pleasure of recounting stories from when she and Charles were teenagers and their parents were still in town. She had told Mrs. Germaine, in installments, about the family times at Hale's Cove, a part of the lake the old lady scorned but nonetheless took a certain interest in because it was where cheap people lived, and cheap people, she said, had to be watched or they made trouble for the rest of us. Louise was not offended. She expected it from a rich old lady like Mrs. Germaine. "Duncan Hale, the one that snatched up that land, he was a son of a bitch," she had told Louise. "His wife got black and blue from him. She didn't last long. And the older boy, the pyromaniac, they sent him away, and the girl, I don't know what happened to her, married her off I suppose, leaving only that young devil Drew. The older brother, you see, set brush fires on cold November days. Did I tell you? They sent him away before the whole forest went up in smoke."

The stories Louise told were about picnics and sand castles and the time she returned for Martin Lanaghan's party. And because today she had given Mrs. Germaine a full account of Martin's latest adventures in the West and even read her the letter he had written with graphic details of the older woman he was living with — Mrs. Germaine loved her spicy stories — it occurred to Louise to stop off at Mrs. Lanaghan's — at Mary's — on the way home and check on how she was doing. It had been a while.

The classical station put Mrs. Germaine to sleep, so

Louise left it on and tidied up, which meant wiping stains and dribbles in the bathroom and folding towels and straightening the bath mat and the throw rugs in the hall that her own feet tended to turn up because she was too large in front to see where she stepped. It was Mrs. Germaine's major complaint about her; Louise told her she should invest in wall-to-wall carpets like Basswood.

She held the lunch tray with one hand and the banister with the other. Going down was even harder than climbing up with the tray full. Lights out. The first floor would be entirely dark until the early morning nurse came. Sundays no one stayed over with Mrs. Germaine. It was her free night and she looked forward to it, she told Louise. She could die and no one would know. She liked the idea.

Louise made it to Mrs. Lanaghan's in time for what she hoped might be tea, and it was. There was a fire in the woodstove, with almost a whole pumpkin pie warming on top, left over from Thanksgiving. Louise settled onto the bench by the door because the stools and rocker looked iffy. Mrs. Lanaghan — Mary — pulled the rocker over to be next to her. Louise leaned back, but her head hit the picture frame on the wall, so she leaned forward instead and waited for the pie to be ready.

"I heard from Martin," she said. "He's happy as a clam."

"So it does seem," said Mary.

"She's taking care of him. I think he's sort of like her sex object."

Mary looked startled. "I'm not sure that's entirely what it is," she said.

"I don't mean in a bad way, Mrs. Lanaghan, I mean in a good way. He's a whole new Martin." Her friend Mary was blushing. "I guess him being your son, you probably don't want to hear about it."

"No, it's that I'm wondering how long it can last. Martin tends to fall totally into relationships and then something awful happens."

"But it's not your problem," said Louise. "My friend Dave Paasivirta skipped right out on me. Did you know? It was going so good, but he had to get away from that wife of his and I wasn't about to go off to Idaho, was I? Can you imagine me in Idaho? Talk about far away."

Mary wanted to know about her nurse's aide jobs now after quitting training. Louise tried to explain that she was busier than ever. She had so many clients, and it was more rewarding to catch people at one of the earlier stages, when they had a spark of life still. "Look at Mrs. Germaine. Yesterday, she was doing her crostic and she loved the quote. It went, 'Don't tell me to get ready to die,' and so on, by Waldo somebody. Isn't that perfect? When I got up to finally go, she was chirping away at me, 'Don't tell *me* to get ready to die, don't tell *me* to get ready to die!' She was full of beans."

They discussed what it was like dealing with the elderly. Louise caught Mary on the run at Basswood now and then, but she always seemed harried and had no time to hang out the way she had at the hospital. "That's what comes of being paid," she said, so Louise said, "Isn't that the truth!" But Mary was not happy with her paying job at all. She did not get the same boost from being in the helping professions that Louise did.

She was serving Louise a large slice of warm pie to go with her tea, but she was sad-looking, sad about everything. Her other children had been there for the weekend, and now they were gone; that was it.

But the old people — Mary could not relax around them, she said. She did not know how to take it slow and let them gab and fuss and stumble. "At least, you're not scrubbing them down in the shower," Louise said. "Try that for a pretty sight."

"I don't know how you do it, Louise."

Louise did not know, either. She thought about it and took another bite of delicious pie. "I think of them," she said, "as big old saggy babies. My poppa always came home covered with grease from working on cars, so I figure working means you get your hands dirty. But you've got a clean job at your desk making schedules and posters and arranging bus trips —"

"I'd do better at a job where I got dirty," Mary said.

"Wouldn't recommend it," Louise said, thinking how nobody is satisfied with what they have. Look at Mary Lanaghan's big cozy house and her kids having love affairs and growing into happy people like Martin, with computer jobs where the real money is, and this woman is sad.

"I could work at a nursery," Mary said, meaning for plants, not kids.

"Might be nice," said Louise. She had scraped her plate clean and was hoping for another slice.

Mary was staring above her head at the painting. "Maybe it's only that Thanksgiving's over and the world's closing in," she said.

"You had a good one?"

"We had our own Lanaghan Thanksgiving on Friday because I had to be on duty Thursday. That's a tough day for people without much family, and Rosa and Nat were at the lodge and didn't get in till midnight. It was better for us. It was all our own. I made too many pies. More?"

Louise was relieved it would not just sit there tempting her. And Mary poured out more tea. Louise felt at home. Mary might not like taking care of the elderly, but she took care of the young. Mothers got into that habit, or else it was part of them from the start. Louise wondered if she and Dave had managed to have a kid what it would have changed in her, but she did not let herself think about it much because she was likely to get tearful imagining her big fat self holding a baby. It could have happened with Dave; he said he would not mind. The problem would have been Charles.

Louise did not want to leave, especially since Mary was being so quiet. She should not have told her about Martin. At least, she had kept the letter itself folded in her pocket. "I'd better get on, Mary," she said.

"No rush," Mary said. "Why don't you take the rest with you, though? I was saving it for Bryce, but I can't take any more pie."

"Where's the dog?" Louise asked. "I expected her to be begging."

"She's sleeping off the weekend." Mary pointed toward her bedroom.

"You better rest, too."

"I suppose," Mary said. "I'm a little low. But it's good to see you, Louise. I don't mean to be so unscintillating."

Louise was not sure what *scintillating* itself might mean. It sounded like *titillating*. "That's okay," she said. "If I want scintillating, all I have to do is listen to my brother."

Mary told her to come back again and she would find her in better spirits, and Louise promised and said she would write Martin and tell him to keep his nose clean.

"It's a tribute he writes you an actual letter," Mary said, handing her the warm-bottomed pie so she could take it by the edges. "He e-mails his siblings and calls me collect. A letter means something, Louise."

"I love Martin," she said. "I saved his postcards in my bureau, and now I'll save the letter. Dave Paasivirta sent me a card from Idaho of a potato. Just a brown potato in full color. He thought it was funny."

It was dark enough for Mary to flip on the balcony light so Louise could make her way down without missing a step. She tooted the horn as she drove off and put the lights on because the pine trees were darkening the road. Another set of lights was coming at her down the way, so she pulled way over and stopped to make room. It was Mr. Hale in his red Chevy, and he was rolling down his window. He reached his gnarly old hand out to hers, which she held out as far as she could. They squeezed tight.

"What are you snooping around for out here, kiddo?" he said.

"Visiting my friend Mary Lanaghan. What are you doing? It's getting dark. It's almost winter."

"Checking on the property," he said. "Holiday weekends bring out the vandals."

"You wanted to sneak off from Mrs. Hale and be like a kid again, I know you," Louise said.

"Could be," said Mr. Hale.

"Sleeping over?"

"One last time before it gets too cold. I like the smells of the old place. Sometimes, Louise, you get to missing how something smells, and you've got to go take one last good whiff."

"Don't get foulmouthed on me, Mr. Hale."

He clucked at her. "Louise, listen to me. I mean it. You should learn this, seriously. Once a place goes, you never get that smell again." And she could tell he meant it; he even had a tremble in his voice. "The smell of that old cottage," he said, "let me tell you, it's made up of equal parts mattress, tin plate, what else — dead mouse under floorboard, pathfinder and deerslayer" (Louise did not know what that was), "forty-eight-star flag, wool blanket, down quilt, soot, birchbark, pine needle, goldenrod in mason jar, oilcloth on oak table — see what I mean?"

Louise had never heard Mr. Hale talk so odd. It was scary to listen to him name each thing as though he saw it clear before him, not just the word for it.

He was going on: ". . . calico curtain, rag rug, flypaper, lotto game, dust mop, mothball, wicker basket, candle stub, drained-out water pipe . . ."

VII

MARY RETURNED to the rocker when her visitor had left. The warmth of the woodstove settled over her like a silken sheet. She heard Louise's car rumble off, nearly dozed, then woke to the report of another car, backfiring up the road toward the cottage. She imagined, as she sometimes did late on dark nights, a carload of drunken men, hunters or worse, stalking about the woods, dangerous, till she remembered that Ron's brother Henry's car sounded like that; he had probably run out of beer at home.

Mary drifted back toward a snooze, but right before she got there she found Martin in her mind and he was feeling neglected, even after her Thanksgiving call. She could try him before weekend rates went back up at five, so she nearly sleepwalked into her bedroom and lay down beside the snoring dog, who had her head on the pillow. Midafternoon in Santa Fe, sunny and springlike, Mary supposed. She punched the number, not expecting him to be in, but he was.

"So, Mom, what's up?"

She told him about the remainder of the weekend, the Foosball tournament, Shirley outracing Nat on the railroad bed, the piles of food. She mentioned that Louise Thibault had stopped in when it was over and made off with a pumpkin pie. "She misses you," she told Martin, but he switched the topic: "What's the verdict, is Rosa getting married?"

"Not that we know of," Mary said. Martin made his usual comment on his mom's partiality to Nat. She knew that outsiders did not fare well in this family. And she knew that she was too close to Bayard, too touchy with Martin, that she babied Shirley, and that sometimes Rosa was almost like her other younger self, though she never had told her so. Mary did not know how to improve this psychology of hers, but there it was.

Martin, naturally, moved the conversation to Suzanne. He wanted his mother to think he did not miss his home, a form of rebellion Mary could accept as necessary, but she wondered how true it was. "Because she's not like us," he was saying, "doesn't mean you wouldn't like her. Don't say she's flaky. You have to loosen up, Mom, let some different ways of being enter your life. You live on that beautiful lake, but do you ever go lie under the night sky and imagine yourself part of the whole universe?"

"You must see amazing stars out there," Mary said.

"That's what we do. We take our sleeping bags into the desert."

"I've been hearing coyotes around here at night," Mary said. "They've been moving down from New Hampshire, even with all the development."

"We hear coyotes, all sorts of animals," Martin said. "There's nothing scary about the desert at night. We love sleeping out in it."

"I hope I'll meet Suzanne someday," said Mary.

"You should fly here. Really, Mom."

"Don't you think you'll come at Christmas?"

"It's too soon," he said. "I'm getting the hang of it here,

and my boss wouldn't let me off yet for more than a three-day weekend. Dad's flying out with Julie to Aspen, so they'll come down. I got them a room at Rancho Escondido. But you could fly out now and crash at Suzanne's to save money. She suggested it. My room in town's a pit."

"Exactly what age is Suzanne again?"

"Come on, Mom, she's thirty-six. What's your problem? Ten years' difference is nothing."

"I'm not criticizing, Martin." And she quickly added, "I'm entirely happy about you."

"Okay, Mom," Martin said, "I believe you." Then he asked if Shirley was still coming on to little Gus.

"That's a unique take on it," Mary said.

And he asked, cynically, about Bayard. "And don't tell me his new one's for real, Mom."

"I try to keep clear of your brother's romances."

"Sure, Mom, sure."

No mention of Bryce. It had been a warm enough phone call despite the sniping. She could let Martin be. But when they had said good-bye, Mary felt a terrific chill creeping up from her feet. She snuggled close to the dog and pulled the quilt over them both. Hilda huffed once and slept on. It was not Martin, it was her own life that was numbing Mary. These were physical symptoms, the blurry watery feeling, the submerged slowness, cold fingers, the drifting. Was it the new medication? She did not like messing with her insides; it made her question what she herself was. She did not want to lose whole feelings. She wanted all her body at once, no veil about her.

In sudden loneliness, she dialed Bryce's number to see if he was back yet from visiting his brother's family in Providence, but his machine picked up and said, "You've reached the Murtagh home. Neither Bryce, Fiona, or Sean can come to the phone at this time, but leave a message and we'll be in touch." After the beep, Mary said, "Happy Thanksgiving, Bryce, Fiona, and Sean. It's Mary the Dog Lady. I'm home, Bryce. My kids are gone if you want to stop by." She paused, then added shyly, "That's all."

And, of course, there was Christina. She quickly punched out the tune of eleven notes to anchor her back in place.

Kurt answered and passed her right over, but Christina was in the kitchen fixing dinner; the Friedenheimers were there, so she could not talk long. "Gus is going off to visit Shirley," she said.

"I gather."

"All right by you?"

"Shirley can handle Gus," Mary said.

"Gus is driving me nuts lately, Mary. He's so antsy. I wish he was out of the house for good."

Mary gave her a holiday rundown while Christina clattered about in the background, chopping vegetables, running water, stirring a pot — the sounds of home. Then she asked if Kurt had called Drew Hale about the cottage. It was such a good idea, Christina said, but they had to think it over. "And how are you yourself doing, Mary?" she finally asked.

With her friend busy cooking, Mary had been afraid there would be no time for it to come up, so before she could think she said, "The sun's been coming and going all afternoon out here. I feel as if I'm filling and emptying, filling and emptying. What's the weather like in there? We've had some rain, and it's colder. I feel as if something's lost and gone. I suppose it's the season."

"Or it's hormones."

"I can't tell. It doesn't matter. I have to get through it."

"Want me to come visit next weekend? It's Gus's conference, and Kurt has business in New York, so I'm alone."

"Yes, come," said Mary. "Oh please, come. Or I could come there."

"There's a thought."

"Should I? Ron and Victor could look after the dog. Or Bryce — but Bryce doesn't see the point of Hilda; he says she just lies there. Ron would do it. You know, Christina, I think I'm using Ron to bother Bryce. I pretend to Bryce I totally approve of Ron even though, frankly, I don't know if I do. But I tell Bryce it's possible to be wild like Ron and still be a loving person. And it is. Ron's very loving, so's Victor in his strange way. I tell Bryce his idea of morality is oversimplified. Who of us is justified labeling things right and wrong? Ron's as justified as anyone else."

"Cool it, Mary," said Christina. "You're on a toot."

"Am I?"

"You check with your neighbors about the dog and call tomorrow night. I have a committee till eight."

So Mary Lanaghan had something to look forward to. It had brought her above the surface, and her mind began to run through what she had to do tomorrow. The last Monday in November. And there would eventually come a Tuesday in December, and on it would go, her life, day by day and month by month, forty-nine, fifty — she began to sink again. It seemed that her life was always before anything happened. It did have its turning points — marriage, birth of children, divorce, the move to this silent country road. Each had happened in an instant and was irrevocable. The births of her children had set new threads weaving their colors into a pattern of her future, even if at first a baby was a creature to hold close and care for and all of her making; Mary had been such to her own parents once, and she was so far away from them now — they were scarcely wisps. Death made other turning points, the deaths of others in her life. No one had died this year. No child had been born. No one had divorced or gotten back together. This was a year before everything. But most every day of her life was like that, and when an event happened, it happened too fast for her to take in. It hit her a blow, and then she went on.

Mary was not tearful, though she felt a well of water pressing inside her. If Bryce came in later and hugged her, then she would cry. Nature girl. And he would fill her again and make her forget, in the moment of his touching, her outside and inside. She would be Mary then, whole for an instant. Another instant. He would lie then patiently, happily, beside her, the instants passing slowly, imperceptibly.

She was drifting again. She imagined Rosa playing her flute in the loft those last days before she gave it up entirely. It soothed Mary to hear it, snatches of tunes, nothing that quite fit together in her mind. Mary had a deep belief that there must be a truer companion, even several, unknown to her, out beyond her woods somewhere, not too far, who might make an answer to her longing. But she had as deep a belief that in all her remaining days she would never chance to meet one of them. The world has possibilities for beauty, she thought, and nearly as many for disappointment. I have had my share of luck, she told herself like the good Catholic girl her parents had once expected her to be, and I must be thankful for it.

As Mary approached sleep — it was right there, waiting for her — she was reminding herself that tomorrow she had to run up to Dowland on her lunch hour because she was practically out of health-diet dog food, which could only be bought there at that unnoticeable crossroad with its gas pump and general store and post office with a sign for the town library in back.